Praise for *The World*

WINNER OF THE ETHEL WILSON FICTION PRIZE
A *GLOBE AND MAIL* TOP 100 BOOK

"Oh, is this a book! What stories, what writing, what feeling, what depth, what humour.... The craftsmanship is superb. There is not one plot thread left to draggle; not one character is left behind. If it's possible to cram a world of human existence into a single piece of CanLit, and to do so with grace, understatement, wry humour, respect and love, then Bill Gaston has done just that."   —*The Globe and Mail*

"[*The World*] is a novel about the wages of love and attachment, and the fact that life is really about disappearances.... That Gaston can send us on this journey without leaving us bereft is a testament to his powers as a novelist."   —*National Post*

"*The World* is perhaps Bill Gaston's greatest work, and Bill Gaston is one of our greatest writers."

—David Adams Richards

"I did not want this book to end.... *The World* is a touching, joyous, heartbreaking and clever-as-hell novel.... This heart-breaking love story is perfectly tuned." —*The Winnipeg Review*

"This is a rich, rewarding novel with many deft touches and more than a few twists and turns.... A classic."

—*Vancouver Sun*

"*The World* is something of an understated marvel, an exploration of mortality, morality, loss and acceptance under a veneer of dry humour, a stylistically complex work that reads almost effortlessly.... In Gaston's hands *The World* unfolds with a breezy ease that belies its power. Far from an academic or stylistic exercise, *The World* will break your heart, and begin the slow process of putting it back together."

—*Times Colonist* (Victoria)

"There is no denying Gaston's gifts as a storyteller, and one of his great strengths—the pleasure of perceiving closely while living in the moment—becomes a recurring theme here."

—*Quill & Quire*

"What makes this the Vancouver Island–based author's best book ... is that it operates, very successfully, on many different levels.... [Gaston] plumbs the nature of existence with such delicacy and compassion that *The World*'s subtle lessons are inhaled as easily as air."   —*The Georgia Straight*

"Gaston is a deft hand when it comes to drawing a line under the stark reality of circumstance, often heartbreakingly so."

—*Toronto Star*

"It's a triptych of stories that build upon themselves. And possibly, it is Gaston's best yet."   —*The Sun Times*

Praise for *Sointula*

"Compelling.... Gaston's passion for Vancouver Island shows through.... The mountains, the wilderness, the sea life, even the threatening rainstorms take on an enchanted quality that balances the human drama." —*Edmonton Journal*

"It's a precisely woven tapestry.... Characterizations are particularly rich and searching, and the resolution of their quests, in an extended dénouement comprising one brilliant scene after another, is virtually beyond praise."
—*Kirkus Reviews* (starred review)

"Gaston is a hugely skilled storyteller, but describing the technical tools he uses here ... would feel like explaining a magic trick, and equally disloyal to his art."
—*The Georgia Straight*

"[Gaston] is that rare writer who can peel back the deepest fears of Nature (abandonment, pain, futility) and find a vision of vehement, imperfect beauty." —*Publishers Weekly*

"A full, rich tapestry of characters. [Gaston] also manages to bring together snugly the divergent plot lines and different thematic threads by novel's end, no easy narrative feat in a book this long and structurally ambitious."
—*The Globe and Mail*

"Each new book by Bill Gaston reminds us that he is one of our best writers—original, versatile, skilled, wise, surprising, and fearless. In *Sointula* he travels elegantly—navigating below the surface of things as he tracks two troubled souls on their separate journeys north to an uncertain future. In joining him, the reader is rewarded on every page." —Jack Hodgins

"Gaston really gets Vancouver Island. He gets it more than any other living Canadian writer, and his love of the place seeps into the pages of *Sointula*." —*Quill & Quire*

"[Gaston's] writing is sharp, and his observations comic but revealing…. Fans of Gaston will find the same backhanded observations, the same surprising insights and gleeful perversities shared by the characters as in his previous books. He excels at getting inside hearts of all ages…. Gaston has crafted a celebration of B.C.'s coast, heavy with insight and all the passion of an islander's proprietary eye. His latest book vividly captures the coast's rhythms, its natural beauty, and its challenges." —*Books in Canada*

"The author is a master at creating characters with deft understatement and dead right dialogue. He is also brilliant with images and symbols that lace the book like the wildlife that leaps and pounces through the landscape…. In addition to a riveting plot and characters that intrigue and often anger, the language urges you to languish even as you speed along to that unimaginable ending, that inevitable final paragraph that seems so right in retrospect." —*January Magazine*

PENGUIN

THE WORLD

BILL GASTON is a Canadian novelist, short-story writer, and playwright. His short-story collection *Gargoyles* was shortlisted for the Governor General's Literary Award and the Ethel Wilson Fiction Prize, and won the ReLit Award and the City of Victoria Butler Prize. In 2002 Gaston was a finalist for the Giller Prize with *Mount Appetite* and the inaugural recipient of the Timothy Findley Prize, awarded by the Writers' Trust of Canada. He teaches at the University of Victoria.

THE
WORLD

BILL
GASTON

PENGUIN
an imprint of Penguin Canada

Published by the Penguin Group
Penguin Group (Canada)
90 Eglinton Avenue East, Suite 700, Toronto, Ontario, Canada M4P 2Y3

Penguin Group (USA) Inc., 375 Hudson Street, New York, New York 10014, U.S.A.
Penguin Books Ltd, 80 Strand, London WC2R 0RL, England
Penguin Ireland, 25 St Stephen's Green, Dublin 2, Ireland (a division of Penguin Books Ltd)
Penguin Group (Australia), 707 Collins Street, Melbourne, Victoria 3008, Australia
(a division of Pearson Australia Group Pty Ltd)
Penguin Books India Pvt Ltd, 11 Community Centre, Panchsheel Park,
New Delhi – 110 017, India
Penguin Group (NZ), 67 Apollo Drive, Rosedale, Auckland 0632, New Zealand
(a division of Pearson New Zealand Ltd)
Penguin Books (South Africa) (Pty) Ltd, 24 Sturdee Avenue, Rosebank,
Johannesburg 2196, South Africa

Penguin Books Ltd, Registered Offices: 80 Strand, London WC2R 0RL, England

First published in Hamish Hamilton hardcover by Penguin Canada, 2012
Published in this edition, 2013

1 2 3 4 5 6 7 8 9 10 (WEB)

Manufactured in Canada.

LIBRARY AND ARCHIVES CANADA CATALOGUING IN PUBLICATION

Gaston, Bill, 1953–, author
The world / Bill Gaston.

Originally published: Toronto, Ontario : Hamish Hamilton, 2012.
ISBN 978-0-14-318086-9 (pbk.)

I. Title.

PS8563.A76W67 2013   C813'.54   C2013-903590-7

Visit the Penguin Canada website at **www.penguin.ca**

Special and corporate bulk purchase rates available; please see
www.penguin.ca/corporatesales or call 1-800-810-3104, ext. 2477.

ALWAYS LEARNING   PEARSON

For my mother,
who forgot

THAT GOLDEN GLOW

Few men realize that their life, the very essence
of their character, their capabilities and their
audacities, are only the expression of their belief
in the safety of their surroundings.

—Joseph Conrad,
"An Outpost of Progress"

The night before his world went up in flames, Stuart Price sat reading an article in *National Geographic* about Egypt's mummified animals—shrews to gazelles to longhorn cattle with statuary built to encase them. Most of all, the Egyptians mummified pet cats. Tensing imperceptibly in his easy chair, Stuart read how, in 1888, treasure hunters uncovered many thousands of mummified cats, layered twenty or thirty deep. Deemed worthless except as fertilizer, these dry-husk cats were piled to the gunnels and shipped to England, where they were plowed into English farmland.

The article had an odd effect on Stuart. What struck him more than its wild facts was the simpler fact that he had never heard of this. How was it possible?

As he sat in his scavenged chair, reading from a borrowed magazine, he was most made to feel boring. Not bored—boring. An affront to life out there, a life from which sprang such colourful stories. He saw how his own life had narrowed, and in the past five years ridiculously. It might look like asceticism but it just wasn't. His simplicity had no purpose other than thrift. After two decades as shop teacher at Lambrick Park High, at age fifty-one, a year behind schedule, he'd retired and, today, paid off his house. Since the divorce he had dedicated his life to exactly those two things—pay off mortgage, retire—going so far as to borrow magazines, drive a thirty-three-year-old Datsun, and neither eat out nor order in. So what—Stuart considered with feet up on the coffee table he'd built himself—what did this sphincter-like frugality mean in a world where mummified, three-thousand-year-old cats were packed in schooners, shipped to England, dug in with the peas and carrots, and no one found it remarkable enough to talk about endlessly or put into history books?

As colourful as all this was, Stuart Price wouldn't recall the article or these thoughts until weeks later, when he would wonder if he'd cursed himself by wishing for a less boring life. The curse of the cat mummies' tomb, he'd say to Melody. Mel would want no part of curses, or notions that we bring about our own misfortune. Which was understandable, given her health.

After reading about the cats, what Stuart did was go and look in the bathroom mirror, which confirmed how boring he'd grown. He wasn't a drinker, yet his face had widened to blandness. His hair, once a rich chestnut, had fallen to gunmetal grey. No, make that the colour of lead. What he did next was go out on the sundeck to conduct a corny little ceremony. It was nothing much; he thought he recalled his parents doing it in their barbecue. He found some matches in the junk drawer.

Sitting on a deck chair, in his white socks, he crumpled the document into a dirt-filled plastic planter. Touching match to paper he felt hollow, realizing that this was something you did with a loved one, clinking champagne glasses and sitting back to watch the bank's paper shackles curl and blacken.

He hurried in to the kitchen and returned with a bottle of beer that he tapped against the wooden wall of his house, his clumsily square and rooted ship. He sipped and watched his mortgage papers burn, legalese only dimly understood and too boring to ever read.

But it was fire, which is never boring, especially when it turns away from the feeding human hand to find its own fuel.

Dawn, Stuart woke instantly, something wrong, something yanking him headfirst from bed, he was up and walking fast. His head felt out of its socket and his vision three feet in front of his eyes, and he understood the wrongness to be smoke. He sprinted to his kitchen, its white walls bright though the lights were off, and he saw through the double glass doors his sundeck and outer wall on fire. He grabbed the phone while yelling *Jen! Jen!* and jabbed 911, shouted his address twice, and then he was out on the deck with his garden hose, standing in full Halloween-orange glare, half the time dousing fire at his feet and half the time spraying into the bigger brightness of the flaring wall. He was making a dent in it, too, was getting somewhere, the flames as he extinguished them making the roar of a pot of water poured on a campfire, but ten times as loud, a true roar, that blasted water back at him, his glasses—getting out of bed he'd somehow put his glasses on—catching the dirty spray full of ash. Again he said *Jen*, but to himself, odd to have shouted for a daughter who had never set foot in this house. Spraying, he saw where the

fire obviously had begun: there against the burning wall was
what used to be the plastic planter, reduced now to a melted
blob of green, silent purple flames hovering over it. Finally,
distant sirens rose over the fire's cracking and roaring and the
blood pounding in his ears. When the first fire truck came
and the men shouted at him, man with little green hose, to get
off the deck, Stuart stood on the lawn counting the seconds
between the firefighters ordering him away and getting their
bigger hose clamped on and pumped full and then gushing,
and in those nineteen seconds—Stuart thought then and
continues to think now—the fire really bloomed, got control
of his house by eating through the wall, the skin, entering the
house itself, exploding into its innocent vulnerable body.

Next he was shouted off the lawn. From the street he
stood watching the swarm of men—there were four fire trucks
now—don spacesuits and oxygen tanks and heft axes, plunge
in and out of doors, while thigh-thick jets of spray blasted in
through windows, or through two black mouths the fire had
made for itself. Other people watched too and a woman, it was
Vicky from across the street, squatted behind him to tie a pink
bathrobe around his waist, for he'd been standing in nothing
but underwear, briefs, white briefs at that, wet and charcoal-
smudged. Somewhere along the line he'd stepped into his
leather dress shoes, which were now heavy with water and ash.

"It was my boy Chris knocked on your door," said another
woman more behind than beside him. He turned to her long
enough to see he didn't know her, then back to the fire, the
swarm of men who were maybe winning the battle, for though
columns of smoke tumbled ceaselessly and filled the sky, now
only rare spurts of flame popped up here or there, and weakly
against all that water.

"Chris saw the flames and just pounded away, Chris told me. He's the paper boy."

Even saying it, Stuart knew it was stupid: "I don't get a paper."

"He saw your *house* was on fire," she said, angry amid the swarm of enthralled people, the fire trucks, the news camera, the smoke and shouting, and Stuart himself intent and stricken dumb, "so he went up and banged on your *door*."

When he turned and said, "Sorry … Where …" she was already walking away, shaking her head. One side of his glasses bore a soot smudge the size of her retreating figure. He'd wanted to ask where she and Chris lived because he did want to thank him—and it was strange having somebody angry at him at a time like this. Pink fuzzy robe tied by its arms round his waist. Watching, with all these neighbours he didn't know, the smoke billowing from his house. It looked exactly like an erupting volcano. The fact dawned on Stuart that the smoke *was* his house, his house and everything in it—his clothes, his floorboards, his chair, his food, his books, his pillow—burned and changed into particles of smoke pounding up into the sky. There was something undeniably grand about it, something more powerful than anything he truly understood.

STUART WAS TO LEARN THAT, incredibly, burning his house was not the worst of it.

All but one truck had left. Stuart was allowed back into his front yard. The insurance adjuster, Bradley Connington, righted two lawn chairs Stuart had apparently heaved off his sundeck while battling his fire. Sitting here in his yard, in their chairs, Stuart still with Vicky's pink robe on, Connington discussed the claim and thumbed away at his BlackBerry, snatching facts and figures, a font of information. Despite the old-school moustache he was a nice guy it seemed, killing time by finding out for Stuart the cost of new kitchen cabinets, pulling up figures for granite counters, because Stuart might not want to simply replace but to upgrade. He somehow knew Stuart was a woodworking teacher and he made a decent joke about how Stuart could conduct classes here at his house, getting the kids to do the work for free and Stuart pocketing a pile. An hour earlier, when the deputy chief gave the go-ahead, Connington had donned a spacesuit and gas mask and gone through the house snapping upward of two hundred pictures. Tomorrow a crew would drag out and throw the smoke-damaged contents of Stuart's house into dumpsters, but Connington would know about the already-stained orange carpet downstairs, he'd have proof of a slightly tattered bedspread. He knew that the blasted hallway lamp was a real Tiffany and knew its replacement cost within five dollars. He was impressed by the quality of tools in the basement shop, especially the lathe, and except for the band saw, which was "toast," Stuart wouldn't need to claim for the tools except if water damage necessitated a rewrapping of the copper coils. No one, "not us, not you," can cheat this way, Connington said, smiling cheerfully, tapping his camera. He brought to Stuart's swimming mind the notion of a Swiss diplomat. Connington also gave Stuart the impression that he had never once been wrong. He was an angel of order in a smoking boneyard.

Connington was waiting for some kind of word from the insurance company. Apparently he got it because suddenly he squinted hard into his BlackBerry and uttered, "No no no no no—you didn't. Mr. Price. Stuart. Tell me you didn't."

"Didn't what." Stuart was staring at his house, thinking it not too bad. Much of the roof was gone, but there was only one other hole, high up the side wall. The glass had all been smashed, but the one living-room window left intact reflected the September blue sky and his neighbourhood's turning leaves. It was a beautiful day.

"Stuart, I'm getting a notice from your insurance company, from Best North, and I've double-checked it, as have they, that as of 5 A.M. this morning you are five weeks behind on your policy. They *cancelled* you, a week ago. Your yearly premium was due August 15th. Five weeks ago." Bradley Connington looked up to announce a great mystery. "You didn't pay your premium, Stuart."

"That's impossible."

His stomach was falling and falling. This was different from the fire. He'd spent the last hour hearing Connington tell him, all smiles, how good his new house was going to look, how his hotels were paid for, how even today he could start rebuilding his wardrobe, and how, since state-of-the-art computers and flat-screen TVs were the only thing available in stores, it didn't matter that he had old clunkers. State-of-the-art was what the insurance company would buy him.

"Can you, can you prove, I don't know, that"—sitting in his chair, Connington threw his arms out—"that you did pay it? Or that you didn't get your notices?" He thrust his face at Stuart's. *"Can you prove you didn't get your notices?"*

"I don't know!"

"Did you get your notices!"

"I don't know!"

"Whoo boy!"

Stuart stood up, Vicky's pink robe falling away. Connington stared straight at Stuart's white sooty crotch, not seeing it, shaking his head.

"What does this mean?" asked Stuart.

Connington was already tapping an idea into his BlackBerry. He brought his cell out and readied it on his knee. "The industry secret, not really a secret, is that they send out letters, they make calls, and they allow a four weeks' lenience period. Four weeks, not a problem. After four weeks? Maybe a problem." His cell rang and he was on it with hunger. "Joyce? Policy Larry33-Xray27-Bob18. That's right. That's the one. Who has— Who has—"

Stuart couldn't help interrupting. "*Maybe* a problem?"

He'd been religious with paperwork. He'd been so good. He'd just paid off his mortgage. He'd converted his lump-sum pension to a monster mortgage payment. He'd hunkered down and consolidated debt. He'd— How had he not paid his house insurance?

"Okay." Connington was looking at him. Stuart suddenly felt less than highly regarded. It was as if, before, Connington was the servant. No longer. "So we wait. Time will tell." Staring into his feet, talking as if to himself, Connington said, "They would have *called*."

"Well I—I changed my number. And had it unlisted."

"You did?"

Stuart didn't answer. He was realizing he didn't get the mailed notices because, ever since he bought this place, he kept getting his mail at work. He hadn't bothered with the change-of-address paperwork. All summer, the high school was basically abandoned. He could picture, just inside the door to the general office, the pile of mail with his insurance notices in it.

"So can I—can I talk to someone?"

"You are. I'm your liaison in this."

"Is there something I can do?"

"No."

"Can I, you know, still just pay it? My premium?"

Connington seemed not to know if Stuart was being funny. He decided he was, and laughed. But then shifted gears. It hadn't occurred to him. "Couldn't hurt, I guess."

"What if I put August 15th on the cheque, would that—?" Stuart tried smiling too, then wondered if Connington was the person he should be saying this to.

"Right, dirty the envelope, give it that 'lost in the mail' look." With a snort, Connington looked away. A firefighter with a pry bar came from around back and flicked the adjuster a peace sign.

"I suspect we'll be having a conversation about this for a while," Connington added, to end it. He packed away his BlackBerry, his phone, his camera, his gas mask. No more smiling chat about upgrading from lino to Italian tile.

A FEW DAYS LATER, only ten feet from where he'd stood watching his house burn, Stuart sat curbside in his Datsun, the old car idling roughly. He turned it off and rolled down the window, better to hear what the men on his roof, or what was left of his roof, were yelling to each other. He heard "the Leafs," he heard "the fuckin' Canucks." Under the September sun they were shirtless, tanned, and arguing hockey. He also heard himself ridiculed. "*Geez*," said one worker in a moron's voice, mocking Stuart's, "*I didn't know dirt burned.*" Stuart had actually said that to the deputy fire chief about his planter, and these men had adopted it as a mantra to remind themselves whose house they were working on.

Mel's letter lay on his lap. It had arrived one morning and his house had burned the next. Though the two things could not be connected, he couldn't help feeling they were. Her letter also grew larger because it was one of the few things he owned. It had survived the fire only because on his way to do an errand he'd read it in the car and left it on the passenger seat.

That he could ponder an old friend's letter was a bit astounding—he'd almost died in a fire. During the front-lawn interview where Stuart understood he was being subtly prodded about arson, the older guy with the white moustache, apparently the deputy fire chief, had said to him, "One minute more, one *half*-minute more, you were toast." Stuart was about to explain how the fire had started, the little fire he'd made in the plastic planter, "full of only dirt," and apologize for it, and how last night after his little ceremony he'd shoved the planter up against the house but it seems the fire wasn't completely out and smouldered all night in the dirt and— The chief put a hand up, smile dismissive, to say, "We know how it started." Well, not exactly, thought Stuart, but he was too embarrassed to explain further. Still wearing the pink wrap, he was instructed to go down to the ambulance for tests. There a young woman took his blood pressure and had him breathe into a tube. He'd apparently inhaled smoke, was warned about a few days of headaches and was handed a brown paper packet of Tylenol 3s.

From his car he continued to watch the crew rip away what remained of his roof, baring the rib-like peaked rafters, some charred, some not. That was the first step, he'd been told. Get a new roof on right away, so no more water damage from rain. The hardwood in the living room was already warping from firehose water, edges curling up like long potato chips, but any more water would get into walls and joists and all the rest of it. The house was maybe almost a teardown. "It's pretty much a coin toss," Bradley Connington had said to him in a cheerful tone to describe jagged ruin and cliff-edge implications. The worse the damage sounded the more sheepish Stuart felt, he being the lame-brain who caused it. (When, puzzled and smiling, Connington asked him what the hell he'd been burning in that planter, Stuart was ready and told him he lacked a shredder so was burning important papers. Almost the truth.) Actually he felt more than sheepish. It was a yawning, frightening guilt: he'd torched his own shelter and was now naked and homeless. More than once he'd cried, usually in private, but the first time in the presence of Connington, the sobs erupting out of what began as a sigh. Connington gave one shoulder a manly squeeze that somehow told him his crying was typical. But today it was hard to watch these guys work overtime, fixing what he'd ruined. Though it looked like all they were doing was stretching a huge blue tarp over everything and anchoring it. He couldn't not watch. Look at it, the charred part so black against the sky-blue. His poor, wounded house. He loved his house. It had become his partner in life. The coffee smells as he read his Saturday paper. Its knowing mood as he watched late-night TV. The chatter of his old fridge, the side window with the bird feather stuck to it—the house surrounded him with textures, like clothing. It knew his routines, and more and more he'd become his routines. Now six guys with pry bars and sledges were going at some remaining shingles and plywood as they shouted training-camp opinions at each other. Some guys had heavy accents but were eager to talk hockey. The Leafs would never win another Stanley Cup, simple as that. Burke was *not* a genius. And another, "Who'd start a fire on their fucking *deck*?" Lithe and efficient at dismantling his house even while shouting things, these shirtless young men were wiser than Stuart, it seemed, in all ways. They were cocky, tattooed doctors who knew everything about his hapless life and what he should have done with it.

STUART STARTED THE CAR, revved it, listened as it fell to idle. There was that little random bump, every ten or twelve seconds. It wasn't a worry, his car was too old to die on him now.

With some fresh excitement he pictured cassette tapes in the glovebox. All his music had melted or warped and was trashed along with the rest of his life in the dumpster in his driveway, but he remembered he had some old tapes in here. He searched in the bills and ice scrapers and found three. An Elton John's *Greatest Hits* Vol. 2, Roxy Music's *Sirens,* and, good God, a Mel, one of her bands. There was nothing he'd listened to in years. He wasn't sure this car's deck even worked. It might be fun hearing Mel again. All you got of her was the deep backbeat. Funny when you thought it: Mel played what made the speakers thump.

In the back seat sat his new suitcase full of new clothes, shirts still in plastic wrappers. After three nights in a hotel he'd decided to drive from Victoria to Toronto to visit Mel because she was sick, maybe dying. He'd decided on the trip also because what else was he going to do? With a last gaze at the charred house and its shirtless doctors, and with a self-disgusted head shake that had become habit, he pulled away from the curb. The Datsun was coltish for a block or two.

The frightening conversation with insurance people could just as easily take place long-distance. One thing he'd learned about life-changing corporate decision-makers is that they'd rather not see your face.

THE DAY BEFORE THE FIRE, in his car when he pinched up Mel's envelope, he could tell it held a single sheet. It had been addressed to the old place but had somehow found its way to Diane's new one, because clearly it was her writing that had crossed out his old address and supplied his new.

How long since he'd had a personal handwritten letter? The year of their divorce, before switching to email Diane had written him a long one, her recent life course charted with exhausting honesty. Careful to take half of the blame. It had been an astounding eighteen pages long.

Mel's was a single paragraph, but revealing in its own way:

Stu Price, it's been way too long, and I
needed to say hi. You're important to me.
And it shouldn't be much longer, the
cancer came back, so. You work too hard,
live a little, or even more than that. Wish you
were here. T.O. has decent restaurants now.
416-604-5995.

Trufflepig down,
Mel

Yes, much too long. He hadn't heard about the first cancer, never mind it coming back. And she didn't know he'd retired. This wasn't time flying, this was decades, *poof.* He could picture Mel easily, could summon vivid 3 A.M. belly laughs. He could see her, thin and tall, hunched gawky over her white bass guitar. Fretless, how was that even possible to play? It had looked to Stuart like earthy genius, her finding perfect notes on an unmarked board. And her bands with the funny names. But the camping trips they'd taken. The food! Mel was one of the few good friends in his life.

He called her, on impulse, right then. Mel's deep voice! She sounded a little shy or confused, and said she thought she'd written the letter months ago. It sounded like she had a sore throat and it hurt to talk. He said he should get over there for a visit, and she said great, he'd have a giant futon couch for a bed. He was too wary to ask if she was married or any of that, still unclear about her and what these days was called an "orientation." She said she was back at her parents' old place. Her mom died two years back and her dad had "moved out" just a few months ago. Alzheimer's.

"Meaning," she said, "I did the North American thing and put him in a home."

Stuart said, "I remember his book, it was great." A painful romance. A leper colony. He hadn't read much of it. *The World.*

"Actually I've started reading it to Dad, when I visit."

"His own book?"

"It seems to spark things."

Stuart said again that he'd try to maybe visit, she said great, and that was that. Stuart remembered how the phone had never been good for them.

And today his decision to hop in the car and drive across

the country. It seemed a house fire will do that for a person. Live a little, or even more than that, she'd written. He'd just show up, like the old days. Appear in her doorway breathless with singed eyebrows and smoking clothes and say he'd burned his house down. Maybe he would even admit to her how it happened.

He approached Swartz Bay and the Vancouver ferry. Her words "giant futon couch" had sounded nicely teenage, and made him feel young, but now a deeper vacuuming sensation was revealing to him that, from the ocean behind him to the vastness he was heading into, nowhere was there a place he could call home. All he had was a couch. If it was vacant.

That sob again. He was getting tired of it.

Especially when it continued in the ferry lineup. He was shaky paying the marmish woman in the ticket booth, she scowling in her uniform while he fumbled fives and tens, passing an ugly clutch of them, on a windy day, from his car window. His credit card, which he'd left on the counter after a phone transaction, had warped. This morning he'd signed up for a new one, which would be mailed to him when he could give them an address, and was issued a new debit card for access to the $4,136 in his bank account. It felt like quite a lot, actually. Way more, anyway, than any other homeless person for miles around. One thing he really didn't want to think about was his pension. Which, upon retiring, he'd taken in a lump sum. Which he had used, the entire lump, to pay off his house. The idea, the dream, had been to retire with no mortgage, no debt at all. For income he'd work piecemeal, only at stuff he liked—simple, yellow cedar coffee tables and pedestal end tables built lovingly and one at a time out of his basement shop. He'd long ago taken a stab at guitar-making and seen that he could do that level of fine work, and for decades had shyly and tenuously held onto a notion of a Stuart Price line of acoustic guitars.

He couldn't entertain any of that now, none of it. The thought of his vanished pension hollowed him out, brought him close to an actual faint.

He sat in the lineup of cars. It was warm so he rolled down the window, put his arm on the ledge. The seagull loitering on the concrete divider ten feet away eyed his open window and tapping hand. When Stuart tapped harder, then banged, it waddled away, never not looking.

At the bank he'd taken out five hundred, including two hundred-dollar bills, and those he'd slid into an envelope cadged from the teller. (He was beginning to learn what the words *I had a house fire, and lost all my* could do.) On a piece of cadged blank paper he'd written:

> Dear Chris,
>
> I'm leaving and don't have time to give you this in person, but I'll come back and visit and shake your hand. I want to thank you for being brave and banging on my door and saving my life. Please let your Mom help you buy something you really want. Or save it in a bank. Anyway, thanks again. I bet your Mom and Dad are proud as punch. They should be.
>
> > All the best,
> > Stuart Price
> > (Mr. Price on Winchester Rd.)

He got another piece of paper and wrote the letter again, changing "your Mom and Dad are" to "everyone at your house is," remembering the Pro-D retreats where he heard about the insensitivity of "taking a two-parent home for granted." Stuart discovered from neighbours where Chris the paper boy lived and managed to sneak up and slip the envelope into the mailbox without being seen. He knew kids well enough to know that Chris would prefer it this way too. Not many kids like a grateful adult looming all over them, especially one who might start blubbering.

The ferry began boarding and when he lurched forward he finally scared the seagull away. Inching along, he counted his life off on his fingers. His checklist was scant and it was this that made him cry a little. What he had, other than a lingering headache, was his health, check. He had a daughter safe in Montreal, check. He had this good old car, check. He had four thousand in the bank, check. He'd emailed Diane up in Comox; she'd be angry if not told because what if she happened to drive by and see the charred shell, etc., check. But there was no one else crucial to contact. How was that possible? How had life gotten so ... streamlined? Odd how it was September and he didn't have to notify work. But he'd left the paper boy that money. Check.

Maybe later he'd call a couple guys on his Wednesday-night basketball team. At least Ryan, check. He'd get his number somehow. He had Mel's number, there on her letter on the passenger seat, check. He had a number for Connington, the adjuster, check. Maybe he still had a house. No check quite yet.

HIS SPASM OF SELF-PITY passed and he tried to get into the spirit of whatever this was. This adventure. He rode the ferry, didn't know all the names of the small islands going by, ate his first cheeseburger in a while, moved to the passenger lounge for an oddly peaceful nap sitting up, and disembarked to start the drive east. Radio tuned to an oldies station, he thumped his thumbs on the wheel and took his place in the stream of cars. He was getting better at forgetting. This could be a vacation. He worked at it. Twice in the first hundred miles he stopped specifically for grapefruit pop and then a chocolate bar.

An hour and a half down the highway, just past Chilliwack, he stopped and checked into a motel, The River's Inn. It was four in the afternoon. He wasn't tired. Something had made him turn in, maybe the deep blue of the sign, or the old-school humility of the building, its rounded corners a bit hobbit-like. Maybe it was the healthy adolescent sequoia towering over and guarding the parking lot.

In his room when he caught himself immediately drawing the curtains to shut out the sun and a decent view of the Fraser River, he stopped. He stood still and noticed his fast breathing, his clenched nerves. Nothing in him was ready to rest and yet he'd wanted to come in here and barricade the door. He stood with his fist full of curtain and could feel it, urgent as hunger—the need to shut everything out.

He threw the curtain open, took in the view, and then one long, fake breath. Nothing felt right.

Back at the front desk he said only that he'd changed his mind, and sorry. He hadn't mussed up the bed or anything. The proprietor, Stuart's age but stern and wiry in a way that brought to mind a dust-bowl farmer, said nothing, not a word. The motel had no other cars out front being guarded by the sequoia. Stuart offered again that he'd touched absolutely nothing in the room, and the motel owner kept pouting. True, he'd done Stuart the favour of overlooking his lack of a credit card to conduct a more complicated check-in that involved his debit card, and now he had to reverse the process. He took his time, turning his back while the computer beeped and chugged, still the grouchy farmer. The transaction took five silent minutes. Stuart didn't get a you're welcome to his thank you, and he hated the long walk to the car with an honest farmer that mad at him.

Maybe to compensate, Stuart drove too far and too long this time, even going off-route to sightsee around the lakes north of Kamloops, at dusk. He got out at somewhere called Pinantan Lake, stretched, sighed, pretending to bask in the sunset beauty. Just past midnight he stopped in Revelstoke, a blinking vacancy light pulling him in like a fishing lure. He groaned climbing out, his back kinking from two angles. He was fifty-one, not a kid. He'd driven this highway more than once in his teens and twenties, and his memory was of nothing but fun. He remembered taking an armpit bath in a gas station washroom around here, coming out snorting with laughter. It seemed you never had to sleep back then. Money was never a problem. There was that time, the outskirts of Lethbridge, siphoning gas from a car beside a well-to-do house, leaving three cans of smoked oysters on the hood as some sort of gesture. And that's right, that was *Mel*, she the kick-ass gas siphoner, they did that trip across one summer, she to see her family in Toronto, and he a girlfriend who'd gone to Quebec to learn French and who, by the time Stuart got there, was enjoying private immersion with someone named Luc.

This motel was called The Vista. Its parking lot was full, and bass thuds and shrieks issued from more than one room. Along the two tiers of rooms, most lights were still on. Stuart didn't think he'd mind this at all.

In his room he stashed the motel receipt in the special manila envelope. Save all receipts, said Connington. He hefted his suitcase onto the bed and opened it to a waft of plastic and stick deodorant.

Smoke and water damage was so severe that he'd salvaged nothing. He'd made it out wearing only the briefs he'd since thrown away and the leather shoes he'd snagged off the deck.

From the suitcase he lifted out the three-pack of T-shirts (black, white, navy), three dress shirts (white, pale blue, grey), a five-pack of briefs (white), ten-pack of socks (black, but thick), a pair of plaid shorts (because it was still sort of summer), white sneakers, disposable razors, shaving foam, toothbrush, toothpaste, floss. All of modest quality, grabbed as he'd pushed a shopping cart through Zellers. Head up, alert, wearing track pants and sweatshirt borrowed from Vicky's husband. His hurry had probably been due to shock, but he must have resembled someone on a spree. He remembered grabbing the deodorant stick because he could smell his armpits even through the smoke wafting off his skin, a smell that would take more than one shower to subdue. He'd grabbed a deck of cards aware that he was straying from essentials into entertainment. It felt frivolous, and loftier, as did the supersize bar of chocolate, even though he bought it with the muddled notion that all survival kits had chocolate.

Stuart unpacked the chocolate, leaving an empty suitcase. Without being aware of it he had stashed the clothes and toiletries in their proper places in the motel dresser and bathroom, as if he were staying more than a night. One kind thing Connington had told him in the first minutes, pointing at Stuart's ruined house, was, "This will be a transition for you. It's like there's been a death. You'll go through the stages of grief. Lots of anger, and guilt. You have to take care of yourself over the next while." Stuart had half-listened, more fascinated by how the firefighters were emerging one by one from the smoke to stand at a designated spot on the lawn where a helper unhitched the spent oxygen tank and placed it with the twenty or so other spent oxygen tanks lined up neatly on the grass. Also hypnotizing were the four fire trucks and their lights that never stopped flashing and that seemed to flash in a connected pattern, which of course had to be an optical illusion. The ambulance had its own flashing red lights with a different rhythm, plus a yellow one adding chaos, or a silent jazz, the whole display penetrating and making Stuart accept in his body that something serious *was* happening. The ambulance's rear doors were ajar and a firefighter sat having his blood pressure taken. The man's mask was off, and the skin protected by it shone white in a black ring of smoke and soot, not unlike the famous faces of 9/11.

ON HIS BED he leaned back against four pillows, his thumb popping the remote in a rhythm and pace that didn't look exactly human. He returned most frequently to a show on fishing in storms for Alaska crab, and a stand-up comedy act wherein a fat comic's shtick was that yesterday he was skinny and today he woke up like this.

It was hard to enjoy images on the screen because memories flashed up brighter. He had never felt this alone.

Between one thumb push and another, he realized that not a soul knew where he was. No one. Other than some neighbours, no one who knew him was even aware of the fire. No one except Diane, and he didn't want to admit to himself how much this made him miss her.

The day after the fire he'd gone to the library to email her. He thought of phoning but knew his voice would brim with emergency and betray other stuff, and maybe he'd cry. And email was Diane's way. After moving out she averaged one or two a week, explaining what had happened to them. "Forgive me," she'd write, near the middle of a five-pager, "but it's how I explain things to myself too." In any case it became her mode of talking to him. "In emails I can edit myself," she said, kindly freeing him from the equation and leaving unsaid that emails were unlike their phone calls, where she'd say "Why didn't you tell me that?" and he'd blurt "Maybe you weren't listening," and knee-jerk escalation made talking impossible.

In the library's cool silence Stuart sat at the screen and tapped in the code they gave him at the desk. He could smell stale smoke rising from his lap. From sweatpants he'd bought an hour ago. Where was the smell lodged, his crotch? His skin? How many showers would it take?

He caught himself shaking his head and mumbling, and stole a glance over at the librarian who'd relinquished the code as if to a potential criminal. He'd tried to show her the face of someone who, like her, abhorred pornography, and it might have backfired. Her eyes were from another era, and had a goat's steadfast warp.

But it smelled so nice in here. It was so clean, and its quiet the abode of angels, where no one had ever lit a match. He also noted an absence of wood.

He had to pause and squint to remember Diane's email address. It had been a while. Three or four months. Maybe it was this lapse of time, or maybe it was the fire, but he found that his thoughts about her, about them, were clear. Their story no longer seemed complicated.

Five years ago Diane decided he was no longer part of her life plan. This plan was vague, and that the plan itself could change was part of its nature. After her earnest probing of yoga and modes of healing and spiritual this and that, her plan as it stood now had to do with a teacher, and a group. It seemed an odd thing for a smart-suited corporate secretary to get involved with, but Diane had always been open-minded. Apparently the group had no name, a fact that for some reason Diane took to be proof of its legitimacy. It had become the Group, capitalized, for her at least, or maybe for everyone, he didn't know. She found a spot with another company and got herself a condo up in Comox. It wasn't mandatory that she be up there, the Group was no cult, but she gained "more energy and guidance from these people than from anyone else." He believed her. Why wouldn't he? He also believed in his anger. All she'd left him with was a blooming sense, right in the gut, of failure. Not just as a husband but as a person. At one point early on she explained that he'd become "an anchor," and though it wasn't his fault, he was holding her back or, rather, she was holding herself back by staying with him, and life was short. She was being selfish, but also not, because if he loved her, honestly loved her, wouldn't he want her to find happiness? Would *he* be happy if she stayed, against her inmost desire? She said she'd left for his sake as well.

In other words, it was all reasonable, middle-age, grey-zone pap, and there was neither an argument nor an antidote against it. He remembered it taking him about a year to be able to hear more of her hesitant reverent spiritual talk without hanging up and then, in the privacy of his new little house, yelling while he paced, the evening's single beer in hand, stereo on, for some reason often old Steely Dan. Those cryptic wordsmiths had a couple of tear-jerkers in their repertoire.

Maybe he should have yelled more to her face. The truth was he never knew how. In the earliest days of their breakup, speaking to him, her face wooden with spiritual intent, her certainty certain, he lacked anything like the right words—or the right yelling—to penetrate it. And the one time he did raise his voice, something like, "Just please shut up," her look was motherly and the closest thing to loving that he'd seen in a while. This was maybe the worst part of the whole thing. Though she was being the villain, she was also in the right. It was a weird contradiction to hold in the gut. She no doubt had some kind of New Age saying to explain it, but he would never in a million years ask her.

Only once did he come close to telling her what he really thought. What he really thought was that, after twenty-odd years, their love had faded. Who was at fault? Only time and human nature. But Diane couldn't admit this to herself, and found a complicated way to think about it, and a Group to fill the hole.

Jen was angry at her mother for leaving. But Jen seemed even angrier with Stuart, for what she saw to be his refusal to fight back. Or, her word, to "try." But she looked disgusted with them both, and it didn't seem a coincidence that a month after the separation she chose to continue her English degree on the other side of the country, Montreal, where she'd lived ever since, five years now. At a loss for words, Stuart sat there watching his life split into three. He was still unclear which leaving affected him most.

He and Diane went fifty-fifty on everything, including the proceeds from the sale of their house, which he'd loved, having built the deck, new staircase, etc. As if on the rebound he went out the week of the divorce and bought the modest pale yellow place on Winchester. Upstairs he liked the coved ceilings, and the wall-to-wall that he would strip for the old hardwood. Downstairs he liked the unfinished space for a lathe and table saw. And he loved the tiny basement suite for Jen, in the unlikely event that she'd come back and use it.

Thus began the five years when Stuart's life became nothing but a race to pay off the mortgage as fast as possible, and retire. Who knows why he began this race, which he ran solo, and head down. Was it because, when they were together, Diane wanted *precisely* these two things and he'd been ambivalent? Sitting here in the library, head spinning, Stuart didn't want to think he was that infantile.

His fingers remembered her address and typed it in a scrabbly blur of keys. Now he had to write something. During one of her last emails, Diane had stained his computer with a notion that she and he remained entwined in ways that affected her progress. She was holding herself back by being emotionally attached to him, and what could he do to help further break the ties? He didn't answer that email, figuring his silence might be help enough.

Smoke smell rising to his nose, fingers twitching on the keys, he knew only that he wanted to keep this short. He was aware of feeling the small thrill of the spurned-with-a-secret. He was tempted to tease: *Watch the news tonight. No one died.*

She deserved to know that he was okay, but really that's all she deserved.

> Hi Di— Had a house fire. The place a write-
> off apparently. My stupid fault. I wasn't hurt.
> Don't bug Jen with this, please. Anyway,
> thought you'd want to know. Stu

He pushed send. The "Di" and "Stu" were digs of a sort. He'd never cared for "Stu" himself, but in the era before their breakup she began using longer versions of names and even had a speech about names and one's sense of integrity. She applauded some guy in the Group for having changed Nick back to Nicholas, for instance. Telling Stuart this, Diane gazed into the middle distance, her new oasis of sincerity. (He's re*nicholas*, Stuart said to himself. Jen might have laughed at that, she loved wordplay. And, until puberty, she found his jokes hilarious.)

He did hope she wouldn't tell Jen. "Your father had a house fire but he's okay." It was like he couldn't look after himself in the biggest, crudest way.

Things were still confusing. He had just successfully emailed Diane, his crotch smelled like smoke (he should have told Diane that, but it was a dig she'd never fathom), and images from yesterday still flashed through his mind in herky-jerky rhythm, not unlike the flashings of the fire trucks. Panic came and went. Sometimes Jen's face, and he had to tell himself again that she was safe. A gasp, sudden tears, a deadly sleepiness. Twice he'd wiped away a tear here in this library. He should try to nap or he might fall apart. Last night, whenever he did somehow pass out, he'd jerk awake in full panic maybe only minutes later. Maybe he should contact Jen, after all. She might pay a surprise visit, you never knew for sure, and what would it be like for her to stumble upon his charred shell?

Stuart logged off, his eyes tired of the hard fluorescence. Even firelight—good God, to think this—was softer. Catching another whiff of smoke he bent over as far as he could and sniffed at his pants. This wasn't the source, though the smell down here was stronger. He forced his head lower. It was his shoes, it was in the leather. He grabbed a foot in both hands and got the shoe up a few inches closer to his nose and the smell snapped his head back. He sat shaking his head, wincing, understanding he might vomit. Then he noticed that goat-librarian eyeing him full bore, alert to a maniac.

NEXT DAY, HE CRUISED Revelstoke to hunt down a decent lunch. He'd had a big shock, why not treat himself? "Live a little, or even more." It would be in the spirit of Mel, who always treated herself, who would find the most intriguing place in town, which might be a dump or a glassy bistro, and even if she settled on a burger joint she'd sit up taller as the waitress approached with the platter, eyeing her untasted burger like it might be a new best. Mel always had that hope.

Stuart passed two Chinese places and a Thai. He was in the mood for Asian, but in Revelstoke? Here, Chinese could mean frozen vegetables, ketchup in the sweet-and-sour sauce and MSG up the yingyang. He was starting to sound like Mel, even in his head. He looked forward to going to a restaurant with her. Earlier he did the math—he hadn't seen her in twenty-seven years. Which was unbelievable, because he could so clearly see her face, that reined-in hunger, how she'd unconsciously bring a fork to her cheek and gently tap it. When food or a bottle arrived she would stop blinking, and not speak.

Goaded by a phone booth he saw again in his circling hunt for food, Stuart decided to try calling. In this age of cell-phones, were there fewer pay phones around? It seemed so. At a corner store he bought a pack of gum with a twenty, asking the counter girl, herself a gum chewer, for as many coins as she could spare. She counted out a fistful without meeting his eye.

Feeling archaic, he punched in the number on Connington's card and clunked in the requested four dollars and fifteen cents. A cheerful recording gave him his list of options. One to report a claim, two to renew an insurance policy, and other options on up to seven that weren't remotely about being homeless, about your house burning down and being covered or not, about having hundreds of thousands in the bank or nothing at all. Number eight would give a company directory of names, and he'd have to spell "Connington" using the keypad. Finally, nine said he could push zero at any time to speak to a service representative, so he did, gratefully, only to be answered by a dial tone.

He put his forehead against the cool glass. He stared at his feet, his smoked shoes. He studied the business card, flicked the card over, and there it was, scrawled on the back, Bradley Connington's cell number. Stuart entered it and dumped in four more dollars.

"Mr. Connington's answering service." The voice had a professional lustre.

"He's not in?"

"This is his answering service."

"Can you tell me when he'll be back?" It occurred to him that this had nothing to do with being "back." This was his cellphone.

"I'm just an answering service."

"Um, so, do you take messages for him?"

"Exactly."

"Okay." How to put it? "Could you tell him I'm just very, ah, curious, to know if … Well, I need to know *when*. *When* they might know if … um. Well, actually, he knows what it is I want to know. He knows why I'm calling. I just, ah, need to know if the decision, if the information, is available. Yet. Or not."

There was a pause. "Is that the message, sir?"

Stuart suddenly felt exactly what he looked like, an unshaven man wearing red shorts, black socks, and brown leather shoes, shyly gesticulating in a phone booth.

"Is this, um, is this being recorded for him, or are you writing this all down?"

"Could you leave your name and number, sir?" Her voice had grown even more distant, as if she were pointing her face somewhere else.

"Yes, thank you. It's Stuart Price, the house-fire claim on Winchester Road, and my numb—" He wanted to hang up from embarrassment, but took a breath instead. "I'm on the road and don't know where I can be reached. Please just tell Mr. Connington that I'm curious to find out about the claim, and I will call him back. Tomorrow."

Reading it back as if to tell him what a proper message sounded like, "Stuart Price will call tomorrow," she hung up on him.

After a visit to Canadian Tire where he bought a cheap

tent, flashlight, air mattress, sleeping bag, and knock-off Swiss Army knife, Stuart circled town again but no restaurant beckoned. Then he did what he'd promised himself he wouldn't, which was to buy food to eat from his lap while he drove. He compromised by buying healthy. Late summer fruit was in and he stuffed a bag with three kinds of apples, some pears, and figs. Plus a chunk of roquefort cheese that he cut up in the parking lot. To pare it into bite-sized pieces he used not his new knife, which had proved impossible to remove from its hard plastic packaging bare-handed, but the edge of the knife's plastic packaging, the knife itself red, plump, and sterile, still inside.

GOOD CHEESE REMINDED HIM of Mel. Should he be calling to warn her?

The thrill of the Rockies rising in the distance, he alternated between cheese bits and apple slices and tried to recall when he first met her. He knew it was a beach fire. Cates Park and the usual circle of more guys than girls, each with beers or wine bottle within reach. A joint going around and craziness sparking up, any gems of which no one would remember the next day. Who was there? Arnie, for sure. Ready to argue everything, even when you took his side. Quiet Laura, who'd drag Arnie away simply by walking off. Dave, with his fresh stump-just-above-the-knee, it was that summer. He'd cry once or twice before they helped him home, drunker than he used to get. George, with the ramrod posture, nicest smile in the world. One of those summers George went out with Diane, which was how Stuart met her. Glenda would've been there. Tony. And probably Pink (whose real name was Lloyd, and because he was the only one of them who never smoked dope, the Pink Lloyd was inevitable).

Then this quiet one, Melody, odd name for a tall, angular body. A friend of Zelinski's from work. Khakis and navy golf shirt labelled her a nerd, though it turned out she was way ahead of them, into that retreat from fashion of any kind, beyond cool. For a girl not to care what she looked like? Cool indeed. But she was so tall. She had a round face, with small, pretty features too gathered and central. Big, kinked hair. She would sit there and beat out a complex rhythm on her thigh, head bobbing along, body loose and bent like a reed. She had a tall, loose-goose thing.

He tried to remember what Mel had in that first knapsack. That she'd brought a knapsack at all was odd, as odd as her being five years older than the rest of them, all nineteen or twenty, enough of an age gap to prevent her sliding in as a full member. Not that she wanted to. But a new person bringing food to a midnight beach fire where no food had ever been before looked like effort, like social bribery. Though of course everybody gobbled everything she had. Which, Stuart decided now, was two kinds of cheese, one of them stinky; and there were pepperoni sticks, but bison, hard to find at the time; and there were dates, and some kind of savoury flatbread. Stuart knew he was mixing up fires and knapsacks, but he decided to remember some challenge hot sauce, or at least some pickled jalapenos to pass around. He did have a clear memory of a quietly likeable Mel. In the firelight ring, laughing soundlessly, jiggling, Mel was content to drink wine out of the bottle like the rest of them, though hers was imported. Like the others, Stuart thought her wealthy for all this. As it turned out, all she had was taste.

Stuart had watched Mel walk into the firelight, tall and self-consciously hunched, all that hair, and caught someone whisper, "Sasquatch alert." He saw for the first but not the last time how she put those she approached on guard, as her walk was a bit off-keel, her head pointed one way and her torso another, so that you weren't sure what direction she was going. Mel happened to plop herself down on an empty spot next to Stuart, trusting the log to catch her, and if it weren't for that empty spot, who knows if they'd have become friends. Neither of them said much to the other. They were alike in that way.

No, he remembered: out of an olive-green canvas knapsack, she pulled smoked salmon. They talked about the probable smoking-wood, which Stuart ventured was alder. He also enlightened her as to the cedar drift log they were sitting on. How old it was and how of all wood its resins were rot-proof. They both agreed it would be lying right here, like bleached bone, long after their grandchildren were dead.

FOR HOURS THE SIGNS had been saying "Golden." On he drove, watching the temperature needle nudging up. He wiggled his bum to get pain-free, ate, admired the looming mountains. But today he couldn't escape another, more real world: piece by piece, what he'd lost in the fire leaped at him in full-blown recall. The objects were random, and had meaning or not. His parents' portrait, wherein his mother achieved the impossible by looking reasonable, and his father had something of a unibrow. The unopened box of dominoes, a painful Christmas gift from Jen that looked bought in an airport. On his mantel, the black rock trapped within a winding grey root.

As he came into a curve nearing Golden, it was his bathroom shelves. He banged the steering wheel with a palm. Yellow cedar, the smell of yellow cedar. Red cedar lined chests everywhere but yellow was rarer and smelled weirder and better. Yellow cedar was figs and harems, its honeyed pepper could lure you and make you a bit insane. He'd taken guests to his bathroom to prove it. He'd hunted his own yellow cedar drift logs on local beaches, bucking lengths to just fit the Datsun's back seat. He brought them to his school at night to use the mill and power planer. It took a month to get his nine good boards. He bought a nice floor-to-ceiling steel frame from a Euro-bathroom place and used his boards instead of glass. He left them untreated and butter-soft and oozing scent, which filled the bathroom. With towels and facecloths laid upon them, still the spice came boldly through. Sometimes he would lean, close his eyes, and breathe it in. He never fastened them, they were anchored only by their own weight, so he could sand them every year and have them freshly oozing again.

His breath caught. He banged his wheel with his palm again, but for another reason. He'd built those shelves at his old house. And left them there. He hadn't smelled those shelves in years. It was Diane who wanted him to sand them yearly, and he'd stopped doing it. They were probably at her place.

What was he mourning those shelves for? He wasn't thinking straight these days. Not at all. Well, Connington had hinted at this, hadn't he.

The world roared on outside, the car bouncing through it, the old engine's buzz sounding more and more like protest. Then he heard it, a little tinkle, a beckoning. There it was, dangling from the ignition, his key-chain ornament, his one attempt at carving. It was almost as old as this car. In lieu of toes, which would have broken off, he'd given the salamander little semicircles for feet, hooves really. Its body twisted like a souvenir Mexican gecko, which was the model he'd used. A dirty, tawny brown from the years of pocket dirt and coins rubbing into it. Its real colour, of course, was the golden cream of yellow cedar.

He didn't ease up on the gas as he unhooked the beaded chain, freeing the salamander. Other keys, one his house key, fell in a scatter to the floor. He hunched and with a blind hand found a key and with it, balancing the salamander on his knee, scraped and scritched the key teeth into the salamander's back. He could smell it even from there. When he brought it to his nose and gently inhaled, he remembered why, thirty years ago, he became a carpenter.

He really used to love that smell.

IN THESE VISIONS were no white envelopes coming through the door, no insurance reminders. He could see himself at his desk, just weeks ago, sorting the mortgage stuff, the lawyer stuff, the fruit of years of focus and saving to pay off the house. How was it possible he'd lined up so many ducks, fitted so many pieces of the puzzle, and missed such a big one? His life was a mosaic of responsible detail: driver's licence, passport, debit, Air Miles and grocery-club cards, lists of usernames and passwords. He paid his sewer and water and electric, his property tax, his credit card. He even got his movie rentals back on time. He paid his car insurance, as well as insurance on his ever-beating heart. (If it stopped, Jen might be sad but she'd be rich.) So how had he missed one?

HE WOKE UP to a morning too cold for late September, and too dark for a town called Golden. He checked out in a hurry, told himself to slow down, and cruised the town for a breakfast spot. Situated on a rise toward a pass through the Continental Divide, the whole of Golden seemed to be sloped. He was sure it wasn't, but his senses saw all stores, banks, and trees on a tilt. He couldn't live here.

Sticking out the side of a gas station was a big white telephone on its field of blue, a pay-phone sign. A hollow in his gut told him he shouldn't have left town in the first place, he should've taken care of this insurance matter, should've researched and persisted and cajoled. Stuart tapped in the number, clunked a few dollars of change through the slot, selected an option of the nine offered and, a miracle, on came the adjuster. Hearing his voice—"Connington!"—Stuart saw the two of them standing together in his yard, the man's hand soothing on his arm. And then at a firefighter's word, Connington donning the survival suit to tramp through the ruins snapping pictures of every conceivable thing. Even his showerhead, his environmentally insulting showerhead. Big as a dinner plate, beautiful, like standing under heaven's warm rain. Its face was plastic and it had warped …

Stuart explained where he was.

"A little trip," said Connington. "Get away from it all. Probably a good idea."

Leaning from foot to foot, a tidy dance, Stuart explained further about heading to Toronto to see a friend. A sick friend. He chuckled about his new tent, all tight-packed and not much larger than a wrapped umbrella. He assured Connington he was saving all the receipts.

"Something's come up, Stuart. We need to talk."

Stuart understood that the adjuster had been waiting for him to stop blathering.

"They turned down your insurance claim—"

"What?"

"*Locally*. And that was expected. It was a rubber-stamp thing, because you were late. Someone in the local office sees the date, ticks an *X* in a box. Automatic. But so is your appeal. I put it through myself. I assume you wanted to appeal."

"For sure. Of course."

"So that's done. Next thing—"

"Do the appeals— Do the appeals work?"

Silence from the other end stopped Stuart's little dance. "Yes. They do. Sometimes they do. Worth following through on, anyway. Nothing to lose, right?"

"Nothing to lose …"

"So the next thing."

A lovely taped female voice interrupted to demand another dollar eighty for another minute. Stuart's hand came up with a grab of change and slid in an ugly mix totalling three fifteen, each size of coin earning a different chime note. Connington had been talking through it.

"So the rain damage is what's called a 'secondary event,' not covered by the same policy that covered the fire, since you're no longer 'residing' in the residence, which puts it into another class of policy, so—"

"It's raining there?"

"And with no roof the water is getting into places—nooks and joinery and seams—that can't be dried."

"They put a big blue tarp on it."

"Well their big blue tarp blew off and that is the 'secondary event' I'm trying to explain, so the battle now—well, the *smaller* battle—is to see who pays for it. Your insurance, which you don't have, since you're now a non-resident. Or the company's insurance, but they're saying that that amount of wind falls under the 'Act of God,' so—"

"But if it's a teardown anyway?"

"*If* it's a teardown. It's gotten complicated. If you had paid and your claim had been *accepted*, we would have sent a restoration crew there *now*, first day, still smoking, tarps would have wrapped the whole place, blowers set up, the whole thing. *You* wouldn't have been liable for 'secondary-event water,' *they* would've been. *No* question."

"Right." Stuart felt blown away by a wind himself. "But the house was, um, sprayed. From firehoses. For an hour. Blasted. Everything was soaked. Remember that river flowing out of the house across the yard? Rain seems a bit, you know, redundant?" Stuart made himself chuckle audibly.

"Well, sure, yes, but how will you prove what water caused what damage?"

"How will *I* prove?"

"I'm afraid so."

"It's really complicated."

"As I've said."

"Can I talk to someone?"

"You are." Connington could be clipped at times.

"So even if my claim, my appeal, is, is accepted, I might have to pay for …"

"Now you really have to hope it's a teardown."

"I guess I do." He recalled his walk-through, his small joy at seeing what rooms hadn't burned. His bedroom. Bathroom. Jen's little suite downstairs, never used, cleanly zen-like as ever. Except for the water streaming through the light fixture, mid-ceiling, and the two inches of water on the floor.

The lovely-voice demanded more money and Stuart spoke loudly over it, telling Connington goodbye and that he'd call again tomorrow. Walking to his car he enjoyed a vision of a country farmhouse burned down and neighbours appearing from over the surrounding hills, their wagons filled with timbers and sturdy tools, and dogs and kids playing, and kerchiefed women bearing tureens of stew and pies covered in checkered cloth. They had come to help him rebuild, they were unsmilingly happy about it, they would complete it in two days, the house would be bigger and better than before, and celebrated with an evening of homebrew and fiddling … The vision was brief, having filled Stuart's panic almost as a joke, and its retreat left him hollower than ever. As he sat with hands on wheel he saw what had triggered it, a Cookhouse restaurant across the street. A hand-painted banner proclaimed *"$9.99 Mountain Breakfast 3 kinds of Meat."*

There was always breakfast. Like Mel, he could get happy with a meal. Today he could fill himself up with mountain meat.

HE REACHED BANFF DISAPPOINTED for being exhausted again, for being blind to the beauty and in a hurry when there was none. None at all.

He found the main campsite just outside town. He chose to camp not to be frugal, in case the insurance company had bad news for him, but to slow himself down. Feel and smell the earth. He was on a journey, he was free to take some time and open his eyes. In fact it was necessary. So, here in campsite 22, he did it. He dropped the tent pack at his feet and looked up into the trees. He smelled the pine. Feet not on dirt but on a spongy cushion of old pine needles, he asked himself, "Will I ever be here again?" He knelt to yank the tent out of its vinyl bag and had to turn his face from the smell. Holding his breath, he asked if he would ever again yank a new tent from its bag and smell new plastic fumes from—he squinted at the label—China.

As if to give him another thing to notice, the sun fell behind a mountaintop, instantly hacking ten degrees of warmth from the day. Stuart gazed up at the loss of light. The mountaintop had gained a halo of spiky solar rays, worthy of a painting. He wasn't sure, but he thought that until now birds had been calling, and with this sudden dusk they were silent. How was it possible he couldn't remember if thirty seconds ago there'd been birds?

Though his questions felt a bit cloying, he wanted to ask them. Keep slowing things down. He'd start by trying out this tent that, with its snazzy fibreglass poles, domed up in a minute flat. He zipped it open, entered on all fours, suffered another minor blast of virgin-vinyl, and paused at the unfunny notion that he'd just crossed the threshold of his new home.

Stuart lay on his unfurled bag. Maybe he'd slow down enough for a nap.

HE STANDS REFLECTED in the black square of his sliding glass door, which is ringed by flames. His skin, lit by the firelight, glows bright gold. He is the colour of a steady, underground sun. He is the Devil at his most beautiful. He stops aiming the hose as he catches his eye in the glass. Beauty, despite his stained old briefs. Beauty despite being surprised and big-eyed and equipped to fight absolutely nothing. The gold of his skin glows so brightly that the dawn behind him appears black.

He wasn't sure if he napped, but he lay in his tent for about an hour, head swollen from lying on the wrong slant. He saw the glowing image of himself less and less now. At first he'd suffered it a dozen times a day, but now it was down to only two or three, and he knew he almost enjoyed it. He wondered if he'd ever forget it. It was so vivid, and he couldn't remember the rest, none of it. Things were either vivid or they were gone. For instance he wondered how he got up on the sundeck with that hose. When did he put on his glasses? He could remember shouting for Jen, even the treble rasp in his throat as he did, and then calling 911, but his next memory was of standing in that black square, skin glowing golden, looking at himself spray feeble water into flames. He must have gone out the front door and around to the side, turned on the hose, then climbed the deck stairs. That would be the only way, and he remembered none of it. He did remember—vividly—trying different settings on his plastic Canadian Tire nozzle, clicking the dial while rigidly moaning. "Shower" was good for rinsing lettuce, "Mist" was ridiculous, "Cone" little better. He clicked lastly to "Jet," which was forceful but skinny as piss. Down on the lawn, when it was all over, he wondered if things would have gone better if he'd twisted the nozzle off and used his thumb on the bare hose. That is—the thing is—maybe his thumb could've saved his house.

IN THE VAST TAVERN, which for the obvious reasons was a disappointing place to spend time in Banff, Stuart and this woman Kath sat nearly touching shoulders, a lack of tables forcing them to end up side by side on stools at the bar. Stuart did brighten a bit at the sight of the bar itself, a massive expanse of vintage white pine.

"Wonder if we're safe from the *muons* in here" is what Stuart said to this woman at his side, a little joke to break the ice.

She looked at him with no comprehension then turned away, possibly concerned that she had a full drink still in front of her.

He'd assumed she'd ridden the gondola up Sulphur Mountain. Didn't everybody? So he told her about today's side trip, how he bested his fear of heights and just did it, feeling only slightly strange doing it alone, but who cared if he looked like a loner, he *was* a loner. (He was aware of talking too much at this point.) At the peak he followed Japanese tourists to the old weather station, where a plaque said "Cosmic Ray Gathering Station." Didn't that sound naive? Cosmic rays? The plaque also told him that several muons had passed through his body while he was reading this sentence.

"So we've both had muons go through us while I've been yakking," Stuart added.

Kath said "Yikes," but couldn't look less impressed.

"I mean, have you heard of muons? I've heard of neutrinos, but not muons."

This news aroused her enough to say with a half-smile, "That's my knowledge of physics exactly."

Then they discovered how alike they actually were: she was driving alone from Toronto to Vancouver, to visit a daughter, while he was doing the reverse, except from Victoria, to visit a friend. Kath was a veterinarian, and forty-one (Stuart didn't believe her by a few years). But then the bigger coincidence: not only were they, at their ludicrous age, both camping, and not only in the same campground but, after describing things—past the washrooms? that grove of trees near the river?—they learned they were neighbours, and what were the odds of that?

"Kath?" Stuart said. "This is weird. That we're sitting—"

"In this bar, and a couple miles away our tents are side by side."

"And we're both as old as we are, and 'not poor,' but we're—"

"Both alone."

"I mean how many people our age camp at all?" Stuart heard his voice pitch high and in the long wall mirror he watched his amazement. "We're hermits!" He wanted to shift her word "alone" from its inflection of "available." Saying it, her eyes had gone wide, obvious as a wink—but a two-eyed version that suggested less some quick fun than a kind of awe at something huge and important in store.

"Weird place for two hermits." Kath turned her head at the crowded bar, its eager clamour seeming to agree with her.

"It's weird times, I guess." He went on to describe how, for the past twenty years, at this time of year he'd normally be in the classroom, that is, the shop, to teach "the meeting of wood grain and blade" to a bunch of hormonal maniacs who hoped they'd found the easiest elective.

"How'd *you* end up *there?*"

Stuart tried to take this as a compliment, and went on to explain how, as a journeyman carpenter, he got tired of bosses and, even more, fed up with clients who thought a week's work would take a day.

"Why carpenter?"

He could still construe a compliment in this. She was almost a doctor, and maybe it was true he'd been forcing extra polysyllables into his chat, trying to jostle her concept of guys who worked with their hands. But her question made him revisit that time, there was definitely a time, when he decided to stop deciding which of the liberal arts to pursue and instead admit how much he liked wood. He told Kath it had a hippyish, "If I Were a Carpenter" flavour, where working with the hands was not only noble but romantic. Mostly he'd just come to accept that he felt better building something than he did writing an essay. Even a stupid birdhouse. Especially if he designed the stupid birdhouse, turning it into a smart birdhouse. What size dowel for thrush feet? Humanesque ornamentation or blend-with-surroundings? Back then, he loved that. He needed nothing else.

"The 'and you were my lady' part was also good." He tried to look rakish.

Missing or ignoring the reference, Kath said, "So you've retired."

"And it's a little weird to be on the loose. No itinerary. Except east."

Kath said that she had to be back at work in two weeks, adding in a cartoon voice, "Because all my little doggies need me." She waved an arm at the bartender. She wore a constant half-smile, her left mouth always curled up, cutely pugnacious.

Stuart mentioned the fire.

"A house fire? Good God." Kath squeezed his forearm, leaving her fingers to linger for a charged few seconds.

He smiled, raised his eyebrows for her. For the moment, the two of them here together in this bar felt to him as weird as anything else that had happened lately. He was aware of comparing her on a desirability scale. She might be described as "not unattractive." Maybe that described him too, but he was in better shape. But he wore glasses. She had expensive, up-to-date hair, her bangs a long perfect curl, an amber sausage spanning her forehead. His hair couldn't be more casual, and he owned no hairbrush. She had stubby fingers, he a wood-worker's hands, meaning those of a feudal peasant. She smoked tarry French cigarettes "only when I drink," and he could smell them on her. He wore mismatched Zellers. Her khaki outfit was expensive and tasteful. He was socially clumsy, she was confident. Tonight was easy for her. But her bum was bigger than the barstool, and the excess wasn't sexy. Mostly, she had steady, friendly eyes. Stuart could feel his flying all over the place.

"How'd it start?" She laughed. Not unattractively. She banged back half her fresh gin and tonic.

Stuart smiled and jammed a thumb to his chest. He began the same story, how he lacked a shredder and wanted to burn some paper. Right about here, people often came up with a little joke along the lines of "You think you overdid it a little?" But Kath didn't. Instead, she asked the wrong question.

"What were you burning?"

He considered her. If there was someone to tell, it was her. And on this night of small coincidences, why not unleash the biggest one?

My mortgage papers. I burned my house down the day after I paid it off. He couldn't. There was something sickly sweet in an irony so perfect, and saying the words out loud might nauseate him.

"Just some letters." He stared straight ahead, letting the moment expand, then glanced her way to acknowledge her sad, knowing smile.

He told her that "despite appearances" he wasn't stupid. It was an immense plastic planter full of bare dirt, three feet broad, big as a barbecue. He hadn't loaded it up with that much wood, and when it started to rain a bit he moved it up against the wall of his house. He let it burn itself out. He had a leisurely beer. When he left the deck there was no wisp of smoke, no live ember. But apparently an ember was hiding, and apparently dirt burns, and apparently a breeze came up to turn smoulder into flame, and at dawn his sundeck and wall were on fire.

"I guess these things happen," said Kath, slurring just a little. She tapped one finger on his forearm instructively.

"Not to me," Stuart said, serious. "It's hard not to take it personally."

"It could have been worse." Kath widened her eyes for him.

The fire chief had ended their discussion by telling Stuart that it wasn't a bad fire, as fires went. In terms of restoration, he said, smoke damage was the hardest part. What had burned was mostly wood, with some plastic from vapour barriers and wiring and such. At least it wasn't a protein fire, he added. Protein-fire smell was hardest to get out.

"A protein fire?" Stuart asked.

"Well, you know, sometimes, for instance, grease catches and a whole turkey burns. Happens a lot. Or there's pets. Or—" The fire chief raised his eyebrows and pointed straight at Stuart's chest. "Thirty seconds more," he added.

Protein fire. Protein fire!

And here in the Banff bar, through the window of which a

bank of mountains stood as black silhouettes against a purple sunset, to agree with Kath he said that at least it wasn't a protein fire. When he hinted to Kath what that was, he started to go teary.

"Well thank God for insurance, Stuart Price!" she said. "Now you get to enter the world of interior decoration. I had friends last year flooded out their whole ground floor. They were flipping colour swatches for six months."

Stuart was glad she was making light. No need to mention his other story.

They were nearly tipsy but drove their two cars back to the campsite. The road was empty and, leading, Stuart did some fake swerving to say hi to her and remind them of their apologies to each other about drinking and driving. She drove a new black BMW and he wondered what she thought of his Datsun, a car so old you could read it as poverty or, maybe, as fondness for vintage. In the parking lot they discovered that neither had a flashlight, his being in his tent, so he took her hand, which was only natural, and led her down past the washrooms to their tents.

"Can we go to yours?" Kath asked, freeing him of various questions he was concocting. "Mine's my son's, and there's mildew." She grabbed his arm and looked at him in the dim light, a mother grimacing naughtily. "And it's my *son's*."

"Mine stinks like plastic." There were no other words in Stuart's head. Nothing remotely like this had happened to him in decades.

STUART WOKE WITH BIRDS screaming so loud that, at one point, he thought he heard Mexican horn music. He had one sturdy sliver of a headache. Kath snored confidently beside him, her elbow pressing his shoulder. He remembered her touching him like this all night, not to make contact or even to claim space, but like her body wasn't aware of anything at all.

He squinted at this woman beside him. Her pillows were elsewhere and her head was punched into the tent floor such that her chin was higher than her forehead, like she was trying to see what was behind her, upside down. The posture also caught his eye because of the neck concavity it created. He squinted in harder. It might have been his hangover's own evil slant, or the fierce morning light of the tent, but Kath had a hump. A barest suggestion of one, but it was, more than it wasn't, a hump. Not as curved as Death's scythe—but if it made you think of Death's scythe, it was definitely a hump.

Sitting up, he reached and finger-tapped gingerly behind his pillow for his glasses. Nothing. He searched farther afield.

"*Jesus.*"

"Whaa." Kath woke and half-turned her head, eyes staying closed. She rolled away from him, onto her side.

He'd spied his glasses poking out from under her sleeping bag, badly bent. He brought them in close to properly see them, but he needed glasses for that. They were for far and near-sightedness both, he needed them for everything. His poor glasses were so completely bent at the bridge that one lens almost touched another. He tried to bend them back. The gold-ish metal felt hopelessly flimsy. Gently, gently, he bent them back, bent them back—they snapped, one lens dropping out.

He lay back on his pillow, which was a towel wrapped around folded pants.

He let the birds envelop him again, listened for mariachi horns. A hermit could get his social fill from these birds, would need quiet the rest of the day.

Despite the evidence of a headache and broken glasses, nothing had happened. He let last night's frolic come back into view. The laughing, the dragging of her foamie, sleeping bag, and two pillows from her tent to his, the stumbling and hissed whispers, the yell from a neighbour tent that made them feel like teenagers, the discovery that his bag's zipper, plastic, would not marry hers, metal, but it was really cold so they just climbed into their own bags, "for now." Then some hasty shallow kissing, and her breath, because she had that last cigarette outside the tent. Her stubby fingers on his bare shoulder, then chest, felt mostly odd, didn't feel like more. When he cupped her breast it mostly didn't feel like Diane's. And Kath seemed not too excited by the earnest things he was doing to it. Their hands' meanderings quieted down at the same time. Stuart felt mostly apprehensive and silly, while he sensed boredom from her. They agreed they were both tired, but also that they were still very, very glad they were in the tent together. And Kath said, "Actually I prefer mornings."

The bird screaming eased off as the border of sunlight moved, almost visibly, down the wall of his tent. He pictured an ever-freshening line of birds waking, screaming, and easing off as the sunrise pushed west toward Victoria. He pictured the sun lighting up his tarp-wrapped house. He didn't want sex this morning. Nor did he want to ask himself why. He unzipped his bag as quietly as he could.

He stood beside the coin-operated shower, dancing foot to foot on the cement, hand in the spray, waiting for the heat, which never did get past luke. He'd maybe suggest they drive to town for breakfast. She probably wanted to get on the road too.

She'd surprised him. He thought she'd be a desperate cougar, which was of course his locker-room notion of what all women her age were. But in fact she had a life, and one that didn't include the likes of him. Her marriage had ended years ago and she had no desire for more of the same. She co-owned an animal hospital in Richmond Hill and was a vet on sabbatical, and "seeing the country and pretending to be a teenager on the way." Walking to the bathhouse he'd eyed her BMW again. In ways that counted to most people, Kath was probably more attractive than he was. Last night he'd felt dismissed. She probably just liked the idea, the wayward thing, the here-today-gone-tomorrow. Maybe his Datsun added to her fantasy. It was a teenager's car.

Back at the tent Stuart stood outside and said "knock, knock" to wake her. He suggested breakfast in town. She wanted to shower and there was a bit of a lineup, so he walked the river. He did so holding up the one intact lens by the arm, an opera monocle. He loved the river's exotic milky blue, wondered how fish could see their food in it. Off in the distance on the bank opposite he spotted a small herd of what were probably elk.

In the spirit of the river he ordered the "Anglers Brunch," which featured a side of trout. It's what Mel would order, no doubt about it. Sadly, for breakfast they had ended up in the same pub as last night. Kath looked around and nodded, noting "the scene of the seduction," and Stuart didn't know what she was mocking. She asked what happened to his glasses and he said he'd stepped on them. Kath was hungover, and with her curly hair all flat on one side she seemed to know she wasn't looking her best and he didn't want to make it worse by telling a stout woman she'd crushed something.

During their meal Stuart twice left for the pay phone to try Bradley Connington. When she asked what was so important, and offered her cell for a third attempt, Stuart confided that the matter of house insurance was up in the air.

She leaned back and watched him more keenly, as if he were an interesting zoo animal, and he caught sight of himself through her eyes. He hadn't shaved this morning and lacked a hairbrush. Here in the restaurant he'd been doing a lot of squinting and, when he needed to, using his half-pair-of-glasses monocle.

"It's funny how it's an all or nothing thing in the end," Stuart offered. "Some guy in an office. Someone in Toronto— or Chicago, apparently—will grab a folder from his stack and go thumb up or thumb down, and that'll be that."

"God." She shook her head minutely and laid her hand on his forearm in so gentle a way that it was only sympathetic. Perversely, it made him want the more obvious squeeze of last night. Their tents were still up and sex was still possible. He told her the little joke he'd come up with.

"The one good thing about not paying my insurance is they couldn't accuse me of arson."

Kath offered to buy his breakfast and Stuart said, "Please. No."

"Jen," Kath said at one point, "who's this Jen? You mentioned her last night. She your daughter?"

"I did?" And then, "Yes."

"When we were drinking. It was Jen this and Jen that, and she abandoned you."

He met her eye. "She didn't abandon anybody."

"Jen's a pretty name." Kath seemed to know it was complicated.

When she was little he told her he'd named her Jen because it rhymed with hen, and how good it was she wasn't a boy because then her name'd be Booster. When she stared up at him her eyes shone and her mouth stayed open, because she thought he was hilarious, and maybe she was the only one in the world to ever think that. He didn't even have to try, yet somehow his quiet goofiness drilled into her. How much had he taken for granted when she sat on the couch between him and Diane, a Jen sandwich, and leaned into Stuart's side, liking his little quips about the sitcom. The berry shampoo smell of her head. He'd look at the top of her head from above, inches from it, marvel at the many colours of her hair, from blonde to cedar to mahogany.

Jen grew distant with puberty. He didn't exactly "try" to fix that one either, thinking that's how it sometimes went with daughters and fathers. If she hated you, she didn't necessarily have a reason. If your heart was broken, it wasn't necessarily anyone's mistake. But there she was in Montreal, with close friends she'd never mentioned, and studying, apparently, Jane Austen. Using grad-school words he didn't know and, if truth were told, didn't want to. Would a better father read Jane Austen so they'd have more to talk about the next Christmas she visited? Wouldn't the *best* father read it just to know his daughter better?

And he remembered giving her Mel's dad's book to read. It was maybe the only book he'd ever given her, and he gave it only because he was proud he knew the author, M.H. Dobbs, if only indirectly. (Mel called her father Hal, short for Harold.

His first name was Melvin, that is, also Mel, and this bothered her to no end.) Jen hated the book, so much so that she hated *him* for the book, too. It came up while she packed for Montreal, and he was helping, or hanging around her room to grab more time with her, when he noticed the books being left behind and he innocently asked if she'd liked *The World*. He picked the book up, bounced the ghostly white thing in his hand. He made the mistake of saying he'd loved it. What he remembered most was Jen meeting his eye, not like his equal in this, but his superior.

"That book of your friend's?"

"Well, my friend's father."

"Some white man, writing about Chinese lepers, writing about a Chinese leper woman being raped, telling us what that felt like? Are you kidding me? I wanted to throw it across the room."

"I'm sorry you feel that way."

"I'm sorry you don't." She turned to stiffly recommence boxing books she approved of, and added, "Some people think they own everything."

It wasn't a fight because it was so one-sided. He didn't defend himself because what popped into his head was only childish. "*I* didn't write it." "How can a book abuse people that aren't even alive?" "I don't think I own much. I wish I owned way more." Also, he was more than a bit dumbstruck by what he'd just heard—the biggest sample yet of how much his daughter kept from him now. The distance between them was shocking. There was no other word.

He could clearly remember how her back turned to him like a signal. And her blue-jean shirt, the one she wore for gardening or cleaning. He remembered first being amused, that day, that she had a special utility shirt, like her mother. He always liked seeing the same person in both of them.

He still felt that day's anger, even in her absence, even years later. You don't forget an angry departure. And that angry departure he associated with *The World*. Which, in turn, he associated with Mel. It was as if, at some gut level, he felt that Mel had made his daughter permanently angry at him. Strange how things fuse.

The World. He remembered some of it, and didn't know why he'd put it down. Probably the horrifying subject. But it was a neat idea, and set near where Stuart lived, D'Arcy Island, which, if Stuart climbed a hill near his house, he could see in the misty distance. D'Arcy had been a leper colony in the late 1800s and early 1900s, home to several dozen lepers, all of whom died there. All Chinese. It was an exotic nugget of history, and Stuart was surprised how many in Victoria didn't know about it.

M.H. Dobbs fictionalized the rest. A mysterious tin full of old Chinese writing is dug up and secretly bought by a junior history professor, and it makes his career. First he has to find a translator, and he does, a strange and beautiful one.

AT THE CAMPSITE, packing up—just two friendly neighbours dismantling their tents, chirping about travel plans—Stuart mentioned his friend Mel having cancer and Kath quietly announced her daughter's cancer, which was in remission. Stuart pointed out yet another coincidence, them both driving to visit the stricken, and Kath said nothing. In their quick hug goodbye she chuckled into his ear, "So who knows what *this* was." No promise to look each other up. Maybe his bad car, bad hair, broken glasses, and houseless bad luck had finally got to her.

There was another coincidence just outside Banff. Pulling into a rest stop to rid his car of candy-bar wrappers, cups, and apple cores, he saw a rat scurry from some heaped garbage bags to hide under a dumpster. A rat, here in these mountains. Hadn't he read somewhere that Alberta was rat-free, and proud? That was a rat, he had his monocle up and saw it clearly. A rat, and now he was pulling out and driving east, to Mel. He never saw a rat without thinking of Mel.

One lovely summer night he was at his girlfriend Sheila's basement apartment in Point Grey, and sweet little Sheila dumped him. He pretended to dump her too, driving in some final nails. The breakup was hot, jagged, and wouldn't die down.

There he was sitting out front in his car, freshly crushed, love convulsing inside him. Window open, his elbow stuck out into a vast night, balmy and luminous and full of summer smells, a night pretending to be one of the friendly ones. But it had a clarity that sucked even the possibility of contentment. Its warmth was cold. Stuart knew that you might kill yourself in anguished frenzy but he could see now how you could do it rationally—you see not only how empty your antics are upon the stage, but that there is no stage and never had been, there's nothing.

At this point, the rat. The thing is, it wasn't a ratty neighbourhood, you wouldn't expect a rat here, and certainly not walking on a sidewalk bordered by perfect lawns. Stuart heard an approaching *tuk, tuk* and glanced down to see it, a rat on the sidewalk beside his car. Stuart startled, and startled the rat. It stumbled off the sidewalk and onto the grass, where it had a harder time, and Stuart saw the mousetrap attached to a front leg, pinching the rat at the shoulder. The rat's caught leg flapped, useless, and it swung-dragged the mousetrap like a giant, clumsy crutch. This explained the sidewalk; in the grass, the trap snagged. The rat looked exhausted.

He had the car door open and a foot on the curb before he stopped himself. The rat stopped too, eyeing him. What the hell. How do you help a rat? It would bite the crap out of him. He brought his leg back in, closed the door. The rat dragged itself away. Stuart shook his head, snorted a laugh. He laughed because there was a stage after all, and the rat was a player on it. As far as coincidences went, this was a doozy. Wasn't Stuart caught by the trap of bad love? Wasn't Stuart free but crippled? He sat staring as the rat risked the sidewalk and gained some distance on him, *tuk, tuk*. He wanted to pound on Sheila's door and show her. But Sheila would see only a rat, she wouldn't get it. The thing is, Mel would. He pulled a U-turn in the balmy smells and pointed his car at the distant neon of downtown.

In retrospect the real meaning of the rat was that, though he had other friends, he went to Mel, someone he didn't know that well yet. Maybe he was looking for the female touch, literally and figuratively, who knows. She just seemed to be the person to tell about Sheila and a rat and a mousetrap. Some friends would see it in a big-eyed cosmic way, like they did any number of details in a day, and others would make nothing of it at all, which was the same thing.

Mel let him in with an air that Stuart visited all the time. It was nine or ten on a work night. The first thing she did was sort through a few bottles of wine on the kitchen counter and open one. Then she started cooking, talking to Stuart over her shoulder as things sizzled. On the couch a shabby acoustic guitar sat propped up looking freshly played. In a corner on the floor amid dirty clothes and sheet music lay her fretless bass, apparently a good and expensive one. Books everywhere, no pattern to them—novels, maverick psychology, bios of rock stars. Her hair looked unwashed and heavy for it, an Afro falling out of its tight curl.

Minutes later Mel plopped down unmatched plates heaped with a pasta and awesome sauce, he'd seen her at the counter grating more than one kind of cheese, there was back bacon, he saw her jig wine, squirt lemon, shake cayenne, and it looked like there were bits of wild mushroom in it too. It was a scene Stuart would come to know, Mel using company as an excuse to cook something.

They ate the pasta and drank two bottles of wine. They talked about Sheila and the mystery of love, and Mel loved the rat. They digested and sipped. Sitting tall on the couch, feet tucked up under her, she looked unsurprised and comfortable in her role as confidante. Stuart noted Mel's voice, how soft it stayed, never forcing a point home. You had to listen or you might miss it. You felt equal to her. You could easily feel more than equal. You forgot she was six-one. You forgot she was older. She laughed a lot but silently, jiggling there on the cushions. At one point he burped mutely but hard so his cheeks puffed out, and she called him Dizzy Gillespie, and when she burped, she tried to copy that and made an ungainly fart noise, and now Stuart could say absolutely anything to her. Eventually Stuart got tired and left, remembering in his car that Mel had to work in the morning while he didn't, and so saw another side to Mel, which was that she'd never tell anyone it was time to go.

No, there was one more thing. He finally got Mel to pick up her battered guitar and sing him a song. She did something slow and jazzy. She wasn't a flashy singer, more a low, honeyed murmur, a tune well carried but no frills. But the guitar. He realized he'd never heard a good acoustic guitar before, not that close to his ears. The sound was both bright and deep. It was that song and that guitar that made Stuart wish he could be a musician too, that coolest of things to be. It looked fun, and soul-enriching, and for sure it got you laid. He considered Mel's guitar, excited. He couldn't make that sound, but maybe he could make the instrument. Not long after, he acquired the pegboard mould, a heat machine to bend the wood, a few precision clamps and drill bits for precision sanding. He bought veneers cheap enough to make mistakes on. It was all about clamping, gluing, and sanding. By the time he got one to the stage where its body was sound, could take strings and hold its tune—that is, when he'd made a guitar—Mel and he had lost touch. The plan had always been to give her that first one.

Stuart built three more, each different but not necessarily better than the first. One he sold for less than the cost of materials, two he gave away, and one he kept. Jen found it in the basement and learned to play and got pretty good—she could do a basic "Classical Gas"—but it ended up at some boyfriend's house after she found showing up to reclaim it too painful.

HE FIXED HIS GLASSES with duct tape bought in Canmore. A clumsy pewter bulb the size of a chestnut rode the bridge of his nose and he'd have to hunch in the back of restaurants. But tomorrow was Monday and he could seek out some frames into which his lenses could simply be popped. The ugly repair and restaurant shame was moot anyway when not ten miles out of Canmore a wasp flew in the window and swatting at it he jostled his precariously bound specs and broke them again.

Still a bit hungover, once more holding up his monocle and steering with one hand, he had to fight the feeling that things were disintegrating. Even the Datsun, coming down out of the mountains and allowed to fly, felt reckless and loose-screwed as it hummed its tune with giddy overtones of rattle. He promised himself he'd slow down and appreciate these famous approaching prairies, perversely flat land that people said "does" something to you. He realized he'd driven through all those mountains feeling cowed by them, more bullied than befriended. As the land started to open up, darkness looming only behind him now, Stuart tried to enjoy this plunging out of the mountains' squeeze into a vastness and light.

Zooming, a fresh world coming toward him, Stuart found himself *doing* it, felt himself verging on happiness. It wasn't just the eager car, and it wasn't just that his monocle, which he checked out in the mirror, was so funny. He smiled. He smiled a bit wider. Even forcing it like this, happiness seemed possible. It did. The alternative was to think back only a handful of miles, to Kath, and what that meant. It had been five years since Diane, since any sex at all. What did it mean that he'd turned down sex when it was handed to him, no strings? At his age, transient tent-sex didn't come along every day. If he were actually to ask himself the question, *Could this mean I'll never have sex again?* he knew a scary answer might flutter too close, on death-coloured wings. Other questions, like, *How much do I care if I never have sex again?* might lead to other questions just as bleak. Or lunatic—*After fifty, does sex always involve a dowager's hump? Or, Even if there's the sexy lack of one, will thoughts of a hump now be automatic?*

His attempt at a lunatic smile had no chance against this sudden non-happiness, so he pulled off at a historical-site marker, screeching his tires a bit as he braked and getting long-honked at as he turned in. He got out and stretched. He breathed the sagey lowland air that came at him invisibly bigger than mountains. He tried to touch his toes but couldn't. The plaque was all about the Bow River, which twisted below him like a silver worm. Lovely. But almost as if to worry him with more coincidence, the plaque's main story was about the Calgary Fire of 1890. Hunched close and squinting, Stuart read how the city burned to the ground and was rebuilt from logs floated down this very river.

He squinted east, picturing all those Calgarians as wary descendants of that fire, which of course was ridiculous. No one was wary. Time heals all. But knowing now the godliness of fire, he wondered at other famous big ones, how unimaginable they must have been. Winnipeg'd had one, and of course Chicago. The Halifax explosion. San Francisco. And Vancouver, back when it was small and wooden. Protein fires in wooden cities, honeycombs of smouldering human bodies. Wooden buildings was the problem. Wooden buildings and people burning their mortgages. No, it wasn't funny. Imagine a city-full of survivors. But no cars, and no place to go. Nobody had insurance back then.

Stuart looked back at the plaque, deciding that coincidence was everywhere if you were looking for it, and meant nothing. At the same time, he had only to feel himself in that dark dawn, spraying the fire with his hose, seeing in the glass door his reflection looking back, his big eyes, his glowing skin.

At that moment, if some voice had said *It's all meant to be*, he would have believed it.

At speed again, he decided just to breathe steadily. That was enough. The rounded foothills looked purple in this afternoon light. He remembered seeing antelope around here when he was young. The road was straight; he braved long monocle scans off to the side, seeking antelope. But soon rose the cityscape of Calgary, much bigger than when he was younger. Big counting house in the foothills. Canada was the biggest oil supplier to the U.S. It boggled the mind. He was tempted to turn left, north to the patch, see where they squeezed the oil from the dirt. As he approached the city, its glass and cement shapes clarified and looked bullying. It looked like there was nothing there that could burn.

Stuart turned south. Then he pulled into a vast gas station because of the size of its store. At the counter he asked if there was a pay phone, then negotiated a handful of change.

"Connington!"

"Hi, Bradley, it's Stuart Price. I called a few days ago? The house fire on Winchester? Seven, eight days ago the—"

"*Yes* yes yes."

"I know it's Sunday but do you have a minute?"

"Yes yes, of course. No weekends in my business."

"One thing. I wanted to ask you who it is who decides if the house is a teardown or not. Because that question seemed to be the key to some other decisions down the—"

"That would be me."

"Ah. Right. So, I guess my next question would be—"

"Have I decided yet? No. That won't happen till a certain big something is decided, right? But, when and if, it's simple. Two companies bid on the cost of *repairing* the house, and two companies—sometimes the same companies—bid on the cost of *replacing* the house. Which costs less? Bang. That's my decision."

"Right. Okay." It sounded fair.

"And actually it wouldn't be unwise of you to choose one of the companies."

"Why would that be?"

"You know how these things work, it—"

"Actually I don't."

"Well, yes, it's complicated. Your insurance company might try to choose a bid that's lowballed and then it's substandard work and iffy subcontractors and all the rest of it."

"Right, I see. So, um, when does this bidding take place?"

"Not until there's money at hand. So there's no point yet."

"Right, and so I was mostly just wondering if, about my claim, and the appeal, about when you'll, um, or maybe it's *they'll*, be, ah, honouring the—"

"Yes yes yes. That won't be known for a while still. When it's not a slam dunk either way, it can take some time."

That won't be known by whom?

"Could I ask, are you in some way involved in the decision? I mean I'm not trying to influence things, but it'd be nice to know the process, you know, and *who* exactly—"

"No no no, I have nothing to do with it. I wish I did, but I don't. Well, come to think of it—" Here Connington laughed a hearty laugh meant to include Stuart. "I'm *glad* I don't have to decide stuff like this. Eh? I mean, who would? Though I guess somebody out there does. But how are you doing? You doing all right? I have that list of counselling services I mentioned."

"Thanks, no. Maybe down the road." He'd meant this as a joke and even laughed, but it was a nervous little laugh and

Connington said nothing. "But I guess I am wondering about the 'who.' About who's deciding this thing."

"You know, come to think of it I can't really say."

Stuart felt something tilt just below his lungs.

"*Can't* say, or, or—"

"No no no, I'd tell you if I knew. It's complicated. I mean somewhere in the bowels of the company—no, no, I'm going to say *brains* of the company—some person will—"

"Is it your company? A branch of your company?"

"No. Stuart? Here's how it works."

Connington went on to explain, laughing at the complicated parts, about insurance. The credit union where Stuart bought his policy used a broker to farm out the policies to any of over forty insurance companies, located anywhere in Canada. His insurer was called Best North. Connington himself was a freelance adjuster who worked a region and was hired case by case by any of these same companies.

"Does Best North have an office in Victoria?"

Connington laughed. None of them did. Most of them weren't even Canadian. Or, rather, were Canadian, just not *owned* by Canadians. If Stuart caught his drift.

"Do you know where the head office of Best North is?"

Connington sighed to let Stuart know he was being done a favour, excused himself, and came back to tell him Toronto.

"But if you're planning to contact them, there's really no reason. If they want information from you, you'll be asked."

"By whom?"

"I'm your contact in this."

Stuart could get rude here. His one connection to the looming decision was a man who'd just announced how glad he was that he had nothing to do with it.

"So they'll phone you? The decision-makers in Toronto?"

"Someone will send a piece of paper with a ticked box to someone somewhere else, who will send another piece of paper somewhere else, and someone will get a memo back at the credit union, which storefronts all these companies, and they'll call me."

"Wow. Okay."

"I'm saying 'piece of paper' in quotation marks, right? It'd be a PDF, some kind of secure screen. And who knows if they're even in Toronto. Or the 'they' might have changed seats. You know? Corporate belt-tightening has a way of trickling."

"I don't—"

"The guy who ticks the boxes in Toronto might have just got a call from a bigger guy in Hartford, who ticks the boxes for the bigger company—I mean, Best North might just *be* a box that got ticked on this *Hartford* guy's sheet of paper, and might no longer exist. Economy like this …"

"Jesus."

"Just speculating. Just telling you how it's built. You asked."

"So there's no way of me finding out the person who's actually making the decision about my house?"

"Stuart? There's no way of *me* even finding out."

Stuart was back in his car, driving stupidly. He went maybe a mile before he realized he couldn't see well because he wasn't using his monocle. He'd gone another mile more before it occurred to him that now he was heading east in a hurry not just to see Mel but to find someone he could actually talk to about his house. The actual decision-maker. The human. To whom he could apologize for being late. And be sincere about it, because he was. Students used to apologize for late projects

all the time. You can tell who's sincere when it's eye to eye. Eye
to eye helps you be human.

THE BRIGHT SETTING SUN rode his right shoulder as he drove
south on a minor highway pocked with tarred-over potholes.
It lacked major traffic. There was legitimate desert in southern
Alberta, he was pretty sure. He should probably buy a map,
though he didn't really need one. If he went too far south
he'd be stopped at the U.S. border. Too far north, it'd get
cold. Turned around, he'd run back into the mountains. And
the sun was there as a simple compass.

Exactly this kind of detour was great, this narrower, slower
road. See things he'd never seen. Maybe eat a giant Alberta
steak in some dusty small-town restaurant. Eat an immense
cowboy slab in Mel's honour. Though he recalled Mel's least
favourite meat was beef.

He ripped into his last bag of potato chips. It was hard to
steer, hold his monocle, and eat chips at the same time. He
zoomed by a bright white school sitting alone in a yellow grass
field and looking like the most forlorn place on earth. It was
too easy to picture rows of morose rural faces in there and
it put him in mind of work, his last years at Lambrick Park.
Funny how even his body seemed to know the time of year,
and that it should be standing on that cement floor, gazing
at the room of new faces. It had got to him, that roomful of
kids who'd rather be elsewhere, paired up at their work desks.
Paired up but not allowed to talk. The air was full of *waiting*.
And his was the face of their imprisonment, his words the
useless hoops they must jump through. It wasn't that way with
all of them, but he'd grown too aware of the latent hostility he

was taking in on every breath. Every September he'd had to adopt the toxic habit of establishing his authority with a yell (the chosen victim invariably never forgave him), because if he didn't, the year would be hell. And then the first lecture, the blood 'n' guts show, demonstrating what tools would take off body parts. For some it would be the last time he had their attention. Then on to elementary drafting, a drawing of their year's project: the grade-nine bird feeder; the grade-ten giant clothespin fridge magnet. It was a waste of drafting paper. For the grade twelves, who got to design and draw their own projects, unless he knew the kid it was hard to discern if a grandiose catapult or dog-size coffin was a leg-puller or not. Stuart had grown so tired of shutting down the laughers and pranksters—his main job was to keep kids from having fun.

He remembered his first year. When he left the carpentry trade for the teaching of it, he'd reckoned the job would still involve carpentry. That is, it'd still have all the stuff he liked—the wood, and wood's forgiving exactitude, and the warm-bread sensation of making something. And he'd be out of the rain. And, no boss. The boss was now him, and he'd be a kind one.

So he was surprised by how little it had to do with carpentry, or wood, or making something. The work was all about teenagers, and dealing with male chaos, with hormone management. It wasn't about being kind, though he tried, but it didn't take long to see that to laugh along with their horsing around quickly became a safety issue because, if allowed, fourteen-year-old boys will keep pushing the limits and showing off until there's blood. It's like they don't even have a choice in that matter. And after kindly believing every shy excuse, he saw he was being lied to and walked on. Even the kids he liked were doing it, and he was surprised by how much this depressed him.

But he stuck with it, as people do, and over the years his weekdays fell to that state of grim patience shared by everyone stuck in a job. He couldn't even complain to Diane about it; she'd ruined that option right off the bat by cheerfully offering to support him through school if he wanted to train for something else. And Diane liked her job at the provincial legislature. Assistant to the deputy somebody, it was a day of keyboarding and low-level secretarial, and she did everyone's bidding, even fetching the coffee, because everyone was above her on the pole. Stuart figured Diane went through a day at work with sunny disposition intact simply because she knew how. It was more than just a trick. She seemed to believe that she was having a good time. It was quite the skill, really: she knew how to make her life pleasant. She knew how to put feeling in her smile.

Stuart remembered being only vaguely aware of that discord, of her liking her job and him not liking his but being forbidden to whine about it properly. It sounded funny when put like that but he wondered how much it had eaten at him, over the years. And if it was one reason he didn't *try*, as Jen put it.

Stuart pictured the inside of that school he just passed and knew he'd grown blind to the fine moments. There were kids who were honest and fun and warm. In the last decade most of these had been girls. Maybe it was that boys wouldn't admit to their new-found fondness for wood, while girls could. But toward end it was girls who arrived most curious, who listened brow-knit, and then truly engaged with the tool and the wood. Who enjoyed the precision. Who commented on the smell. None had carried on with it that he knew of. Over the years a few boys had kept it up, a few even becoming carpenters. A few out of over a thousand. There might be others he didn't know about. Why would he know about them? There was that one tiny kid who became an architect. He visited once when Stuart was out, dropping off a note to thank him. Robbie Coleman. The note was somewhere in his bookshelf at home, meaning it had been pitched into the dumpster of charred, wet slop with everything else.

Back when he was younger, a girl had come on to him. Maybe it was her way with all male teachers. Quite pretty, a bit goth, Carol Dixon had lingered after class to talk about nothing in particular and touched her little finger to his wrist and boldly left it there. (He sometimes wondered if he waited too long to remove his wrist. He didn't want to jerk it away dramatically, in case it was innocent. It was maybe a four-second touch.) But some students had become friends. Yes, he could call them friends. One, Richard, turned out to be gay, and so their hushed, eye-to-eye conversations may have been a boy's crush, but so be it.

It was sad to leave in bitterness. But it had been years since he'd felt his words as he described that good violence of a saw cutting across the grain of fir, or of sanding a project to cream. Or the magic of a well-struck nail embedding itself beyond the range of the hammer, in momentum's dimple. The Goldilocks curl of cedar planed paper-thin. It had been years since he cared. Students did their work well, indifferently, or poorly, then they left and he had no clue if he nudged them, if he planted any seeds at all. So, freedom fifty-one.

Stuart flicked the empty chip bag to the floor, mouth burning with salt, ashamed of himself. Then he noticed

something his eyes had seen a million times but hadn't registered in years: his wooden radio knobs. Probably twenty years
ago he'd had a snarky guy—Nick, he was a Nick—serve out
his detention by learning the lathe and fashioning two sets of
knobs, because it turned out he had the same year of Datsun
and the same radio. Stuart showed him, on the spinning wood
piece the thickness of your thumb, how you knifed into it to
make a string of connected spheres, then sawed them apart. If
you got finicky you could even make beads this way. So both he
and Nick came out with a set of radio knobs. Twenty minutes
and a dab of superglue later, they had probably the only two
sets of arbutus knobs on the planet.

He was bouncing too much and *what* was the hurry? He
forced his damn foot to ease off on the gas pedal and got the
needle to drop 10 Ks, from 110 to 100. He could feel the loss
of inertia, could hear a lower roar of air outside. At the same
time he felt the shove of impatience in his chest.

And he could smell smoke. House-fire smoke. It made his
stomach clench, and he began breathing shallowly. It was still
his shoes, these leather shoes. Why were they smelling again?
Was he remembering correctly that someone, some firefighter,
told him that body heat would bring out the smell? Not losing
much more speed he toed off his shoes, tossed them in the
back.

It felt childish driving with stocking feet. He could feel
that the gas pedal had vertical ridges. He could feel his foot
muscles pressing down hard, and he could feel his calf working
too, and even his right buttock, a little.

He zoomed past a country-poor gas station and its side
café, looking too grimly rural. He pictured squinting locals on
stools, tense with bizarre ideas, but he knew this was just TV.

Mel would approve of his detour, she liked the adventure of country restaurants and bars. For his part, Stuart never liked places where locals stared at strangers. He wondered if there was any establishment in this vast land whose door a man of fifty-one could walk through and conceivably face danger because he was a stranger. How bothered and bored would a pack of cowboys have to be? Stuart wondered if that was the one good side of aging, when you no longer showed up on testosterone's radar.

Mel always loved getting well away from it all, loved camping. Which perversely made her pay even more attention to food. It was a funny quirk—the more hardscrabble the trip, the better grub she'd bring. You canoe out to Jug Island for the night, you expect a sandwich, or beans, not prosciutto wrapped around fingers of monastery-made raw cheese, not a strip loin as thick as it was wide, not *smoked sturgeon*. She'd softly proclaim *Ta-dah!* and slide a surprise out of her knapsack. Stuart could remember Mel, two in the morning, an open fire, trying to bake a *moutarde ancienne* crust onto some lamb. There was always something exotic. Stuff he'd never heard of or tried, back before sushi or Thai or pho became the new burgers. There was an even more extreme phase, when the outdoors made Mel see food framed more simply— by the wind, campfire, often rain—so it didn't need spice at all. Stuart remembered a chicken, roasted on a stick, and him tasting, for the first time, *bird*. And one time there was that beef heart. Also roasted plain, on a stick, whole, Mel squatting there like an art installation. Out of loyalty, Stuart had a bite. He dropped a pinch of salt on it, had another.

Anyway, they had some fine trips. Stuart was twenty-two, twenty-three, when they camped near Egmont, an out-of-the-way place if ever there was, and after hiking all day and failing to catch fish off some rocks they ate a midnight meal of porta-bellas with fresh herring (sold as live bait at the marina) and canned lobster sauce, plus a bottle of Benedictine and brandy. That's exactly what they had, and that was the trip where they picked up that hitchhiker, a guy they'd talk about years later.

That hitchhiker smelled a bit rugged and he had the worst beard, the kind that was half bald patches. His constant smile teased their necks from the back seat. He looked maybe thirty. During the two-hour drive to the Vancouver ferry his story came out. He was a true hermit, living up an inlet twelve miles' kayak from Egmont. He'd built himself a shack out of scrap from an abandoned logging camp, and he'd been living there "maybe five years, maybe six." He paddled to Egmont monthly for supplies and to collect his "nut cheque."

"A doctor diagnosed me crazy and I get disability for life. It's superb, it really is. It's half again what you get for welfare. Doctors are gods, they truly are." "Superb," "truly" is how he spoke. Always the little smile and, in the eyes, a bubbling up, a glassy joy. He told them, "I'm Baker."

Once a year he travelled to Vancouver, found a hotel, showered, bought clothes, and began "a week of excellent drugs and food." At this point Baker and Mel commenced a digression on Vancouver's restaurants. Stuart drove, listening to them agree that the William Tell had lost its mojo. Apropos of nothing, the guy shrieked a *"yeehah!"* and punched the air and kept laughing. When asked, Baker explained through his self-amazement that he'd just several days earlier fallen off a small cliff and broken his leg. Lying there helpless and dying of exposure, he finally succeeded in "healing my leg."

Stuart was prone to changing the subject around now but Mel had to say, "So tell me how you healed it."

Baker asked if they'd heard of Jane Roberts and "the Seth material." Mel had. At one point Mel glanced at Stuart and asked, "You never heard of *Seth Speaks*?" Stuart learned that Roberts' books were recorded sessions where she channelled an Egyptian spirit named Seth who delivered all sorts of wisdom, the gist being that we create our own reality. Including, it seemed, a healed leg bone.

"I have five books on my shelf," said Baker. "All Seth. It's what I've been doing. The exercises." He didn't sound insane. He could have been detailing a career in carpentry. "So here I find myself, boom, bottom of this cliff—it was about a ten-foot drop, I was carrying a truly excellent beam I found under some rusty cable, been there *for years*, I could build a porch now, I wasn't paying attention— So here I am at the bottom with a mashed head and a broken leg, and I'm being given this, this 'opportunity.' I knew it right away. It was the universe saying, 'Okay, Ace, time to put your money where your mouth is.'" Baker smiled humbly, shaking his head. "So: I either do the work or I die. I passed out for a while, and when I woke up I started working on the leg."

Joining the party, Stuart asked, "So how do you, you know, actually do it?"

Baker said you visualized the bone, its cells, bringing a certain spark to them, and that meant "focusing so hard it feels like you're pushing a diamond through a diamond." Stuart braved a look back and through Baker's wild hair you could see an ear and upper cheek and scattered scabs.

On the ferry Baker bought them bacon cheeseburgers. After they dropped him off at a motel they agreed how sane the guy seemed. Mel shrugged and said, "Incredible." Stuart asked if she actually believed all that and Mel offered the cowardly, "I believe that if he believes it happened, it happened." But then Mel gave him pause by adding, "If you believe in nothin', that's all you're gonna get." Stuart would get used to Mel dropping her *g*'s when she said anything grand. It was like she had to get tough with the embarrassing bigger ideas. When she came out to him, for instance, she dropped *g*'s galore.

The last thing they said about Baker was sparked by the times. Neither of them had a career yet nor wanted one, so they agreed that Baker had a perfect life. He had guts. No money worries for life. He was a leech on society but so was any capitalist, and at least he was interesting, insane or not. That was worth something. A story-worthy life was worth a ton.

Maybe that's what Stuart could do in Toronto. He could have himself declared.

He decided to pick up the next hitchhiker he saw. In BC he'd zoomed by a few with eyes averted. The thinking was, you just didn't pick them up these days. But, what the hell, there might be another Baker out there. Or just some nice guy needing a ride. Maybe one of his old students. Maybe even a Jen. Anyway, he should come out of his loner shell and rejoin the world.

For Diane, his loner shell had become a problem. His satisfaction with it. She never ventured the complaint but he knew it was true. It was a weird problem, but she simply could not stand that he was satisfied with their relationship, and that any remaining distance between them was fine with him. Basically he was okay with himself, and with him-and-her, and over the years this was probably another thing that made Diane quietly unhinge.

On he zoomed, anticipating a hitchhiker around each
bend. He was empty with hunger and had held a pee for an
hour. Again, why the rush? Why couldn't he stop? Next town,
he would eat, eat something big, a mound of pasta, a steak,
both. He'd get a room. Enough tent for a while. And even
as he thought this, around a bend came a motel, the name
Foothills in the neon, a long building bright and lonely as the
moon landing, replete with a café, and bar. All the cars, pickup
trucks actually, clustered near the bar entrance, nothing at the
motel or café. Stuart registered this while zooming on.

There was that time, maybe it was the second time Stuart
met her, in that Downtown Eastside bar, the Cobalt, a place
they went for the safe danger suburban kids look for. Any dark
corner you glanced into sat some jagged guy not liking your
glance. They'd go as a group. Stuart remembered Mel entering
the place, eyes flicking here and there, almost mischievous. In
those days, to cover a few rounds they'd all "buck up," tossing
twos or a five centre-table, and Mel threw hers in and said
"Tithes." It wasn't particularly funny, no one laughed, and
some maybe didn't know the word. It took Stuart a moment to
register the quiet joke, drinking as organized religion. Mel just
didn't fit. Plus she was so tall. But so it was: entire years would
pass without him seeing Mel. Then out of the blue a phone
call, for a birthday bash, or camping. There was that "hillbilly
luau" in the backyard of some heavy-drinking guy who let her
dig a pit to bury hot stones with half a bourbon-splashed pig,
sweet potatoes, and corncobs.

Stuart was squinting through his monocle at the approach
of what looked to be an actual town, replete with motels,
when he remembered more about Mel at the Cobalt. She had
spotted two huge glass jars on the bar, one with pickled eggs

and the other with pallid white sausages suspended in what looked like brownish formaldehyde, and the cause of speculation about whether those cocks were from moose or dead guys in the alley. Soon Melody was sitting back down with both an egg and a sausage. Stuart could remember the smell—heavy vinegar off the egg and an iffy death off the sausage—and the table's laughing disbelief. Mel nibbled, paused, shrugged. No one took up her offer of a bite, so she wolfed both down, and then went and bought seconds. Some guys likely considered her for the first time.

And it was around then, maybe even later that same night, when he learned Mel's father was a writer, M.H. Dobbs. A few of them were walking along Fourth Avenue, hurrying to catch a band, and there it was in a bookstore window. A little stack of white books, *The World*. Mel said "Hey," pointed, and told them, "That's my dad's book," then kept walking. It was "about a leper colony mostly," she added out the side of her face. Stuart wanted to go back and lean on the glass and marvel at it a bit. Mel's casual air made it even more marvellous than it was, but that's how things happened back then. New things came at you all the time.

HE WOKE AFTER ONLY six restless hours, with a bad taste in his mouth he couldn't identify but sensed it had fuelled a dream or two. The bed had been fine, and while drifting off he'd watched a pleasant movie—despite being a cutie-pie, Jennifer Aniston was actually a pretty good actor—but deep sleep never took over. He was in the town of Fort Macleod. Last night he'd noticed its pretty Main Street with hundred-year-old stone facades, and lots of churches. This morning he showered then headed down to have what was advertised on the sign outside, the Truckers Breakfast, $5.95. He had to start watching his money.

Between his thighs he gripped a large coffee-to-go, which he didn't need. Merely sitting behind the wheel again, before even turning the key, he could feel the road fly below the floor at him and, not only that, he realized that it'd flown all night. He said "okay okay okay" under his breath. Then he stared out the window at nothing, making himself wait, feeling his impatience, feeling a ghost road zooming through. Something in all of this felt stupid. He should be back in Victoria taking care of business. He'd call Connington when he got to Lethbridge, an actual city. Then he shook his head—how did it matter where he made a call? Why a city? He could make the call naked in a field. He wasn't thinking straight.

The Datsun took a while to start and, leaving Fort Macleod behind, it bumped and chugged and took too long to get up to speed. How was that possible? Last night it was humming. How could a good night's rest do a car harm? Overnight, could some hot metal cool down and warp, touching something it shouldn't? He didn't know metal, didn't trust it. Though he trusted his Datsun. This chugging felt too much like a faithful old dog in his death throes.

A mile out of town he chugged past a hitchhiker, the one he told himself he'd pick up, but the guy was shaved bald and goateed, one of those thorn tattoos around the throat. Though Stuart saw himself through the fellow's eyes too: a fifty-year-old with a weird monocle in a poverty car. Who should be warier?

The car got to speed and the chugging turned into hesitations, like someone yanking on the back bumper from time to time. But going this fast he settled into his hurry and it felt only good and natural. He loved being in his car. He liked the world shrunk to car size, seedpod size. He could feel it as a tiny replica of his house. Buzzing along, life coming at you, was progress, endless progress. To stop, to get out, was to invite complications.

But he had to. In Lethbridge he found a Canadian Tire with an empty bay, was told to come back in two hours, and he went off and spent a half hour hunting a pay phone. During his hunt, one drugstore cashier shrugged and had no suggestion where one might be found but announced with undisguised pride that Alberta had the highest per-capita cellphone use after Italy.

Connington didn't answer his cell, so Stuart tried the man's office. After negotiating the menu of choices, he listened to a message from Connington proclaiming his absence for a week and giving a number for emergency assistance.

"Name and file number please?" asked a friendly female voice that sounded seventeen.

Stuart had to dig for the file number in his wallet, difficult while crooking the phone in his neck and holding a monocle to one eye.

"Mother's maiden name please?"

"Winter. But, um, I just need to ask if—"

"Winter?"

"Yes. I wonder if maybe Mr. Connington left word if—"

"Can you spell that?"

"What, *Winter*?"

"Well there's no listing of your file under—oh here it is. It says this file is no longer with us."

"No longer with you?"

"No."

"But that's probably— Is there any note from Mr. Connington that—"

"Maybe it's gone to head office."

"That's exactly what— Are you aware of my particular— Did Mr. Connington get you up to speed on what's going on with my, um, my file?"

Stuart had difficulty keeping quiet while he listened to shuffling paper. And then computer keys popping.

"All I can find— It just says here that it's been flagged for head office."

"Could I talk to someone?"

"Well, you are."

"I mean at head office."

"I don't think so. It's not 'our' head office. It's the head office of the insurance company handling your file." Then he heard what sounded like a hand over the receiver, and some whispering.

"What are you?"

"Excuse me?"

"What are you if— Are you employed by the insurance company? Handling my file?"

"I'm employed by an insurance *adjuster.*"

"Is Mr. Connington—" More whispering. Stuart waited.

"It says here— It says here you want to appeal your policy? You, let's see. You're appealing, um, you don't want to pay your premium?"

"No I was late with my payment and had a fire and it's being appealed and Mr. Connington told me to phone and—"

Stuart was asked to deposit more money.

"Hello? And I'm just trying to find out who—"

"I have to put you on hold. Excuse me."

The hold muzak was Santana's "Black Magic Woman," a spooky xylophone rendition. Stuart thought it an above-average song to spend this kind of time with, so he waited. He remembered as a kid thinking it was the singer named Santana, not the guitar player, and having an argument with a friend and losing, and he never heard the song without remembering this. The song was interrupted by an ad for financial products at the trust company Stuart had bought his insurance from, then more Santana. When the machine-voiced operator came along to ask for more money, Stuart gave up for the day.

He located an optician with a big stock of frames displayed on three walls. He entered to the tinkle of an electronic bell into a room smelling of fresh paint. With each step, his leather shoes whacked the spanking new laminate floor. A young man with dyed hair, perfect teeth, and the snappiest eyeglasses shifted out from a nook, smiling. Was that pointy hairstyle not called a faux hawk?

Stuart presented both halves of his glasses.

"You had a owie," said the young man.

"What I'd love, is if you could find something to pop those lenses into," said Stuart. "Instead of me buying completely new everything."

"These are really old lenses. They're pretty scratched. You sure?"

Stuart explained that he was only in town another hour and the young man walked away in deep study of Stuart's lenses, nodding. And returned, five minutes later, shaking his head.

"These won't fit anything I have. Nothing."

"I don't care what it looks like. Can you maybe just ram them into some plastic ones? Maybe grind them down to fit?"

"We don't do shaping here. We use computerized grinders. In Regina. Nor do we 'ram.'"

"I *really* don't care what it looks like. It's a danger driving this way." He grabbed an arm and monocle from the young man and demonstrated, grimacing with his head at a tilt as he did so, clearly a highway menace. "Even shim it in, and some crazy glue. Do you know what a shim is? Usually it's wood but—"

"I do know what a shim is," he said, taking Stuart's gear into the back again.

In five minutes he returned with an alarmingly ugly contraption. After popping the lenses back into their holders, he'd connected the broken bridge with a length of black plastic that went up at each end like evil eyebrows. He'd bound the whole mess together with lots of gold-coloured wire and solder, some beads of which, big as peas, blobbed at intervals along the bridge.

"It might hold till you get where you're going." He waited while Stuart gingerly studied what was in his hands. "How far are you going?"

"Toronto. How much do I owe you?"

"I can't take *money* for that." The young man laughed in horror, put his hands up in a protective cross. "Ssssst!"

Even lunch was in its way disappointing. The Best Burger in Alberta sign in the window drew him in, and while the beef was probably good, there was simply too much of it. More loaf than patty, it was two inches thick and cooked legally grey, and it made Stuart realize that he liked burgers mostly for the stuff around the meat. He could only imagine how he looked trying to get his mouth around it, and he figured that this combined with his glasses was the reason no one glanced into his corner of the restaurant twice.

Eager for news about his Datsun, he got some good mixed with some bad. The car had "lost a lot of blood," the wry mechanic explained, because it needed a head gasket. Stuart noted the man's homemade tattoo, which was either Christian or a plus sign. They could do the head gasket for a few hundred dollars, if Stuart wanted, or Stuart could buy some gasket-in-a-can for twelve. The thing was, a new head gasket might be a waste of money, because the head itself might be warped and need to be planed. That was many hundreds more. At this point the mechanic commented on the car's "advanced years," and made a dry funny about letting it die with dignity, which Stuart didn't really register as he was trying to decide about the few hundred dollars versus the twelve-dollar can.

"Does gasket-in-a-can work?"

"Sometimes it works great."

"Okay. I'd like some, please."

"And sometimes it just blows out like shit through a hoop. You buy it in the store proper. Through that portal." Already walking away, he hooked his thumb back over his shoulder toward the door. Stuart was too tired to enjoy these guys who were too witty for their jobs.

Maybe it was the transfusion of oil, or maybe the gasket-in-a-can, but leaving Lethbridge the Datsun was zooming again, no worse for wear. In fact the lesser country road through Taber and then Bow Island proved too narrow and lumpy for its renewed zip, so after a couple more—Purple Springs, Seven Persons—Stuart headed north in search of Highway 1 again, to Medicine Hat, a place worth going to based on name alone. He wanted to go fast. He just did.

And what, he thought, *what* would it mean if the insurance company did turn him down? Would he "lose everything"? Cresting a sudden tiny hill, the Datsun caught some air. It boomed upon landing and a fist of adrenalin shot up his spine and out the top of his head. He didn't let up on the gas. No, he still had "the land." Such as it was. It was a small lot even as lots go, but it was still his. His *land*. The dirt the clay the worms the stones. To demolish the house and have it removed would no doubt cost many thousands. He would be left with a cement foundation, and debt. He could maybe go back to work, pay it off. Could he freelance again? Frame up walls? No. What did it cost to build a house these days? Two hundred thousand? And the demolition, another ten, twenty? What bank would loan him two hundred twenty, he of no job.

The insurance company had to see the light. There was no other way.

Zooming well, a coffee in his crotch and his glasses hideous but working, he pointed north, soon to point east, to see Mel but mostly to see about his house. Talk to someone. Talk to the person whose job it was to tick that box.

At least he wasn't crying anymore.

LEAVING MEDICINE HAT, which looked too ordinary for such a great name, he saw a library and was braking and pulling into its parking lot before he quite knew why. In the stacks he found Fiction, then Canadian Fiction, and there it was, a row up from the bottom. The copy he'd given Jen had been soft, and this one was hard, but the dust-jacket spine was the same off-white, with the same plain black lettering. This would be good, bone up before seeing Mel.

He didn't expect to be granted a library card and was almost saddened at how easy it was and how they didn't care that his address was a motel. The literature business must truly be in dire straits. The smiling older woman—well, a few years older than him—even gave him a free cloth bag. Under a bold Your Public Library, it read, *"Reading Is for Real."*

In the parking lot he turned on the car, revved it while looking out the windshield at what he was about to tackle, then turned it off. He took *The World* out of its bag and turned to the opening, a page and a half long.

At the sight of him, Michael was glad they were meeting at Michael's house and not at his office at the university. He led the fellow into his study, insisting that he leave his shoes on, though they were workboots and not clean. The young man, who said his name was Pete but whose accent suggested to Michael that the real name was Pierre, had called him and described the box's contents. And now, as Pete lifted the battered tin cube from the canvas backpack, Michael was cautious and professional—but a mysterious box will excite any boy. Even from where he stood he could smell the box and it smelled ancient, of strange earth and roots and secrets.

Pete set the tin on Michael's desk, but kept one hand on it. Michael had said he'd pay him when he saw it and was satisfied that it wasn't a forgery. Pete, very much looking the part of a marijuana grower, wore a shapeless ponytail and sported a dramatic hawk nose which he seemed proud of, though Michael couldn't say how he knew this.

"How deep was it buried?" Michael asked, aware that the answer would tell him nothing.

"A foot. Not even that."

It did tell him something. A liar would have made it deeper, more hard-to-get. "Was it in a clearing? Or old garden site?"

"No idea. It was off the beaten path. But who knows what was where a hundred years ago, eh? D'Arcy Island's not small." Resting his fingertips on the crusted lid, Pete paused. He winked when he asked, "Think we can still catch it?"

"No," said Michael, sombrely, though he realized he didn't know for certain. Leprosy was a bacterium, and didn't they die after a while, unlike a virus?

"Too late for me anyway," said Pete. "I've had a boo at least ten times." He quickly added, "But I didn't tear anything."

"Did you xerox it?"

Pete looked at him quickly. "No."

The lid came up with a rusty screech which at the same time sounded sweet.

Michael leaned and peered in. There were ways to artificially age paper. But this was old. He could simply smell it, the smell of a hundred years underground. And this man was an innocent dope grower, so to speak, and the amount was only five hundred dollars. Good enough. He leaned in closer, his face six inches away from the top sheet, the faded characters coming clear. It looked like one hundred spiders had posed geometrically on the page and then been squashed flat.

"That's definitely Chinese," he said.

"It's definitely not English," said Pete. As if he were a legitimate businessman, used to transactions of this sort, he held out his hand to be shaken.

Michael took the hand and said, "Okay." Then he opened his drawer and took from it the envelope thick with twenty-dollar bills.

Pete bounced it to gauge its weight. He smiled at Michael and said, as if to let him know what a good person he was, "When you saw it, I could have doubled it and you would have said yes. I could tell."

And so Michael Bodleian, Assistant Professor of History at the University of Victoria, came into possession of a box of paper that would change not only his professional life, but his heart. He of course knew none of this, and even less did he know that, as an old man, he would think back on this day and wonder at the shape of his life had the box remained not only shut, but forever safe and deep in the haunted ground of D'Arcy Island.

Stuart placed the book back in its bag, smiling at "*Reading Is for Real.*" He remembered the book's wooden style. Old-fashioned. It was a classic kind of story. He remembered Mel telling him that her father named the character after a famous library, and that Michael Bodleian symbolized knowledge. The limits of it. Something like that. She also said that the book was about the head versus the heart, though whether any of this was her idea or her father's, Stuart didn't know.

And, yes, he did meet Mel's father once. Hal. He'd come out to visit. Tall like his daughter, sitting mischievously in her stupid beanbag chair with his knees sticking up. Stuart remembered him clearly now. Hal Dobbs had been odd for the way he sat there interested and smiling, but never saying anything unless spoken to. When he did say something, it was fast and funny, surprising.

HE STOPPED FOR LUNCH at yet another gas plaza. The restaurants attached to them weren't part of any chain, so each one was a surprise, the kind of place you checked other tables to see what the waitress set down. What did the fries look like, how big was the seven-buck bowl of soup. It was hard to do that here, with only one other person sitting over near the wall, a young fellow in a hockey jacket, one of those loud Canucks things with the torso-sized *C*, the top arm of which sprouted what looked like an angry killer-whale finger puppet. Catching Stuart trying to study his lunch, the Canuck fan stared back and Stuart looked down. But the Mexi-burger turned out not too bad, the salsa and guacamole juicing up a dry patty. A side of gravy did the same for the fries. And one thing the café had going for it was its chairs, at least fifty good knotty-pine chairs looking freckled but standing solid. Stuart hated it in walls and other broad planes, but chairs, yes. He and Diane once had a knotty-pine table in the kitchen nook, stained a kind of orange, and one morning he'd commented to Diane that it was like eating breakfast off of a giant freckled Archie face. Diane said nothing but might have been disgusted subliminally, because a month later the knotty-pine table was garage-saled and they were eating off white melamine.

The guy in the Canucks jacket stood with his thumb out on the ramp back to the highway, a small red knapsack at his feet. Despite his urge to not waste a second, Stuart couldn't not stop. They'd shared a look, they'd been aware of each other, their relationship couldn't be frailer yet somehow it seemed to count. Their eyes were locked again now. And Stuart wasn't up to speed yet. And he'd promised himself.

"I know these things look nuts" was the first thing Stuart said, pointing at his face. "Quick repair job."

"No problem," the guy said, still not looking at Stuart or his glasses. It seemed that the guy might not have noticed the glasses at all. He had a unibrow that dipped in a slight V, which made him look permanently concerned. And he did seem concerned. Distracted in any case. Glaring constantly at the road ahead. Stuart considered the small coincidence of his glasses' connecting strip of black plastic, his own unibrow.

"Where you headed?"

"Shaunavon."

"Not sure where that is."

"Middle Saskatchewan."

"Well, just tell me where to let you out."

"Okay."

"Give me ten yards' lead time, though, okay?"

Stuart had meant this as a bit of a joke but the guy merely said he would.

The guy was from BC, which was disappointing, and his name was Johnny. Stuart identified himself as Stu. Johnny was going to Saskatchewan because Saskatchewan was the new Alberta. He had a girlfriend there, he added, in Shaunavon. From the way Johnny crammed this in, Stuart suspected Johnny was telling him he wasn't gay.

Johnny seemed fine with glaring at the road, not speaking, but Stuart didn't think he could stand much of this, not hours of it anyway, it would make him ill. He sped along, pondering this car-filling edginess, and it was his own body that realized, *This isn't Diane.*

He didn't want to but he could feel her so clearly. He had courted her in this car. How many hours had they spent here? He could feel her hand light on his wrist as she let him in on a friend's story. Or the two of them riding in a silence that was just fine, that felt like a small, shared smile. Cars were so intimate—thigh to thigh on this little couch, looking out the same window, sharing the same *horizon*, even, and maybe your sweet little girl is floating questions from the back— What was he even thinking, letting this guy in here and expecting something comfortable?

He took a calming breath. Then a sustaining one. Then a third for bravery. He gave Johnny a cheerful rendition of things, that he was on a surprise vacation because of a house fire. Johnny wasn't interested but said "*That's* the shits" at appropriate times. Stuart punctuated things with the house-insurance problem.

"Good luck on *that* one," said Johnny, as if he'd gone through exactly this himself. He turned away to look out the side window, the subject at an end.

After five minutes passed, Stuart asked him if he was a Canuck fan, and Johnny said no. Another minute passed and Johnny told him he just liked the jacket. For the next while, the engine whining at him, in lieu of any more conversation Stuart forced the Datsun a bit faster than he should have. The car bounced in and out of dips in the road where the prairie underneath had warped it, likely something to do with its extreme mood swings of winter to summer and back. They did manage a string of words when he asked Johnny what kind of work he was looking for and Johnny said "Probably construction." Stuart was able to ask some of the right questions and ascertain that Johnny had experience framing houses in Surrey, so then Stuart was allowed to go on about his own woodworking life. In case he'd come off as too much the expert, and as a ploy to keep Johnny talking, Stuart offered that his own framing skills had lapsed, seeing as he was a couple decades removed from that work, and weren't they using metal studs these days, and even plastic? Johnny confirmed that they were, but seemed unsure saying it.

They drove through some plain, wide country. Apart from a dried salt lake with a piece of broken machinery beside it, there was nothing, not even tractor ruts through the fields. "Construction boom" drifted around the car in irony. Not much of the land looked even arable; maybe that grey stuff was wild grass. The only part of this landscape that looked capable of becoming something else was the wall of clouds to the west, which had been changing colour in his rear-view for a while now. Thunderheads, and maybe headed this way. He remembered he liked prairie storms. You could watch the storm coming at you for miles and miles. The atmosphere swells and roils and charges with spirit. One minute you're in sunshine and the next the world's gone black and you're bombed by icy raindrops the size of marbles.

"Look at that wall of cloud behind us," Stuart offered.

Johnny turned as if the wall was in the back seat and about to get him. He watched it for a while and said nothing.

They eventually approached a turnoff to Gull Lake and

Johnny said Stuart could let him out there. Stuart slowed and Johnny bent back to grab his little pack.

"Where is it you're going? Shawna—?"

"Shaunavon."

"Far's that?"

Johnny looked south and thrust his chin at it. "Couple hours that way."

"Ah hell," Stuart said, stepping on the gas. "Let's just do it." He took the exit south.

"You don't have to, man." Johnny sat stiffly with his red pack in his lap. It was the kind of thing middle-school students used for bookbags.

"I'm in no hurry," Stuart said, mostly to himself. "Sort of an expedition." He was going to say "walkabout," but guessed Johnny might not like that word. "And there's a storm coming." He hooked his thumb at the clouds to his right in as manly a way as possible, because Johnny was looking uncomfortable with his generosity still.

Johnny shot a look through his window to the west, probably too briefly to register anything. But the clouds were closer.

"I'm sort of on my way to visit my old girlfriend too," said Stuart, not technically a lie. "Melody. Haven't seen her since my divorce." Still no lie, though the implications were false as could be. He was eager to set right any "gay" question that might have clammed the young man up. Thus the manly capper, "So I guess I should be in a hurry, right?" A lascivious chuckle. "Dunno why I'm not." Another chuckle. Across a vast psychic distance, Mel was snorting at him in disgust.

"Okay. If you want to."

"Actually Mel's sort of sick. *Melody's* sort of sick. Maybe that's why. Anyway no problem. I'm just sort of exploring. Our home and native land."

Stuart had to be careful not to babble. Maybe his glasses were the problem. Maybe he looked absolutely bent.

"Why don't you throw on some music." Stuart tapped the dash over the radio with his fingertips. "Find a station."

Johnny complied. Not commenting on the arbutus knobs, he turned it on and popped "scan" like he knew this radio intimately. He turned to toss his pack in the back seat. As Stuart had feared, Johnny stopped the scan on a country station. It wasn't even the good old Hank Williams stuff, which was bizarre enough to be interesting, but the kind that sounded like lame rock 'n' roll with a steel guitar and a singer, who was likely from Calgary, trying to sound like he'd never left Arkansas.

Johnny leaned his head against the window and pretended to be asleep. He even let his mouth fall open.

Stuart waited a few minutes before turning down the music. Turning it off or changing the channel could be construed as an insult, whereas reducing the volume was obviously to help his guest sleep.

His girlfriend Melody. It was fun to think about that one again.

After the evening of the limping rat, they saw each other a few times at parties or the bar, and she invited him to watch her play in her latest band. She was purportedly very good, but also it was cool to have a girl bass player, especially a tall one with a junkie's hunch. Looking almost sleepy, she'd gaze down, seeing nothing with her eyes, bobbing her head, all in service to the music, playing a simple style but pitch-perfect, fretless, never watching her fingers and using the whole neck, going up fast and treble sometimes. You could tell it was in her bones and belly. But she rarely stuck with a band, not seeing it as her life's work, or something like that. She loved music but not the stage. Or the ambition. He remembered her describing some singer's ego "billowing like a big black cauliflower." She tried an all-girl band and that was no better. But as she explained to him more than once, bass needs a band.

Then Mel invited him canoe–camping. Actually it was an open invitation to everyone, a "Next weekend anyone want to …?" and Stuart was the only taker. They paddled Indian Arm to Raccoon Island, got soused on good wine and had a feast, Mel bringing a Dungeness crab and Stuart some spicy chicken wings, the shells and bones of which they could flick like royalty into the inlet at their feet. She had some pâté too, liverish and somehow floral, and it might have been here that she first called herself a trufflepig.

They each had a little pup tent, and when they were yawning as much as talking it wasn't clumsy just to say goodnight and crawl off in separate directions. Mel was good-looking enough. Her skin reminded him of pearl, some hint of luscious colour beneath the surface. She had these nice, baseball-sized— well, she *had* breasts, she had the required gear, and that was enough for a loveless guy of twenty-one. He could ignore the height, the two-inch difference. She was pretty, she really was. And sexy. But maybe they were already too close as friends.

Then they were on their second camping trip alone together, a road trip to Port Renfrew. The whole thing felt engineered by Mel. The long drive took them to a curved talon of wilderness beach on Native land, where apparently it was okay to camp. There was no need for Stuart's tent because Mel had borrowed a big one. This time her main fare was fresh Digby scallops wrapped in thick, unsalted bacon (deadpan, she called it kosher bacon, and Stuart didn't get it), skewered through with sticks hand-held over alderwood coals, then dipped in a bean can of melted butter, then a dribble of lemon. Both Mel and Stuart groaned, eating them. They smoked narrow black cigars after, and drank Greek brandy, which Mel thought foul.

It began to blow and to rain, and even in July this meant jackets. The night felt off kilter, and maybe it was the brandy, but all along Stuart wondered if Mel was flirting with him a little. She had eyeliner on, a first. When they stumbled to the tent, which wasn't so huge after all, and paused side by side on all fours to consider the readied sleeping bags, Mel said simply, "You wanna?" and gave his thigh a little squeeze.

The next morning they were quiet over their coffees, hungover, staring out at surf breaking into the bay. The sky was the deep grey that hints purple. Stuart thought things had gone well last night and wondered what might happen now. Then Mel blurted an apology for "an experiment gone wrong." When she declared her sexual preference he thought she might just be rejecting him in a creative way to make him feel better and at first he didn't believe her. He was hurt, of course he was. She suddenly seemed much prettier and sexier. And while over the years he would hear about other experiments with other men, he would also see her with a girlfriend or two, so it turned out she wasn't lying.

Anyway, the scallop night, as he came to think of it, didn't make him wince for long. It didn't seem to trouble Mel at all and maybe it helped make them the good friends they became. The first time Mel heard the term *angels on horseback* to describe scallops and bacon, she asked, "Is *that* incredible?" giving him

the naughtiest look. Who'd been the angel and who the horse
wasn't clear to him, though he knew he shouldn't take things so
literally—yet why she enjoyed a glorious image for an event that
hadn't moved her much, well, it was curious.

Probably until Diane came along, Mel had been Stuart's
best friend. They were like two men—the humour, the indirect
intimacy where nothing needed to be said so it wasn't. Yet
because they weren't two men there was a certain civility, a
caution that their friend was another species and in the end
mysterious. They could joke about this, though. She claimed
that "the diff" kept him from revealing his depths of selfish
sexual depravity common to all men, and he claimed it kept
her from spewing the endless emotional pornography of
womankind.

Stuart couldn't remember exactly what happened to
them. Mel moved to Toronto for a year or two but then came
back. She was in that band. The Revealers, The Revellers,
something. She showed up, bizarrely, at his grad party. She'd
send him invites to record launches, some of them bands
she gigged with. Sometimes he went. They wouldn't see each
other for a year at a time. He'd forgotten that. And then he
moved to Victoria. He remembered hearing something about
Mel up in the Queen Charlottes, or Haida Gwaii as the islands
were called now.

THE DATSUN HAD WHINED forever and here they were in
Shaunavon. Stuart read the sign like a train conductor and
Johnny woke up. He'd fallen asleep for real. Stuart peered out
his side window while Johnny wiped an alarming amount of
spittle from his cheek and shoulder.

It wasn't much of a town. Spread out, with clusters of houses here and there. Johnny knew the place. When Stuart asked him where to go, he mumbled, "Ten more klicks," and jabbed his finger forward. He sighed loudly and looked nervous.

Suddenly he volunteered, "Haven't seen 'er in a while."

Stuart offered that that can be tough.

"Kayla," Johnny said, as if reminding himself. And then, "*Ah* it's not like I'm askin' her to marry me." He hesitated, his comic timing good. "Not this time." He turned and met Stuart's eyes for the first time and laughed boisterously, desperately. It was like sleep had made him a new man.

Johnny confessed that their last "go-round" was a fight.

"You're surprising her, aren't you?" Stuart asked, a little surprised at himself.

"Best way," said Johnny, turning to look out the window.

The storm chose now to overtake them and blacken the ground. The Datsun's right wiper squeaked cruelly. It wasn't one of the grand storms, with the thunder and lightning, just a ragged, blowy mess, a shitty dog with bald patches.

Stuart turned where Johnny said, up a dirt road that he followed wordlessly through a grove of poplars until it opened up again and stopped at a farmhouse backed by fields of something. It was almost night.

"Okay, thanks," Johnny said, grabbing his red pack. He jumped out, slammed the car's old door and didn't look back.

Stuart circled out of the big gravel yard but stopped just short of the poplars. Maybe he was being nosy, maybe he wanted to make sure someone let him in and things went right, because it was raining and almost dark and far from any town.

Johnny stood waiting at the door, and then there was a young woman, light streaming out behind her. It looked like words were going back and forth, and then the door closed hard. Johnny wrenched it open, and now an older man, who would be Kayla's father, stood blocking it. Both men yelling. The father clamped a hand on Johnny's shoulder and Johnny clamped one on the father's. The father shoved, Johnny's hand shot up and hung in the air, a held slap. The door slammed and Johnny walked backward off the porch and down the steps, yelling. His red pack stayed on a deck chair beside the door.

Down on the gravel, Johnny spun around and yelled incoherently at the trees, at the storm. When he saw Stuart's car idling thirty yards away his reaction was instant. He put his head down and charged, screaming, angrier than real anger gets. He ran at Stuart bent over and neck out like a charging goose, his fisted arms like wings trailing behind.

Stuart got into gear and away just before Johnny reached him. He could hear the screaming through the glass. Dodging poplars, he kept watch in the rear-view to see if the man was chasing him.

When he reached the small highway and turned east his heart was still pounding and his breathing shallow. That was it. That was it for hitchhikers. That was it for snoring veterinarians in tents. That was it for coming out of his loner shell.

ASSINIBOIA, A CHEAP MOTEL, he sat on the bed restlessly watching TV. He hadn't wanted to stop but the storm made driving a strain. The awful bed made him miss his own. Which, of course—his stomach fell to picture it—sat dead in some landfill, clotted with smoke and hose water. Odd that you get attached to things. His old chair, from which he watched so many movies, read countless newspapers and magazines. Mummified cats filling ships bound for England. Oh, he missed his shower, his plate-sized showerhead and its warm rains of heaven.

Mostly he didn't want to think about Johnny, huffing around crazy in this weather, out there in the night. Just the thought made Stuart feel cold and afraid, and an even more horrible thought arose: Had Jen ever been stricken with a man like that? He felt helpless, then angry with himself that he didn't know even this much. Jen was out there in that darkness somewhere, out past these walls. She felt lost out there, but of course that was only because he had lost her. She was probably fine. Of course she was.

He could hear wind out beyond his curtains. It wasn't just his burned house that was out there, Jen was out there too. And Diane. And so was the way she'd come up behind him to leisurely scratch behind his ears, always when he wanted it, sometimes making a gentle joke about her favourite dog Stuart. The scratching behind his ears was gone too, lost out there in the dark and wind and rain. And so was his work, and all this September's new kids, they were all out there.

He sat on the bed, too forlorn to cry, crying was easy now. It was more than his house—why had he thought it was just a house? He'd lost what was far bigger. Who knows why, maybe because of Johnny, or that storm out there, but tonight it felt like everything he'd lost over the years by vague degree had just now been snatched from him whole, leaving a huge, raw gouge in his body. No, the gouge was the size and the shape of his body, it *was* his body.

There was nowhere to go and thank God he was exhausted. He was too afraid to leave a ground-floor window open, despite the unhealthy stuffiness of the room. Its wood gave off a fifties cottage pong. This homey modesty made him miss his house again. His ease within it. Wooden skin is what a house was. You could float around in it, mindless and safe. It was like living happily within your own armpit. In his house he'd been able to be himself, whatever that was.

THAT NIGHT HE DREAMED it again, he saw himself reflected in his deck window, naked except his underwear, skin lit golden by the fire. This time he had a beard, and fireglow made its curls golden, and it grew more curly and golden and Zeus-like the more he admired it. Then instead of hosing the blaze he was pissing into it, and there was the burned-urine smell of dousing a campfire. Then Vicky was behind him, wrapping him up with the pink robe. He peed on that a bit and she yelled, mad at him even while his house burned down. He didn't know how to respond to her and she began biting him, ripping into his arm with little shrieks that he joined with shrieks of his own. This woke Stuart up.

In the morning he wanted the big road again, Highway 1, so he headed north to Moose Jaw, another little city to visit for name alone. A place you wished your parents were from, if only to drop that name, especially among Americans, keep their version of us alive. He parked randomly centre-town and walked, peering at door menus from behind his hideous glasses, trying to locate some actual moose to eat. He settled on a bison burger and on the paper placemat read about tunnels under these very buildings, and Al Capone's probable hiding out here, "to escape the heat, and we don't mean the hot Saskatchewan summer!" And, of course, a fire had destroyed the downtown core. Moose Jaw was shaping up to be an intriguing little city, but not enough to keep him.

Back on the big road, and maybe it was the speed, but not many miles from Moose Jaw the gasket-in-a-can apparently blew out like shit through a hoop and the Datsun began grabbing and missing again. He slowed down but it got so bad that the last few miles into Regina he had to cripple along the paved shoulder with his flashers on.

This Canadian Tire mechanic's diagnosis was the same as the last but delivered without the humour. Stuart decided to go with the new head gasket, to the tune of a few hundred dollars.

The mechanic, whose solid-looking glasses Stuart coveted, spoke slowly. "But you know that if the head's warped, the new gasket won't help? It'll fail pretty quick. I'm duty bound to warn you."

Stuart removed his own glasses for this transaction. No one had ever said "duty bound" to him before. The young mechanic was six-four, six-five, and Stuart hoped he didn't look too weird as he squinted upward for more details. He was told the car would be ready in two, maybe three days. Stuart tried to get it down to one day, but the mechanic explained things, painfully slowly.

"Only two of us here can do this job. First we have a Ford Focus with a timing belt, plus the tuneup that has to go with that. Then we have a Dodge Caravan, an old one, with over-heating problems, and it's probably a head problem too, I *know* it's a head problem, like yours, but we have to take it right apart to see, and then we have a Subaru that needs not only a new rad but probably all the belts changed, and they want wires and plugs, too, and then …" It was hard to stand there politely, but Stuart did. Saskatchewan felt like a friendly place. He let his squint relax, and the mechanic's face widened and faded as it talked.

REGINA WAS A TEST of his impatience to get somewhere that wasn't here, to leave his skin. He tried striding the city in random directions, stopping when he could see open prairie. He tried and failed to reach Connington, the fucker, and no one else was willing or able to tell him if a decision had been made yet. But the three showers a day felt great. For some reason his head itched. Maybe it was too much cheap motel shampoo. But, some good news, his leather shoes hardly smelled anymore. Time was healing some wounds. In bed, though it was easier to read newspapers, he read more of *The World,* and how, growing up, Michael Bodleian was poor, and embarrassed by his father's little stall in Kensington Market, selling cheap scarves and belts and purses. His father was illiterate. Almost to punish him for it, Michael sat at the cash register reading books, the thicker the better, while ignoring customers. Back in Victoria, the professor Michael Bodleian was having trouble finding a translator for his mysterious tin of pages, and the pressure was on to publish or perish.

Day two, Stuart set off along Regina's main streets for the fourth or fifth time. He'd already walked some of the suburbs. Today's walk took him past the Canadian Tire where he eyed the bays in vain for a faded green Datsun getting her gasket. Two blocks along he had another coffee in "The Largest Tim Hortons in the World." He kept walking, recognizing the streets. Anything to keep him away from daytime TV, which he felt drained him of all self-esteem, intelligence, and luck.

Through a window of some sort of gallery he'd not noticed before he spied a sculpture of a kingfisher, made of smooth coloured glass, maybe eight inches tall and hefty looking. Strategic little spotlights shone under it, and the effect of the blue-orange-beige was glorious. During one of their camping trips he and Mel had watched a kingfisher work the shore of the riverbank in front of their tent, screeching unbeautifully and diving headlong underwater to grab minnows. Mel knew lots of facts about the natural world, and not only was this a kingfisher, it was the only bird in North America and one of just several in the world whose female was more colourful than the male. This one, with its orange collar, was female. She stayed the whole weekend, and sort of became their bird.

Stuart entered the shop to get a better look. The white price tag was maddeningly tucked under it—why did they all do that? Willing to part with as much as a hundred bucks, maybe one-fifty, for this decent curio for a stricken Mel, Stuart heard from the young Asian woman that it was normally one thousand six hundred, but on sale this week for twelve hundred. Plus tax. Stuart stood nodding. He became aware of his track pants, then his glasses. He'd actually been forgetting the splendid ugliness, the rococo horror, of his glasses. This morning in Tim Hortons, a cashier girl who looked no more than twelve had bitten down her smile while sliding him his double-double and change. Not one eyewear place in town could get him new glasses in a day and a half.

But, as it turned out, today he decided to change his life

for the better. What decided for him was an accident with some ice cream.

Outside a corner store, there was something about the old-school sign, the three fat scoops of brown, white, pink, like a simple heaven. He got a two-scooper, rainbow on top and chocolate on the bottom. He left the store licking. He was a kid, it was hot boring summer, the ice cream blanked everything out. A few blocks along he suffered the paradise-lost of the cone getting boring itself, the sugar burning his mouth. Then he did something he hadn't in years, which was to bite off the bottom cone-tip and suck the melting ice cream from below. To do this he had to contort his head sideways to keep the cone up while sucking—and his poor glasses, tent-smashed by the clumsy Kath, repaired by the flippant artiste, tumbled off his face to the cement and exploded. One lens broke in pieces and the other popped out and flew five feet.

Stuart was calm. In fact he finished sucking the remaining chocolate out, then chewed the soggy cone. He picked up the unbroken lens, held it to his eye, and looked around. He could see with it and admired the clarity of the billboard for a half minute before the sign registered. It was a before and after photo of a man his age. On the left, a scowling codger wore out-of-date horn-rimmed glasses, behind which his eyes swam like goofy plums. On the right was the same man smiling sexily, hair suspiciously darker, at peace with himself and, most of all, glasses-free. Under the photos he read The Vision Clinic. He had to get closer to the billboard to read the phone number, as well as the words Same Day Laser Treatment.

THE NEXT DAY, his third in Regina, Stuart sat in the waiting room tapping a foot with *The World* balanced on his thigh. Something had screwed up and he was an hour early. The receptionist at the desk had let him sit here for a half hour before asking who he was. So he had another half hour to wait.

Yesterday he'd learned something remarkable about modern life: eye surgery, using beams of light shot through a ruby, was not only easier than finding a new pair of glasses, it was quicker. At the pre-operation assessment he passed with flying colours due to his "classic astigmatism and good, thick cornea." In three hours he'd be walking around glasses-free.

Stuart sat there surprised and pleased with himself. Apparently he was going through with it. Well, it was time he did something like this for himself. It was overdue. He'd worn glasses since grade seven. He'd survived a house fire! In this age of contact lenses and easy surgery, what is a glasses wearer but someone who's used to low self-esteem and a constant, background-noise kind of suffering? A contraption hanging off your face? Barbaric. Yesterday, after learning the surgery was a tidy fifteen hundred dollars per eye, he'd slapped down his debit card to prepay. He now had five hundred left in the bank. More than enough to get to Toronto, and Mel, and the big bag of money waiting for him at the insurance office, because Connington would come through.

Legs crossed and a foot bouncing perkily mid-air, Stuart picked up the pamphlet again, turning to the "What Are the Risks" page. Blindness resulting from this procedure was "theoretically possible." It didn't explain what ectasia was, but there was a $1/10,000$ chance. Infection with scarring was $1/50,000$. He read a chart under the title "Comparable Common Risks (Over Lifetime)" that risk of death by lightning was $1/50,000$,

death from "chocking" on food 1/5,000, death from falling
down stairs 1/3,000, and death from car accident 1/80. Not
only were the stats misspelled and questionable—did one out
of every five thousand people really chock to death on food?—
Stuart had to wonder why all this talk about death.

He opened *The World* at its dog-ear bookmark, page
twenty-three. Last night he'd read how virtually nothing had
been written about the lepers of D'Arcy Island, and that the
contents of the tin could result in a book that would instantly
make Michael's career. He was alone and friendless. From
Eastern Canada, he couldn't get the hang of the West Coast.
The story backtracked and described Michael as a lonely child.
The suggestion was that a tall bookworm was somehow more
pathetic than a short one.

While attending Queen's, in Kingston, Michael
dreamed about the life of a professor, which seemed
to him a mix of nobleman and magician, in the way
of Merlin. Over the years, with scorn and pity Michael
had watched his father's humble business falter, and he
wanted no part of the world of buy cheap, sell dear. He
would be no middleman. He wanted to contribute to a
more exalted world, and if he didn't yet know the challenges of that world, he knew it was the world of ideas,
and its gate was university. As a first-year student he was
impressed by the knowledge he began encountering,
but he was just as struck by the professors themselves.
In a roomful of smart people, they were the smartest.
They were confident, if not arrogant. Even if they
were nervous in front of the class, you could still see
how they rested in the self-worth and safety of their

knowledge. They knew what you needed to know, and wasn't this gulf as glaring as that between the rich and the poor?

And one evening he encountered paradise. It was a cold, November dusk, and he was walking with head down to the cheap basement apartment of a prospective girlfriend. Though no romance ensued, he would forever remember the vision he encountered on Salem Street, as the Jaguar cut in front of him to turn up a driveway. He watched it park and heard its deep purr die. Out stepped his English professor, Doctor Wellborne. Perhaps forty-five, smugly wise, owner of a perfectly trimmed beard and smoker of exactly two cigarettes per class—one at the beginning, and one signalling the end—Dr. Wellborne cast a glance about his neighbourhood and looked through Michael like he wasn't there. The professor turned and trotted up the steps of what was very nearly a mansion, a perfectly kept Tudor with uncharacteristically large windows, from which glowed a warm and golden light and through which Michael could see walls hung with fine art, a fire in the grand stone hearth, leather furniture, a slim and elegant wife—and, waiting for him, a life like no other. And while Dr. Wellborne apparently did very little work, spending all class reading Wordsworth or Coleridge to them out loud, entertaining their stabs at commentary with a scant smile and eyebrows held high, and marking their earnest essays with a simple B, unaccompanied by helpful words, there was no doubt in Michael's mind that the professor deserved this life. He had worked hard in the world of ideas and had earned it. But clearest to Michael was how cold and windy it was out on Salem Street, while inside, where the professor was throwing his coat over the couch, it was perfect.

Of course, the ladder to tenured life in academe promised nothing like that. In fourth year, when Michael heard that a plumber just out of apprenticeship made more than a university professor, he wasn't deterred. Nor was he deterred by the great debt incurred on the way to his Ph.D. The difficulty in finding a niche in his field—labour history in the Pacific Northwest—was no insurmountable barrier either, nor was the scarcity of jobs. A combination of luck, connections and good, hard work landed him his tenure-track post at the University of Victoria, a job that now hung by a thread. What was proving elusive was that idea, that piece of original scholarship, that would see him granted tenure. He had to get tenure within one more year or he was gone. Gone! Booted out of not just this university, but all others. Denial of tenure was a globally shut door. It meant ejection from the world of ideas. It meant an endless walk in the cold wind of Salem Street.

Stuart was put on alert by a rusty, scraping sound coming from a backroom. Then a clunk. It sounded nothing like lasers or, for that matter, modern medicine. It sounded medieval.

He skipped a few pages, to a fresh section.

In her phone message, in shy and only moderately accented English, she said her name was Naomi, Naomi Chan. She was studying English Literature at

UBC, she was twenty-four and an exchange student from Guangzhou, "or Canton, as you might know it." Michael's advertisement had asked for knowledge of "old Cantonese dialect." After a full week of waiting he had received only one other call and it was depressing; the young man's accent was so thick and his short sentences so garbled and pinched that Michael could tell no good writing would come from him. This Naomi's English must be excellent if she was studying its literature.

To make the call, for some reason he rolled his chair over to the window and drew his office blinds. He knew his level of secrecy was absurd, but you never knew. He'd advertised nothing in Victoria or his own school, not wanting any word to reach his own department. He'd gone to Vancouver himself to tack up the notices, posting them both in Chinatown and on campus, and they said only to "call Michael," with his home number. Nor would he tell the translator, once he located one, where the tin came from or what the nature of his work was.

He dialled the number.

"Naomi Chan?" she said, and he was tempted to make a joke and say, No, it's Michael Bodleian. Her accent sounded stronger than in her message, and he understood that she must have rehearsed it. Of course she did. Who wouldn't?

He identified himself, told her he was working on scholarly research (though did not identify himself as a professor), and in order to agree on a price, he laid out the barest details of the translation task: it was thirty-nine pages of old Cantonese dialect, on very faded and fragile paper. He asked how long the translation might take, in hours.

"How many characters on a page?" she asked.

"Umm. Of course," Michael said. He was embarrassed he hadn't thought of this. "Maybe, ah …"

"Are the characters bigger than a postage stamp?" she asked. He thought he could hear a smile in her voice.

"Um, no."

"Smaller than a pencil eraser?"

"Bigger than a pencil eraser." Her voice was dusky, and her confidence threw him. He had expected the shyness of her message.

"It depends on how idiomatic it is, and how clear the writer is, and what the subject is, but …"

"Of course."

"I think I could do a page, good page, in two hours?"

"I can tell you that the subject is leprosy. Or at least that the writer likely *had* leprosy. Was a leper. The pages are roughly one hundred years old."

"I see."

Michael was troubled by the silence that followed. He asked her if something was wrong, and quickly interjected, "You can't catch leprosy from the pages."

"The writing will be very difficult," Naomi said.

"How so?" asked Michael, not sure what she meant and wondering now about her strengths in English.

She ignored that question and asked, "Is it from a grave?"

"No, it is not." Michael realized he wasn't entirely
certain of this. Nor did he like this line of questioning.
"It was found in a garden." Not exactly a lie. Pierre had
probably planted a garden of sorts.

Wanting to reach the end of Chapter 1 before his name
was called, Stuart skimmed. Arrangements are made. Because
of Michael Bodleian's almost paranoid need for secrecy, the
pages can't be copied, he won't mail them to her and all work
has to be done at his house. He will pay her ferry and expenses.
Because she's a student, Naomi can come only on weekends.
She agrees to do the job for scandalously low pay and Michael
feels the "thin remorse of a cheapskate."

Not twenty minutes after speaking with his new translator, Naomi Chan, so good did Michael feel that he
sat down to type. He rolled his chair to the window and
opened the blinds onto a crisp spring evening, onto
fresh budded trees that edged the campus parking lot.
He chewed a pencil while staring at the blank page
in his typewriter. He saw his nervously tapping fingers
and caught himself smiling. He knew he should wait
for Naomi's first translated pages, but he couldn't help
himself. This stood the chance of being a popular book.
A popular book. Leprosy was a gruesome disease, but an
old and almost mythical one, and there was no longer
any need to fear it. So it could be "entertaining," it
could be the Great White Shark of diseases! No matter
what the pages revealed, Michael had no doubt that
he could slip in many of the poignantly gruesome facts
he had been gathering in his reading. Officially called

Hansen's disease, it was caused by *mycobacteria leprae* and *lepromatosis*. It could rot your eyelids away (God, imagine), causing eventual blindness due to infection. Actually it was hard to catch. Ninety-five percent of humanity was naturally immune. It caused total numbness in the extremities. Fingers and toes didn't "drop off," but were torn or cut, and because they couldn't be felt, wounds festered and then digits rotted off, or, more commonly, rats ate them while a leper slept. Humans could catch leprosy from armadillos. There were still over one thousand leper colonies in India. The proper, and rather elegant, term for a leper colony was "lazaretto." Leprosy could easily be cured, but such was the stigma persistent to this day that many stricken people still did not come forward to seek treatment. Syphilis was often commonly mistaken for leprosy, and many a syphilitic was thrown into a leper colony, where they would eventually contract that disease as well. In the old days, a not uncommon religious self-sacrifice involved committing one's life to working with lepers, as was the case with the famous Father Damien in Hawaii.

If his D'Arcy Island leper was short on helpful information, there was plenty of room for anecdotes of the most gripping, sad and heartfelt kind.

Michael placed his fingers on the typewriter. All books needed an introduction. He decided to start. He wrote, brazenly eschewing academic style and adopting a more popular voice: "The magic of any ethnology, or study of a sub-group of people, is its insight into human nature itself. The microcosm reveals the macrocosm: in the faces of pygmies, prostitutes or pirates, we see ourselves. The study of a leper colony, and its portrait of contained suffering, doubtless shines a light on our own, larger "colony," as it were. For aren't we all"—swelling with feeling, Michael Bodleian took his hands off the keys, wanting to get this sentence exactly right—"as we conduct daily life within a circumscribed farm or village or even city; as we practise our fear of strangers; as we witness our finite lifespan; as we suffer our onset of age and decrepitude—aren't we little different from lepers? To put it more clearly: *might not a leper's situation be seen as the essential version of ours?*"

THERE WAS NO PAIN except the clamps to keep the eyes wide open, and the eyedrops stung. Fear of moving his eyes at the wrong time—"When I say 'now,' *do not* move your eyes. Ready? *Now*"—was by far the worst thing. Otherwise, as he lay there, he was self-conscious about his track pants, and the belly of his T-shirt and its grand grease stains. When the laser got going he thought he smelled smoke, though that was probably impossible. Painless destruction within his eyeball. All in all, it felt less like medicine than science. He was paying three thousand bucks an hour for this, so someone in here was making a decent wage.

What came next to his mind was deeply adolescent. What he pictured was his young self sitting on a towel, sucking in his stomach, it was summer, there were girls around, and he was wearing no glasses. His gaze was middle distance, he was just giving them a chance to see him.

A young Diane came by. He gave her the first bare-eyed inscrutable look of his life.

ON HIS WAY TO his motel, he probably shouldn't have had the extra-large coffee from The Largest Tim Hortons in the World. He doffed his clothes at speed, anticipating his shower, head itchy again. His vision wasn't great and he was trying not to worry about that. Not only had there been no eureka moment, as in the movies when the bandages come off and the world is clearer than ever before, but the edges of desks, windowsills, and his own eyes in the mirror were all a bit iffy-looking. His focus was not quite double but verging on it. As part of the price package he was permitted two post-operative checkups in Toronto—or Thunder Bay or Orillia if he wanted, they were a chain. He could drive starting tomorrow.

He was standing in the middle of the room, naked, trying to get the wallpaper's grey diamonds in better focus, when the phone rang.

"Mr. Price," Connington sighed. "I tracked you down."

"Stuart, please."

"All right, Stuart. You're in, where, Manitoba?"

"Saskatchewan."

"I'm afraid I have some news, and it isn't good."

"What's the news."

"Your appeal has been turned down."

"Ah. Right. Hmm."

"I thought you'd want to know as soon as possible."

"Yes. Thank you." Stuart tried hard for some appropriate words. "Is there— Is there another appeal I could, I could launch?"

"I'm afraid there isn't. Not that I'm aware of, in any case."

"Could I talk to someone?"

"Well, I'm your contact person here, Stuart. And I'm just relaying the message down from on high."

"And here I am standing here naked!"

Connington didn't address this, or Stuart's odd barked laugh. He said only, "I'm sorry to be passing on bad news."

"Well, it's not your fault." He did wish he knew whose fault it was. Who finally ticked that box?

"And I have a bit more news that isn't so hot," said the adjuster.

"Hit me!" said Stuart, bouncing from foot to foot, cold. He shook his head violently again just to feel no glasses fly off.

After the call he showered and tried to digest things. The additional bad news had to do with him owing some restoration company fifteen thousand dollars for the work they'd done on-site—the partial teardown of the roof "for safety sake" and wrapping the house with tarps against further water damage from rain. Stuart had Connington clarify that, yes, these were the same tarps that had failed to keep out the rain that did cause further damage. Stuart only half-listened to Connington's abstract explanation of the secondary claim, which was still pending, and for which Stuart might be reimbursed, though likely not. Connington also explained that, yes, the work *was* expensive, but that was because it was emergency work, much of it happening on a Sunday, when workers were paid double time, "which is only fair." Stuart agreed it was only fair. But when Stuart offered that he hadn't asked for any of this work to be done, Connington explained that it was contracted automatically, on the assumption that Stuart's insurance company would be paying for it. The *erroneous* assumption, Stuart offered with a chuckle, but Connington didn't laugh. When Stuart asked *who* had automatically made the call to the restoration company, and Connington allowed that it was he, Stuart wondered aloud if Connington had assumption insurance that would pay for it, and hung up. Aside from a few seconds' giddiness he didn't feel better for it. Bradley Connington had made no mistakes and didn't deserve a cheap shot like that.

STUART COLLECTED HIS DATSUN at five in the afternoon on the fourth day and he wouldn't let the tall mechanic explain why it had taken longer or how the repair had gone. He'd had enough talk. He paid, roared two blocks to a store, parked hard, bought a lap-load of snacks, hopped in the car, and headed to the highway and east.

Indian Head. Grenfell. Moosomin. A sign reading Friendly Manitoba.

"Can I talk to somebody else?" he'd asked Connington, softly, after calling him back. Explaining that there was no reason to, Connington's previously human voice shifted to opaque, the aural equivalent of a one-way mirror. Stuart saw himself in it. He was the enemy, he was the living dead, a zombie stumbling at Connington in slow motion from the twilight fringes of the insurance world.

"I want to talk to somebody in Toronto," the zombie insisted, and in the end Stuart got a long sigh, an address, and two phone numbers out of the man, and now he had a place to go, or at least phone, in Toronto.

He drove and drove and no longer had to ask himself why. A thousand miles to go. Get to Mel, get some sleep. Then, marvel at things. He and Mel had been good at marvelling at things. Along with some weird cheese. Bread more black than brown. Some rib-sticking beer. Or mead, alchemical honey that warmed the heart.

Then he'd talk to somebody about his house.

He drove, imagining Toronto. The likely scenario kept coming back: he's standing in the vast glass lobby of a Toronto tower. There's white noise and his ears feel pressurized. He can't get past the curved marble desk where three uniformed guards sit verifying people's appointments. There is no directory on the wall, just two bronze signs inscribed Tower One and Tower Two. Men wearing identical suits, adepts of this world, murmur on cells as they emerge from or disappear into the bank of soundless elevators. Not only does Stuart lack an appointment, he can supply no company name. Nor does he know the vocabulary. *I really need to talk to somebody,* he says, but the guards are immovable, well-trained, Soviet. They are even good-looking, and smart, the job wasn't easy to get and they're climbing a corporate ladder of their own. They even act friendly, which hides their immovability, which is absolute, as if they're bolted to the very foundation of their building. He holds out a stained scrap of paper. *I think, I think I need to see this man, a Mr. Moore. He works either for Great Asian or maybe Shield Patterson Buck, Inc., which owns Best North, Mr. Connington wasn't sure, that is, "Brad" wasn't sure and*— Mr. Moore no longer works in this building. *Can you tell me where he's*— I'm sorry. *So then I need to talk to somebody up there in order to find out who to talk to.* I'm sorry, I'd like to help. *Well then why don't you?* If you don't know who to talk to, sir, how can I possibly know? *My cellphone melted, I did own a cellphone, it melted in a fire, can I use this phone here?* I'm sorry. *Is there a pay phone some—?* No, there isn't. *Do you know where one might be?* No. *Could you find out for me, please?* He gestures to the glass walls now because, at this point in the scenario, all four walls are buffeted by snow and wind, and Stuart lacks a coat. The guard says that if Stuart would wait a few minutes, he could check with his colleague, who might know someone who might know about pay phones in the area, and he should be back from lunch soon. Maybe ten minutes. Fifteen at most. *Thank you.* Stuart is genuine in his gratitude. *Thank you!* he says again.

And realized he was zooming through friendly Manitoba.

Face to face. He needed to see somebody face to face. How could one human ruin another when they were in the same room together? They've mentioned last night's big game, which Canada won. Someone has a shirt-button thread unravelling. It's late, they're both hungry. On the desk, the picture of a daughter, they have daughters the same age and they compare notes, smile dreamily and shake their heads for the same reason. The storm out the window will make it hard for both of them to get home, and the feeling is that life is far bigger than this office. How can someone X another's box when the glaring fact is that they're someday both going to die and the world out there will go on happily without them?

VIRDEN. BRANDON. CARBERRY. Now Winnipeg, with the choice of a bypass, which he took, and it was such a good bypass that Winnipeg remained just a glow to the north.

The dash clock flipped to exactly midnight. He looked left to the city glow, remembered the trip with Mel, and the bar they'd stopped at somewhere on the outskirts, a huge thing sprawling with boozy tables. The band had played the best music they'd ever heard, a jazzy pop that was truly strange in a loud way. The lead singer was shaved bald and had sequins glued to his head and one bare shoulder, but the effect was dangerously macho because he was ugly. For the finale this singer rode around on the beefy bass player's shoulders playing two saxes at once, and they ran around the tables to the length of the bass player's extra-long electric cord. Mel screamed about the labouring bass player: "*And he's playing Jaco Pastorius!*"

He should be sleeping, but there was no way he could. In a room he would pace, he would pop the TV remote like Pavlov's hungry chicken. He might as well drive. Lifetime chance of dying, one in eighty.

Ste. Anne. The Brokenhead River! He remembered the name from that trip—Mel made a joke about it, something about their hangover from last night in that bar.

Falcon Lake. The Ontario border. "Yours to Discover." He'd take them up on that. Rat Portage, the best name yet. Nothing open in Rat, not even for nibbly snacks. Maybe in Kenora, Kenora was bigger. Wasn't there that twenty-foot leaping Muskie in Kenora? He could picture it, a favourite of books on freakish roadside sights, the giant potatoes, space-ships, hockey sticks.

A postcard for Jen. That's what he used to do, send post-cards to Jen. A funny one, whenever he travelled. He hadn't travelled much, but whenever he did. That's right, and a certain style of funny—he'd buy a postcard of a Mountie, and he'd write in the card, "I think this is what they call a Mountie. Love Dad." Or, "This appears to be a snow-capped mountain. Love Dad." She thought it was great, to be invited into making fun of the adult world. It must have felt a little naughty. "Someone has painted that house yellow and that boat bright red. Love Dad." "They have sunsets here. Love Dad." It was the first thing she'd show him when he got home, where she'd taped it up in her room. They were friends with a secret, because though Diane thought it sweet that he'd sent his daughter a card, her smile was dubious, like she didn't quite get it, or approve.

IN WESTERN ONTARIO, dead middle of the night, Stuart zooming along in bug-eyed half-sleep, two things happened simultaneously. One, his new head gasket failed and the Datsun began chugging. Two, someone was walking across the highway right in front of him, a guy with— He pounded the brakes and during a long skid somehow missed him. Of all things, it was a TV Indian, wearing buckskin and moccasins, carrying a canoe over his head. Pale, ghostly in the glare. Stuart pulled over and idled on the shoulder, heart going good. Middle of the night, a guy carrying a canoe across the TransCanada! Stuart grabbed the rear-view and angled it this way and that but there was just darkness back there. Jesus. That was close. That was weird. The guy was running with the canoe, kind of jerking it up and down to keep balance. Crazy bastard. Even from that distance, from the way he moved you could tell the guy was loopy and insane.

Stuart checked the dash, it was 3:45. He made to pull back onto the road, and there the guy was again, ahead of him, still carrying the canoe but now he was twisting around and thinner, and it wasn't a guy carrying a canoe at all. It was something wiggling right in front of his face. He swatted at it, slapped on the dome light, peered into the rear-view. There was something hanging on a hair—there—he pinched it between thumb and forefinger. He peered at it. Was that—? It was some kind of bug he was squeezing. He had almost gone into a spin because a bug dangling on a hair in front of his eyeball was a Native guy carrying a canoe.

Squinting with his new eyes, which were for the first time excellent, he peered at the bug closely. He had lice.

He was losing. He was still losing. He sat beside the wilderness highway, pinching a louse. Now his head itched, deeply. He knew it had been itching for days, like bad background music. He had lice. And his car was dying, this time for good. This trip was no fresh start. Whatever had begun was still happening. His house was still burning down. Its glare was a taunt. His future was withering away faster than he could drive to it. This felt like the end of things.

Not bothering to look in the rear-view for what might be coming—who else would be here, he was obviously alone in this—he floored it back onto the highway. The Datsun took ages to chug up to speed. Stuart breathed hard through his nose. Several times he made to adjust his glasses, and when his fingers met nothing but space he poked himself in the temple, and one time right in the eye.

IT WAS DAWN of that same morning. He'd made it to Kenora's leaping muskelunge in time to check into a cheap motel. He'd lost his louse, so before he tried for sleep he lay in wait with the light on and in time managed to pinch out another one when it scurried behind an ear. He pinned it to the side table and then dropped it into *The World*, ready and open at page one hundred, slammed the book shut, switched off the light, and passed out in a kind of fever.

He woke up unsure what to do. Checkout was eleven and it was already noon. He climbed into a scalding shower, blasting what he couldn't help but imagine was a forest of lice. Even after blasting and scalding, even after towelling off so hard with all three towels that he gave himself cramps in both arms, it took no more than twenty minutes for the itch to begin afresh. They must hide in holes like prairie dogs.

He checked out and found a walk-in clinic. In the waiting room, he remained standing. Why was he here? He had vague questions about lice. He wasn't sick. He was fine, what was sick was ... his *life*. In fact it felt like his life might be dying. But when he was taken to an examining room and the doctor arrived, a small man surrounded by his private cloud of diligence, and he asked Stuart what was the problem, Stuart couldn't speak. He got his face turned away and the tears blinked to a stop but he knew the doctor saw. He probably presented a disturbing case: a healthy-looking man of fifty, crying, unable to speak, clutching, and now trying to hide, a book called *The World*.

"Actually I'm okay," Stuart said. He stood up. He managed a sheepish smile.

"Sit down," said the doctor, with no answering smile.

Stuart complied. He looked up at the doctor, who hadn't himself taken a seat, and shrugged. Then he adjusted his glasses, which weren't there, and who knows what the doctor made of that.

"Are you in pain?"

"No."

"Sick with anything?"

"Not that I know of." Stuart smiled and met the doctor's eye, but he was fooling nobody. He almost, as a joke, blurted that he'd been cursed. Because that's what he'd considered this morning. Jen and her lepers, and how he hadn't taken her seriously. She had so fiercely insisted that they were being abused by someone writing about them, as if they weren't a hundred years dead.

"Are you under some stress these days." The doctor didn't pose this as a question.

Stuart shrugged again. "Sort of."

And so began the story of his house fire. No, he hadn't been hurt. No pets had been lost, no. Yes, he'd lost pretty much everything. Telling this to a doctor didn't feel at all burden-lifting, especially when the doctor glanced at his watch and saw that Stuart had seen. Stuart didn't bother going into the details of insurance. He figured now that the doctor had come to the conclusion that he was here for the drugs.

"One last thing," said the doctor. "Are you married?"

"Not anymore." Stuart wondered at this question, and the doctor surprised him by volunteering some detail about stress and marriage and longevity. It seemed that married men lived longer, quite a bit longer. From this information, and the way it was given, Stuart knew the doctor was worried himself.

Looking more boldly at his watch, and with unfelt professional grin, the doctor held out his hand to be shaken. The prescription he gave Stuart was "Try and take it easy."

IN THE KENORA PUBLIC LIBRARY the woman at the desk told him he couldn't bring that book in.

Stuart had merely asked for the computer code. Maybe it

was the look on his face. He was aware that he carried a stolen library book. He saw her read its *Fort Macleod Public Library* stamp, which had slid beyond the heel of his hand.

Stuart closed his eyes. "Why?"

"It isn't ours."

"Then why do you even care?" Stuart had rarely heard himself so stern.

"Well," the librarian stammered a bit, "it's hard for us to keep track of thefts and such. It's, it's just hard to keep track of things."

"You're afraid I'll steal it? Haven't I already stolen it?" Stuart tried to get her to smile. No doing. "How—come on— how do people steal things with those there?" Stuart jabbed the book at the two radar poles. "*Why* would people steal books? They're free! You're a library!"

The librarian gazed blinking at the pen she held in front of her with both hands. Big-jawed and freckled, she reminded Stuart of a previous principal he'd worked with, Jane McKeetchie, who was, more than anything, kind.

"Are you afraid I'm going to leave it?"

Now she looked only sad as she shook her head and met Stuart's eye. "I don't know."

"I just need to compare what's in it. To something else. I promise to return it. To here." He tapped the Fort Macleod on the spine.

In the end she not only let him in with his contraband book but surrendered the online code, for yet again her argument that he needed a Kenora library card did not hold up against Stuart's logic that you needed a library computer if you *didn't* live here; if you lived here, you'd be online at home.

Upstairs, once the old machine chugged past the passwords,

Stuart thought to check his email first. The entire notion startled him, especially as his list of unread messages came onscreen, that he could still get messages though his home computer was a blasted ruin lying on its side in a recycling pile.

Aside from spam and two queries from the organizer of Wednesday basketball, the second one churlish and clipped, Diane had a week ago sent him, all in caps, "GOOD GRIEF! WHAT HAPPENED! BUT YOU'RE OKAY??? PHONE ME!!! 250-971-7499!!!"

Despite the exclamation marks, Stuart emailed.

> Hi Diane,
>   I'm okay. Believe it or not, I started the fire on the sundeck. Insert laugh track here. Or that guy on the Simpsons who goes HA-ha. Tho you didn't like the Simpsons. Hope you're well. Maybe you could explain this all to me! Oh, and, still don't tell Jennifer. Maybe I will, do you have her email? I seem to have lost it.
>   Love,
>   Stuart

He'd been aware of the "Love, Stuart" while writing it, thinking, why the hell not? How could that word possibly hurt anybody, ever?

He googled "images lice." Waiting while it chugged, he noticed at his elbow a newspaper article, circled in red marker, about a new edition of a junior dictionary that had culled words such as *dandelion* and *willow* and *nun*. Words added included *lol* and *facebook*. The article had a tone of rousing the reading rabble. Stuart found amusing the notion of some kid not knowing what a nun was called. A willow tree, not so much.

Narrowing his search to "head lice," he found the mother-lode site, a big section on not only lice, with many pictures of various kinds, but also how a person catches and gets rid of them.

He scanned to an image of an ugly thing that, if you were addled enough, might be mistaken for an antique Native portaging a canoe. He picked up *The World*, thumbed to page one hundred and opened it warily. Near-dead, the creature wriggled and jerked itself along, threatening to leap. Stuart snapped the book closed with force. And then again. The sound shocked the place. He was alone up here; he thought he heard concerned librarian-murmurs from below. He half wished the young woman could see him snapping his book of death. He'd smile at her and snap it again.

No he wouldn't. There was no point dragging anyone else into this.

ONCE AGAIN STUART was hunched over the wheel, headlights boring into a black world, illuminating it with what looked like dire frost. The car whined in a deeper, more visceral way, sounding seriously angry with him, accusing. He decided to see how far the car got. Its grave might be a ditch beside the road. It was only early October, he wouldn't freeze if he had to hitchhike.

Hitching might be trouble, given his new look. A Safeway had all he needed, and he'd shaved his head as best he could in a gas-station bathroom. Now he drove, head mostly bald and glistening with grape-seed oil, all bonneted with a plastic shower cap. Dribbles of oil traced his neck and tickled him under his shirt. He should have bought a tuque in case he did have to hitchhike. But he really hoped he could keep this gear on. If he stayed capped for twenty-four hours, all lice and all eggs—technically nits, hence the term *nitpicker*—would be dead. He would be clean again.

In the library he'd learned a lot. Because of the stigma, having lice was like minor-league leprosy. And the stigma was similarly misplaced. It turned out the main attractant was *clean* hair. It now seemed likely that he had caught lice from a semi-wealthy veterinarian with a BMW. Apparently, at middle age, you didn't have to have sex to catch an STD.

Despite what he looked like he felt rational. Sober as could be. On the passenger seat rode a bag of crabapples (washed in the same gas-station bathroom), a bag of dried cranber-ries, and two wheels of Laughing Cow cheese. A third empty wheel lay on the floor. He'd learned to peel the little triangles one-handed.

In the glovebox, two postcards. On one, the famous leaping muskelunge, named Muskie, and because it was already ripe for satire, all he'd written was "Here it is. Love Dad." The other postcard was loaves of pink granite sticking out beside the highway. On this one he'd written, "Canada is made of this. Love Dad." All he needed were stamps. Even after five years, her address—321 Bonneville—he remembered as easily as his own. He would have heard if she'd moved. Probably. Of course.

He was seeing clearly. For instance he noticed now, for the first time, the green glow from the dash radio light reflected on the back of his wrist. His new eyes were working, his vision felt steady, strong. It was as if he could almost see beyond his headlights, deeper into the night.

Maybe it was the shaved head, or the non-glasses, but he could see things as they were, not as he wanted them to be. He saw Connington's neutral face clearly. He saw the evil of corporate bureaucracy. Everything had gone corporate. Kids at school volunteered at all sorts of good things not to do good but to pimp their resumé, to "better position themselves"— at an assembly he'd heard a career counsellor say that to the student body. The kids were scared. Back when Stuart was in high school he didn't even know what a resumé was.

The corporate world was a monster. No, it wasn't even that. A car engine had more feeling. Insurance companies in the States denied claims to dying people because of "pre-existing conditions" like pregnancy or childhood measles. But the evil was *natural*—this was what Stuart saw, chugging into the frost-white tunnel his lights made. The evil arose naturally when people weren't face to face in the same room. The evil could not grow during that awkward little shock of being human together. Stuart apologized to himself for the drama of this thought, but would Hitler have been able to kill a leper with his own bare hands? No, but he could tick a box.

Looking hopeful, a sign said: Sudbury 53.

He did know a few things. Life becomes a search for pleasure that doesn't bite back. Moderate pleasures. Loyal pleasures. Stopping at two glasses of wine. Sex that's friendly. If you're a monkey, you sit amid your clan, on the rock outcrop, having your nits picked.

He figured he'd been pretty good at finding loyal pleasures. It was maybe his only success. He enjoyed a walk in any season. He could name maybe two dozen types of tree, from their shape, or leaves. He enjoyed food, the first few bites anyway. Basketball with the guys, whom he didn't need as friends. A newspaper. Coffee he blended from two cans, a regular roast and an espresso. He even enjoyed—why not admit it?—the bowel movement that followed the coffee. There was an art to the small. He enjoyed the drive to work if he was prepared for class. He enjoyed the smell of any kind of wood, yellow cedar the best. He used to call it the smell of pumpkin pie from another planet.

There was little pleasure here, zooming east. He was truly broke. His head sparked and popped with what might be the death throes of lice. What had gone wrong? Why was he being denied not just the big pleasures but the modest ones too? Why had life ended his family, his careers, his friendships, and now burned down his house?

Family was supposed to be a loyal pleasure, maybe the best.

His clarity felt cliff-edge, like it could burst forward, through the windshield, at any moment. At least it wasn't hard to keep pointing straight.

Instinct told him that to turn off the Datsun would be to kill it, so he let it idle roughly as he filled it with gas, spending the last of his money at a gas station just east of Thunder Bay. He had enough left for a final lap meal of chips and two bananas. Whether this tank, or this food, could get him all the way to Toronto, he had no idea.

THE DATSUN DIED IN Parry Sound, "The Birthplace of Bobby Orr." It chugged to what sounded like a strangled but at the same time relieved stop a block past the sign. Across the street beside a convenience store there was a pay phone, and Stuart felt mocked. He tossed the shower cap in the back and rubbed a T-shirt over his head to suck up the oil.

He got a wrecker on the line and wondered if they'd like an old Datsun, a BC car with almost no rust. The fellow told Stuart that even if he didn't, he'd tow it away free for scrap. Stuart found one last quarter in his pocket and, seeing no humour or romance in the act, he put it in the slot and called the bus depot. He learned that buses to Toronto left four times a day and cost forty-nine dollars.

The Royal Towing guy, about forty and needing a shave, hopped out smiling and waving. He looked fit, and wore a faded Bruins cap, backwards. He struck Stuart as the kind of man who would smile while fighting. A foot from his truck's rear bumper he dropped an orange traffic cone.

"Jesus, you're right about a BC car. I could sell those plates to a few guys for lots of money." He noted Stuart's incomprehension. "They get to say their car's from BC, eh? No salt there? Sell it for more?"

"Ah," Stuart said. He thrust his chin at his car in what he hoped was a tough and businesslike way. "What d'ya think."

"You just drive 'er across?"

"Trying to make Toronto, yeah."

"She dead meat?"

"I guess so. Head gone."

"Dead meat."

"So is it worth something?"

"Not unless you parts it out. You could parts it out, but unless somebody had the exact—what is that, a '78?"

"'76."

"Jesus, then. Unless somebody wanted a starter for their

'76 fucking Datsun, and there won't be many those left—*any* those left—in Ontario, 'cause we use salt here, so, no, it's not worth anything to me at all." He laughed while adding, "Hey, drive 'er back to BC somebody'll give you five, six hundred bucks for that thing!"

"Hmm." Stuart didn't know what to say. He was clenched up with feelings for his car. The green faded to grey. The click of the glovebox. The arbutus knobs.

The guy punched him lightly on the shoulder. "Wait a couple more years, you got a collector's item." He laughed and pointed to the bumper. "One those fuckin' *black and white* plates, eh?"

"That'd be crazy."

They both stood staring at the old car for a moment more and then the guy asked him what he wanted to do.

"Okay, well, I'm totally broke now," Stuart said, managing a smile, making sure he wasn't being pathetic. "So what I *want* you to do is give me fifty dollars, which'll get me to Toronto on the bus."

"Jesus it's fifty bucks now?"

"Actually forty-nine."

"One way?"

"Yeah."

"Jesus, used to go down, grab an Argos game, twenty bucks round trip."

"Yikes."

The guy laughed over-loud. "I guess I was a drunken teenager then. And *that* was a while ago, eh?"

"I guess it was."

"Okay, I'll give ya fifty bucks."

"Really? That's great."

"Believe it or not, I can get twenty-five apiece for those tires. Those are pretty good tires. Double my money *today*."

"Well, thanks. That's great."

"An' a few years I'll have an antique, eh?"

At this he stuck his hand out to be shaken, to mark their transaction. He dug out his wallet and pulled a red fifty from a wad of them. Stuart signed something. He grabbed his suitcase, and coat, and the three cassette tapes from the glovebox that he'd never, in three thousand miles, remembered to play. He lifted Jen's postcards from the passenger seat.

It didn't feel bad walking through town lugging his suitcase. He'd been sitting too much. He hadn't slept but the sun was warm on his stubbly head, and it was never a bother learning an unknown town. Parry Sound was a mix. Perched on a lakeside, parts of it looked like a million bucks. As always with bus depots, this one was in the beaten old middle of town. He walked by the Sally Ann, cheque-cashing joints, rough-looking loiterers, a faint waft of urine.

There was a decent-looking café inside, with a grand display of sandwiches, and Stuart wished he'd lied to the wrecker about the fare. As it stood, he should have lied, because the woman—young, alarmingly pretty—slid him his ticket and asked for fifty-four twenty. Stuart told her he'd phoned just minutes ago and had been told forty-nine.

"HST," she said.

"What?"

"The harmonized sales tax?"

"I was told, over the phone, that a bus ticket to Toronto would cost me forty-nine dollars."

"Then you add harmonized sales tax?"

And *harmonized* was a nice word. "If I'm told it will cost me forty-nine dollars for a ticket, I would logically think that forty-nine dollars will buy me a ticket."

"We have sales tax in Canada."

"I'm, I'm *from* Canada." He was aware of his shaved, oiled head, his lack of a shower, and armpits of rage. He focused on keeping his voice and hands steady. "If a ticket, costs fifty-four twenty, why don't you tell people, who phone, that it costs fifty-four twenty?"

She widened her eyes and spoke slowly, insolently. "The ticket, costs forty-nine? The tax, goes to the government?"

"You have my forty-nine dollars, please slide me my ticket. And a dollar change."

She'd touched the fifty in the till to return to him. She looked on the verge of calling security, if there was such a thing in this building.

"Okay." Stuart held his hands up. "Will you get in trouble if you give me the ticket? If you will, no problem, just give me the money. But I drove across Canada, my car died, and I just sold it for fifty dollars, because that's what I thought the price was. I could have sold it for fifty-four twenty. It's no one's fault. It's just that—" Stuart shrugged and smiled for her, trying to keep all strategy out of his face. "—fifty is what I have."

The young woman didn't move through his speech, and she continued to look at her hands. She pinched the bill, held it, let it go. She released an angry huff and slid him his ticket for the night bus, as well as a dollar change. He thanked her, then thanked her again, trying not to sound pathetic, and he only wished that she would have looked up at him, not sent him away on a breath of anger.

Down the block in the convenience store he didn't push his luck. You couldn't quite buy two stamps for a dollar so he didn't try. He bought one, and left the ancient Chinese woman the change, though she seemed disturbed that Stuart did so.

Outside at a mailbox, Stuart thought a moment then affixed the stamp to the granite postcard, not the fish, and thumbed it through the slot.

AS THE SUN ROSE ABOVE Toronto's office towers and the street gained warmth, Stuart walked downhill, to the lake. In the distance it looked lovely, a tranquil ocean. He'd forgotten it was blue. It felt good to walk, and even better to be walking downhill.

He hadn't slept much on the bus but he hadn't expected to. He hadn't had a good sleep in days, and the proof of this was that he couldn't calculate in his head when his last good sleep had been. In the depot he'd bummed a quarter and phoned Mel but got only her message. He really should have phoned ahead. Was she even in town? Was she at work? In the phone book there was no listing for her, no address.

He walked some of Yonge Street and enjoyed its mix of wealth and seedy commerce, the giant garish signs like come-ons to hillbillies or other innocent types. He felt clean of that when he reached the waterfront. The actual lake was accessed between enormous condo towers, and on the other side of them were some nice spots. He remembered that big bodies of water were actually wilderness, and exciting for it. The shoreline was a concrete wall, and there were tie-ups for big boats, so the water here, the wilderness, must be deep. The city had seen fit to sculpt some nice parkland, with a wooden walkway along the shore, some clutches of small trees, and hearty benches, and a few moulded and manicured hillocks. He spied one such mound a hundred yards away, the sun hitting it such that it glowed like a soft warm emerald. It looked welcoming. He made for it, the perfect place to sit and wait before trying Mel again.

As he walked the wooden boards edging the shore, the lake to the left, the towering, rich-people condos to his right, he peered into the depths for fish, for anything alive, but saw nothing. A few seabirds paddled calmly within crust-tossing distance, eyeing him.

Halfway to his hillock, Stuart saw that his spot was being taken. For a moment, to Stuart's unsteady eyes, it looked like a tall black nipple changing shape up there upon a soft green breast.

Stuart got closer and watched a man get himself settled. His black coat and pants were thick and crusty, such that the fabric's wrinkles were exaggerated and permanent. He looked maybe Stuart's age, though age was hard to determine in a man like him. You could tell he wasn't drunk, though he did look tired. With a clean black blanket the man made himself a little nest and lay down. He pointed his face into the sun with a look of satisfaction you could tell was rare to him. Then he made prayer hands, rested his cheek on them, closed his eyes and began what looked to be a well-earned nap. The bum's face was perfectly round, and dark-skinned, Native perhaps, and so puffy and scrunched that you thought of a fleshy baby. Now a sleeping baby. The sun shone full on the sleeper, and the grass around him was lit up green-gold. Stuart felt jealous. He wondered if he shouldn't just climb up and flop down and share that spot in the sun.

From the other side of the hillock appeared a policeman,

striding up with purpose. Now he was nudging the sleeping man with a toe. Not a gentle toe either.

"Let's go. Up."

Surprising himself, Stuart yelled, "Leave him alone!"

"Excuse me?"

Stuart approached quickly. For some reason he dropped his suitcase. He spoke while he hustled up the hillock. "Why don't you just leave the guy alone? He's just having a nap." Stuart shrugged and smiled for him.

"You telling me my job, sir?" The cop looked half Stuart's age. His eyes, though, looked old enough.

"Why can't a guy have a nap? I want a nap myself."

The officer put a finger six inches from Stuart's nose. "*This* is city property and *you* get out of my face."

The bum was awake now. Moaning a tired "fuuuck," he rolled twice to get himself out of range of whatever was happening. The next time Stuart looked for him, to bring him into the conversation, he was gone, his blanket left behind.

"How is this private property? It's a perfect napping place. Look at it."

Stuart didn't know why he was enjoying himself but he was. Meeting this man eye to eye. Sticking up for the bum, offering the logic of justice and reason. He enjoyed saying the words.

"You been drinking, sir?"

"It's ten in the morning. I just haven't had much—"

"Where are you heading, sir?"

"Nowhere."

The cop pointed his chin. "You're carrying a suitcase."

"I'm visiting a friend. I don't see why a man can't lie down in his own city, his own country, and—"

"Address, sir?"

"Actually, I'm—I'm between addresses."

"Last address?" The cop had a pad and pencil out, not unlike an old-school waitress.

Stuart pictured a charred house. "Is that any of your business?"

He barely saw the elbow to his stomach. His wind gone, he was on his knees, the sun red through his closed eyelids, his words an ugly painful coughing.

STUART WAS SURPRISED at the size of the cell. Before sitting down on the wire mesh of the bed he stretched his arms out to easily touch both walls at once. It was a bit longer than it was wide. Then he was glad it was so small, because this meant he would probably be alone. He really didn't want to be caged with violent men. They'd be insane here, and age wouldn't help him.

Everything smelled of disinfectant. A sick pine.

No one would tell him anything. Nor did he argue. Not with anyone. Waiting in a chair, then fingerprinted, then waiting in another chair, always with a different bored clerk, he understood the size of this machine, and could see that none of these people had an answer to even one of his questions. One clerk, a kind of class clown, wore an immense and comic moustache, and when he winked at Stuart and stage-whispered that "nobody got killed" and that he wouldn't be here long, Stuart imagined he was watching TV.

Because it was all so bright in here. Banks of fluorescent lights cast hard white everywhere, through your shoe leather and around corners. A white so energized it was blue, and you could hear it. You could feel it on your scalp.

He was led to a phone, where he attempted to call Mel. He wasn't restricted to one call, nor did he need to bum a quarter. They wanted him to reconnect with his world, or maybe just see if he had one. He called Mel and left a long, sometimes coherent message. At one point he laughed, not knowing what to say. He didn't cry.

In his cell, the funniest thing happened. Stuart had no sooner sat on his mesh bed than someone actually knocked on his cell door (there were no bars, it was hollow metal, with a tiny window) and then opened it, but only after Stuart called, "Come in."

An immense beaming man, dressed in institutional whites, his head fat, round, and bald, leaned in on an angle that suggested he was walking backwards pulling something. He asked Stuart if he cared for some lunch. Stuart said sure. He couldn't tell if the man was a prisoner or an employee.

"Well, here ya be." The man handed in a plate covered with a tin warming top, on which was placed a plastic knife and fork tucked into a folded cloth napkin.

The food was pretty much perfect. It reminded Stuart of an airplane meal but it was homelier and better. Real mashed potatoes, left a little lumpy. On the potatoes a butter pat, melting in a hole someone had pressed in with a spoon. Peas, from a can, which he hadn't had since he was a child. Two plump and decent sausages, not too salty. So it was bangers 'n' mash. Edging the potatoes, a sprig of parsley. When he was finished he would chew it for his breath.

He hoped someone else was sitting on that sunny hillock. Someone who might nod off and safely go to sleep.

As for himself, as he sat amazed on the metal grate that apparently had become his new bed, he saw that the world as he'd known it had come to an end. He understood that a vast, over-filled toilet had been flushed. He saw that what had come to take its place was vast and bright and terminal. It didn't want him here particularly, but nor was it disturbed by his presence. For this, it reminded him of wilderness, it had that size and shape.

He could almost say he felt good here.

TRUFFLEPIG DOWN

Has any one supposed it lucky to be born?
I hasten to inform him or her it is just as lucky to
die, and I know it.

—Walt Whitman

The call from the police station felt like good cheap adventure, the kind that reminded Mel of earlier days with wilder friends. But mostly this emergency outing, to go get Stu Price, meant a break from dire but humdrum routines and showed Mel how completely they'd taken her over: the five feedings a day, two tube cleanings, usually a doctor's office, the scheduled rests. Then, only a bit less medical, the visit with her dad at Royal Elms. Lately she even had TV shows she tried not to miss, something she hadn't done in over a decade, back in the money days, as she thought of that time, with her second husband, Bryan. Bryan the Brit. Who held those conversations with whatever TV show he watched, arguing with it, or predicting a punchline. And, the worst thing, often sort of winning the argument, or getting the punchline right. God, here was yet another thing she hadn't thought of in years. These days old memories revived like loud flowers, needing to be seen a last time. Bryan's cute accent: *Oh, right! Right! You stupid bastard! You are truly unbelievable!* No, the worst thing about Bryan's TV watching was he seemed to think his witty commentary was a kind of foreplay for them, even if she was hardly watching and barely amused. The more he won his arguments, the more he shot slick glances her way and the more he figured sex was a given. She'd liked most of Bryan's Englishisms, not just the accent and weirdly perfect grammar even when pissed to the nines, but his lame approach to sex also seemed rooted in his being English. James Bond notwithstanding.

In any case the call from Stu Price had been a surprise and, maybe since he was a former lover, technically at least, Melody found herself dressing up a little. The black jeans, the open-toed leather shoes, dull gold blouse, and the black scarf with its calligraphy of gold bamboo stems and pale elephants ghosting through them. In her private shorthand she thought of it as her "Hindu scarf." (*Scarves* were the easy gifts from friends: she had a party scarf, a tooth-fairy scarf, and one she called her Johnny Depp scarf for the sails that could be pirate ships. Her baloney scarf, that of the lunch-meat hue, was now bound around the washer hose, stopping a drip.)

She wore scarves not just to cover her scars but lately for the fresh breeze swirling in the leaves. Her front yard was probably the street's new disgrace, despite everyone knowing the situation. Owner in dementia wing of a nursing home, prodigal daughter down the drain with cancer—no matter, in this neighbourhood you hired somebody and your yard looked it. In any case, earlier when Melody conducted her little ritual of stepping out onto the porch to greet the morning, it blew back cold in her face, cutting right through the morphine, *nice* actually, and she said aloud, "It's October out here."

After checking a city map to find the main police station, Melody barged into the leaf-scramble October morning and walked, almost strode, the ten minutes to her mother's subway stop. Passing under the ROSEDALE sign and entering the tunnel, she didn't look up to read the word. Since leaving home almost forty years ago, she felt a pang whenever the neighbourhood got mentioned. The place of her mother, Rose Dodds. It had never been determined whether or not her mother was named after the place she'd been born and lived her entire life. Rose had never tired of Hal's joke that it was named after *her*.

On the platform Mel's legs felt cold and doughy from the walk and she had to sit on the bench. This was new.

The train burst from the tunnel, thrilling with a blast of colder air it pushed along with its flat face. She found a seat inside. The posters and ads were familiar. She'd read the Random Acts of Poetry poem enough times to understand that it was about a love affair, not birds. None of these ladies with shopping bags at their feet inspired her to imagine life scenarios. No more than three stations went by before the novelty of Stu Price wore off too and things felt normal again. That is, entertainment over, she settled back into her body and what was actually going on.

She still felt ready. The feeling remained good. It still felt like certainty, and bigger than her.

It had come on suddenly, and shocked but didn't scare her. It seemed to have a lot to do with her father. For a few months now Hal no longer recognized her, not a bit—so he would not miss her, would not have to grieve a child. This was a big part of it. All heart ties cut, Melody could float free. She was already floating free.

Oddly, closer to death, this was the best she'd felt in these past eight years, or cancer-time, as she called it. And because this contentment had come as a surprise, and wasn't something she'd manufactured or cranked up, one of those feel-good strategies to beat disease, she trusted it. It felt not only natural but irresistible, like ice melting back to water. It had risen in her only after all her conniving toward happiness was exhausted. It wasn't the state of giving up, it was the state after giving up. She felt good, and this feeling alone felt like a miracle. It felt like the only miracle possible.

It was the extinguishing of both fear *and* hope, which she now knew to be the same thing. Fear and hope were the same cruel fire.

But she needed to hurry. At first, the word *chemo* had an almost friendly ring to it, but as a route taken three times now it had sent her down tunnels of nausea, and warped sorrow, a sluggish psychotic flu that could still erupt and easily break her. She had to hurry—any good feeling, even one this big, could be overwhelmed by the evolving damage that turned comforts upside down (this week her strawberry protein drink smelled like feces), or by a new brand of unimagined pain that could benumb or shatter and take her to a place where she would have to rely on the kindness of strangers.

She had the way. Amazing what you can learn online these days, and between her GP and oncologist it was easy to double up a prescription, no questions asked. Maybe they knew. The pills were a noble forest green. Shaped like elongated diamonds. They looked authoritative, like they knew what they were doing.

Yesterday, she'd decided on a date. For memory's sake she wanted one she wouldn't lose track of, and since Christmas was too distant she chose Halloween. It would leave time to write good letters to the dozen or so who might welcome one.

It would be enough time to ensure her father's memory of her was truly gone. It would also leave time to choreograph her wake, where whimsy would rule. She had the menu and song list almost ready. She saw how she'd been working on her song list all her life.

She would stick with her plan. This contentment felt wide and strong. The proof was that she didn't have to look to find it, or prop it up. It had arrived like morning light, and continued like wide sky.

So Stu Price was not just a surprise but a complication. His calling today felt somehow part of her plan, though how could this possibly be? It seemed she now had a house guest. During his call, when she asked if he needed a place to stay, his relief had gushed out as an exhalation of breath that ended with the flip of a sob. Before hanging up he added a laughing shout, as though he was being hauled away, "Don't let 'em hang me!" She didn't recall him being funny.

MEL REMEMBERED STU PRICE wearing glasses, and when he came through a door into the bright waiting area he paused to take in his surroundings, all big-eyed and blinking, like some kind of baby Disney animal emerging from a cave. He looked possibly unstable, and that had never been her sense, at all, of Stu Price. Stu Price was steady as oak.

The shock of seeing a friend instantly twenty-five years older—wider face, wrinkles, fallen shoulders—pulsed through her without much effect. She was used to it these days, having contacted old friends from here, there and everywhere to say versions of goodbye. She hadn't expected Stu Price to come, of all people. And she certainly hadn't expected him like this.

Fresh from jail, startled by everything. Black track pants, new white dress shirt tucked in, and severe bald cut that looked either Buddhist or fascist. She'd always thought him the type that nothing would ever happen to.

He saw her, suffered his own twenty-five-years shock, and came at her smiling, hand up in a wave the whole while.

MEL PATTED THE BACK of the L-shaped futon couch. "This really is the best bed in the house. You sleep like the dead on this thing. You don't even dream."

"Futons are great," Stu Price agreed.

She also patted the folded blankets and sheets on the coffee table where she'd piled them. Making up the bed for him would be weird, she didn't know quite why, maybe because it would make him feel more like a guest, less like a friend. But it was a comfy bed, she wasn't lying, though it also felt a tad weird putting him downstairs, with three official bedrooms upstairs. It was just that one bedroom lacked furniture, and she occupied the guest bedroom herself. The master bedroom, she couldn't see putting Stu Price in there. It was childish to see Mom and Dad's room as sanctified territory, but she liked keeping that feeling. You don't let drunken buddies sleep in your parents' bedroom.

Stuart stood hunched at her guitars, one her white Fender bass, the other a crummy old acoustic, both on their stands, both impotent with thick dust. They sat exposed like that only because she had no proper cases; both had arrived in the back seat of a car.

"That your old white one?"

"That's her."

"Still play much?"

"No band."

"'Bass needs a band,' right." Stuart nodded.

She pointed her chin at the TV. "You can drift off to the tube, if you're into that."

"Great!"

"Or," she indicated the universal gym, "you can work out and get in shape."

"What a concept." Stu Price patted his flat stomach then pivoted his body, not moving his feet, looking here and there, smiling, absurd in his track pants and dress shirt. He hadn't put down his suitcase yet.

"Or you can help me unpack." She pointed to the boxes stacked to the ceiling and obscuring a substantial part of this very large rec room.

"How long you been living here?"

"Almost two years." Why she had shipped everything from Montreal she didn't know. Her last delusion of longevity.

"Yikes. Do you actually want some help unpacking?"

Mel snorted, then saw this tamp him down so she added, "*God*, no," and with her fingers aimed a cross at the wall of boxes. Stu Price smiled but kept gazing around in too wide-eyed a way, now with one hand on his head. He looked like a man wondering what might be expected of him.

"So, you're starving. The bathroom and shower's right over there. How about something seafoody? Tuna, anyway. With melted cheese. Pickles." She'd bought cheese and a tomato at the market by the subway, put them in her purse. She had bread in the freezer and could picture various jars of stuff.

"That sounds unbelievable."

On her way up the stairs she called down, hurting her

throat, "Or, you can build me that guitar. In there." She
pointed under the stairs to the recess leading to what they'd
laughingly called her father's workshop, a huge cement room
with virgin workbench and tools, replete with industrial-sized
exhaust fan to vent all the potential industry. It just came to
her, how Stu Price promised, more than once, to build her a
guitar. She heard him put his case down and go check out the
workroom.

In the kitchen, her own hunger pangs rising, she mixed
a can of tuna with mayo, Dijon, a drop of habanero sauce, a
few capers, spread it on bread, topped it with thin gruyère,
and put it under the broiler but didn't turn it on. She heard
the downstairs shower start so she decided to eat first. It would
make things easier when she watched him eat for real. She
grabbed a tin of the chocolate, rather than the strawberry. At
the sink she popped the lid off and poured the goo into a
clean food bag.

She kept her rig, as she thought of it, in the TV room,
because she sometimes watched while she ate. She rolled
the contraption over to the easy chair and sat. It was a basic
rack on wheels, the kind used to hang a blood or antibiotics
drip. She clipped her bulging brown bag to the rail, plugged
the clear hose into its bottom, hiked up her blouse, tugged
the neck of her feeding tube out so it extended its full inch,
popped its top, plugged the hose in. Amazing how the incision
had more or less healed around this piece of plastic that was
now part of her. She reached and flicked the stopcock at the
bottom of the bag. Tic-tac-toe, automatic. Her lunch began
its glide down the hose. Would you like some fresh ground
pepper on that, Ma'am? Now it was entering her stomach.
And now she was eating. In two minutes the bland-bag would

be empty and she would be done. If she decided to prolong this life and endure more operations, chances are she'd end up with a colostomy bag, in which case food would both enter and exit in plastic bags, nothing touched, tasted, or smelled at either end. The new necronaut. (Morphine was good at gallows humour.)

She caught herself blinking at the blank TV. The curtains were drawn, the light was low and pleasant. Her parents' books lined one whole wall, looking long untouched, like the TV's quiet, orderly victims. Friends said TV had suddenly gotten good, all the real writers working for the offbeat cable shows. It was something she wouldn't be finding out for herself.

She was already feeling full. She hated meals. For what they weren't. The only other sensation was a slight cool at one side of her stomach. It had been months since she'd been able to properly drink this stuff, glug, glug. Now she could only dribble a little water down to keep her throat moist, and even that amount of swallowing hurt. It had been over a year since solid food. In a long battle between pain and taste, pain had won. It was maybe the defeat Mel felt most.

Bag lunch (ha ha) done, it was reverse tic-tac-toe. She took the hose to the sink to clean out. On the way she flicked on the broiler. She'd be able to smell when the gruyère bubbled and began to brown, an earthy and wonderful smell.

She heard the shower stop downstairs. She'd tell Stu Price she wasn't hungry. Or something. She didn't know what to tell him yet. On the subway ride home the subject didn't arise. Stu had kept up a manic banter about his house fire, his car, and his stupidity. He said his big plan here in Toronto was to see some insurance people. Shaking his head and apparently free of irony he referred to the integrity and

honesty he felt certain was still alive at the heart of the insurance business.

Mel hunched at the open oven door, took in the bubbling
gruyère. More and more, she could smell only the crude,
the gross, the heavy perfumes, or smoke, or her own weird
urine. She closed her eyes and inhaled deeply, trying to
smell the just-browning cheese, taking in the barest waft like
nourishment.

SCRUBBED AND ROSY-FACED and his buzz cut still wet, he ate,
groaning for real and then a few more times for thanks. He
told her how strange it was, someone cooking for him, because
it had been five years since Diane had done that. He went on
about meals he and Mel had apparently eaten on camping
trips, details she'd forgotten entirely. She guessed he was
wrong, or exaggerating, about the Cornish game hens impaled
on sticks, stuffed with mushrooms and the cavity corked with
a lemon. Cedar-planked sockeye she sort of remembered, but
then she'd planked lots of sockeye. She ate so much salmon
on Haida Gwaii, or the Charlottes as they were then, that it
sickened her. Still didn't like it. For fatty fish, give her shark
any day, or even a can of tuna to doctor up. Stu Price was sure
wolfing his, but please stop the moaning. Actually, the best
fatty fish in the world could be mackerel, if it was fresh that
day. That time in Goldilocks, the first Charlottes restaurant
she worked in, when mackerel schooled through and some
made their way into the cooler and she improvised a barbe-
cued mackerel salad niçoise, people thought she was magic.
Even RJ, her boss, sometimes let her "fuck with the menu"
after that.

"Well, jeez, Mel," Stu Price was saying to her. "I have an embarrassing request."

He sat with his hands folded in his lap like a boy. He had pushed his plate to the side, and on it his fork held down his neatly folded napkin.

"Shoot."

"It's kind of intimate."

"Well now you're scaring me."

"No, the thing is, I want to take a nap, I *need* to take a nap and …"

Melody had no idea what might be coming, none, and she found herself smiling.

"The thing is, I don't want to bugger up your sheets and pillows, and your nice futon couch, because I *probably* don't, I think I killed them all, but—I might have lice."

"Oh! Okay."

"So what I think I need to ask you to do, embarrassing or not, is to check my head. I think I got rid of them. I mean I basically drowned them with oil and suffocated them, but, um, there might still be nits. Eggs."

She shushed him and made all the right noises about lice being no problem and of course she'd check his head. She dragged a chair up behind him, more than a little creeped out. But interested enough. Stu Price, old friend. A just-showered, clean head. In Montreal she had a friend, Gina, who, though childless, for years volunteered to nit-pick at the local elementary school. Said it both relaxed her and, a shy confession, she found it "rewarding."

"Okay." She raised her hands behind him, a praying-mantis pose. She could smell her shampoo on him. His close-shaved hair was dull brown and grey, and dense. No balding at all.

She'd read that men went bald due to excess testosterone. Did this mean Stu Price had no testosterone? It might explain a few things about him.

"I hope you don't find anything, because you *really* don't want to see me in my shower cap." He turned and made a crazy grimace that had nothing to do with shower caps but maybe showed some kind of buggy tipping point.

She put her fingers to his head and leaned close. She parted the bristles, peering in. She swept, she brushed with fingertips. She made it something of a massage, until he moaned again, then she made it all business. It was relaxing enough, but she didn't feel rewarded when she found the nit. Then another. Little white sesame seeds, clinging to a hair at the base. She stripped them off with her nails, laid them on the table. Like all eggs, they looked pregnant and clean.

Stu Price apologized. He assured her he'd oil his head again and wear the shower cap whenever he lay down.

"You're worried that I'm worried you have lice?"

And then, still behind him, hands at work, she told him everything. The eight years, the three rounds. That it had long been inoperable and her throat had been blasted to raw bits. That it was in the liver and now, apparently, the lungs. Stu Price grew sombre, then disturbed. He apologized for coming and she told him nonsense. She said she was glad, and she was surprised to see that in a way she was. Stu Price still loved her, or something about her, and he was the most trustworthy man in the world. She'd picked his nits, and it was no problem showing him her scars. She told him she hadn't eaten solid food in almost a year, then hiked her blouse to display her feeding tube, which made him close his eyes and softly shake his head. Trying for the right words, and doing not too bad a job with it, she described the recent friendship she'd made with death. Then she told him she would soon be ending it, ending *this*. When she put her palm to her chest to show him what *this* meant, she was smiling and she felt stronger than ever. It was her first time telling anyone her plan.

Then she quit talking. Her throat hurt and she told him so. Stuart put a finger to his lips and shook his head, serious.

She hadn't mentioned October 31st.

SHE HAD AN IMAGE of her freshly dead body lying on the living-room couch. Pale, literally still, unoccupied by her breath or spirit. Roving trick-or-treaters gather outside at the front door, ring the bell, wait, then murmur to themselves, ring again before leaving. What enters the house are the noises, some-times swear words, of children, the disappointed pirates and zombies and ghosts. With the real stuff of Halloween lying there inside. She adds to the image, and on the front porch she leaves a heaping salad bowl of the very best candy, or rather three bowls, with a sign asking that they take only "enough" and leave some for everyone. What torture, that "enough" word. Some, who can't yet read, or who simply cannot consider that word, soundlessly stuff their bags, big-eyed and feverish in their sin. From others come little peeps or squeals or groans of good joyous greed, in any case pure sounds, and these are heard by her hovering soul, releasing it from its bonds to go and find other places. Just like music, when truly heard, spreads itself, lives. She is starting more and more to believe that a soul, if it exists at all, won't travel so much as it will spread. Widen out in all directions at once. Soon to have the scant awareness of wind.

MEL DIDN'T HEAR HIM come upstairs but here he was in the kitchen, wearing his shower cap. He pointed to his head, smiled, shrugged.

"Stu? You go see those insurance guys wearing that," she said, "I think you'll get everything you ask for."

He made his crazy-grimace face for her again. Then fell to quiet. Sheepish.

He said, "Weird when you call me 'Stu.' I don't know. I haven't been called that for so long. I forgot I was ever called that." He paused. "I don't know if I *was* ever called that."

Mel panicked a little. She wasn't sure what she used to call him.

"I think of you it's always 'Stu Price,'" she said. "As in one word: StuPrice. In my head, that's you."

"'Stu' just sounds like the *food* stew. The home-cooked meal."

Well, that's not so bad, Stu. "Do you want me to call you Stuart?"

Stu Price scrunched his brow as if unsure. "Sure. Why not."

"Hello, then, Stuart."

"Hello, Melody Dobbs." Then, "I have something funny for you." Stu Price—Stuart—held out a cassette tape, which she took. The label read, in faded ballpoint, in Stuart's writing, *Mel's Tape.*

"Holy cow. I wonder what's on this." She flipped the tape over, and back. For some reason, she smelled it. "What's on it?"

"Found it in my car. I don't really know. I think it's you in one of your bands." He played an air bass guitar, thumbed it nodding, cool rhythm-section dude.

"We'll have to give this a listen." She was pretty sure the

stereo system here had cassette doors. "I'm due for some public shaming."

Stuart tapped a hand on a thigh, glanced around at nothing, spun and ducked to gaze out the window over the sink, took in one second's worth of the backyard, and spun back. "So. What have you done in the last twenty-seven years?"

"Is that how long it's been?"

"I did some high-power calculations." He touched his temple.

It was a question that could be answered at boring length or with a shrug. Stu Price looked prepared for either. It was also a question whose answer wasn't a stranger to her. It had become rote, really. With cancer's onset came much fearful summing up and, after eight years, whenever she summoned her past it arose as if organized in a photo album. And lately she found that, maybe because she'd dropped all judgment of the pictures, her album had a simple clarity and she could flip through with detached fondness. I was a lonely, storky child. Those were my university days in Vancouver. I did nothing with my English degree, even less with my Philosophy. The music, the bands, that was lovely and indulgent and I risked my health but that was normal for that kind of fun. I was (still am) addictive, I smoked deeply, I was a good and proper smoker. Waitressing, sometimes cooking, up and down the coast, how brave I was, how comfortable to be alone; how I avoided both ambition or career, and how proud I was, actually, to stay clear of all that. I took *On the Road* seriously, good for me. The five or six excellent, in-the-moment years in the Charlottes, good friends. Expansive times. Two bad years of fun-that-was-no-longer-fun in Prince Rupert. A few years in money-Alaska, cooking on the big trawlers, lots of storms, a few men. One good woman. It was highly unlikely Ruth was still alive.

For Stu Price she chose the shrug, but said, "One of these nights I'll tell you. Some of it's good."

Some wasn't. Returning to Toronto at thirty-five, partly to clean up her act, partly to help Mom when Dad left for Nepal. Marrying Danny, and the fun of owning a restaurant and planning the menu, of feeding people what might delight them. But Danny put profits up his nose, it was that kind of time, and then her having to do the business side of things, which in her perverse way she always seemed to sabotage. Then her and Danny sabotaging each other. Hello Bryan the Brit. A kept woman. The years blending, passing, who knows what she wanted or how the hours filled. Then, yay, Montreal. Her throat started hurting soon after, but thank God for Montreal. When you arrive in Montreal the angels descend, hand you a beer and inform you there is nothing serious enough to be sober for.

Stuart was still standing there expectant and Mel realized her rudeness. "And I want to hear about your twenty-seven years too."

"Okay." Stuart looked at his feet, then back at her. "Here: wife, job, house, kid named Jennifer." He paused, pleased. "Then no wife, kid gone, retired, now no house. Boom, done."

"No, seriously." To which Stuart shrugged, still looking pleased, not willing to edit his story. He absently scratched a spot on his head through the shower cap, caught her watching, whipped his hand down quickly.

"It doesn't really itch, I just …"

Stuart was a good egg, with not a lot of confidence. He was a man you could see was stuck, and where.

"Stuart? I'm on my way to go visit my dad. He has Alz-heimer's, he's—"

"You told me on the phone. That's really sad."

"I'll be back in a couple of hours and I'll make you dinner." Stuart was staring at her, impossible to read. "Unless you want to come. But you probably have those insurance phone calls to make."

"I'd love to come."

He'd love to come to a dementia ward.

"What about your nap?"

"I picked up his book," he told her. "M.H. Dobbs."

"That's the man. I call him Hal."

"I'm really liking it. I didn't get to it the first time."

"I've been reading him that book." Mel went to the table and into her purse for the book, its white cover rough and almost tan with wear. It had been weeks since she last read from it. Her throat.

"You mentioned that. You're reading him his own book." He shook his head in amazement for her.

STUART DROVE THEM in Rose's Mercedes. It was an older car, with deep rattles and a long gouge in the leather so it leaked its kapok stuffing right where Stuart sat. But it still had its muscular German charms and he leaned forward with hands high on the wheel as if to be extra careful. Moving down their street, Mel realized how relieved she was to be driven. She still called it exercise, but lately the walk to the subway and back had been draining her. With the morphine patch she'd had to relinquish her driver's licence. As she'd had to relinquish her daily bowel movements, most pain, and the background-music concern for things like politics, weather, and the turmoil she read about in the paper. She hated morphine, but not really, because morphine dulled that feeling too. And music—only the bloodiest kinds of minor-chord ballads could cut through. "The Valley of Strathmore" was a good one. Sigur Rós, even after she heard that sometimes their lyrics were just noises, not Icelandic at all. The Russian Easter Overture for a while, but it no longer penetrated. Edith Piaf *sounded* like morphine. Anyway, the drug was a spongy wall between her and hell, and it sometimes made her jolly, even goofy, in the bloodstream.

Stuart was a good, fluid driver. He rarely blinked. She saw that he had rubbed up most of the olive oil with what looked like toilet paper because tiny bits of it were stuck in his hair. "Don't mind me," she told him, and picked them off.

"It's funny," he said when she finished. "I was sitting right here, driving, and you were sitting right there. Remember that guy we picked up, we were camping up in Egmont? The guy who said he cured his broken leg with his mind?"

"I actually do!"

"Had himself diagnosed crazy and had a pension for life?"

"I do." She could remember, could hear, his bubbling voice. And how his words came out sounding shaped by his smile. A bit much.

"It's so eerie—so many years ago? We were exactly this far apart"— he took a hand off the wheel to touch her shoulder— "and looking out a windshield, like this, and it could have been yesterday."

"I know."

"It could have been *five seconds ago*."

She murmured that time sure flies. She'd been ready to hear him ask about healing yourself, and if she'd ever tried to.

"No, it's more than that. It's like time doesn't even exist." He seemed genuinely troubled. "It's like looking up at the stars. When you sort of see past them. *That* feeling."

She almost said, I live that feeling, but didn't one-up him. Time vanished for her years ago. It was replaced with shock. She'd been awakened by life's snapped fingers. It's a secret that shocks over and over, to learn that life takes one second to live. But morphine did its muffle job on that one, too.

Strange how Stu Price—Stuart—had nailed that feeling, here with her. He was an empathetic man, even if he didn't know it. And it was going to be an honest and sincere visit. She might have to loosen things up. If death had no sense of humour it would be *death*. But first she told Stuart—in case he was wondering—that she had tried to heal herself, too. She had tried and tried, in tandem with the standard brutal treatments. You can't help but try. But with cancer you never know what works. You meditate and visualize and eat nothing but black grapes and curcumin, and the tumours shrink for a year—but was that the radiation, or what? It can go away fast and come back fast and you don't find it until it's rooted in tight places and it's suddenly a dangerous time again. What do you hit it with now—the breeze of a diet, or the hurricane of chemo? And all the while you're the shocked child waking up in a tired old body.

Stuart's face was wooden.

In her case, medicine had tried and failed. Her throat flaring, she told Stuart how, if you researched the industry, despite its many wonderful and smart folks, you'd be horrified to see how arrogance survived such ignorance. She told him a favourite story, about the discovery of "farmer's lung" by British medical researchers not much more than a hundred years ago.

The Industrial Revolution had peaked, the skies were filled with coal smoke. Some autopsies were showing an "odd pink" in the lungs of certain men, who were determined to have come from rural areas, so they called the mysterious disease "farmer's lung." Incredibly, it took decades to realize that pink, not dark grey, was the healthy one. That they not only could be so wrong but backward told Mel how blindly science trod its path, and drew in cartoon lines the ramshackle brutality of her own medical journey. They'd hacked at her throat with knives, radiated whatever raw meat was left, then pumped poison into her whole body for good measure. It sounded like bad science fiction, and a hundred years from now when these cures were described to doctors—if doctors still existed—they would cough into their elbow joints and change the subject.

Stuart pulled gently into the parking lot of Royal Elms. Mel decided that she had complained enough to him, if complaining was what this was, and she would do it no more. She was free of it, of complaining. Dying had its benefits and this was another. From here on in, she didn't have to do anything she didn't want to do. This was clear as clear could be. She still felt like a lens.

Stuart parked in a Visitors' stall and the car chugged once before falling silent. When Hal left Toronto for good, he called the Mercedes pretentious, symbols of wealth being one of his and Rose's main sticking points. Years later when he returned, forgetful, he thought the car was noble, "a good machine," and he related warmly to its wear and tear.

"Stuart." Mel put a hand on his knee. "It's okay. I packed a lot in." She pointed to her mouth. "I drank and smoked, I crammed and crammed. Everything." She smiled for him. "It's kind of perfect. It decided to close itself off."

THEY WALKED THROUGH the two main wards before reaching
the thick and locked door of Forest Grove, Royal Elms'
dementia wing. Mel thought the name fit—a dark cavern deep
in the woods where the lost could see neither the forest nor
the trees. She popped in the five-digit code, 1967*, which she
remembered by referencing the summer of love, this place
being some kind of ongoing opposite of that. To exit, the
code was entered backwards and was foolproof—it sometimes
stumped Mel too.

The lock light flashed green, a mechanism clunked. Mel
pulled the heavy door open, this movement hurting her
deeply in the chest and back. She didn't know she'd gasped
aloud until she saw Stuart watching her. This door was one of
her gauges. She didn't even know where inside it had hurt,
what newly invaded terrain to visualize.

"Okay. Stuart. A few things. He doesn't know me anymore,
so I'll sort of slide in who I am when I introduce you. He'll
forget who we are right away but he'll pretend he knows. He
gets embarrassed, he knows you're supposed to know your own
children. So I slide information in. Blunt honesty can hurt."

"Okay."

"But sometimes it's good, too."

"All right."

"He also doesn't know where he is, not really. He hallucin-
ates, usually that it's still Nepal. He thinks any brown person
working here is Tibetan. It was sort of a monastery. For visiting
Westerners. He was a meditation instructor. He's still there."

"Okay."

"He'll probably give you pointers about meditation, like
get you to sit up straighter. He's trying to be helpful."

"All right."

"If you say the wrong thing it's no big deal. Nothing sticks and it's back to square one. He's usually pretty happy. It's his default mood."

"Nice. That's lucky."

"His last twenty years he was a hardcore Buddhist. I don't know if that has anything to do with it."

"Interesting."

"Lived in Nepal fourteen, fifteen years."

Stuart didn't appear to hear her. He looked nervous as they entered, and Mel saw the place anew. The scattered amblers, wearing anything from pyjamas to suits, most women carrying empty purses. The gentle gargoyles in wheelchairs, stalled mid-corridor, often habitually saying hello, or pleading about going home, their eyes too bright. Though Mel hardly noticed it anymore, an endless music tape loop of craftily chosen oldies and smoothies tried to put a pillow over the face of the general anxiety. Early on, Mel had recognized some Mel Tormé, and Sinatra, and a voice that was probably Perry Como, and perhaps Michael Bublé, but sometimes whole Beatles albums played, and occasionally, maybe as a joke, "Purple Haze." She asked, and it turned out the playlists were made by Frank, a night janitor who was, she was quickly informed, gay. As they made their way in, *South Pacific* was on, and Mel saw that Stuart had already blanked it out.

Somehow, a good mood prevailed among staff who moved from here to there, rarely in a hurry. A floral scent battled an earthy tang. Furniture and paint was more practical, plain, and sturdy in these halls than in the other wings, the residents here no longer alert to decor. You didn't often see it, because most patients were hobbled by drugs, but mood swings and violence could be sudden and severe. Then staff hurried. Even the frailest could scratch someone's face or hurt themselves trying.

The bedrooms were identified not with numbers but with a recent snapshot of the patient. They reached Hal's picture and Mel pointed at it. It was one she liked, Hal beaming playfully, his hair freshly washed, the long single braid draped over his shoulder in front.

"So that's your dad."

"They keep wanting to cut his hair off."

"Why? It's great."

"It's inconvenient." Their argument was that he wouldn't know anyway. But he would. He preened it constantly. He'd feel the absence, he'd know something else was missing.

She knocked, listened, opened the door. Hal wasn't in his room. Mel hoped he wasn't in the lounge staring at the TV, which happened more and more lately. It was an awful scene, that lounge—fifteen, twenty people sitting around the perimeter, subdued by a blaring screen, the program not important. They couldn't use locks here and sometimes Hal was found asleep in another patient's empty room, which because of the gender imbalance was usually a woman's, and this kept the staff ripe with jokes for a shift.

"Has he written more books?"

"*The World* was it. One book. Dropped writing like a stone." Along with most everything else. "He doesn't know he wrote it or anything. He doesn't remember it one day to the next, or where we left off."

"Ah."

"*I* wanted to read it. It was a whim." Half-truth. The whim was Hal's.

"Sure, why not."

"I noticed how he remembers little phrases and things. Little word combinations. Or gets excited by them. It's funny, he rarely remembers the ideas or characters, but he seems to remember putting one word with another."

"Interesting."

Yes. What did it say about the brain, or creativity, or maybe selfishness, when you can't remember your own daughter's face, but an adjective you stuck on a noun over thirty years ago makes you smile? Sometimes he'd nod with recognition, sometimes exclaim, "Nice." Once it was "tight-fisted spring," describing a cold April.

So far he'd given her no clues that he remembered the big stuff, which was the real reason she tried reading him the book. He'd told her just the one time. They were downstairs going through his stuff, both of them joking too much to compensate for the sadness of it, a mere week before his big move here, and the end of them keeping house together. "Melody? That book wasn't fiction at all," he said, and it shocked her quiet. He held her eye to pound it home. She never did know exactly how to ask what he meant, and the next thing she knew, it was too late.

Stuart hadn't yet spotted Hal, who Mel could see holding court with Bea and Vera in the dining room, hair resplendent, a dark silver waterfall down his back, time for a shampoo. Or maybe Stuart thought that despite the shoulders Hal was a huge old crone, as sometimes happened. Then Hal laughed his explosive deep laugh, and Stuart looked and saw him.

Two years ago, just in time, her father had come home. He became real to her. And even something of a hero, which is how it's supposed to be. Maybe it was because they started fresh, almost as strangers. Maybe the Buddhism had made him new enough. People do change. Whatever the cause, he was the ripest combination of funny and sad. When his eyes welled up you didn't know which way it might go. The tender way a smile grew. A laugh leaping out, like they'd all just survived another one. There he was now, leaning hungrily forward. Even in a chair he never relaxed. You'd think a professional meditator would relax. She wondered if this, his refusal to sink back, might not be another of his Buddhist things.

Some of which surprised her. The first time she saw him, back after all those years in Nepal, in the hospital for a hip replacement, his hair tied up in a bun that looked all-business, the mala beads wrapped around a wrist, his glasses smudged almost opaque. What used to be called granny glasses. In the first minutes he identified himself as "a broken heart." He wasn't talking about a woman, or romance, or an abandoned child, which would be her. He was talking about his general condition, but not just his—he meant Mel's and everyone else's heart, too. And the past, and the future. Not the present, the present was fine, he said, and laughed easily. He was on heavy drugs and ideas were spilling out, but he could make things clear, or as clear as this sort of stuff got. There in the hospital bed, hip freshly replaced, offering her his vanilla pudding along with his broken heart.

Her mother had just died, a heart attack, sudden, on the front steps, and Hal came back for the funeral and stayed. Actually, he admitted, smiling at her from the bed, for some time he'd been meaning to come back to get his hip done. Rose dying decided it for him. He also told Mel, raising his eyebrows in humorous self-amazement, that he had "the start of Alzheimer's," and was going to "take advantage of famous Western health care because I can't put my friends through it."

All of this said through a mischievous smile, one that included some in-your-face irony that he might now be putting his daughter "through it." He said he might seem "oppressively open" to her because he'd forgotten how to act since he often spent months at a time in solitude. He was "a self-proclaimed mediocre teacher of the holy Dharma," for whom "sitting as still as possible" was his primary occupation. He laughed summing up, saying, "So I'm here with my begging bowl out."

When he was able he moved back into the family home in Rosedale, which felt only natural. Her parents had never truly split up, not legally in any case, and when he told Mel "she wants me back in here, believe me," Mel did. And she gradually moved over from Montreal, one of her doctors being in Toronto in any case. News of her rebounding cancer hurt her father to the quick and he could hardly speak of it without choking up. The two of them "convalesced" together, both ill with what would deepen and end them. She learned from him how to laugh about it—not bitterly, not from the nihilistic perch, but from a kind of astonishment at how colourful one's situation could be. They called their shared downhill slide "the slow toboggan." The year and a half of getting to know each other wasn't a sad end to either of their lives, not at all. Though this shifted when they had to face facts. Eventually, no matter how much help they hired, he couldn't stay with her in Rose's house. He started to wander. There were hygiene issues. Once he was fierce on the phone and tore it from the wall, a minute later having no clue why. And then it began: sometimes he wouldn't know her. Those first gaps were horrible, but only for Mel: entering the room and Hal lifting his face to her, the quick friendliness, the charisma he used to greet a stranger.

She wouldn't soon forget his first reaction to Royal Elms.

Because of his hip history they made him use a wheelchair for his grand arrival and Mel pushed him up the ramp, her first real sense of the wide shoulders on the man. He worked his mala and Mel could hear whispered repetitions of *om vajra-sattva hum*, a mantra she hadn't heard since his time in the hospital. When the glass doors slid open and they crossed the threshold, he interrupted himself to mumble, "I am your blushing bride," one of the little jokes he didn't seem to care if she heard. They'd come in from the rain, and as they travelled the first hallway he wrapped his mala around his wrist and dried his glasses on his shirt. A nurse named Mary walked with them from the front desk, pointing out in singsong the water fountains and activity rooms, adding from time to time, "We are not in your wing yet, Mr. Dobbs," but eyeing Mel as she did. She had an accent Mel came to learn was Vietnamese. Her father ignored her, wiping his glasses. When his glasses were done he unfastened and shook out his ponytail, which spread flat on his back as if on display, like an old peacock's last feather.

He'd been in before to check things out, more than once, but didn't appear to remember. When they got to his special wing and he saw the old men and women shuffling, wheeling, and sitting about, some chatting to no one, some open-mouthed, he studied the situation for a disturbed five seconds.

And said, "So that's it for getting laid, then."

Mel laughed out loud, startling the nurse.

The thing is, he meant it. Jostled truth was key to his kind of humour.

"Hey, excuse me," he said next, to Mel, forgetting her again, confirming for her their decision. "Am I staying here?"

"Yes." When her father forgot her it was breathtaking.

She wanted to tell him then that this facility, this *home*, was his reason for coming back after two decades away in Nepal. She wanted to say that things had worked out as planned, that his whole life was a success. But she didn't have to. It was strange how he both knew things—everything—yet didn't know anything. The big part of him, not the thinking part, knew. Awareness seemed to radiate from inside his body in a way that bypassed his brain. She couldn't describe it any better than that. She was still struck by how bright a mind could be with its memory gone. She often felt like Hal was fooling her.

Before leaving him here that first day, hoping he wouldn't see her tears, she squatted beside him and took in his face. He also knew this was a big moment and his eyes flicked here and there, absorbing the heavy-duty linoleum, the wooden bumpers running the length of the corridors so gurneys and wheelchair arms wouldn't hurt the institutional green paint. She saw him minutely panic, which he would do when he forgot where he was. Then she saw his eyes clarify, and he took a deep, controlled breath. This "coming back" was something he could always eventually do, even if his own name didn't come back with it. Sometimes his brief awareness would bring forth an insight, often a sad one—"I thought I could do it anywhere, but I don't know if I can"—"it" perhaps meaning meditate, or perhaps live. But sometimes it brought a joke, even the gallows variety, as it did that day when he lifted a finger, pointed to the wall and said, "That colour knows my fear."

After his first minute in his horrifying new home, he took a deep breath, much like a swimmer about to jump in. Then either deciding something or forgetting everything, he smiled at Mel and rolled off in the wheelchair, maybe also forgetting he could walk, to begin joking with the various staff, trying to make them feel good about themselves. One thing he did first was instruct them all how to properly pet his ponytail, whose name, as it turned out, was Hal.

"Stuart, I'd like you to meet my father, Hal Dobbs?"

The two men shook hands. The word "father" didn't spark anything so she stepped in and hugged him, saying in his ear, "Hi, Dad. It's Mel."

"Well, of course it is. It's been a long time!" Hal smiled earnestly, even lovingly, both acting and not.

"I come as much as I can, Dad." Part of her wanted to fall on her knees and assure him that she's come every day he's been here, but you don't want to remind them about their memory. Even if they don't remember nightmarish information, the sadness lasts. And sometimes thrashing anger.

"And where are you living now?" he asked, the usual question.

"I live in our old place."

Her father nodded pleasantly, picturing nothing.

She conducted introductions all around with Vera and Bea, and they were delighted to meet her for the hundredth time.

She still didn't always know. With seeming sincerity Hal had just asked Stuart if he was a monk, pointing to his shaved head. He had Stuart bend down so he could "fuzz" it, which he did, rubbing Stuart's head briskly, chanting a monotone "fuzz fuzz fuzz" with the stroking.

When he first moved here he would phone from the nursing station, and one thing he often asked her was, "Okay, Mel? So where am I?" Laughing, but serious. Another time, "There's a doctor here telling me I have Alzheimer's with a capital A. He can be pretty funny, that guy." The pause. "Whoever the hell he is." The pause, the timing, was the main indicator of Hal being funny. The other was the way he looked at you, deadpan, with wink implied. Once he said to her, and this was after another visit from the doctor, "Now you can call me Al."

What sort of man was Stu Price seeing? What was left of her father? It was crucially hard to know. Sometimes he still seemed almost wise, with the calm that signalled it. But could wisdom be a kind of vacancy?

"Hal?" she asked. Then, louder, "Earth to Hal." He always liked that one, maybe because it explained and excused everything. He looked up smiling. "Hal? Do you want me to read more of the book to you?"

He pretended to understand. "Yes! Of course!"

"We're at an important part."

"We'd be grateful if you would." Reverent, he adjusted himself in his chair and placed his hands in his lap.

"Is it storytime?" asked Vera. Mel couldn't tell if that was vague mockery and Vera was acting superior, but when she sat she adjusted herself for a story. Bea looked distracted, primly clutching her empty purse on her lap. She had a pinched, brow-knit concern about her that made everything she said dire, even "hello." Both wore heavy cardigans though it was hot. Both ladies were proper, perhaps moneyed. Their shoes looked expensive. Vera had on her violet sun hat. Mel didn't like feeling condescending toward them but at this stage in the game they both had the look of children playing dress-up. Hal wore grey sweatpants and a white T-shirt. Mel eyed Stuart's attire without meaning to. He didn't look out of place. Even his age. There were three or four in here younger than he was. That new pretty one, Julie, looked barely forty.

Hal was out of his chair now to stoop beside Stuart and whisper in his ear. He put a hand in the small of Stuart's back, and Stuart instantly shot upright, laughing nervously, then Hal put a hand on Stuart's shoulders to get him to relax them.

"Now tuck your chin. About a half-inch."

Stuart dropped his chin into his chest.

"Way too much. Here." Hal lifted Stuart's chin with a gentle finger. Then asked, "What practice do you do?"

Stuart looked up at him, smiling helplessly, and shrugged.

Hal snorted. "I know what you mean!" He patted Stuart's shoulder. Returning to his chair, he passed close to Vera, who contorted her body away from his dangling hands lest they touch her too.

Mel held up the book and showed them all the cover. Stuart pulled up a chair as well.

"This book is a novel called *The World*, by M.H. Dobbs." From her father, a small anticipatory smile but no recognition. Both ladies offered a polite, "Oh!" Stuart was staring at Hal.

"Ambitious title," Hal said, turning abruptly to Stuart, scaring him in two ways.

A young staffer Mel hadn't seen before rolled up a cart and offered juice and cookies. Bea and Vera had apple, Stuart pineapple, and as always Hal had tomato. The thick plastic cups were built for children and the beach. All three women refused a cookie, Hal took a sugar cookie, and Stuart a chocolate chip. Mel noticed a new earthy tang to the air and she wondered who it was. Her father, supposedly, still had control.

"Okay," she announced. "This part I'm going to read is about a woman who lives in a leper colony, on a small island, over a hundred years ago. She can't leave, and she's afraid, because she's the only woman there."

"Why can't she leave?" asked Bea.

"She's a leper," said Vera, staring straight ahead. Vera was one of the only doubt-free people Mel had ever met. It was a trait difficult to maintain with Alzheimer's, but she did.

"Is this—" Stuart interrupted, unable to help himself. "Is this one of the early translations? Before—"

Mel gave him a wary eye. "Yes." This shouldn't be complicated. But Stuart wanted to be read to.

Hal said, "It's a translation? From the what?"

"Okay, here." Mel figured, why not. You never knew what might stick. And this might kindle something bigger. "The story's this. There's a young history professor, Michael Bodleian. Michael happens upon an old tin, dug up on D'Arcy Island, a leper colony a hundred years ago. The lepers were all Chinese. It's full of old Chinese writing, and Michael hopes he can publish it—"

"And be lured onto the rocks of fame and riches," Hal said, matter-of-factly.

"He hires a translator, Naomi. And since the work is secret she has to stay over at Professor Bodleian's house. Which sets the stage for?"

Bea tried to share a look that Vera didn't return.

Vera asked, "How old is this Bodely?"

"He's maybe thirty. She's, I think, twenty-two or three."

"It could be worse," said Bea.

Stuart couldn't help asking, "They have an affair? I'm not there yet."

"What show is this?" asked Vera. She looked off after the cookie tray, as if wanting to call it back.

"So Naomi translates the papers. They're both madly in love but neither knows it." Mel thumbed through the book, searching. "The part I'm going to read is some translation Naomi has just given Professor Bodleian. The first was lists of food and supplies. Professor Bodleian was very disappointed. This second one is more promising. It turns out to be by a woman leper whose very existence was in doubt. Her name is Li."

"I don't know about any of this," said Vera, agitated. Hal, not looking at her, reached over and put a hand on her wrist.

"Stuart?" asked Mel. "Would you mind?" Holding her finger to a section on the page, she passed the book to Stuart. "My throat's a bit sore."

Stuart said sure and quickly took it from her. He was nervous as he glanced up at these people who were now an audience.

"Really slow," Mel said, and Stuart nodded.

Mel listened, but most of all watched her father. Reading, she'd never been able to do this.

Hands minutely shaking, Michael Bodleian began to read the typed page for the second time, this time aloud. His voice rang clear, and overly slowly, as if he didn't believe what he read:

I hardly remember the first week, or the second, or the third, except that I slept outside under a cedar tree, in the rain. Up against the trunk, the raindrops did not find me too often, unless there was wind. I was more wet from the heat and anger of my own sweat, because I lived encased in a ball of heavy blankets. We all had many

*blankets. It was the one item we had too much of. I saw
that some blankets were used to strain food, like the broth
of soup, or bean curd, and then were just discarded. Of
course we*

"This is good," interrupted Hal, gazing at the floor. As
usual, Mel didn't like her father's self-congratulation, even if
it wasn't exactly that.

"I like it too," said Stuart, who leaned toward Hal, nodding
rapidly.

"And it doesn't stay so sad," Mel thought to add.

Bea smiled falsely while Vera regarded all of them with
suspicion. She rose and strode off, and soon the air smelled
only floral.

Stuart settled back and continued:

Of course we burn the blankets of the newly dead.

*   I could have slept inside either of the two main huts,
but I chose not to. It did not matter where I was, truly,
because for many, many days, I cried. To find myself in
this place. To look upon the faces of the other prisoners,
and see not just their disease but the emptiness of their
eyes. It is the eye that cannot show sorrow, or hell, which
because of its great weight stays below the eyes, down in
the heart. The heart too heavy to rise to the eye and show
itself. I know that my own face would puff and pox and
break open like theirs soon enough, if not this year then
the next, and my eyes would show the same nothing. So
I cried. It didn't matter where I was. I had already been
approached by two men, San Yu and Fong, and it was
terrible, that they would want me in that way, though*

one of them even explained in his wheezy fumbling that he hadn't even seen a woman in four years. But it was yet more terrible that I did not really care, and even though I swatted and punched a little, the main reason the men gave up was that they could not manage to peel away many of my blankets, could not find the edges or grip them with their dead hands. But my life's sorrow is so vast that these two men and their evil hide lost within it, like two small insects.

"Naomi," said Michael Bodleian, too excited to look up from the page, "it's her. It's Li, the woman. It really is. This is unbelievable."

Naomi smiled, happy for him.

"There are some verb-tense issues but no matter." He followed his finger back to his place, and read:

Still, I did not want to sleep in one of the huts because to do so would be to admit that I truly lived here now, which I could not bear. Also it would be like throwing myself to them, like fish skin to dogs. Under my tree in the woods, at least, they would have to search and find me, and fight through my many blankets, and my fists. Most will not bother with me or with any of that, because at this point in their disease I am stronger than many of them and, though I do not care to think and picture it, I also knew that some of them, whose disease was well into the middle of the body, could not take pleasure from a woman any longer, could no longer even feel what wolves and ears of corns do.

Excited as he was, Michael stopped his reading to ask, "'Ears of corns'? Are you sure, Naomi?"

"Yes. Yes, I think." She grew concerned and hunched to rustle daintily in the pages, still housed reverently in their original tin.

Michael reread the sentence to himself. "It's just so weird. And then with the 'wolves,' it's weirder still."

"It *is* weird," said Hal. Staring into the middle distance, he shrugged by way of explaining, not agreeing. "And Bodleian is uncomfortable."

Stuart waited in case Hal had anything more to say. Then asked, "Should I continue?"

Bea, brow-knit and like much depended on it, said, "Oh yes!" but eyed the approaching cookie tray on its return run.

Mel smiled at Stuart and nodded. Her father closed his eyes.

Naomi pointed to two elaborate characters on the dry parchment, tapped both and it sounded like the tapping of thin wood. "It is exactly that," she said. "*Yat kung kuut.* Ears of corns."

"Corn. All right. All right, that's fine. Thank you, Naomi." Seemingly unaware of it he laid a hand briefly on her shoulder, and Naomi dropped her head.

But I am fearful now. My fear grows from hope, isn't that strange? When hopeless, there is nothing to fear. But now, after some weeks, I have begun to see that the sea is not so cold, and the waves not so large, and that one day, if I focus my heart, I will get away. My disease is not so bad. My nose has thickened a little, and my lips, and most days my toes do not feel much, but the rash is hidden. In Victoria, people meeting me for the first time could see nothing wrong. It was only those who saw my face change. But now I have decided to leave, and to hope. And so I care about not getting sick to death in the rain, and now I fear not getting my share of food, which these men would happily deny me. According to the night-time stories at the fire, some here have chosen to die that way, weakening themselves with hunger until a killing sickness comes. But the garden here is good, and some of the men, I see, tend to their vegetable plants like their babies, mounding seaweed as fertilizer around the plants, sometimes even in designs, like artwork. I have seen the smiling mouths of seaweed built as if eating a cauliflower.

Of those first weeks, I also remember hearing for the first time the awful music of the wind in the tree-tops, and its cruel roaring. I say music, because what is wind in trees but a monstrous wind instrument? I say awful, because what is this music but the voice of nature, and so it is the voice of the hawk snatching up the baby rabbit and tearing it apart while it is alive. It is the music of storms drowning men at sea. It is the music of fruit rotting to release seeds and it is the music of the heartless stars. It is the music of what brought us here.

I have never heard human music, here. I have heard no one sing. Of course, who would? And I sometimes imagine that, if by magic someone found a flute and had the good fingers to play it, the flautist would either be attacked and killed on the spot, mid-song, or else there

*would be instant tears, and he would be worshipped, and
he would never have to work his garden or cook again.*

*I know everyone now. Mostly I am fearful of Quince.
There is a belief, commonly held, that the stupid are in
their nature more honest and kind than the clever. Why
does the myth persist? It hurts me anew each time I am
leered at by Quince, because in all of my life he is the
stupidest man who has come within touching distance.
Quince is not merely uneducated, he is a man who could
not learn to read no matter the skill of his teachers. You
can see his stupidity in the shape of his face and the bone
of his head. His eyes shine with erroneous light. He looks
like he could kill me and begin to eat me but be chased
away by a thunderstorm like a dog. This is a man I
heard about even in Victoria, a man so hateful that he
was tricked onto the boat to this place, and who arrived
several years ago without the disease but has it now as
a gift from these men, and as a punishment from his
enemies in Victoria.*

Mel waved for Stuart to stop, and he looked at her ques-
tioningly. She asked if he could skip forward and into the next
chapter, to the third piece of translation, which she liked.
Stuart joked that he didn't want to miss anything, and she told
him it was all university stuff, Michael contacting publishers,
telling them he had a great secret, and them wanting the hard
evidence. She saw that Bea was asleep though bolt upright.
Her father's eyes were still closed. His lips moved, but his mala
was still on his wrist. It was probably time to stop but she did
like this part. And there was something about being read to.

She wondered who last read to her as a child, her mother or
Hal.

Stuart found the place and began:

> *In my first eternal month on the little island, on Foo
> Hoi, I had not noticed him much, because he was quiet
> and kept to himself. But Sang Seen had noticed me. Then
> the first good hour of what remained of my life occurred
> when his unfeeling hand took my good one and he led
> me up a small, hidden hill, and in one day he built my
> heart, my mansion.*

"That is exactly what is written," said Naomi,
not giving Bodleian time to ask the question when
he looked up from the page at her. "I checked and
checked. *Sam* is 'heart,' and it is also 'deep.' *Ahk* is
'house,' *gwai*, 'expensive.' 'Mansion' is an expensive
house, Michael?"

The way she said his name, *Myco.*

He thought a moment. *Mansion,* used figuratively.
He nodded, and returned to the page, though he
appeared to regard it differently from before.

> *There was a flat space already prepared, some of it
> dug to make it level. New blankets waited for me, folded
> clumsily and resting on a rock. He had already cut the
> poles and bound them with leather ties to make the frame
> for a simple, leaning roof. I knew that he had to have
> tightened the knots using his best hand and his teeth.
> Together we found cedar boughs enough to layer, and
> keep out the rain. More cedar boughs we laid upon the*

*ground, which now became a proper floor, and maybe
the best part of the mansion was its smell, because the
cedar we had ripped from the neighbour trees bled sweetly
into the air of the clearing, so richly that we could smell
nothing but cedar, and this was a rare treasure in a place
whose living spaces were crowded with men who had not
put soap or water on their skin in years, whose bodies
were rotting on their bones, and whose very words, and
indeed minds, seemed to exude a badly warped odour, like
the poisons of Violet Hell.*

*We lay back on the cedar boughs, just breathing. I
smiled. I may have laughed. The man who lay at my
side, respectful, two feet away, was missing the tips of
all of his fingers, and some were openly bleeding, as were
his cracked lips. I knew his name, but to be polite asked
him anyway, and it was Sang. Sang Seen. He looked at
me and smiled, not with his thickened mouth, but his
entire face, and mostly his eyes, and it was the smile of a
sunset.*

*The next day we built a good fire pit. We began to
carry boards up the little hill and stack them. Sang had
a shouting fight with a man who wanted the boards to
remain below, though there was no use for them there, nor
a plan. In the World, insanity can be dressed like logic.
The next day I traded all of my opium ration for the five
months to come, for private ownership of a pot, a frying
pan, two plates, two cups, a glass, a small bowl, a big
bowl, teapot, and spoon, fork and knife for four. Cutlery
is easy to acquire, since most men simply use whatever
they can grab and hold, like a thick stick, to push food
from a bowl into their mouth. I will enjoy myself like an*

*English lady for years to come. In the meantime, the walls
of my mansion go up. I have put in an order for cedar
shingles. I am told that if I make demands for a feather
bed, I will at least get a pillow. So I have demanded not
only a feather bed, but a canopy to encircle it, claiming
that my modesty is at stake. If I can shame the authorities
even a little, how can this be a bad thing? I have also
put in an order for fish hooks and line. The several men
who can still handle a fish-line have grown lazy, and
have lost theirs or let them lie where they fall, and the salt
water rusts them thin and then to nothing. It is said that
one man, Lu, walked around unfeelingly with two hooks
in his foot until he died. The joke, that he called himself
"a baited hook," is I think false.*

    *No other man but Sang Seen will come up the hill to
see me. I have seen that he is a leader here, and perhaps
men are afraid of him. I do not know why this is so, but
how wonderful he is. Sang cannot do the fine work of
pinching a nail to be properly hammered, but he is a good
teacher. He places the board and I hammer home the nail.
He is such a good teacher that, one day, interrupting our
work on my house, he taught me to build a kite! It was
windy, and his immovable face looked almost excited.
He told me to peel that branch, and that one, and bind
them together like so. He called it "ironwood" and said
you could even make fishhooks from it, which would be
stupid, he added, if you lacked a boat. Laughing, he
removed one of his own shirts for the fabric, told me where
to cut it, and with string I tied it to the frame. Before
long I was knee deep in water at the north beach, letting
more and more string be taken by the offshore breeze as*

the kite rose, and rose, and it soon became the tallest
thing anywhere in the World. Sang said, I think only
to himself, "That is my skill up there." The kite danced
and danced, and I was not the only one looking up and
laughing at the happiness of it. The kite could have been
a signal, a wave, to anything alive beyond our island,
but it wasn't that. It was just ours.

Sang Seen is a father and a brother to me. He is
my head. Perhaps I am his heart. He speaks only on
occasion. I once heard him shout wretchedly and in
hateful anger from inside the main house during a meal,
and it scared me, because it was a voice I'd never heard.
He never has to shout, and never has to cry, when he is
with me.

Bea's mouth was open and she snored softly. Hal had his
eyes closed still but had his mala off his wrist and worked the
beads between thumb and forefinger. This was a prayer or reci-
tation of some sort, and Mel suspected he could do it in his
sleep, or that the state he was in now was a kind of sleep. Stuart
smiled and raised his eyebrows for her, closed the book, and
stretched. A stout nurse bustled by and gave Mel the smile that
said Mel must be pleased to have gotten the children down at
last. As she passed, doing a job Mel didn't envy, the machinery
of her hips rustled loudly in stiff white fabric.

When they rose to go, Hal put his hands together and
bowed to Stuart. To Stuart, because he had just read them
something and had been their teacher. Then he said, formally,
"We are very grateful, and please visit us here again." Here
being the meditation hall. His eyes on Stuart were open, warm,
welling up with a gratitude that he truly felt. She could see in

this the love he gave freely to strangers, and this hurt her as it always did. Her father was a lovely man. Stuart bowed back to him, and Mel bowed too, which closed Hal's eyes and had him on the mala beads again. His lips moved.

As always, the bowing made her feel good. A kind of respect in the air. And, for the visit, punctuation. Better than ending things in grim confusion, which was often the way visits ended here. Poor old souls who "feel better now" and want to come home from the hospital.

With Stuart in tow Mel hoped it wouldn't be awkward getting out of the ward but it was. The usual cluster of residents (thank God Hal wasn't one of them today) had gathered at the door, the door that led to their freedom, they knew this much. They often took turns trying it, stepping up and giving it a good rattle. Someone might toss out, a bit arrogantly, "You need a key. Someone get the key." Someone else would announce that she had the key in her purse, and she'd dig and dig but never find it.

Another reason Mel hated exiting at this door was that in her hurry she sometimes couldn't work the dementia code herself. It should have been funny but it wasn't. Hal might be at her side, smiling benignly, no clue as to what was going on but happy to be a part of it, while Mel tried to punch in 1967* backwards, excited old folks pressing at her elbows, all trying to help. Flustered, always worried her dad might figure out this time that *my daughter is leaving and I'm not allowed to,* her fingers were fine with the star, but then someone would say, "*She's* got it," and the murmur would start, and the shuffling forward, a geriatric rush to the lifeboat, and she'd be embarrassed for herself as well as for them and pissed off that a nurse hadn't come by yet to gather them with the trick, "Who wants a cookie!" which worked dismayingly well on these once-capable folks who had themselves been nurses, or realtors, or mothers, and she knew of a couple of lawyers, and a city alderwoman, and one lapsed writer who'd been living in Nepal.

Today a nurse strode out from her station and stood between Mel and the rest, and smilingly asked them who was hungry for dinner. Mel heard no response, but it worked, and she escaped again, Stuart silent and quick-stepping beside her.

PERCHED BEHIND THE BIG Mercedes wheel, Stuart said he'd forgotten how sad the book was, and Mel said, "It's a leper colony."

"True," he said. Then, reconsidering, "And there's weirdly happy parts."

"Well, yeah," Mel said. "One of his intentions in the book was to see if it was possible for humans to have a good time even in a leper colony."

"He said that?"

"Not in those words." She added that mostly it was a tragic love story and that's why it made its minor splash at all.

When Stuart went on to say how good a writer Hal was, and what a shame he'd stopped, Mel said his greatest strength as a writer was probably that he knew how good he wasn't. She thought it hadn't been so difficult for her father to leave writing behind. She told Stuart of Hal's confession to her, that the proudest time in his life was when he found himself teaching Buddhism to Tibetans, getting some to meditate again, and being called, by a few, Rinpoche. *Rim*-po-shay. In daily use it meant teacher, but literally it meant Precious Jewel.

She didn't tell Stuart that Hal told her this on her birthday when they were in a bar on Queen Street drinking cognac, and that he wagged his eyebrows at her, stabbed his thumb into his chest and said, "*Boo* yeah, *preshiss* jewel."

Mel directed Stuart to a grocery store and they pulled into the lot. She turned to Stuart as he parked. She wanted to clear up what might be another assumption.

She said, "Hal's hair?"

"That hair's great."

"It's not old hippy hair. His teacher in Nepal had hair like that. It was a lineage tradition. The teacher died ten years ago. It's Hal's gesture of respect, or devotion."

Stuart nodded. "I guess then it's even better."

Stuart hadn't turned off the car and he looked disturbed as he stared at nothing through the windshield. Mel asked him what was wrong.

"Sorry, nothing." He smiled falsely for her. "It's the Buddhism part of things, I guess. Not wild about it. Diane left me for sort of a Buddhist thing." He closed his eyes, and shrugged so that his shoulders stayed way up. "Actually it's not Buddhist at all. Never used the word, anyway. It's some sort of spiritual deal, though. I know they meditate."

"I'm sorry to hear that."

"Nah." Stuart laughed and shook his head at his own idiocy. "It's not why she left me at all."

He probably had it right the first time, Mel figured, walking through the parking lot, hunching in the drizzle. There were worse reasons to leave people.

Back in her kitchen, as she sautéed the pork tenderloin in butter, port wine, and garlic and was busy chopping the mushrooms and shallots, when Stuart realized she had shopped and was cooking just for him, he exploded with protest and apologies. She told him it was worth it to her just for the smells. To prove it she hovered over the bubbling tawny sauce and inhaled rapturously (unable to escape, for a moment, the image that she was Li inhaling her cedar boughs and Stuart at her side was the stinking and wooden Sang) and she didn't cease inhaling and moaning until he said he believed her.

SHE WOKE LOST in a cocoon of pain. Pain was everywhere, pain was her past, pain was her future. When she slept too long it could do this, it could take over, it could shove her off, king of the mountain. She tapped her patch ten times, hard. They told her there was no way this could speed her relief, but it seemed to.

She was getting better at finding the level of pain she could live with. She wanted to stay clear, especially when the time came. She would not become a glassy-eyed loaf. But nor would she be like one of the Buddhist teachers Hal had told her about, who apparently would go—would relish going—to the dentist for some drilling or a tooth pull, all with no novocaine or anything else, bring it on. It was against his religion, so to speak, to inflict torture on himself, but any time he could legitimately challenge himself with pain he took the opportunity. After, he would bow to the dentist, "smiling like he ate the canary," said Hal, who clearly had his heroes.

There. Okay. Back on top of the mountain. Pain was still the mountain, but that's how morphine worked.

She stretched, trying to luxuriate in what she'd dubbed her harem bed. In her search for comfort she'd gone through

all kinds of sheets. Satin felt slimy when she sweated, which
was often the case, so she settled on a buttery eight-hundred-
count white cotton bottom sheet and a navy blue satin upper.
It felt like a nurse below and a party above, but somehow this
combination wicked away the wet.

The light coming through the window ivy, fluttering
almost musically in the breeze, made her think midday.
Sometimes she slept late. This no longer panicked her, no
longer felt like a tragic loss of time. She'd discovered that that
was just ego, to think that if she was awake it somehow made
existence better.

She could hear Stuart in the kitchen trying to be quiet
with the faucet and a pot. Today he was off to Bay Street to
do battle. Last night before bed, he had another sheepish
request, wherein before asking her for the obvious—money—
he prepped her with a story of melted bank cards and busted
glasses and manic eye operation and selling his car for a bus
ticket. *Less* than a bus ticket. Even after she asked how much
he needed and was rooting in her purse he continued his
blather about being good for it, and how his ex, Diane, could
wire some, but he needed some now, he needed to buy some
pants, and subway fare, but he'd pay her interest, he'd—

"Are we friends?" She caught his eye and watched his face
collapse as he had an inner moment.

"Yes."

"Then don't insult me?"

"Okay. Sorry, I—"

She put her hand up to stop this apology too, and went
on to say that if he only knew how little money meant to
her now, and that she was looking for good ways to spend
it, and helping a friend was one, and if he ever mentioned

paying her back she'd kick him out of the house. She gave him eighty of the ninety dollars cash in her purse and wrote him a cheque for a thousand, then ripped it up, told him he needed to buy shoes and a sports coat too, and wrote it for two thousand. Taking it from her and reading it, he swore and said, "This is it? After all that?" Another side of him came back to her and she remembered how funny he could be when he tried. Then in an odd moment he told her, reading the cheque like an amazed boy, and as if it hadn't been Mel who'd given him the money, that he'd been thinking only fifty or sixty dollars.

She could hear him in the kitchen still trying so hard to be quiet. Funny how that made it louder.

Money. In the long dark she'd lain awake fine-tuning her plan, and Stuart now had a role in it. The food, the wake. And, maybe, her father. He did seem to like Hal. Stuart would not only agree, he would be honoured, she was sure. But she'd also decided to surprise him, giving him no chance to think about it and for whatever reason decline.

She tested her memory with the menu. Three more recipes last night. Her rule, and she didn't know why, was that she had to invent them in her head and not test them out. They were all canapés, and they all had funny names. Her Montreal friends would expect this. She wanted nothing of her wake to be serious. Nor did she want anything to be frivolous. Babette's feast, but Babette wouldn't be there.

It took a while, breathing steadily in her harem-bed sheets, but she recalled all three:

"Forest Floor" *(this could be great, or a disaster)*. Portabella caps stuffed and baked with goat cream cheese, lemon zest, horseradish and whole steamed fiddleheads. After, embed whole peppercorns, slivers of raw garlic, hints of raw ginger, tiny scatter of rosemary leaves. Dribble truffle oil.

"Duck Satan" *(bad pun on devilled eggs)*. Hard-boiled duck eggs, halved, the yolk mixed with garlic aïoli, kosher salt, Spanish paprika, dribble of piri piri sauce, and warm capers embedded.

"Macaroons DNA." Egg whites, coconut, chocolate, butter, demerara, slivers of real vanilla bean. At the blender snip in a single tiny piece of my salty eyelash, one of which I will supply.

Mel still wanted to do some variation on ants on a log. What could you fill a celery stick with besides peanut butter or cream cheese? Some kind of weird pudding? Foam? Pâté? Marrow! What could the ants be besides raisins? Maybe she should just do … ants on a log.

In the bathroom mirror she looked like a ghoul. Judging by the crusty matte of her hair, she'd been sweating on and off all night. As she stepped into the shower she heard the front door close, and Stuart was gone when she called his name.

In the kitchen, his note thanked her again for last night's meal, and said that he had made himself a huge and great breakfast, thank you again. He explained that he was off to "hunt down" some insurance people about his house, and he thanked her for the use of her father's clothes.

Opening a can of pink food, setting up her rig, Mel wondered what outfit, or costume, Stuart had worn downtown. When he first arrived she offered him the use of Hal's clothes and showed him the closetful. Stuart tried on a single shirt and swam in it. Hal was a wagon and Stuart a bike.

She was glad she'd missed Stuart going out the door; it would have been sad. She wished he'd had time to buy some clothes before this morning's meeting. When you fought City

Hall you had to dress like City Hall. Clothes were the first hurdle. She didn't know much about men in power but she did know that. And this: if they saw they were dealing with a loser, they'll shake his hand and smile, and Bozo won't even know he lost.

While she ate, again not watching the TV, she decided she felt up to the walk to the subway, to visit Hal. Nothing else on her schedule today. She would try reading him some more *World.* Maybe the next section, when the affair starts, see if he reacts. Watching the chemical-pink course down the tube, she smiled at her father's possible affair. It was like he was teasing her, tricking her—it was entirely possible. What exactly did *It's not fiction* mean? They were downstairs, discussing what of his stuff to give away, when he pointed at a boxful of copies of his novel then said two things, holding her eye. The first was "Melody? That book wasn't fiction at all." The second, said with a snort and a half-smile, "This is my Bengali tea boy. You should read it to me when I'm up in the clouds."

It was easier to ask him what he meant by the second thing. She heard a brief tale about a great teacher who hated his Bengali tea boy, a servant who was travelling with him. A constant irritant, the tea boy asked impudent questions and spilled things. The teacher soon discovered that all the nice, smiling, respectful people he encountered put him to sleep, while the Bengali tea boy was far more helpful for waking him up by keeping him uncomfortable. "The tea boy," Hal concluded, "makes you see the parts of yourself you don't want to see." And so, somewhat magically, the Bengali tea boy became the great teacher's teacher.

Mel figured any book could be a Bengali tea boy, if it showed you yourself, but what about this claim of non-fiction? Was it

Hal's braggadocio, a "My book is full of truths about the human condition," or confession, a "When we lived on the West Coast I actually had an affair with a Chinese translator and ruined my career and marriage and I still cringe with remorse"? Because he had been an academic, in history. They'd lived in Victoria when Mel was two and three years old. She'd never once heard her mother and father talk about those times.

Years ago on first read she'd found it creepy, the book's seduction and sex scenes, because even then she couldn't help picturing Michael Bodleian as her father, if only because he must have experienced the touching, the breathing, likely with her mother, and so it was all genetically repulsive territory. Now it was less repulsive than mysterious. If Michael Bodleian was Hal's version of himself, it would be a hard mirror to look into. Michael Bodleian as Bengali tea boy seemed to fit.

She saw she was finished eating. Mmm-*mm.* She unhooked the tube to clean it, and wondered what to cook for Stuart tonight. Perhaps because she'd been picturing the West Coast, she came up with another one:

"Prawns Afterlife" *(wear gloves during prep).* Fresh BC spot prawns, peeled, deveined, dabbed lightly with inner flesh of ghost pepper. Grill 30 seconds per side. Drizzle with lime, toss some kosher salt. Eat with knife and fork.

It would burn lips, but maybe the prawn's sweetness would come through. It'd be a shame to ruin everyone's tongue for the rest of the food. (Though she did want Bryan to grab one and just bang it down. She could see that stiff upper lip beading with sweat.) Maybe serve with a shot glass of cold buttermilk? Would that fix it? While in his monastic life spicy food was frowned upon as "entertainment," it was Hal who told her about ghost pepper, and she found some last week in one of the high-end market stalls. Apparently it was the hottest edible pepper in the world, leaving the bird pepper in its dust. It came from a valley in the lower Himalayas and got its name from the idea that, if any outsider mistakenly ate one, they would burn up on the spot, but their ghost could never leave, since the pepper was at the same time so damned good. For some reason she'd clung to this story like a talisman, and not just because it was funny. There was something true about loving what killed you. Not in the pathetic way, where the conquered worship the power of their master, but in a real way. Could she ever love her tumours like that? Some of the self-help books called it a necessary step, not for survival, but peace.

The ghost pepper itself was bloated and wrinkly and had the bleached-out hue of dog shit after the thaw, like this plant had never exactly been alive and was something else entirely. She likewise pictured her tumours as belonging to some other dimension of ugliness, the overlap of ugliness and evil, like something shit by a vampire. Sometimes she saw them as a mash of crushed insects, sort of alive, clicking away with legs and mouths, mining her good flesh. Sometimes, to her surprise, she found herself feeling sorry for them, because, well, what a thing to be. This wasn't "loving," but perhaps it was close.

Anyway, ghost peppers. Stuart said he loved spicy. He claimed she introduced him to that whole realm, on camping trips. So, let the camping trips continue.

Today was new-patch day. She showered first, then towelled her right shoulder hard, leaving the skin pink and soft as a baby's and, so she imagined, more absorbent. She broke a patch open and slapped it on, leaving the old one on the left.

You weren't supposed to wear two, even if the old one was weak, but she found a painful gap in there sometimes if she followed those instructions. And who cared what she did? Who cared if she got a little high? Drooled a little and hummed a tune? Whose business was it but hers?

She brushed her hair, grabbed her things and, closing the door behind her, decided not to lock it, anymore. She missed those places, and those days. Leaving it unlocked made her feel a little breathless in a good way.

She not only visited every day but tried for the same time, one o'clock, right after lunch. She knew a visit, by anybody, pleased him, and he enjoyed her presence even if he was napping and she simply talked or read to him. She could tell he felt it and felt it in his body. It's the pure kind of happiness, and maybe the stronger kind, an animal kind. And if it made her happy to do that for him, maybe it was in the end selfish, but so what.

And she would be visiting him only twenty-three more times.

The walk to the subway wasn't fun, was a mistake. She was grateful for the station bench. She sat back, closed her eyes, tried to gather herself. She realized she felt a bit guilty because she wouldn't be at her best for him. To fix this, she pulled out *The World* to read herself a section that made her not like him so much. Michael Bodleian was kind of a pig. And if Michael was Hal, or Hal's version of himself, how odd, or maybe it made sense, that the writing was often so bad. Like he was all thumbs trying to pin himself down.

And how had her mother felt, reading this? Reading any of it? If Hal was Michael. If she was sitting home with a baby when this was going on.

Michael checked his watch again, though she wasn't yet late. He watched for her out the window, almost willing her to burst past that corner of hedge. Everything was laid out on the table, ready, including a roll of candies that suddenly embarrassed him. Naomi's breath had always smelled inexplicably of lemons. He'd grown romantic about it, imagining that her breath didn't smell like normal breath, and he asked her—actually, praised her—about it, and she'd pulled out her favourite candy and offered him one.

He grabbed the lemon candy he'd bought and hid it in the utensil drawer.

He still had reservations about Naomi, and they were at war with his feelings for her. Last time, after she had delivered the first instalment, which was, after all, a kind of probationary or trial run for her, she confided—or admitted, or confessed—that she was no longer a student. Her grant from home had run out, or been denied—she wasn't clear on it herself—and because of her new status her visa was up for reinterpretation. But what rankled Michael was that, as a non-student, Naomi's status on his D'Arcy Island project changed, too. Professors could and did use students, graduate students, whenever they could, as research machines, and they sometimes thanked them in print, but weren't in any way obliged to acknowledge the nature of their work or, even more rare, cite them as co-authors. Naomi now fell into a grey area, possibly one of collaborator, and as such her professional qualifications might come under scrutiny. Not to mention his having to share some of the credit. (With this in mind, he would continue to keep Naomi in the dark about the true nature of the project.) But he had decided to push on with her. For one thing, it was sheer luck that her knowledge of late-nineteenth-century Cantonese dialect was so good. For another, she could write English so well. For yet another, he could afford her; she was translating for not much more money than you paid someone to type your thesis.

He thought he'd heard someone stepping up the walk, but he hadn't. He checked his watch—she was now late, by two minutes.

But the main reason Michael Bodleian was willing to overlook her status, and one that he was just realizing, was that his stomach hollowed out whenever he laid eyes on her. To imagine her breasts under that loose tunic made him feel faint. To glimpse her eyes meeting his was an unbearably pleasant shock. That was the only word for it, "shock." Her looks weren't striking; in fact he'd hardly seen her at first, but now how he loved that impossibly perfect skin, her long lustrous hair, her face, with its larger than typical nose, approaching not cuteness but almost a classic kind of beauty. And now, whenever he heard her voice, he felt bathed in warmth. When she was at his side, softly explaining a finer point of idiom, sometimes he got her to repeat herself because he'd simply been listening only to her voice, not the words. But his favourite time—he realized now—was when she fought to pronounce a word properly. The way she would briefly look up at him, frustrated, apologetic, and try the word—last week, "schedule" had been one—and

say it again, and then again, louder. It was a weakness
that she abhorred, and her diligence was so sweet.

But when they were conducting business, it would
be all business. He would not pay her more, now that
he was becoming involved with her. That would be in
some way immoral. He wasn't sure in what way, but
knew it was so. Nor could he risk losing sight of that
darker possibility. He didn't want to mistrust Naomi,
but there was the possibility—it came up so commonly
in cases like this that it didn't even have to be
mentioned—that through marriage, with a random
anyone, Naomi could move to Gold Mountain. He
could not shake the memory that, on first meeting
her and after they had shaken hands, her second or
third sentence to him had been "I very much want to
stay in Canada." Michael knew he must never forget
this. He must not lose his head, no matter how perfect
her voice, her skin. No matter the joy that might be
coming in the deep of the night. Maybe this one.
Maybe tonight.

IN THE KITCHEN, still wearing a hideous, pale rose dress shirt
of Hal's that was probably two decades old, Stuart sat down to
the meal she'd cooked for him and had waiting. He moaned
"Mmmm," and continued to chew. Maybe four or five more
chews, then he stood up. Then the pain registered on his face.
He spun once, raced to the sink and took tiny steps on the
spot while he drank from the faucet.

"Ghost pepper," Mel said. "Sorry." She'd made a simple
Thai chicken stew, over basmati. She'd laid a quarter of a

pepper in there to simmer for fifteen minutes, then lifted it out with chopsticks. The rest of the pepper sat in the fridge crisper, double-bagged in plastic. Stuart straightened at the sink, then sank down for more gulps.

"Sorry," she said again. "I'm living vicariously."

Stuart put a hand up to say it was okay. Mel dished him another bowl, from the second pot, the one not injected with ghost pepper. She even used a new bowl, throwing away the first one. It was thrilling to throw away a dish. Maybe she'd burn a hundred-dollar bill. No, she'd give one to a panhandler. Or maybe a passing kid on a skateboard. Maybe one day she'd give out twenty hundreds, make a day of it. Good mischief. Anyway, she'd rethink ghost pepper at her wake. Bad enough to choreograph people's experience. She wouldn't let it veer anywhere close to pain. Maybe some discomfort. For instance, Ravel's *La Valse* might be a truly creepy piece of dinner music. Though with a piece so hauntingly disjointed already, who knows, at a wake it might sound just sort of logical. Maybe she should hire a magician. Or a clown. No, that would be sarcastic. And lame.

"How'd it go today, with the insurance stuff?" Mel rifled the upper shelf, not hurting her chest and back too much, searching for any cans of vanilla-food.

"It's a story," said Stuart, still dabbing his eyes with a napkin.

Mel had a theory that, though she couldn't taste her canned food, she could somehow feel it; that is, vanilla made her feel slightly different than strawberry. Lots of food-sensitive types could feel the diff. Not that it meant much, a tiniest mood shift, a faint nudge of some kind. But she wanted to try some vanilla and pay attention. It was a last thing she could do with food.

"And not a very good one," Stuart added. "You feel like a beggar. It's everything you own." He dabbed the napkin harder for a little joke. "And I'm crying."

Fingertips on a bright orange tin, Mel considered its contents. She should give this to someone who could use it.

"Smoke any weed these days?" she asked. "I've got a whole smash of it here. Grade A choice from your neck of the woods."

"Thanks, no. I don't. Not much, anyway. It's been years. But maybe I will." He laughed, surprising himself. "I'm on vacation!"

She got a medical licence for it five or six years ago but it didn't really do the trick and it gave her, of all things, insomnia. Her heart raced and thoughts spiralled. Still, it was fun in moderation, though she hadn't smoked any lately. She didn't want pain but she wanted clarity. Clarity most of all. Which was why, after smoking it with her for novelty's sake here in the kitchen, Hal also rejected it. He said it made even his smallest thoughts and emotions grow a kind of Velcro, and "everything clings and grows, for no good reason." That's right, he also said something funny—"It puts the glue on the sequins." Which made him laugh, proud of himself. He was quite high at the time.

"It's probably a year old, so it might be weak," she said to Stuart. "Anyway, it's here."

She found a can of vanilla, which she took along with her rig to the TV room. She could have stayed in the kitchen and "eaten," with everything discreet under her blouse, but Stuart was tucking into his unghosted stew and she didn't want to ruin it for him.

She set up, cracked open the vanilla, smelled it. The can said "Real Vanilla Flavour." She always forgot how much she liked vanilla. She remembered the washroom in a glitzy gay bar in Puerto Vallarta with whole vanilla beans dangling from the ceiling (*just* too high to grab if you jumped) and its heady, glorious, urine-bustin' aroma. And that's right, she'd been high the whole time in Mexico, high on something or other. She also didn't want to smoke pot because if it took away her clarity she might panic. When clarity faltered, it allowed fear of death. No, it was instant: lack of clarity *was* fear of death.

Hal had helped her with death. Her understanding of it. She'd come upon the basic logic herself, and had death reduced to a maxim she could call on when she needed: either there's something, or there's nothing. "Something," any form of it, she was fine with, because it meant you didn't die. "Nothing" took more work to accept. When she was first diagnosed, and even before that, probably all her life, the thought of non-existence floored her. She could not even think about it. You ceased to exist. For infinity. Nothing left. For *infinity*. It would be like you never were. No, you don't live on in people's memories. The kind things you did might matter to others, but they no longer have anything to do with you. You don't become the spirit of the tree over your grave, you aren't the song of a nightingale. You die, disappear, you never were. You're less than gone. You're nothing.

Gradually, the panic about nothingness began to lose its edge. Blessed logic took over. If you were nothing, there would be no pain, nothing at all bad, because it was nothing. Why worry about nothing? Why worry about something that had no qualities at all? Nothing would *matter*. No—ha ha—nothing *wouldn't* matter. And, everybody did it. You had plenty of company in infinite nothingness. So, logic—why worry about nothing?—gradually, gradually wore away panic.

It was the "something" angle that her father gave some flesh to. If not quite flesh, skin. They didn't talk about it a lot. Mel saw Hal trying to be skilful and pick his spots. But he never avoided the pithy stuff, and he was relentless with "the now." For instance, it was far more important to him that she be aware, here *in this moment*, than it was to speculate about anything else, like death, like Buddhism. The whole point, he told her more than once, was to "feel your bum in that chair, and all the muscles in your face, especially the small ones, and the back of your neck, and your soft breath coming in, going out—all that at once. Keep doing that, and witness thoughts come and go."

One night, after an hour or so of such talk, Hal looked at her fiercely. He was near tears. "I would love it, if any words I say make you less afraid. It's really all I care about."

And he did help with her fear a little, with this possibility of "something." He'd read about and met "all sorts of people smarter than you or me" who had experienced something beyond death. Some Tibetan lamas predicted their next incarnation, saying they could be found, three years hence, in the body of a two-year-old, with a mother named this and father named that, in a hamlet north of a certain village, with a yak corral of yellow stones on the south side of the house. A clutch of the dead lama's colleagues would show up armed with an array of malas and ceremonial objects (she said nothing, but Mel had seen this very thing parodied on *The Simpsons*, though she didn't know if this made her think more, or less of it) from which the child would gleefully pluck what was familiar, and he might also greet his old friends with delight, and a touching of foreheads, that sweet Tibetan mind hug. Hal had met these people. Talk of after-death—actually, talk of between lives, called *bardo*—was everywhere, it came up in their conversation the way a trip to Cuba would come up in ours. Even Carl Jung had stumbled across this bardo realm, when under hypnotic regression his patients described pre-womb states of being that included formidable lights that became demonic or angelic challenges.

"Carl Jung wrote an introduction to *The Tibetan Book of the Dead*," Hal told her, with a quiet intensity, as if this fact proved everything. They were sitting in this very TV room. For whatever reason it was where they had most of their good talks.

Mel asked him if he believed all this. Hal said that he tried not to believe anything at all. But "from all available evidence," it was clear to him, or "clear enough," that this version of events, of afterlife, is what happens.

No, what really proved the "something," he added, was that, to Tibetan Buddhists, an afterlife wasn't good news at all, but quite the opposite. To them, the whole purpose of being here was to try to get off "this endless wheel of life," and not keep coming back. The First Noble Truth was, in fact, "life is suffering," and the whole idea was to be free of this, to not stay here. Death, or bardo, was just the gap between painful breaths. After Hal's long description, Mel thought it was interesting that there was a similarity between the bardo and the Christian judgment, because, in the bardo, everything you had amounted to in life was put to the test.

"Apparently it's overwhelming," Hal said. "One teacher said the bardo was like being surrounded by twenty teenagers, all playing ghetto blasters, all at different stations, volume 'turned up to eleven,' he knew that joke, and all of them are poking you with pins the whole time. And sleep never enters into it." Hal laughed, shaking his head, believing all this. "And the idea is not just to keep it together, but to be magnanimous and compassionate." He added, scientific, "It's how and when you freak out that determines which direction you go."

"It's an up or a down?" Mel didn't hide the censure in her tone. This was sounding like the severe side of any old religion.

"More or less. A better next life or a shittier one. Apparently there's all sorts of nasty beings that don't live here or have physical forms. Good beings, too. What we'd call angels."

"Can I be a dirty angel?"

Hal wasn't ready to humour his daughter's cute wish. He said, straight-faced, "It's mostly bad, and it never stops. But"—the father regarded the daughter's face now, and softened—"for us who cling to the idea of a continuous self, just to hear that there's something that continues is a comfort."

"It is," Mel agreed.

And it was, and it continued to be. And either the something or the nothing she could live with, so to speak.

As long as she didn't get knocked off her clarity. Her tube was clear and she unhooked her rig, feeling no different for the vanilla in her stomach.

She made herself aware of her bum on the chair, and the feeling of her breathing. She startled. It would happen here. It would happen here in this room. She didn't know why she felt most herself in this room, but she did. Most alert. Maybe it was the blank TV and book spines, all mounding out at her, promising something. No, it was more like the room expected something of her.

So it would be here. This seat. This room. This air. A moment would come when she would say goodbye to herself.

It would come, the moment of goodbye. Goodbye to *this*. She couldn't quite imagine it, though it would be simple.

Calmed by three, four extra patches. Sitting here, she would lift her hand, and thumb ten pills down her tube, chasing them with something liquid. Cognac. But the *moment* of doing it, of inserting that first pill—not thinking it, actually doing it. It would be a now, like this one. No different from now. It would be *this*. She knew she would think, *Now I'm actually doing it.*

Picturing it in a way that almost leaped time sent her close to panic, but it was also a thrill. It would be the last thrill. It was really all she had to look forward to.

STUART WAS STILL at the kitchen table, sitting at his empty plate, staring straight ahead. Probably not seeing his life as a thrill.

"Stuart, sorry, you had a story to tell me. A not very good one. An update on your house."

"Right."

The poor man did look glum. The living do have worries.

Her plan for him took on a sudden new dimension. She tamped down a smile. She was certain. Why not? Who cares? Hal had already signed the house over to her. She could do what she wanted with it. It would mean a visit with the lawyer. She stood behind him and put a hand on his neck. Which felt hot. Which meant, to him, her hand felt cold.

"Not good, eh?"

"Ah, who knows."

Stuart explained to Mel, who asked, that if his house insurance didn't come through, and he sold the land, his little city lot, after paying for the demolition and what he owed the insurance company to pay the restoration company, he'd have maybe forty thousand dollars.

"Well that's something."

"Yeah. It's a down payment," Stuart said, slowly, sounding more depressed with each word. "I can start over. Look for some kind of work. Job."

The amazed way he said it, "job," made her hear what a funny word it was.

"But, you know?" asked Stuart. "It's just the principle of the thing now."

"Really?"

"I don't know if I even want to go back there." He looked at her wide-eyed, afraid of what he was saying.

"Really!"

"I think my, my anchor rope has sort of, I think it's boinged free."

"So you're adrift, then."

"I don't know what this is. It's new."

"Welcome to the club."

"Yeah, I guess so." He looked worried that agreeing with her might insult her. "Not that my thing is anything compared to …" He gestured with his finger in her direction, afraid to actually point at her.

"Stuart? I want you to actually believe me when I say I'm okay with it. Please?"

"Okay." He smiled. "I'll try."

She took his dishes and, though he tried to stop her, brought them to the sink. "Starting tomorrow you're living here. You're not a guest. You can do all your own damn dishes, damn it." She smiled to make certain the joke. So tender was he.

Stuart saluted, then sat, sighing loudly. "So, anyway, who knows." He resumed the glum stare, then remembered something. "Okay, tomorrow, if I'm out, if a man named

Connington calls? Tell him I didn't mean what I said in the message I left."

"Will do."

"And I might be getting another meeting, with someone else. It ain't over."

Stuart wrenched his face around so she would see his game attempt at a smile. He was no actor. Since her problem was Death and his a mere house, it was not in his constitution to let himself feel as bad, or add to her burden. But she lacked the energy tonight to suggest that her burden, if she even had one, was lighter than his and that she was almost free, because she had literally nothing to worry about.

"And, ah," he added, "is it okay if I send an email or two?" He tilted his head in the direction of the TV room, where on a desk in a corner sat her mother's huge old computer.

"No," she said, teasing for a moment. But the question showed how she had severed ties with the world already. Emails had become an emotional drain. Every email, not just with friends but acquaintances too, had asked a decision of her: either you suggest a final reunion or you don't. Either you write a final email or you don't, and you identify it as such, or not. Either you tell a white lie or you explain things. So she'd stopped paying the monthly bill, and let the service provider pull the plug for her. The internet died a week before Stuart showed up.

"We're not online," she said, happy to include him.

Stuart mumbled something about another library.

BEHIND THE WHEEL of the Mercedes, on the way to Royal Elms, the route to which he knew well already, for he was evidently that kind of driver, Stu Price exuded the confidence of a man wearing new clothes he was proud of. Not only had he agreed to visit Hal again, he seemed eager. Excellent. He also agreed to go clothes shopping first. And it was fun taking him. He confessed to little sense of current style for guys his age, and joked about his lack of sense in general. Mel had done this drill with a few women, but with neither of her husbands, who were both good at clothes. It was fun, waiting while Stuart thumped and zipped in the change room then emerged, impatiently sombre as a ten-year-old, for her appraisal. Once, as if she were his mother, he looked skyward and sighed. A couple times he emerged in shirts he thought, for reasons not visible to her, less than masculine, and once he swanned out loving what he modelled—the black jeans and tan linen shirt he was wearing now.

Mel also had a small moment—a guitar note bending up, a bluesy gut tug—when she delivered to the change room two more shirts that Stuart took from her through the parted door. She glimpsed skin and boxers, and he looked in shape, but it was mostly the public place, the naughtiness of the thought— and it was only a thought. Sex just wasn't in the cards, wasn't anywhere on the agenda. Though Stu Price looked a prime and easy candidate if it was.

She couldn't remember what it had been like with him.

Behind the wheel, Stuart sat straighter today. He also had a pair of Euro sunglasses tucked atop his head, because his new eyes, as he called them, were still tender. Mel could smell the fresh raw leather of his shoes, mid-priced but rough-looking loafers that said California sand-stomper more than Toronto toe-tapper. Mel had always opted for the stompers herself, the desert boots, the Docs, avoided the tidy little gems costing a fortune, the collusive taking advantage of girls. She'd tried heels exactly once, hating that extra inch. More collusion, that she was made all her life to hate her height.

"Stuart. My throat's iffy." It felt fine. She deceitfully fingered her scarf, the Johnny Depp schooners. "Could you read to him again?"

"His book?"

"I like just to be able to watch him."

"Sure. Of course." He nodded, then smiled. "But I'm instantly sort of nervous now."

"You are?" She pictured them as the most helpless people on the planet.

"It's his book."

This was funny. It felt more like Michael Bodleian's book. It felt more like Li's.

She told him, "Only amateurs aren't nervous." She'd heard that from Hal, in a Buddhist context.

Stuart seemed to consider this as if she were serious.

"You have a daughter, you said? Montreal?" She hadn't been doing very well at the job of catching up.

"I do. Jennifer."

"So what's that like?"

From his glance she saw how stupid her question was.

"You mean generally, as in a daughter, or specifically, as in a Jennifer?"

"Sorry, I'm not that great at small talk." Or, lately, big talk.

"I remember."

"I guess I meant a Jennifer."

"Ah." He paused for the words. "We drifted. It was great when she was small. We were buddies." Then, making light so as not to burden her, he said, "It's one of my sadnesses."

"That's too bad." Then Mel added, pretty sure it was true, "She misses you."

"Well, we don't seem to, ah, neither of us seems to know how to bridge that gap."

"Montreal's only a five-hour drive." Mel slapped the dash, which was either the most rigid German leather or a bad plastic. It hurt her hand.

"Actually I just sent her a postcard. From Parry Sound."

"You can borrow this any time." She watched Stuart eye the car anew. He looked positively afraid. What would it be like to be scared of your own kid?

ONE TIME HAL CAME closest to apologizing for the past. Not for what he'd done, but what he'd done to her.

Since she'd already flown the coop his "periods of absence" hadn't affected her nearly as much as they had her mother, though evidently her parents maintained a truce. More than once her mother told her, though rather grimly it seemed to Mel, that she supported what he was doing. Over those couple of decades when Mel made it back to Toronto for a Christmas here and a visit there, usually en route to somewhere else, sometimes her father was home, generally he wasn't. At first it was upstate New York and then it was Nepal.

Hal apologized to Mel almost formally. Not long after her mother died, when he was out of the hospital and his hip was good to go with a cane, he took her out for coffee and a pastry to spill the beans. He fell sincere, though the jokes bubbled up and the eyes glistened when he got going. He wore good jeans and a quality jean shirt. His hair resplendent, tied back with a mother-of-pearl clasp.

"I want to explain myself," he said, not loud but in a tone that made the couple at the next table stop talking.

He told her about reading something when he was fifteen. Two things, actually. Both from "the exotic East." The first was a sort of autobiography, *The Third Eye*, by Tuesday Lobsang Rampa, who claimed to be a Tibetan lama inhabiting the body of a Cornish plumber and now living somewhere in Ontario. The book was about boyhood in Tibet—the horse riding, kite flying, sky burials, and intensive training in the mysticism for which their land was famous. It was written in a language and pace easily savoured by fifteen-year-olds. Rampa described at length a coming-of-age ritual wherein he'd had a specially fermented piece of wood implanted in his forehead, resulting in the rebirth of his "third eye," which let him see people's auras, a bit of the future, and other cool things. The book talked of astral travelling and reincarnation, and basically made a young teenager feel like there was nothing in the universe or in his budding life to be troubled about. If he screwed up this time around he would have infinite tries getting it right. Plus, if he meditated in a cave he'd become enlightened, and people would seek him out.

"Even then I sensed it was bullshit," her father told her, "but I let myself bathe in its glory." And, "I put it on my secret shelf for later, knowing I had a key to the meaning of life, and it was great, because now I didn't have to *be* wise—just knowing I could do it someday was enough."

The second thing he read back then that also sank in and took root had to do with Hinduism and how a man led his life. In India, a supreme life went like this: a man had a physically active youth involving sport and sexual conquest, then he married and had a family, at which time he worked hard to master business affairs and attain wealth, and then, while still vigorous, he left his family, career, and wealth to go seek the truth, living out his years in poverty but most of all relentless meditation, until he woke up to reality in all its inherent radiance.

Her father stopped talking, met her eye, held it, and popped in what remained of his strudel, as if he'd saved that piece for punctuation. He lifted his hands and shoulders in a massive shrug, eyes glinting.

"Hey," he said, doing his Brooklyn voice. "So what am I s'pose ta do?"

"So that's what you did." Mel felt herself nodding, noncommittal. She felt her face fall lax in judgment. Here they sat, a funky Queen West eatery, surrounded by soft-talking cool folk, most of whom no doubt did yoga, or had a mantra, or had tried versions of that stuff. Who in any case knew this kind of talk. But her father, the man sitting here, had gone and really done it, full out. Most of these people would say that what he'd gone and done wasn't necessary.

"Okay," he said, shaking his head to negate whatever her face showed him. "So if you thought there was a way to find a meaning to life, I mean literally, *the* meaning of life, something that would give purpose, vision, utter sanity—"

"Enlightenment," she said, which made him close his eyes and lean forward, interrupted. It was clear he'd said all this before to someone, just like this.

"I don't like using that word, it's so loaded, but okay, 'enlightenment.' If you thought such a thing *existed*, and that you had some real understanding of it, and you had a *shot* at it, wouldn't you be stupid not to try?"

"You'd be completely stupid."

"I hit forty. It was now or never. I jumped. And wouldn't anyone who loved you, truly loved you, push you to go and try your best? I know it looked like pure selfishness. I'm extremely aware of what it looked like."

"Are you saying Mom didn't love you?"

"I'm saying she did. At first. Then it got harder. I was away a lot. Then your mother didn't know who she loved. I think it was too big a change, when an academic-turned-writer-turned-realtor became a monk."

"Well, wasn't it a big change?"

"Yes and no. It felt like coming home, so to speak. It felt like me becoming more me than ever. Real me. Which meant dropping lots of early me."

Mel still couldn't smile along. She didn't think she knew this man, who claimed still to be uncomfortable in Western clothes, having worn robes for years. His hair looked great against his jean shirt, which had the old-school pearl buttons. Where had he found that?

"Melody, it was a long long process, me leaving. I left for years and years. Your mother could have come, any time. I asked her and I asked her."

"She couldn't sit still."

"*Your mother could not sit still.*" Hal nodded at her vigorously, vindicated on this peeve. Long ago, her mother had told her some of this.

"But Mom stayed right where she was, and you didn't. Which is sort of ironic."

"Well, it is ironic. There's lots about the whole thing that was ironic. She'd say I changed so much and for the better, but she didn't really want to be with me as much. And the most ironic thing of all—you want to know what I really think but promise not to hate me?—the most ironic thing is that by staying where she was, same house, same habits, same everything, she chose to leave *me*."

"Hmm." She smiled for the first time she was aware of. "I'll buy that, I guess. Because it sounds ridiculous."

The Brooklyn. "Good, *good*! Now eat your little tart, why don't you."

She pushed her pastry across the table at him. "Not too wild about it. Sorry."

"Never been a fan of marzipan myself. 'Nother little confession for ya."

Hal sat, staring off, and Mel let him. It didn't take him long to come back to being serious, to get something over with.

"Your mother and I dealt with this. We had our reconciliation. In the end, she was very kind to me. But I need to apologize to you."

"For what?"

"Well, you came home, you visited, and I wasn't there." He smiled, half-joking. "Even an *old* kid comes home expecting it to be just like it always was."

Mel reached across for both his hands. She squeezed them, then withdrew. They had never been touchy. That wouldn't change.

"Apology accepted."

It was true they hadn't seen much of each other for twenty-five years, but Mel thought it was she who should apologize.

There were a slew of Christmases where her parents just didn't cut it as a priority. She'd fly to visit friends instead, often in Mexico. She'd call Christmas day, and from their wintry huddle the snowbird thing always made good sense to them. Good for you, they'd say, get a tan, come when you can. But, accepting Hal's apology here in the bistro, what stung Mel in particular was that one Christmas, when they made sure she knew her father was arranging to come all the way from Nepal, which meant almost three days of travel each way, and he was staying a week. Mel had just met someone, Joe, a geologist quartered in Masset for a month, their hearts were on the upswing and, a few days before Christmas, hungover and spaced out, she blew her flight and didn't renew. She convinced herself that a phone call would be enough, but all Christmas day she kept forgetting and when she did remember it was nine or ten at night, which meant after midnight in Toronto, plus she was out of it again. But even now she could hear her hip Nepalese father's voice on the phone, his bottomless cheer, like disappointment just didn't compute. Her mother wasn't so cheerful and wouldn't come to the phone.

Anyway, her apology would ruin his. And it didn't matter, she was adoring her father again, this man who just wanted everything good for all sentient beings, or was trying his best to want that. It had been her mother's grudging observation that her father's footloose ways, and his eschewing three careers, was daughter Melody's tacit permission to be similarly fancy-free and, in her mother's disparaging words, "above it all." It had taken years for Melody to see and admit this. And in this café she admired her dad's new mystery. She decided that what he exuded most was discipline. But an odd discipline. Sitting here in chic-ville, spending twenty dollars on tea and a pastry, a possible ex-womanizer who wore a feminine clasp to hold his ponytail, a seventy-two-year-old garbed in old hippy gear was more his own person than the carefully curated individualists hunched at their laptops and smartphones. His discipline was that, after all these years of meditation, though he was reasonably clear and confident, he was at the same time impossibly tender, vulnerable. His discipline was vulnerability. She could see it in his eyes. She could see that if a fly landed on his skin it would touch his heart. Saying a harsh word to another, he would hurt himself. It was something no one could feign, and it was the least she could do to forgive him for what he'd done to her mother, and for what he thought he'd done to her.

MEL AND STUART FOUND Hal sitting in his usual corner in what was called the lounge, in the big wingback chair. He sat up straight, not leaning back, hands resting out wide on the chair arms, a regal posture he sometimes took, Mel thought, playfully. Vera sat on the couch three feet away, beside another woman whose name she didn't know, a mouth breather. Mel had never come upon Hal sitting with a man, an oddity despite women outnumbering men five to one.

He and Vera were having a chat, staring straight ahead not looking at each other. Mel had suspicions that Vera could hear mostly, or maybe only, sibilance.

Patting his pocket, Hal said, "I can't seem to find my glasses."

Vera: "Well, you missed the bus."

"I don't really need them. But it would be nice."

Vera, glaring at him: "I have my car but I don't think I'll be lending it."

Hal patted all his pockets. "Hmm. Well."

Vera, turning away: "I know who's sitting beside me again

at dinner." Vera checked her watch, which no longer worked. "You'll miss it again."

Hal pointed near her watch. "Look how you can see your things there, coming from under your sweater." Hal meant her veins presumably. And he'd been wearing his glasses the entire time.

It wasn't always this sadly funny. Mel walked to within touching range of her father's shoulder.

"Dad?"

"Well hello!" His smile rose incompletely, held back by what it felt like to have a stranger call you Dad.

"Dad, it's your daughter, Melody, and I brought a friend."

He smirked like she was being ridiculous. "I know who you are, dear." He turned to Vera, whom he no longer knew either. "This is my daughter, Melody."

Vera rose and held out her hand, halfway. "Pleased to meet you," she said, as always. "I'm Vera."

"Nice to meet you, Vera. I can see my father has a good friend."

It was pretty much word for word, every time. Sometimes Mel had the feeling that they knew it too.

"Dad, this is Stuart Price. An old, old friend. Stuart, this is my father. Hal Dobbs."

Stuart smiled and dipped his head and said how pleased he was to meet him. Hal leaned forward and offered his hand to be shaken in that odd way he had, which was to hold it almost shoulder height so that the hand was pointed down, cocked, resembling a horse's head, thumb up like the ear. It looked like the handshake of someone doing it for the first time. But Hal shook hands often, and often with a hint of mischief on his face, like he was instigating a game. The brain, the brain. How could he have no memory, but shake hands that way every time?

"Pleased to meet you, Mr. Dobbs."

"No, I'm not," he said, with the little gleam. "You can call me Hal."

Sometimes he said "You can call me Al," and Mel still had no idea if he was joking or forgetting.

Stuart commented on "the nice teak work" in the wingback chair, running his hand over its main sweeping curve. Vera spoke over him to tell them about a pending election, the basic time or place of which never became clear, though Israel was mentioned. A young woman with "Maria" on her chest arrived with the rolling juice-and-cookie tray, drinks were poured, Vera gave hers back angrily for being too cold, and both men received a chocolate-chip cookie. Mel handed the book to Stuart, who cleared his throat and shyly offered to read to them. From his big chair, Hal said rather formally and loudly, "We would be grateful."

Michael Bodleian had to stop his hands' shaking as he inserted the five copies into the five envelopes and began addressing them. The manuscript sample was only ten pages long but it was enthralling, it was dynamite. One to his History Department head, one to an important colleague in Berkeley, and three to interested publishers. Had there ever been a bidding war among academic presses? He didn't know. It wasn't the money in any case. It was his career. Which *was* money: a book like this meant promotion. It meant conferences, less teaching, more research time, more books, a name. A name.

It still wasn't a book, and wouldn't be until he'd written his eighty or so pages of contextual analysis and scholarly argument, his anthro-ethnology, around the translation, itself comprising only about forty, maybe fifty pages according to Naomi. Among his added sections would be some colourful history of the Chinese in Victoria, their Chinatown warrens and opium factories; something about the language, differentiating the old Cantonese dialect from the Mandarin—Naomi would help with that, too. And of course some scientific thumbnails about Hansen's disease. The mythology surrounding it. Leprosy as metaphor. How easily it was cured now but, because of the stigma that persisted as in Li's time, countless thousands around the world did not come forward and their disease progressed down its hellish path. Some anecdotes about Father Damien in Hawaii

Hal interrupted. "Father Damien! Went to live with lepers, caught leprosy, died of it. Pure compassion. Second *bumi*. He was a saint. Hawaii. It was a small island there too."

Stuart waited for more. Then offered, "It sounds like he *was* a saint," to which Hal smiled and nodded.

Some anecdotes about Father Damien in Hawaii and other tales of missionary zeal (he thought he had heard of one connected to D'Arcy, a minister's wife; he hoped it was true). He could write up something poetic about the *experience* of D'Arcy now. His research could and should take him to D'Arcy Island itself; he would stay overnight, soak up whatever ghosts wanted to present themselves. Because he had the hard goods, the facts, he could get away with a section of something personal and intangible. Poetic. Perhaps he could take Naomi with him. He could borrow a tent from Simmons, and sleeping bags. Or just ... blankets. A ball of blankets. Good God. He could picture, could feel, her small body up against his side. They could hunt for the little hill out behind where the structures were, and they could build a little lean-to. Of cedar boughs. He would build it for her in one hour. A mansion.

Yesterday he decided what he would call the book. It was tricky, seeing as it seemed possibly a bad title, a blandly bloated one, until the context was understood. He had grilled Naomi about it and she had been clear. When he called her to him she came face to face, too close, and he could hardly listen to her. Oh, her skin. It made him feel the weakness of words, in particular, *skin*. The thick and smooth wonder of her skin should have been called *cream*, or *golden*, something rich in the saying. Naomi was saying that the lepers called their island *foo hoi*, which meant "the whole world," as in, all that existed. Naomi still had trouble meeting his eyes. But she sheepishly confided in him that she had been tempted to use a different character than what was actually there, *waan ne*, which meant "the world as nothing but a sea of troubles," which she said "also might be the meaning that was intended." She put her head down to continue. "And it wasn't logical, *foo hoi*, since they could see the other world, they could clearly see Vancouver Island, maybe even houses, structures, and there was a supply boat from the other world that …" Michael stopped her here with a finger under the chin, and moved his hand to cup the side of her neck, so warm under the blanket of rich black hair. It was the first time he had touched her. She went deathly still and dropped her eyes again, whether from outrage or to savour the touch, he couldn't tell. How was it possible that he couldn't tell? But he had never felt so brave. In any event, he didn't dare kiss her. In one sense, he was relieved.

"If that's the word they used, that's the word I'll use," he told her, hardly hearing himself. "You don't have to edit a single thing. In fact, I don't want you to."

"Translation is not so simple as that," Naomi said. "I have to choose all the time, always," and Michael told her he understood, he knew there would be difficulties with certain expressions.

"And, poetry of the heart," Naomi added softly, and Michael Bodleian had no answer for that.

But it had thrilled him, the section he'd read today. Just as the second batch of translation had differed so much from the first, so this differed radically from the second. This woman Li had gained a depth of vision, of inward seeing, that would cast a deliciously subjective light on the objective history, for certain. One so often saw in historical records a merely wooden reportage— weather, crops, legal gossip—and this was so much more than that.

He removed the package to Oxford Press, found the pages he wanted, and read them to himself again:

More than a little embarrassed with myself I went to see Chin, because I wanted to know about love. Love! For the first time in years, I was curious about love. It is a sweet hunger like no other, and to even think of it in this place! How many love auguries had Chin been asked to perform here? Even one? But to Chin I went, because I know enough about our disease now to know that he will not be with us for much longer—cold phlegm rattles in even his stronger breaths because his throat cannot easily swallow it—and I wanted his gift of augury while he could still give it.

I knew he would be eager to help me, because in payment I offered to repair some clothing. My mother laughs from her grave, such are my sewing skills, but among these dead-handed men my wielding of a needle is nothing short of a miracle. I have seen him augur for far less, for almost nothing, for instance when men come to ask if the boat will bring, this time, what they asked for. For that one, Chin floats two old acorns in a bowl of rainwater. If they touch, the answer is yes. If they float apart, no. And I believe that all of his healing spells he conducts for free. They come to him, on each month's new moon I think, and he takes from his ragged bag certain sticks that he touches to their bodies and then places in the racing tide, anchored with a stone, to be cleaned, and then touched to the body again. And though no one's body has been cleansed of its curse, of course, certain smaller illnesses were helped they say, enough perhaps that people forget their monthly disappointment. In any case they are free, so Chin was very happy with my offer of two repaired garments. And it was odd sewing the smock and

the tunic, because I know what shop they come from in
Chinatown, and I know that man, the silent Mr. Wing,
who tailored them. Feeling the fabric, I could see Mr.
Wing's face, and smell the grocery store beside his shop.

Chin's augury for love I will not describe in this
writing because part of its art is that I am not to speak
of it to anyone, and though no one reads this, writing
is speaking, certainly. All I will say is that it involved
sea shells, some broken and some whole, along with two
bizarre objects I will not name. I will also say I was
not happy, not at first, with the augury. It told me that
Sang's love would not be what I wanted it to be. This
message I had to digest like tough but healthful meat.
Because—and here is its wisdom—what good thing is
ever what we want it to be? To want something is to
assume knowledge of what that thing is. As if we can
know a thing before we have even seen or touched it.

So. I wait for Sang Seen's love to become what it will
become.

And I must be patient, because maybe his love is
simply to teach me to be patient. What Sang Seen began
also to teach me, after my first month in the World, was
that this was a place where I could love. I could love
Sang Seen, but since his love was quiet, and not selfish,
I could love other things of the World as well. I have my
own house, which is small but now has hard wooden
walls and a roof of cedar shingles. It has also the promise
of a wooden door, which is coming, Sang said, on the
next boat. Similarly, I can love the hunger in my belly,
which makes the rice cake, and the boiled crab, taste so
wonderful. I was proud to learn to love my hunger, and

in this same way I have also learned to love my pride.

I can love being here because everything has become comprehensible—it is a way of life so honest that it puts an end to perplexity.

And so I can love the dawning of the day, and the blissful snores of the men, down the hill, and the noisy birds, some of which always make the World their home, and others which have come here searching for something more.

Stuart put the book on his lap, checking the faces of his audience before closing it. Mel had watched him enter this happier section and instinctively slow down, apparently also enjoying Li's "poetry of the heart," and not questioning how absurdly and impossibly grateful it is. At first she had heard in it what she thought was the voice of altruism and broad insight that perhaps signalled Hal's early attraction to his Buddhism, but then even she had listened harder to it, to Li's voice and words. And that was part of her father's skill at fiction, or maybe that was the skill of fiction itself, that someone like Li had felt for a moment almost real.

She watched him, his thumb nimble on the beads, mouthing some Sanskrit repetition, eyelids fluttering with an intense hidden gaze on—what? How less real was Li than Hal's inner world right now, or for that matter Stuart's? Stuart sat tapping the book's cover with a finger, staring at the floor, far away. And there was Bea, digging through her empty purse, again. And here she was herself, lost in studying these people, forgetting once again that the 31st was fifteen days away.

THE WIND AND RAIN pummelled the Mercedes on their way downtown. She'd forgotten how cold this car was and how loud its brutally practical heater and fan. In its noise she could hear an old German engineer in your face shouting endlessly, *YOU VANT HEAT, ZISS NOISE IS NECESSARY!* She couldn't shake the voice-in-the-fan. Morphine could make imagination real, and she didn't want to spend her time there.

She was in and out of regretting that she'd come with Stuart this morning on his probably futile quest. A meeting with an insurance-company executive, high up a glass tower on Bay Street. It might be someone's version of hell. What decided her was the shop she knew of within walking distance, a trendy new place that stocked bamboo dishes and cutlery. She'd seen in their ad some flat little plates perfect for canapés. And she wanted to test a bamboo knife-edge on her thumb.

The car coughed and hesitated, and Stuart hissed, "Jesus!" He turned to her, serious. "I really don't want to kill another car."

Mel told him it was nothing. She knew he didn't believe her but she was too tired to explain the big puddle back there, the splashing up and under, moisture getting to an old-school carburetor. The car might stall but still it was nothing. In Haida Gwaii, you learned about old cars and big puddles.

No, it wasn't nothing. She was too tired to get out to hail a cab in the rain. And they were both dressed up and looking good for the meeting. She wouldn't let Stuart go under the hood.

She had also insisted on coming with him to indulge her urge to be kind. Kindness was a sort of prayer and, if done right, not a selfish one.

In the underground parking she had to take his arm

the first several steps until she steadied. He let her hand go reluctantly.

"You sure you're okay?"

"I'm good."

"You really want to do this?"

"And you have to come to the kitchen store with me. And decide things." It was more than obvious how squeamish Stuart was about anything to do with the wake.

"I honestly don't know how you can help," he said, again.

"Maybe I'll think of something to say. Who knows."

Global Assurance occupied several top floors of the tower, and Mel was struck by the artfulness of the place. She'd expected the usual corporate ritz, something like a glamorous bank. But the reception area was all hidden spotlights and muted browns, with enormous earthen jugs and other pottery, all in creams and rusts, to give things a rural and even ancient look. It was clear where artists and designers made their living these days.

They were ushered right in, no "take a seat please" to wait like cattle. A Mr. Ben Masters, second office to the left. Walking down the darkish hall, Mel whispered impishly, "*Please* Mister Masters," but Stuart didn't smile. His walk was confident and strong.

Before reaching the lit doorway and making their presence known, Mel removed her scarf, stuffed it into her purse, then shifted her shoulders to lift her glaring neck out of its low collar and make sure everything showed.

Ben Masters rose from his desk to rush them, hand out to be shaken. He said to please call him Ben. He was a couple of inches shorter than Stuart, several inches shorter than her, with a round face, like a rosy apple, a jovial kids' show host.

But his eyes didn't match it—they were bright, unsmiling, and missed nothing. It was like talking to two people at once, one of whom lived inside the other. So forceful were his eyes that you could easily miss that he wore a headset, magically attached to his head such that only a wire-thin mic crept round his cheek to be ready for his words. His office was spacious and tasteful, and despite the micro, Euro-style lamps hanging from the ceiling on pencil-thin stems, it felt more businesslike than the reception area. Yet there wasn't a piece of paper or file folder to be seen, not a pencil or phone, and Mel guessed that this man was probably brilliant at some aspect of the insurance business that she wasn't even aware of. A secretary appeared to ask what they'd like to drink, then went to get Ben his Earl Grey, Mel her water, and Stuart his cappuccino. Ben Masters was alertly looking everywhere but at Mel's neck, especially the side that wasn't entirely there.

"I'm glad," Masters said to Stuart, "that we could have this talk." He added, "Some say persistence is a virtue," and smiled with his eyebrows raised.

Stuart thanked the man for seeing him and, as it turned out, Ben Masters was a nice fellow, insofar as it was possible to tell. He was "an Associate Vice-President of Accounts, here with Global, which does indeed now own Best North Holdings, which controls Best North Insurance, but you can well understand that me pulling strings way over there at BNI would be like—well, Stuart, it would be like you asking a fellow teacher to change one of his student's grades, all because that student's mom or dad asked you to help. That teacher, now tell me if I'm wrong, might just tell you to mind your own business, and he might be right in saying so. Correct?"

Stuart nodded seriously. "Correct."

"Except," Mel heard herself begin, "what if the mark deserves to be changed, and the student was suffering? Does the rest matter?" Mel expected at this point to be asked what her own business might be in this meeting.

"Well that's a good point. So let's get to the bottom of this thing."

Still not referring to a single note, Masters reviewed Stuart's case, listing the pertinent dates, claim amount, and their own pending water-damage counterclaim against the restoration company. Bradley Connington was quoted twice. At one point he asked Stuart to explain, honestly and frankly, why it was he had not checked his mail, or arranged to have it forwarded, mail that contained numerous requests not only for payment, but "requests for contact, for a phone number, an email. Anything. They really did try, Stuart." At this point, Masters' eyes changed, as if focused on another, unseen world. He said, inexplicably, "No, we cannot and will not do that, Marilyn," and it wasn't until Masters' eyes focused on this room again that Mel understood he'd been talking on his headset. He hadn't turned anything on or off, so it was likely that he was working on all other business at the same time. She pictured a whole backroom of Lily Tomlin secretaries plugging wires into a wall, everything funnelling into Masters' ear.

"Sorry," he said, and looked genuinely sorry. "I had to take that one."

So beautifully earnest was Masters that Mel had a sudden vision. In it, she saw how out of date she was; in it, money had finally been acknowledged as the only true religion, and it was no longer shameful to worship. All the best, most truly good and spiritual people—like Ben Masters—had been altar boys when young, but now no longer waited for their manna from heaven but rose up in these towers, nearer to heaven, to meet manna halfway. All the genuinely good souls on the planet were up in these towers doing sacred business. They were all fair. Her vision cracked to a nasty end when she decided that Masters had pretended to take that call and he wasn't plugged in to Lily Tomlin or anyone. She also understood that her morphine was a little wibbly today.

But Stuart had begun explaining himself, smiling sheepishly to tell the man that he'd gone into hiding, more or less. Mel had to close her eyes. Stuart told Masters how his marriage had died, and his child left, and while looking for a place to live he arranged for his work, his high school, to be his mailing address, something he liked so he never had it changed over five years, because the secretary, Deborah, who was a saint, automatically recycled the junk mail and put the important stuff at the top for him, but these days there didn't seem to be much important mail, so much stuff was online now, weeks go by without any real mail, and then in June when he retired, he naturally didn't miss getting mail at his house because mail never had come there, and they had a new secretary filling in for Deborah, who had cancer, and the new one didn't think to ask what to do with this retired guy's mail, or even know the guy was retired, it being summer. And, the thing was, not that it should affect this decision, but in May when he retired, he took the lump-sum option on his pension and put it all into paying off his house.

"Oh, God, no," said Masters, and he sounded genuine.

So, Stuart explained, not just his house burned, but all his years of work in the high-school shop.

Mel thought that, all in all, Stuart did an excellent job. She was proud of him. He capped it off by saying, "I'm fifty-one. I've never missed paying a bill in my life. I had the money to pay. It was an honest mistake." Here Stuart leaned forward, and spoke slowly. "I really, really just want to speak with the person who is actually making this decision."

Masters sat back in his chair, keeping equidistant, Mel saw, to Stuart's lean.

"The one problem, Stuart, is that the decision has been made."

Stuart was quick. "'Has been made.' By whom, exactly?"

Masters was just as quick. "A case like this, rest assured it crosses lots of desks. It's a process."

Stuart leaned in another inch. "Teachers change grades all the time."

Masters met his lean with one of his own. "A business won't survive if it tosses hundreds of thousands of dollars into the fire every time somebody out there makes an honest mistake."

Stuart spoke steadily and it sounded rehearsed, but that was okay. He looked like a man physically incapable of lying. "People hide behind the word 'business' too much these days and it isn't good for anyone. This might sound corny, but this is an opportunity for someone to feel really, really good about themselves." Rousing all the heart he could, Stuart stared at the man across the desk. Mel was spellbound. It was like he transported them back a hundred years, before irony had been born, when naïveté could be the truth. She could picture offices well made of polished wood, lit with oil lamps, bright-eyed men smiling gloriously through their moustachios and handshakes all around—in other words she was imagining some old movie.

On their way down the elevator Mel asked Stuart how he thought it had gone. It occurred to Mel that, with her overt scars and Stuart's haircut, not to mention his sincere ways, that Bay Street pro might have thought he was seeing two dented naïfs just come down from the hills. But, really, she had no idea what she'd just witnessed up there.

"He let me talk, it felt okay." Stuart thought a moment. "It felt about as good as it was going to feel."

"You think Mr. Masters will change your grade?"

"I don't have a clue in the world."

"Is that the end of the road, or is there more?"

Stuart sounded apologetic. "I've put calls in to a few other people, and one or two might see me."

In the kitchen store, which was more gallery than retail outlet, Stuart's confidence vanished. He trailed Mel as she browsed, respectful of this perfect marriage of art and function, gently touching the faucets, sinks, countertops and even cookware that was beautifully displayed and was not, technically, for sale. If you wanted to buy something you spoke to one of the two impeccably dressed sales associates—the mature woman was rather handsome and the young fellow quite pretty—and they would arrange delivery. But shelves in one bright corner of the store held the small stuff, the single-cup coffee presses, Himalayan pink salt, five-second corkscrews and, there they were, the bamboo cutlery and compact plates.

"These are perfect." Mel showed Stuart a plate the size of a bagel.

"Wooden plates. Amazing." Curiously, he smelled one.

"No dishwashers. Best just to wipe clean. Apparently they last awhile."

"They're so thin. I can't imagine what sort of lathe." He looked grossly uncomfortable.

"So you approve?"

"Man." He shook his head and looked away, his eyes finding a window onto the street. Mel felt right in her decision not to tell him the timeline. Not only would a ticking clock drive him crazy, but she could see now that he would try hard to stop her.

"Stuart, I'm sorry. This makes me happy." She could explain that to see and hold these plates was to see and hold her immortality. Stuart and her other friends would go on into the future, holding these plates and the food she'd dreamed onto them. At the wake, these plates might be the most solid thing left of her. No—when they picked up and ate her whims off these plates, when they were chewing, taste erupting in their mouths, it would almost be like being alive. It was how Catholics kept Jesus going.

Stuart looked skyward. "Okay. It's hard." He smiled for her. "It's *different*."

"It's fine. I've been living here for years. This is almost fun."

"Okay."

"Okay, so, I've got five, six different things to serve. God, I don't know, twenty, thirty people. How many of these do we need?"

"Man."

EVEN FIVE SILENT MINUTES in the warm leather car seat rejuvenated her. They agreed not to drive home but go directly to visit Hal. Eating meals with the residents was encouraged and she sometimes did so, if only to sit at Hal's table and turn down endless offers of sandwiches. Today she'd be an hour early.

They arrived near the end of "morning activity," and it was the clown-head beanbag toss. Stuart actually said "Wow" to see it. Mel was fairly certain it was a campy gift from Frank, he of music tape-loop fame. A pretty young staffer shouted "Martha got one! Let's give Martha a cheer!" when Martha threw a bag through the gaping mouth of the six-foot clown head on wheels. A few residents clapped dutifully but with little sound, and Martha said, "I did?" The others waited seated until a beanbag was handed to them.

"Remember," shouted the staffer, whose name was Elise, and who always seemed to run the bag toss, "hit two out of three and you get … a *cookie*!" Only Bea exclaimed "Oooh!" and looked around at the other limp-faced gamers, who either were or weren't onto Elise's in-joke that they lived in a place where a cookie was maybe the only thing that could be had for the asking.

Mel thought, why a clown? It was a cast-off from an old-school fair of some sort. It could have been worse, she supposed, if it had been one of those hugely smiling creatures, but this one had a neutral mouth, horizontal and hot-dog-shaped, and for some reason this wasn't so bad. Though, one day, Mel had to watch this awful bag toss with the Carpenters' sugary "Close to You" coming on in the background, which shoved her brain a noxious half-inch off-centre, and made her close her eyes and not like Frank.

Elise handed a beanbag to Hal. He took it without looking up, and threw it at the clown. Usually he made a small show, a baring of teeth and a funny "Grrrr," which Mel took to be his commentary on contests in general, though who knew.

He could almost reach the damn mouth with his long arms, and he always got the bag in. But this time he didn't bother looking up at the target or throw with much effort and the beans barely thumped the chin. His other two throws hit the same spot.

It was maybe the saddest thing Mel had seen here. She led Stuart out to the garden walk, which was shaped like a figure eight, and around which grew only edible plants. Not, she told Stuart, trying to get herself in a jollier mood, for use in salads and such, but just in case a stroller decided to eat something. The figure eight was brilliant, though, because to anyone with no short-term memory, it was a complex walk that went on forever.

She and Stuart waited and joined the residents when they were all freshly sitting at tables, Hal a head higher than the three ladies at his. Staffers were only too happy to "set two more places," though they had to tell a quiet old thing, Meredith, that she'd received an invitation to join another table, and then guide her away by the arm. Bea and Vera remained there with Hal, who still looked tired, and who only lifted his hand in greeting, perhaps not hearing Mel say "daughter." His eyes looked milky. A kink of hair shot out sideways above his ear. He looked old. When the tray rolled up to their table and they were given a choice of soup or salad, and grilled cheese or chicken sandwich, Vera demanded the liver and onions, something she often did, and Hal mumbled "Soup, grilled cheese" out of turn, not looking up.

She watched Stuart and the rest of them slurp their vegetable soup, which she knew to be bland and saltless. Mel still found it surprising how many of these people ate hardly anything, a nibble here or there, sitting through lunch simply because they had been led to it. The room echoed with off-kilter swallowing sounds; this disease did that. Some of the more advanced residents were spoon-fed by relatives or staffers, and occasionally one swallow took a half minute and involved gasps and retches. Living here landed you in a pit of horrific intimacy, the worst noises and smells, like it or not. Losing the ability to swallow was an ugly but common cause of death. Back when Hal first came home to Canada, he would tell her, "Buddhism ain't for sissies." Then he took to saying, after one of their heartfelt talks, "Dying ain't for sissies." Coming here, it became "Living here ain't for sissies," but that faded in the first weeks.

She watched her dad chew. Denial was an amazing filter. She remembered when she thought he didn't belong in this wing. When he arrived, Hal was alert, vivacious, sometimes even wise, and the others were not. Three weeks in, Mel collared a staff person, the head nurse as it turned out, to ask if her father belonged.

"Vere vould he go?" the nurse asked back. "Do you know someone who could give him care?" No pointed look, and in any case Mel had already done her time with guilt.

"I meant another ward. He doesn't seem to fit here."

"He has Alzheimer's." The nurse, whose name tag said "Hanna," and who might have been Swedish, implied that no other explanation was needed.

"He just doesn't seem that bad." Mel lowered her voice. "He seems way higher-functioning than the others." She caught herself a breath away from saying that he was by far the best at ring toss, for instance.

"You're his daughter?"

Mel nodded. The nurse guided her into an office, closed

the door, then listed all of the "disruptive behaviours" her father had committed since coming here. An event at lunch involving a thrown dish. Twice he'd tried to slap a nurse, the same nurse, in the face with a slipper. Many refusals to leave his room for meals, "when he sits praying wit his beads." And once when someone took these beads away for cleaning, he was very abusive. The staff should not have to suffer that. And, at night, he often paced.

"Out of boredom?" Mel heard herself ask.

"I see it as an anxiety," said the nurse.

Through the door's reinforced glass window, she could see Hal ambling back from a visit to the bathroom, looking for action. "I haven't seen that," Mel said.

"The brain dies, bit by bit," said Hanna, pinching two fingers a hair's breadth apart, but smiling rather happily now. "It opens hidden areas. Loss of memory is one ting. Mood swings, another. They can become somebody new. Or they get stuck in an age of their life. Usually, teenage, or young." A good word came to her. "Embarking. Ven they were embarking on life—this they can remember. Precise memories."

Mel watched her father bring his palms together and bow to Alexandra, the ancient woman who pulled herself along in her wheelchair with little pitter-pat steps of her feet. Hal did start a life, maybe the real one, in Nepal.

"He's safe here," added the nurse.

Mel nodded, though Hal's notion of safety had nothing to do with the nurse's, and Mel was about to say this, though there'd be no point, when the nurse offered something horrifying: "Your father will fit in nicely soon."

They re-entered the hall, Mel noticing the office's air freshener because of its sudden lack. The nurse shifted into josh-with-family-member gear. "He told me, he told me he flew twelve t'ousand miles, to be wit us. He's quite the flirt. He said—" She touched Mel's arm. "He said, 'I have come all dis way, Hanna, just to be wit you.'" Hanna laughed loudly to affirm that it had been just a joke. "Isn't it amazing? How long he vas over there? In Asia? Twenty years, no?"

"Fourteen," Mel had said, still feeling certain that her father would never fit in here.

She still sometimes thought that, though today was an off day. She saw that Hal had more than finished his grilled cheese sandwich, he had stolen and eaten Bea's untouched half as well. The food seemed to be perking him up. But, fourteen years. The number made Mel think, painfully, of her promise.

About a month before moving here, they were in the TV room and he was talking about his name, like he was trying to cement it in his memory. "For fourteen years I was called How." His eyes began to tear. "They're speedy talkers and 'Hal' is 'How.'" He smiled. "How Rinpoche, sometimes." (And Mel was thinking that a real smile, plus teary, shiny eyes, was the most beautiful human face.)

Barely taking a breath from his story, it was at this point he made Mel promise that she'd never—*never*—come visit him unless she truly wanted to. "It'll poison the whole thing," he said.

During that last month at home, in the Rosedale house, he made her promise this at least a dozen times.

The dishes were being cleared and stacked in the rolling cart with a noisiness Mel hated. They were plastic, and more or less tossed, clack-and-bang, and she could tell the ladies were disturbed by it too, though Mel thought maybe that was because it broke the illusion that they were in a decent restaurant, which most of the diners seemed to believe. Stuart, ever helpful, exclaimed, "Well, *that* was good," and Mel agreed, causing dear Bea to lean in, face pinched with concern, "You didn't eat much, love."

"I think I ate hers too!" laughed Hal, back in action. Then, abruptly, "Did we do the closing chants? The meal chants?"

"No," said Bea, concerned anew, "no, I don't think we did. I'll ask." She craned around hunting for a staff person, and it was Hal who put a hand on her arm to settle her.

Mel felt off, herself. Colours were too bright and might be throbbing. Her hands and face were hot and she had the urge to grab herself tight with her own arms and squeeze. She wondered if this wasn't a little seizure. A surf of blood roared and ebbed a rhythm in her ears. She made herself breathe steadily. It wasn't too bad, whatever it was. She could just sit here, with the others. Funny how no one was moving from the table. These old ones would sit here forever.

"You okay?" asked Stuart.

"I might lie down." Everything had taken on a yellow hue, one that created its own light. It had edges of purple. Her heart was going pretty good, but that was just fear.

"You want to go?"

"No."

"Are you sure?" he asked, leaning at her. Bea got up and was coming at her with a hand out.

"If I have to I'll go lie down."

Stuart looked around, seeing himself alone with these folks. "Do you have the book?"

She lifted her purse onto the table and slid it at him.

"Does anybody want me to read more of the story?" asked

Stuart, to murmurs of assent and Hal's formality about being grateful. "I know *I* want to find out what happens."

He'd learned not to bother trying to catch his audience up on where they'd left off. He'd apparently been reading some on his own at home. Hal was sitting up straight again and his face had uncrumpled and filled out from within, from a wellspring of vitality, or maybe it was just alertness alone. He had his mala ready. He looked poised, ready for a workout.

Stuart began, and Mel told him to "Slow down for us old folks." Stuart began again:

Michael was more excited than usual at the thought of her knock on his door. He tried not to, but kept finding himself staring out the window, eyes glued to the sidewalk and corner of hedge from which she would first appear. On the phone several days ago she had been so happy to tell him about the good dictionary she'd found and the university had let her take out. "It smells just like … more really old paper!" She laughed, and it actually was funny. And when she said, "It is so huge and heavy to carry, can I leave it at your house?" he had become instantly hard. He didn't know what he was looking forward to more, reading Li's next pages or Naomi's next kiss, and their mind-toppling hug.

Nor did he know what might happen. It would be the second time she would spend the night in his house. Last weekend, when they both complained about the short, short work time and the complications of her making the ferry, he unfurled a foamie in his little dining room, said he would flip her for it, and lost, and though she claimed she couldn't possibly take his bed while he took the floor, she had shyly crept away to his bedroom after a second cup of hot chocolate. On his foamie, unable to even think of sleeping, the thought of Naomi in his bed made him swell with a warmth he had never felt; it wasn't only carnal, it was protective and it made him smile. The next day he was disappointed when he could not smell even a trace of her on his pillow.

Michael had come to understand something about Naomi: she was beauty in human form.

He was indeed watching when she burst past the hedge, lugging an overnight case as well as what must be the big smelly dictionary in a plastic bag. He hesitated at the first knock, even trotted through the kitchen to bang a few dishes in the sink. But when he opened the door, pretending surprise, she brought with her a bigger one. As he approached her for his kiss and his hug, smiling and moaning low, Naomi put her face down and her hand up, halting him several feet away.

"Michael. I have to say something. I am sorry. It is something I need to say."

"Okay," he said. And when she merely stood there, apparently composing her words, he couldn't help but say, "You're scaring me, Naomi."

"I want—I want to ask you to stop this. Your project. This project I am helping you with."

"What do you mean?"

"Can you, please, stop doing this project."

"I don't have the remotest idea what you're talking about."

"The project that we—"

"I know the project. Why? What's your reason? What the hell!"

"It's wrong for us to do it. It's not your story to tell."

"How is it wrong, exactly? It's a wonderful story. It's fascinating. It's enlightening. It's not grave robbing. It's Li's story. It deserves to be heard."

"*Li's* story, yes. You are not her, and you are not the lepers. You did not know their life. It's wrong."

"I don't know what to say." He didn't. "I'm unconvinced." He was. "Let's—" He reached for her arm and took it. She allowed herself to be led, and Michael didn't feel as scared. "Let's talk inside."

Naomi wouldn't take off her coat, and stood in the entryway.

"In China, it's very different. How we think about the dead. Only with respect. Also, it's because we fear the dead. We think they bring us luck. When we don't respect them, there's the other side. Other side of luck. I think the word is 'curse.'"

"That's ridiculous." The curse of the mummy's tomb. This is Li, an unfortunate but forgotten young woman, her memoirs. And—yes: "If Li didn't want us to read her words, why did she write them?"

This seemed to have Naomi stymied. But, no. After a time she said, "If it isn't yours, it can't be true. It's impossible." She met his gaze with a look of fearsome neutrality, the look of the correct. "If it can't be true, it has to be a lie. And isn't that one kind of curse?"

"You better listen to her, boy," Hal blurted, not looking up from his mala beads. He could have been watching a western on TV. Bea echoed him with an "Oh, aye!" and Mel realized, for the first time, that Bea was Scottish. Stuart waited for anything else that might be coming, made eye contact with Mel, then continued. He looked eager to get to it.

"Well, so why did you translate this in the first place?" Michael snorted. "If I'm stealing from lepers. Who are long dead. *Who can't be stolen from.*" He musn't get too angry. He couldn't bear her walking away from this.

"I ... At first, I thought it was innocent. I thought, I thought that ... you were innocent too."

"What's that supposed to mean?"

"I thought that the World, I thought that the D'Arcy Island story, would just be for your studies. Your interest."

"And that's what it's for. My studies. My research."

"But you are trying to sell it."

"Naomi—you've been going through my things?"

"Michael. I have heard how you talk. Your piles of notes. You are writing a book. You are writing a book with this in it. With ... my work."

Michael spun away from her. He thrust both hands in his pockets and stared out the window, breathing precisely.

"Ah. So it's *your* work."

"I did not mean it that way. But, isn't it my work, too?"

"Li's writing, which I own, and which you are

changing into English, will be little more than a half, a third, of the book."

"That's not what I mean."

Michael spun back around. "Do you want your name on the cover? Done. Do you want more money? Done." Because, truly, these were trifles. It dawned on him that, if asked what would pain him more to lose, the book or Naomi, he didn't know what his answer would be. There was no answer. But nor would that question be necessary!

He stepped up to her and took both wrists in his hands, and she let him. He shook them while he spoke, and her hands flipped with words he emphasized. "Naomi. I want us to be partners in this. I just want us, I want us to …" Michael's eyes teared up, and he gazed intently into Naomi's face, but she looked down. "I just want this to keep going, like it's been going. This is the best time of my life."

"I … think that, too. Also."

"Because, I love you."

"I … also."

They embraced, and held it for a long while. At one point Naomi began to lurch against his chest, and Michael held her gently through her crying. He had no idea what it meant. It frightened him, and he wished he could help her. But it stopped. And then she shook her head and laughed, embarrassed. Another minute passed before she asked if he wished her to work on the new pages now. He said only if she wanted to. Her cheek pressed against his sweater, she nodded so slowly he barely felt it.

No words were exchanged as he took her coat. Simple things, physical things, they still found awkward together. She took her leave of him for his study. He hoped she would notice the tidied desk, the cut flowers in the vase, the thermos filled with oolong, her favourite tea—of course she would. He hoped it would shake her out of her mood, erase those thoughts. Cursed. Good God.

She disappeared down the hall with a weak, unfelt smile, lugging her new dictionary.

Michael hoped he could find something to do over the next few hours, until the first pages came. He decided to make them a nice dinner. Perhaps oddly, she loved Japanese, especially teriyaki salmon.

Several hours later, fish wafting from the kitchen and Michael reading an archived report on the BC medical system circa 1903, Naomi appeared soundlessly from behind him and handed him two fresh pages. He was amazed at her speed, and praised her for it. She whispered to him that they were rough draft only, but that the meaning would be clear.

They remained standing for him to read them, as had become their custom. Something Michael added to it now was to stand behind her, almost draping himself over her so that she was tucked in against his front. She didn't resist. To his delight, when he began to read, she let her head fall back onto his breastbone.

Michael read slowly. When it dawned on him what he was reading, he was overcome with a fresh tremble that came from fear, or gratitude, or both:

I could not bear to open it, the letter from my father,
who will by now have heard what has befallen me. He,
who worked in a mine in the north near a place called
Revelstoke, if that is still where he is. He, who can not
read and who would have spoken his tearful words to a
friend who wrote them down. I held the envelope in my
hands, could feel that it held one thin sheet only, but
still I could hear my father's voice in it. I could hear
his anguished pleas for whatever calm or contentment I
could still squeeze from the parched years that remain to
me. My poor father. I burned his letter, I could not read it
so I burned it. To the ears of Heaven, isn't this the same
thing?

"Naomi! Letters! They got letters!" Michael
reached up and squeezed her shoulder, shaking it a
little. "Did you know I was wondering last week about
letters, if they got them at all and how bizarre it would
be if they didn't?" He could feel her nodding against
his chest. "Here it is! Letters! This is great! Maybe we'll
have more. Maybe we'll have some actual words, from
the outside world, to a leper, *attitudes* …" Michael
skimmed ahead, unable to help himself. "Maybe,"
whispered Naomi. Michael began again to read slowly,
in exalted amazement.

I burned his letter because I knew that upon reading
it I would so desperately want to comfort my poor beloved
father as best I could, instantly, with an answer, and I
can not. Whenever they arrive, the men in the boat may
be a welcome sight to our eyes, other humans who bring

us our hemp-woven bags of supplies, but they remain carefully away, they heave everything onto the dry rocks on shore while they ride two feet deep, daring come no closer. They bring us things but they will never agree to take anything away—though we shake important messages at them, and letters for families—so fearful are they of our contagion. I know well the contents of these letters, for I write many of them.

Once, so the story goes, an old one, Menmen, who was among the first to come to the World, threw a stone at the boat, not taking aim at a white man but simply lobbing it in, to give them something to scurry away from, and worry about all voyage back, a little leper among them, mute on the boat's floor. It is not part of the story whether he was teasing, or laughing, or shouting curses. But supposedly a sailor screamed; perhaps it had brushed his foot. In any case Menmen was set upon by the other three men here, and beaten badly. They worried about their opium supply, and perhaps their food.

"Of course they would," Michael whispered to himself. "Of course they'd beat him." He reverently began a new page.

We are all still shaken by what we saw. Last night, though the sun had fallen, the western sky stayed all aglow, and after some initial puzzlement we understood without trading words among ourselves that Victoria was burning. Now we also understood the heavy smell of smoke certain winds had brought us that day, smoke we thought to be from burning forest. We lined up on the

*shore and watched. And began to speak, each in our own
way.*

Why did I assume we all felt the same?

*Some watched in silence. I heard several quietly
laughing, laughing scornfully. I heard the word "good."
Others moaned names, of family, and wondered aloud
at the hardships they would now face, and perhaps
injuries. More than a few glanced harshly at Wan,
who last month had with useless hands knocked over
the latrine lamp and burned the fetid structure down.
Then some—and this would become the main conversation—soon realized that what we were watching might
soon affect us too, perhaps severely. With Victoria thus
stricken, would they think of us at all? How would
this affect the supply boat? How long would delivery
be disrupted? Would some supplies be cut off? Opium,
they used opium for victims of burns, didn't they?
Would there be any for us? For some, this thought was so
fearsome they could not speak at all, except to demand
an augury from Chin.*

*And so I saw that this fire was not just there, but also
burning here, in the World. I was saddened to see that we
were still connected. When connected to the outside, we
became lepers. Alone, we are simply what we are.*

*I was crying, but no one would know why. Sang Seen
came to my side, finally, and slid his arm through mine,
so that his inner elbow—a place he could still feel—
touched mine. I did not know what he was thinking. I
never know what he is thinking. Perhaps I should have
taken some meaning from the fact that, even while I stood
and watched another world burn, I wondered at this*

man at my side, and what he felt for me, and if I was
merely his hobby, his plaything against boredom or, worse,
his garden that he watered and weeded diligently, but
with thoughts of the profit to come.

"Excellent," Michael said. "Good work, sweet-heart." Emboldened by having used the endearment, he squeezed Naomi's shoulder.

When they sat to eat, the salmon was dry and the salad dressing had pooled in the bottom of the bowl and Michael didn't think to toss it. He had trouble thinking at all as he faced Naomi across his table. She had last week agreed to his suggestion that they position themselves not at the ends of the table but the sides, so they could be closer. Saying this, Michael was aware that it was likely the most forward thing he had ever said to a woman, and all through the meal he thought that, if he felt her foot touch his, he would drop a fork. By meal's end he had dared edge his foot her way, but found nothing.

Tonight he knew he had to be more forward still. He could see it was not in her nature to do it for him. It had to be him. He saw that neither of them were eating, not really. He knew it wasn't because the salmon was dry.

It was as though she already knew his question and was ready with her answer.

He barely got it out, but he said, "Should we flip for the foamie?"

"No."

He rose, and so did she. His neck swollen, all his senses on fire, he stumbled as he took her hand, which was already halfway to his. Crossing the threshold to his room, somehow not missing a step, she kicked off her little slippers, as if what they were about to do was worthy not only of respect, but haste. He knew now that she had been waiting too.

FROM THE LEVEL OF HER KNEES, Mel gave Stuart a little wave, stopping him. She hooked her thumb back to indicate the corridor, then put her hands together as a pillow against her cheek to tell him she was off to have a little nap. Stuart raised his eyebrows to ask if she was sure, and maybe didn't want to just go home. Mel shook her head and pointed to the book.

Stuart looked over at Hal and watched him. The clicking, the lips moving. Just like a high-school teacher, Stuart asked suddenly into the silence, "Hal. What is it you're counting?"

Hal smiled at Stuart and lifted the mala. "These."

Mel made her way down the corridor, which brightened and faded with her heartbeat. Her father was a trickster. Even now it was hard to know what went on. This section of *The World* had shown her nothing and it was a part of the story that should have. The mutual seduction, the first time. Had he been listening? She didn't even know that much, let alone whether this was non-fiction and had happened to him. Though how much did it matter to her? Did she really want to find out why her father had been scared into Buddhism?

SHE WOKE, SWEATING because of the plastic mattress cover she could feel and hear crackling below her. Her hands and face were no longer burning, and her vision was back to normal. Feeling logy, like she'd slept a long time, she snorted at the dream she'd just woken out of. In it, with boyish and buck-toothed enthusiasm, Tom Cruise had his pants down to show her his clean doll crotch, glossy and smooth. Then it was Stuart, and he tapped a finger to draw her in closer and he showed off his Harley-Davidson tattoo there.

She sat up on the narrow bed, feeling a sharpness in her esophagus that wasn't nice. It was time for a new patch. She had one in her purse, which sat over on the chair, but she delayed getting to her feet. It was a discipline she clung to, this tasting the pain long enough to understand again where it would lead, and not just blindly grabbing for something like a junkie.

She remembered enjoying coming in here and falling asleep in Hal's bed. It was narrow, and noisy with plastic, but it was her father's bed and for a moment she'd been his little girl again, protected, delicious, a feeling so real it was time travel and—yes—it was why she'd been able to sleep.

She rose, determined not to rush to her purse. In his closet were enough shirts, some with his name sharpied in the collar, some with other names. Lots of thievery here, though of course it wasn't exactly that. One shirt was a woman's floral print, the name "MacArthur." Bea's last name might be MacArthur.

His dresser had a decent supply of socks, and undershirts. Some sweatpants still with store tags, neatly folded, not yet used. In the same drawer festered a pair of beaten-up dirty slippers, which she removed to the closet floor.

On the wall, a picture of her mother, smiling pleasantly

enough, but nothing in her eyes. For that reason alone it didn't look like her mother, whose presence was a good match for Hal's. Beside that, a picture of herself, a studio portrait in graduation regalia. She remembered being higher than a kite for the shoot, though you couldn't tell. Her parents had pleaded with her to get such a photo done, and she quoted them twice the price, which they happily sent, though they probably knew, they weren't stupid about such things. She wore the gown just that once, never making it to her actual ceremony which was scheduled in the aftermath of all the good grad parties going on.

Mel cracked the window to let more air in. She was aware of taking stock, of getting Hal's world in order for her departure.

She felt good. Rested. It would be a good afternoon. She left the room, saw Hal and Stuart and a few female heads at one of the dining-room tables, playing cards it looked like. Mel turned the other way, checked the wall clock, went to the nursing station, and called the restaurant.

STUART DROVE EXTRA-CAREFULLY, it seemed, with Hal in the front seat. Her father liked giving directions, always had. After hitting the brakes a couple of times when Hal pointed at a corner they were already passing and said, "Go there," Stuart learned to ignore him. At a red light, when Stuart turned off the windshield wipers that had been shrieking on dry glass, she could hear the mala clicking.

"Do you remember this car, Dad?"

"I don't remember anything anymore," Hal said, his usual answer to a question this direct. He was quite cheerful saying it.

"You do remember some things," Mel corrected him, an encouragement she sometimes couldn't help giving. ("I remember that I have no memory," he used to say to that one, very aware of the irony. And she'd say, "No, sometimes you forget that too," keeping it going. "No, I don't, dear. I don't forget things like that," he might say then, getting her to study him for further irony or confusion, because he could lose awareness halfway through a sentence. But they hadn't had a good string like that for months. That was over now too.)

"I remember I grew up here," Hal said, turning to tell Stuart. He gestured to the dashboard with a palm-up sweep of his hand. Mel saw Stuart's brow furrow.

"In, in Toronto?" Stuart asked.

"Right here," said Hal, wobbling his head in an odd way and smiling.

"Dad, you grew up in Niagara Falls," Mel offered. "And you were always proud of that."

"I was?"

"You were proud because people came from all over the world to see where you grew up."

"Niagara Falls is not a very uplifted place. It really isn't."

"I agree with you there. But don't go telling Stuart your Viagra Falls joke, please."

"I know a joke?"

"And, hooray, you've forgotten it." Mel squeezed Hal's shoulder from behind. Stuart looked wary of all this veering into honesty. It did make her feel breathless. A tightrope walk, heart in throat.

"Is it any good?"

"It's the punchline to the question, 'Where do retirees go for their second honeymoon.' So, no."

"Viagra is that, that—"

"Erection medicine."

"Yes." Hal smiled sadly. Then he was looking out the window where a hot-dog vendor was running on the spot, and from the slight tilt of Hal's head Mel could see that everything was now new.

As they drove, Mel hoped Stuart would find her father funny above all, and realized she had always felt this way. She wasn't sure why. Maybe because humour seemed to fix everything, even the air. If only for the moment.

Her new patch felt warm on her shoulder. It also felt like everything that food, tobacco, and alcohol had ever done for her. It felt as warm as friendship. It felt like when you saw you had a bingo, just before you shout. But with morphine you never do shout, you stay right where you are, bubbling up.

IT WAS MEL'S WHIM TO SAY "Turn left here," but she said it in time enough for Stuart to comply. They had a half hour before their reservation, and Mel wanted to see it again. She enjoyed, and didn't enjoy, Hal there.

The sign, in painted red and yellow wood, said *Karmê Dhatu Chöling*. Hal pronounced that last word "churling." Mel had no idea what any of it meant. She could see from the lights on that it was open.

Mel thought she remembered the pale, red-haired woman who popped out from a side office to meet them in the hall and explain with a precise smile that the centre wasn't open, exactly, but since the door was open, it was open, and they were welcome to do whatever. She pointed to a bright blue door and said, "The shrine room."

Mel flicked on the shrine room lights and closed the door behind them. Stuart stood speechless, looking at it. It was this shrine that drew Hal to this place in particular, its objects and even colours telling him that this was closest to his congregation of Buddhism. Hal called them "schools" of Buddhism. Mel knew only that his was Tibetan, of which there were several schools, even here in Toronto.

About twenty cushions sat in neat rows facing the shrine, waiting for people to sit on them. The shrine itself was an elevated wooden box, painted bright red, with gold leaf trim and swirls, upon which sat glass bowls, some holding rice and some water, and one what looked like ink. There was a vase with peacock feathers, a golden chalice, a crystal ball the size of a human head resting on a canvas pillow, a mirror propped to face the room, an incense burner, various metal objects, one of which was apparently of solid "meteoric iron," and a hand-held noisemaker that looked like a toy but was made from the tops of two human skulls. On the wall, backing all of this, were photos of various gurus, only one of them female, plus wild paintings of beings with colourful skin. In one, surrounded by flames, ponies, skulls, and waterfalls, a red woman was poised a quarter-inch from a kiss with a blue man, the pair copulating standing up, the man's leg cocked around her bottom such that one could glimpse his testicles.

Facing the shrine, Hal sombrely spun his braid into a bun atop his head, stabbed a stick through it, put his hands together as in Christian prayer, said words to himself, bent forward to fall to his knees, and then slid onto his belly. He flung his arms forward, forehead on the floor. He mumbled something into the carpet while down there, then pulled his way back onto his knees then feet, wincing once or twice. Then he did it all again.

Mel took Stuart forward by the arm to stand at the shrine. First she lit the two large candles—last time, Hal had done that—and then told him what she knew, which was that none of these things were "religious," exactly. Stuart was content to remain quiet, eyes flicking here and there. Every object, she said, represented some aspect of the human mind.

Mel and Stuart watched him prostrate. "So Hal is bowing to himself. To his own mind's potential."

"That's … interesting."

"It's the mind that's considered sacred. And the world it sees."

"Ah."

"So it looks like devotion in here, but it's devotion to your own mind." She'd heard these words but had never said them herself, and just the saying of them felt something like belief. "But it's not selfish, because you see that we all have the same mind, the same, um, obstacles, the same *mess*, and you can't help but feel like you're just like everyone else too."

"Okay."

She knew she was preaching, but enjoyed sounding like Hal. She had just started understanding his world. "You can't help it. That's the compassion part. It's not forced."

"Right." Stuart scanned the objects. "So what is—"

The woman came in, not smiling. "I'm sorry, please put the candles out? The shrine has to be opened properly. If you want to come back at six, to sit, that'd be—"

"I opened it," said Hal matter-of-factly, breathing a little hard, his back to her, hands prayerful with his mala dangling from them, about to dive forward again.

The woman watched him prostrate. She looked at Mel and Stuart to consider them too, Stuart waved and smiled, and the woman, still unsmiling, withdrew, closing the door soundlessly behind her.

Stuart leaned in to the vase of peacock feathers. He bobbed his head to shift the colours, the glorious colours. Mel knew what the feathers meant. The story was that a peacock ate poison in order to grow its beautiful tail, which meant a Buddhist "invited" negative emotions and difficult challenges, fearlessly using them to grow compassion, and wisdom, which were then adornments, like the tail. Hal sometimes called alcohol "poison for the peacock."

Mel took in the beauty of the shrine objects, her father huffing in the back, Stuart daring to touch a skull top. So much here was about death. Death of each moment was a core idea, but so was the big one. Death. Buddhism trained you for it. "You need to bring as much alertness to the moment of death as you can," Hal told her, more than once, in more than one way. He told her how one of his Buddhist heroes had died "just sitting on the bed, died sitting up, they said he wedged himself in pillows in a corner so he wouldn't fall over."

"Hal, excuse me." Stuart got her father to stop. He pointed to one of the paintings, the one with the copulating deities. "What does this red lady mean?"

"Vajrayogini is passion." He regarded Stuart a moment longer, and who knows what or whom he was seeing. "Or you might say *com*passion. But that's a long story."

Mel was struck again. Hal knew a deity's name, not a daughter's.

"And this blue fellow?" Stuart persisted. Mel couldn't tell if he was interested or merely testing.

His chest rising and falling, Hal observed Stuart again until Stuart grew uncomfortable.

"The *nintun* is Saturday and I'll put that in my talk. All right?"

"Thank you," Stuart said.

Leaving Karmê Dhatu Chöling, Mel and Stuart waited near the entrance while Hal visited the bathroom. Stuart picked up a brochure and then flapped it back on the table. He gazed around like he was in an airport, not reverent at all.

Stuart said to her, "You're so devoted to your father. I think it's great."

"I've always been devoted to somebody." She didn't mean to demean it quite that way. But she'd always had someone to focus on. You could call it devotion though it felt more selfish than that. Even with Hal.

They heard a toilet flush. Paper towels cranked from a machine.

"You ever get lonely, Stuart?"

No pause to think, he said, "No, you?"

Mel looked at him harder and saw he was being funny. Of course he was lonely. Was she? She almost gave him the "You die alone, and I've been practising" line. She had Hal, but she also didn't have him, not at all. The first time he didn't know her she could still feel as an emptiness that blasted all the way down to her feet.

"Yes."

And here Hal was at her side, ready for anything.

SEOUL FOOD WAS OFF Yonge down a side street and identified on an outer stone wall solely by a small bronze *s* that you'd miss if you weren't in on it. Mel had read about it twice now, both raves. On the phone this afternoon the young woman had laughed and said, "Wow, there was a cancellation, like, two minutes ago? Usually it's a two-week thing. You should buy a lottery ticket today."

She'd read that its "upscale and unexpected" offerings included almost nothing recognizably Korean except for beef short ribs, kimchi, and the individual table grills. Mel was drawn by this last one. She wanted to watch meat sizzle, shrink, and move, she wanted to smell the scorch to brown, even black, wanted to hear it. She'd have unknown sauces to dip finger to tongue—one reviewer had said the place was all about its sauces and that's what its *s* should stand for. Hal was worldly by habit, he'd get by. Stu Price might remember a camping story or two.

The idea was, she might smell or taste something new, a modest enough wish.

At 5:30 the place was empty of diners but two servers bustled to get things ready and the kitchen was already noisy. The three of them hung their coats on the backs of their chairs though the room was sedate and low-lit and, you could tell, pricey. A young thing came to take their drink order, and before Mel could guide him Hal said, "I'll go with the tomato."

"Would you like a beer, Dad? Beer's good with spice."

Hal looked at her like she was crazy, but then nodded, still in doubt. The young woman began listing available beers, pleased to show off her memory and speed, and Mel realized it was the voice on the phone. She stopped her at an oatmeal stout for Hal, and Stuart opted for that as well. She was quite beautiful, a Deborah Harry face. She could be Deborah

Harry's daughter. No, good grief, that would be grand-daughter, wouldn't it. She asked if Mel would like anything, and Mel didn't mean to but looked at her and laughed, and said, "*Any*thing?" No smile from the granddaughter. It wasn't a good start. Why, after all this time, did Mel assume everyone thought like her?

When the server left, Hal tapped the table's inlaid grill with a single chopstick and whispered, "We have our own thing," as if it were someone's mistake and this might not last. He also began to say something he'd repeat all evening, which was, "I guess we're allowed to eat in here."

The menus were a treat. You could order things—soups, sobas, a kimchi tempura!—from the kitchen. But most were pre-marinated grill-your-own meats and veggies—bison, duck, goose, sardines, and "shark cubes," along with the usual. An asterisk at shark directed one to the bottom of the page where it was explained that the species was "salmon-shark to the English, the spiny dogfish from the Salish Sea, a sustain-able fishery." Everything on the menu was farmed or deemed sustainable.

She began reading off items for Hal's sake but also because she liked doing it and her throat was holding up. She noticed Hal fall silent and close his eyes.

"Did you read to them for much longer?" she asked Stuart.

"Maybe a half hour more. I drove away Vera. Bea almost fell out of her chair. A nurse made me stop. He was just—" He mimed counting beads.

"Did he"— Mel flicked her eyes Hal's way—"react to anything?" At the moment of asking, she realized she wasn't sure if she still wanted to know. If an affair was the reason her parents had gone on to lead the lives they did, did it matter now, even remotely? Would it change how she felt about them?

"Yikes, sorry, I was reading, I couldn't say." Stuart laughed. "*I* did, though. You know how when Michael finds out that leprosy's really hard to catch and the medical people already *knew* that? And there was no reason at all for the lepers to even be there? Ouch."

"I know."

"Everything gets sadder then. That it's all for no good reason. All that suffering."

Perhaps that was her father's point. "It's even more poignant at the end." Well, yes and no.

"Don't tell me!"

Hal said, "Tell me what?" He fiddled with the mala around his wrist as if unsure whether he wanted it on or off.

Watching him, it struck her as amusing, the possibility that his book might even have been written *for* her mother, Hal's public self-flagellation his gift of apology to her. Maybe she even demanded it of him!

Mel closed her menu. "Get whatever, guys," she announced. "It's on me." She added, "But please order sardines, and the goose. And, maybe, the kimchi tempura." She smiled for Stuart. "I want to spectate."

"I just remembered you didn't have any lunch either," said Stuart.

Mel tapped her purse hanging off her chair back, by way of saying she had a can in there, one she could take to the bathroom and tip into her feeding tube, messy but workable. But she had no intention of doing that, eating *that*, in this place.

"What?" said Hal, the New York Jew. "Eat. *Eat.*" His bun was still up, and Mel realized her dad looked like someone who would know Asian food intimately.

Music began, and Mel couldn't help but pay attention. It was something Danny relied on from her at La Tarantula, the playlist for the tape loop. Of all the ways one choreo-graphed the diners' experience, music was as important as the decor and, almost, the service, and the challenge was to find the right formula, an odd *via negativa*: you didn't want to make people feel like getting up to dance, you didn't want top-ten faves, you didn't want classical, or risky experimental. You didn't want to distract people from food, or conversa-tion. But nor did you want vacuous elevator. Mel changed the loop weekly to keep the servers—and Danny, and her—from going crazy—loopy. She often went with instrumental, some-times Eno from his long ambient phase, and David Byrne, and, there was Weather Report, and world beat was often good, the list was endless, really, but mostly easy fusion and solo piano; but then that Fats Waller phase, and of course the later, jazzier Joni Mitchell had been safe, though Danny would sometimes accuse her of picking things with a show-off bass. Which was true, so sue me.

There wasn't much background noise in here yet but you could tell the speakers were excellent, they were so much better these days and probably the size of a shoebox—where were they?—you could hear every word and yet you could completely tune it out, you could return home after a night here and call the restaurant "quiet." Mel knew this song, that moony baritone, it was The National. She liked them.

"Do you know this song, Stuart? The National?" Mel gazed up into the ceiling's corners, couldn't see speakers.

"I don't."

"Where are we, exactly?" asked Hal, looking up in the corners too. Unaware of music at Royal Elms, he wouldn't notice this tape loop either.

"We're in a Korean restaurant, Dad. Are you hungry?"

"I sure am."

Good lyrics, not afraid of melody. A nice yelp about depression; she wouldn't want to be that fellow. She'd watched them on YouTube before her internet died. Any time a band has a non-handsome front man, you know it's famous for the right reasons. She liked the rhythm section, which got pounding and jazzy.

Deborah Harry's granddaughter came to take their order, and Stuart did a good job of it, seeing that Hal looked a little distressed, not knowing what was expected of him. Just as she was turning away, having memorized, not written, Mel called her back, a no-no, but there you go. She asked if they had any sake.

The granddaughter feigned sadness for her as she said, "Sorry, um, that's Japanese?"

Mel didn't want to explain that it wasn't the sake she'd wanted, but the little ceramic pouring flask, with its spout.

"Do you have individual teapots?"

The server looked at her overlong. "Yaaasss?"

"Could you bring me an empty one? Plus a bottle of good Cotes du Rhone? Not over a hundred dollars? But if there's a French with the word 'Bandol' in it, I want that. Please."

The server glared down at the wine list, but didn't say anything. They'd ordered lots, both men were having more beer, now good wine, and a big tip might be coming.

Mel also didn't like the way the granddaughter had ignored Hal. You couldn't blame her, but then again maybe you should. Her father perched in his chair very unlike somebody at a restaurant. He had his mala going. It made Mel remember his first month home, after the hip operation, when they were getting to know each other, how Hal would perch straight in his chair as he spoke, not touching the chair back, hands resting on the arms and elbows a little out, looking like he had triangular wings at his sides and was ready to fly forward. He was the picture of "ready," and this was one of his favourite Buddhist words, as it turned out.

A cook came to turn on their grill and explain how things were done. Mel suspected it was a male's job to do this, simply because of a perception that diners would be more trusting of a man. Fire, a grill, meat! In fact, she was right—as tables filled, the same man came out with the (very simple) manly instructions. He also gave them their windup timer and told them it was very important, especially for seafood.

Their second beer came—it was strong, according to Stuart—as well as a bottle of Bandol, and some appetizers. Mel had to remind the granddaughter about an empty individual teapot and, the girl's smile verging on insolent, was told it was still coming, no room on the tray, a lie. One appetizer was a sampler-sized tempura kimchi, which Mel loved the look of. She chopsticked some up, dipped it in the accompanying sauce—a transparent tan, your basic tempura sauce—popped it in, and chewed. Flavour came, sour, hot, garlic, it was deeply good. It was hard not to swallow. Even the throat's anticipation of swallowing created a tiny spasm that hurt intensely. She brought her empty wineglass to her mouth, hunched over, and as delicately as possible spit the chewed food out.

"Okay!" said Stuart, pretending not to have seen.

"No good, eh?" asked Hal.

Mel unfolded the royal blue napkin and hid the evidence with a shroud.

The food began arriving, most of it small plates of raw meat. The server also arrived, breathless, with Mel's little teapot, saying she was sorry it took so long, and Mel wished such attention hadn't been paid to it because now discretion would be more difficult. Worse, Hal gently though flagrantly touched the server on the wrist, causing her to recoil. When Hal indicated the rest of the dining room with a hand sweep and instructed her, "We should be sure not to forget the meal chants," her withdrawal was mostly angry.

It was the kind of meal Mel loved. Small portions, lots of variety, you had to work a bit so you ate slowly and the evening lasted. It was sharesies. And you could feel the heat of the grill on your face. There were plates of marinated goose, sardines, shark cubes, some lamb, and some beef flank. A big plate of yam, green pepper, eggplant, gai lan, and something like bok choy that wasn't. Each of them received a "sauce wheel" of seven small bowls of sauce, in the centre of which was their eating plate.

"So whose is this," said Hal, tapping the goose plate-edge with a chopstick.

They loaded up the grill with this and that, Hal pitching in, his chopsticks second nature. Sometimes he flipped meat before its time, and Mel simply let him forget and then she flipped it back. They used the timer for the sardines and shark, though she thought this needless and a little gimmicky, because you could just tell. Though you could get drunk and distracted. Maybe you talked about your marriage while the sardine dried and blackened. Hal kept asking whose meat was whose, and several times he removed something from the grill, dipped it in something then put it back, but no harm done. Soon the two men were eating, the thinly cut food taking only a few minutes. Sometimes Hal was shown what sauce to use with what, sometimes not. Twice, Mel tried a chew-and-spit. Otherwise she was happy to dip a finger and touch it to her tongue. There was nothing earth-moving about any of it, no sauce broke new ground. The deep-fried kimchi was still the best.

Except for the wine, which was half gone. Her abdomen had gone instantly and gloriously warm. Two little half-full teapots, and it was time for a third. Stuart had been too busy grilling to notice her first two, and now he looked a little panicked to see her hunch into the table, hoist her blouse, and uncap what they'd both begun jokingly calling her "adapter." She was discreet, but not that discreet. Four tables were occupied now and she knew that at least one had noticed her.

Then Stuart, bless him, was raising a beer to her in toast. She brought her teapot away and clinked it to his glass.

She brought it back and carefully placed the spout to the little plastic mouth. "I basically have to just glug it in," she said. "It's good wine. I wish I could taste it. But it *feels* like good wine." She hoped Stuart didn't see that when the wine wasn't going down the little neck fast enough she had to shift in her chair to reshape her stomach and make space.

Stuart said, "Remember your experiment?"

She rolled her eyes for him, not exactly embarrassed. This was going way back, but she had declared at times, not quite joking, that her life was an experiment to find out how what you put in your body made you feel. One mystery was, if alcohol was alcohol, why did a scotch feel different than a beer? Why did good wine lend that wise glow and bad wine make you harsh and goofy? She "experimented" on food of all kinds—the trufflepig thing. The question had widened to music: How did one bass note make your gut feel that, but another note *that?* She read about harmony, frequency, and the varying density of human organs, the idea being that they were also ears. It was a long time ago. It had ceased being an experiment and became the way she gobbled through each day. And when she first learned of her cancer, it was what made her think, *of course.*

This wine did feel good.

"It's working," Mel whispered to Stuart, settling back, through her shirt pressing the stopcock back into its socket. "I guess it's fast this way." She added, "It's really good."

"May I?" Stuart slid his wineglass over.

"S'il vous plait," said Hal, sliding his over too.

"You basically just chugged wine on an empty stomach," Stuart said as she poured, trying to smile with approval.

"If I don't get sick, I'm going to order some cognac." Which she already planned to do, now that these two were killing her bottle. She wanted to celebrate what she'd just a minute ago heard: Hal saying, to Stuart, "You have a daughter? I do, too. I have a daughter too." Stuart had raised his beer glass to this, and Hal's thought stayed alive long enough for a smiling clink as the two dads shared a look.

"I really hope you don't get sick." Stuart glanced around the dining room as if to calculate that exactly zero people had ever thrown up in here. The loudest noises in this room were occasional titters from someone fumbling their chopsticks, or the soft ding of a seafood timer.

Mel waved at the server.

And there was the music, which was still good. A secular drone. This was—she didn't know who it was. It sounded like synthesized choir, with a gentlest backbeat. No bass. That's what it was. They'd sampled some choir, layered it. Then bent it around, this way and that like warm pulled toffee, nice. You have to love the visceral candy. The warm jets.

"Whose is that?" Hal tapped with his sticks the beige strip that sizzled in front of him. He'd laid it there twenty seconds ago. It was the tenth time he'd asked this question so far in the meal, and with the beer the question was coming easier and faster.

"Yours, Dad. Not done yet." Mel was getting tired of this. "I'll tell you when to flip it, okay?"

Hal threw his hands in the air, palms out. "Jesus take the wheel!"

Stuart, also feeling the beer, threw his hands up too, proclaiming, "Jesus *burnt* my wheel," still on about the chunk of goose he'd let go black on one side.

Hal liked that one. He bobbed with laugher and threw his hands up again. "Jesus blew my mind!"

Then Stuart, almost overlapping him, "Jesus burnt my house down!" and the two men laughed like first-drunk boys.

Stuart noticed too much smoke and giggled, saying, "Whoa, *protein* fire!" and flicked water on a charring piece of meat.

Mel saw off in a shadowy corner a waiter exchange murmurs with the maître d' or owner or someone. It wasn't like they were breaking glass or exposing themselves. Though perhaps that term did apply to her tonight. Five other tables were seated now, a few of them eating. Aware of their table but no one seemed too scandalized. And so what if they were. A tight place like this needed its seams stretched. It occurred to her that the last establishment she'd been asked to leave was also Asian. It had involved Danny at a koi tank, wet to the elbow, pretending he was trying to lift a five-pounder out with his black lacquer chopsticks. He was doing a quick pantomime for their table but he'd already been warned, it was a last straw, he was persistent, drunk, and also on whatever else. Mel, never one to be thrown out herself, had always enjoyed the company of the playful.

Stuart and Hal were going through the food at a workman-like pace. Stuart claimed the goose was his favourite, like mild beef, so Mel asked the granddaughter for another plate of it, and more lamb, which Hal seemed to favour. She'd always been attracted to the arrogance of carnivores. The server spun away on her heel, Mel said "*And*," she spun back, and Mel ordered three cognacs. Hal lifted his empty beer glass and beamed at the server, getting no smile in return.

When the girl spun away a second time, looking put upon, Mel knew she was precisely the kind Danny would have hired, and flirted with. That one waitress—they were called waitresses then—he more than flirted with. Mel felt nothing for that now. Danny meant well. He scrambled harder than most to fill up the silence.

Hal watched her. "Are you not feeling well, there?" He pointed his chin at her wineglass and the chewed food in it, which she hadn't covered well this time. "Why don't you try some of this. It's *very* good." He slid his plate her way an inch. It was smudged with overlapped sauces, and held only the vegetables he hadn't liked. A strip of charred zucchini with a bite out of it. Mel's heart caught in her throat.

"Thank you. I will."

She chopsticked a shiny bok choy lump, dipped it in the hot one, then took it with careful lips, throat already hurting. He'd forget in a moment.

"Are you liking this, Dad?"

He looked around, nodding. "It's a great spectacle," he said, and as if to prove it he went still to watch Stuart turn a sizzling shark cube, which sent out a wisp of white smoke that curled on itself while it rose and disappeared.

He caught her replacing the cloth on her wineglass and wiping her mouth on her hand.

"Are you not feeling well, there?"

She did feel too light from too much wine and she needed to slow things up if there was to be an experiment with cognac. She didn't like the thought of unchewed meat in her stomach. The menu offered a "Korean pho," but an order of soup at this stage of the game might send the granddaughter off the rails. The shark cubes looked best, mashable even when raw. She drew the plate to her and took a cube. When Stuart saw her form it into a pencil shape and break it into two chunks, he looked away. She scooted up against the table then hunched over herself as discreetly as possible. She brought a single chopstick into the mix. In the Charlottes her good friend Kenny, from St. John's, liked to eat and sometimes he'd go all Newf for her pleasure—"I loves the halibut and I loves the moose sausages"—and he'd speak of a mythical "scoggin stick" you push down your throat to tamp down too much food. This chopstick was her fine little scoggin stick, sliding the shark down her tube neck till it disappeared. In her depths she felt a nudge, a rude jostle for position. Umm, my my, that was good. She rolled up another one. Maybe this was what public breast-feeding felt like.

Perhaps to be outrageous himself, Stuart had grabbed the book out of her purse.

"Hal, can I read you something?"

"I'd be grateful if you would."

Hal asked what "text" it was and Stuart ignored him, thumbing through the pages. Stuart was a little drunk. He cleared his throat.

"'Michael looked down. Naomi, up. He knew what was coming. It was a first kiss. Here came her lips, which he could not even think about. Her smell, of almonds, lemon, and earth. She stared at his mouth, her target. Now as their lips touched, and their mouths opened, he was kissing through to the other side of the world, he was kissing uncountable millions of others—yet he was kissing only Naomi. He felt her breath, soft from her nostrils, on his top lip. He opened his eyes. Hers were open already. Irises, brown as wisdom. He could read nothing in them except that he was being read fully. His body was without weight, because they met in the centre of the earth. He felt doomed, yet he would choose this kiss again, and again, and again. He wanted nothing more than to be doomed.' Hal, come on, *yikes*. Do you remember writing that?"

"Of course." Hal, shifting and uncomfortable, stabbed at some grilling lamb.

Mel watched his face. Had she just seen a memory sparked, or had he been thrown by Stuart, something impossible expected of him, like he'd been asked a question in a foreign language. Well, of course, that's what it must be like—she and Stuart speak gibberish to him! She had promised to get him back by nine. He was on a strict meds schedule. "He usually takes his pills nicely," a nurse had told her, with reprimanding lilt, meaning sometimes he didn't. Meaning sometimes he remembered his main vow, not to sin against the light.

Stuart mumbled, "That was quite the kiss, I want one of

those." He thumbed through the book some more, but gave up and put it back into her purse. Mel had an original thought: only a man who'd had a good marriage would go so casually into a woman's purse.

Oh, bullshit. Who knows what's true. It was just another storyline of hers. To go along with her big one. To go along with Stu Price's storyline about wanting a real kiss. Once, Hal told her that the main goal was to stop our storyline about ourselves, and see what's real. Because all of us had storylines going and they were mostly fantasy. It wasn't just the babblers on the street, whose fantasy surrounded them like a halo, it was everyone, we all have versions of ourselves, always. Mel watched her father calmly chew. He had a cow's dumb contentment, much of it coming from the belief that he was in Nepal with a bunch of other seekers, his storyline about as solid as it could get. She hated to think that he had failed utterly, but it sure looked like you needed more than half a brain to stop your storyline. It was awful, really. After all that meditation, to be sunk so deep in fantasy. Deeper than the rest of them. Probably. Maybe he did snap out of it in ways she couldn't see—well of course he did. Or maybe his dreams were real. Maybe there was no real, maybe it's all storyline. Maybe all that can stop a story is a palmful of forest-green pills.

A young man, his fawn suit so linen and perfect it was hard to know if it was business or pleasure, approached their table, hunting the bathroom. Hal looked up, caught his eye, chuckled conspiratorially, and said, "I know!"

Cognac arrived for her to continue her experiment. She rinsed the little teapot with water, poured that into her wineglass, which was half full and looking pretty rugged, then tipped the snifter of cognac into the pot and brought it under the edge of the table. She suspected people might be watching. Certainly the granddaughter. She had the sense of being on stage. She poured, steadily, spilling none. The glow was almost instant. Courvoisier. It felt like the wise brown of Naomi's eyes as she kissed. Beer would have been bloating, and too slow. Wine redundant. Scotch had always confused her. Vodka, she might have sung aggressive songs. And then become suicidal!

"Have we done the meal chants?" said Hal.

Stuart asked her father something and Hal was making some kind of Buddhist confession, about killing, about how he had killed so many fish. She heard "bounty of the sea," and "snagging its nuggets of protein." To Mel's knowledge Hal had never fished. But he was saying, "Nuggets that are so beautiful. Fish are beautiful things. There are brown jewels, and there are grey jewels. I loved loading my boat, dead fish all around my feet. Stiffening and losing colour."

What the hell. And now he jiggled meat from his chopsticks to tell Stuart about the karma of eating meat, about it being fine (he used the word "kosher") for a Buddhist to eat meat if it first passes through three sets of hands, which Mel found false, a passing of the buck if ever she heard one. But she couldn't help listening. She could almost picture pockets of his brain dying as these voluble bursts got rarer and rarer. She savoured his voice itself, the baritone she'd grown up with and loved. Not loved, it was simply Dad, resonating in her chest. It probably fed her, in a way. It was her bedtime story. What was odd about his voice, though, was that, like all deep voices it was the sound of solidity, of roots, of staying put. Not leaving careers and family and flitting to Nepal, chasing Buddhist whirligigs. Mel wondered if people heard his voice and then his wayward story and were thrown by the contrast.

Voices—voices should have been part of her experiment. Or maybe they were. Why did we like certain singers? The velvet fog.

The National were playing again, same song. They were hearing a second loop and overstaying their welcome.

Stu Price, whose voice you instantly trusted, though it wasn't a confident voice. Good-man Stuart. They'd been real friends for a while. As they were again, but it was different, because they were different people, ungainly with passed time. He had the hang of her father, in fact was now engaged in a brief sword fight with chopsticks, both of them deadpan but going at it rather hard. Despite Hal's bun, Stuart looked the more eagerly demented of the two, this schoolteacher who'd shaved his head, an excited, clean-slate look in his eyes, like a kid's. She could read him as damage. A man whose wife leaves and out of silent anger he buys a house and sits down to eat it all by himself.

Mel had the legal details written up two days ago. It hadn't been hard, a will can contain anything, it's all wording. She hoped it would be a nice surprise, even if it was something of a practical joke. He would be legally entitled to remain in the house for as long as Hal lived. There'd be a little cash for food and clothes and upkeep for the car. Also to set up a basement shop "equipped to build the wooden products of his choice, including guitars, either acoustic or bass." This part tickled her. Stuart would cry when he heard this read to him, for sure. When Stuart left Toronto, or when Hal died, whichever came first, the house would be sold, and with the rest of the estate donated to an orphanage in Nepal. Stuart had years in the house, if he wanted them. Hal was a horse.

A missile of yam. A double cognac to chase it. Down the hatch. Now best put a cork in it, so to speak. It was actually sort of a cork! Okay, the granddaughter was on her way over. Be nice.

"Excuse me, but …" The server was bent to her ear, whispering. This was for her only. "Um, I'm sorry, but there have been some complaints."

Stuart, eavesdropping, told her, "Tell me who. I'd like to explain something to them." Stuart sounded friendly, and reasonable enough, even if he looked about as reasonable as a red light when he stood.

Mel put a hand on his wrist and sat him down, apologizing to the Deborah Harry face that Danny would have helplessly flirted with. She was only doing her difficult job. One must think of others. Mel guessed there hadn't been a complaint at all, not actually voiced, not here, it would be more a generic irritation issuing from the diners' shifting bodies, and from the place itself, this shrine of the orderly, quiet, and expensive. It was time to go.

"We'll be going in a sec, if you could just bring the …" Mel told her, miming a signature on her palm, and the server's response before turning away was to briefly meet her eye with sadness and some knowing and the smallest half-smile. Who knew, really, what her life was like.

"It's been a really long day," offered Stuart into the silence when the server had left.

"It has?" asked Hal. "I feel damn good."

"We've done a lot today." He found Mel's eye, and braved what he said next. "And your daughter. She's not feeling well and needs to take care of herself."

"It's taken one second." She found Stuart's eye back. "This

whole thing's taken one second. Poof. It's over. It's unbeliev-able." She enjoyed what she came up with next. "And there's a big trick with time I'm about to do."

Stuart said nothing.

Ignoring their gibberish, professional with his chopsticks, Hal hunted the grill for seared meat stuck to it.

"I'm perky. I had a nap," Mel said, trying to get Stuart to shift gears and smile. He did, and drained his beer, then caught himself and closed his eyes while putting it down.

"Ah, shit. I'm supposed to be driving."

"Taxi. There's no problem." As if to prove it, she signalled the granddaughter, mouthed "taxi," and mimed dialling a phone. The server gave her a thumb's up, Mel's ally now.

There wasn't a problem. There were no problems. There simply weren't.

Hal was standing, looking this way and that. "I need to, hmmm. I wonder if this place has a— Excuse me?" He tried to get the attention of a young Asian woman at the table next to them and she purposely wouldn't look. Stuart rose and took Hal's arm to lead him away.

She watched Stuart guide her father around the tables, the diners' murmurs going silent as they passed. Stuart told Hal some kind of gentle joke and Hal laughed then halted to bow to him, still laughing. A gleam came off both of them. It was like their faces and even their clothing were etched in dark, almost cartoon lines, while flesh and fabric glowed. Even Hal, something about his old, old skin looked fresh and tender, the paleness rich, like pearl. She could see their private colours, or you could say their music, though it was neither of those, and not as grand as a soul. But it was a kind of moving beauty and, yes, the entire room had it. Deborah Harry's granddaughter especially! It was of the same glow she'd had this afternoon before her nap.

She wondered if she could see the world's beauty now because she was leaving. It was heartbreaking to be leaving this beautiful place. Everybody here was perfect. Her thoughts themselves were beautiful, and glowed. She sobbed, once, twice, again, it was delicious. So much heart. Which she could feel too, her heart, its faint beating, it was delicately beautiful as could be, you could injure it just by thinking about it. God, her heart was like a baby. A baby that had grabbed its life but had yet to open its eyes. It was like her baby she had never named.

Stuart was coming back. Mel wiped her cheeks on a fresh cloth napkin.

"You think he's okay in there?" Stuart said. "By himself?"

"I think so. He rarely washes his hands, though. Evidently."

"He's great. He still has his loyal pleasures."

"He does." Loyal pleasures. She liked that.

"This was fun. It worked out okay, don't you think?"

"It's great! We should—" Do it more often. Do it again. Take Hal dancing. Take a taxi. Nothing she did tonight would she be doing again. Everything was a last time, now. Every breath. It was like a wave coming at her.

"—fly a kite!"

"How you doing, Mel?"

She smiled, shaking her head, blinking tears. Drinking was not a good idea.

Because there was no problem. There simply wasn't. There were no problems at all and never had been. Things unfold. She even had a cure for her disease, and this pain. The cure was her clear mind, and October 31st, and the forest-green pills she had at home.

Stuart's hand on her shoulder, clumsy and wonderful. It might be her last human touch. It was dangerous, this lingering in the world. She mustn't be nostalgic. She must not hold on. Not even to seeing with these eyes. Not even to breathing.

October 31st. It should be sooner. It should be sooner, because, if she waited, when the day finally came, when she woke that morning and felt the decision thrust upon her, she might resist. She might panic. She felt a jolt of panic now, knowing what the panic would be like.

"Pardon me, folks," said the granddaughter, at their table in a rush, "but the older fellow's just going into the kitchen?" She stabbed the air and there was her father's back, disappearing through the door, which swung on its spring hinges behind him.

Mel told Stuart that she'd get him. To show the server that there was nothing to worry about, that this was not a situation, Mel calmly reminded her that they were ready for their bill. She rose with grace and aimed herself at the kitchen.

It was a deadly contradiction. *Deadly*. To end it all when you feel at your best. You grow to feel strong and clear about dying, you naturally wonder if you shouldn't live a little longer because you feel so good. To kill yourself, when you're not suffering, to exit on a peak. But that's what had to happen, or it wouldn't happen at all. She had to exit on a peak. Like this one. It needed to be like it was right now. And then she would simply have to do it.

Hal had probably been bowing to the cooks, because one of them was laughing and bowing back while holding a tiny frying pan of bubbling sauce.

"Really," Hal said, a long strand of hair free of its bun and hanging kinked like the wildest musical note, "we're so grateful for your work. We need to free up some time for you to join us in the shrine room."

Mel took her father's arm, and along he came. Out in the restaurant, though he was limping, she leaned on him a little. He took her weight without thinking and she felt that, somewhere in his body, he knew her. And she thought, Oh, what a couple of wrecks.

She needed to go home and sit, and find a time of clarity. Even delight. She needed a wonderful moment. She needed the next wonderful moment, when she might climb in fearlessness.

THE WORLD

Few people come
to this mountaintop;
cranes do not flock
in the tall pines.

One Buddhist monk,
eighty years old,
has never heard
of the world's affairs.

—Chia Tao

He wakes and sees he was thumbing the mala in his sleep, a sign of excellent practice. He's sitting on a bed, wedged in the corner. Doing *tonglen*.

It's hot, he should open that window.

There's something wrong. He's had some sort of brain— He doesn't know what's happened.

He's just here. Fear is extra.

He's sitting on his bed, wedged in the corner. Wiggle things a bit, get comfy. So bright in here, how did he fall asleep? Sitting up! Beads, counting, by habit. There are good habits. It's too hot in here. Maybe that window opens.

Something's wrong. He knows what it is but can't quite— He's just here, the fear is extra. How long he's been doing tonglen he has no idea. On a bed! He feels well-immersed in the mantra. It simply must be done. The suffering of all beings, the poignancy of *that* so heavy in the air, there's really no choice at all, so one does tonglen practice.

It's hot, and he's hungry—he adds this to the practice. He's had some sort of brain injury. Add fear to the practice.

Include everything. He keeps count and it's like a stream of a million little breaths, the world of sentient beings breathing.

She knocks and comes right in, one of the Tibetans who work here. She's not happy with him. Hal thinks she's been in here before with the same message. She's the one with "Leah" written there on her thing, her ornament.

"Mr. Dobbs, you must come now to eat. You miss two meals already."

"No thank you. Please leave." He's hungry, but that's just the small hunger in his body. There's something hanging so black in the air, growling deeply like an invisible bear—he can't miss this opportunity for tonglen.

"You must come now, Mr. Dobbs, or we force-feed and it will be horrible again."

She's not his teacher. She's not even a teacher. "No thank you. Please leave."

She pretends to smile and hums the weirdest little tune as she comes at him. She's pulling his arm but he doesn't give her an inch. She goes for his mala! There's no way he'll ever— She's pulling hard enough to break the string. This was a gift. This is *a sacred object.*

"Please, you'll—" He follows her out the door, or it's more that she's towing him, he won't let her break his mala, the beads are sandalwood, this was *a send-off gift from my wife many, many years ago.*

The hallway is full of people, it's like rush hour, they're all heading to that smell of hamburgers, like sheep, like stiff-legged goats, some are in wheelchairs, what the hell's happening these days, it's— This woman is trying to steal his mala! He takes a little swipe at her big head of hair just as she gives the mala an all-business tug, snapping it, perfect co-emergent action that continues: she yells, curses at him in bizarre language, the mala has broken, and beads bounce, one hundred and eight *ticka ticka tick tick tick ticks* on the hallway floor in every direction. She gave that to him. Rose. *It says I forgive you.*

   Rose.

HE BOWS GRATITUDE to the Tibetan serving them. It's good that they're given most of the jobs here. He thinks he's seen this one before.

   "I just hope we're paying you well," he tells her.

   "I'm union! Is good!" She laughs about money. "But never enough!" She explodes with laughter to tell him it's a joke. Her bronze plaque says "Sally."

   "Well, when is it ever?" He puts his hand on her wrist, gentle as a feather. "Were you born here or did you come over the mountains?"

   "Mountain of Manila!" She laughs again. "Hal you a funny man."

   Tibetans think he's joking even when he's not. They have an excellent sense of humour. He's seen them laugh— He thinks he's seen them cheerful in the most horrendous situations, blood and feces.

   The tuna sandwich is excellent. He's hungry and they don't get a lot of protein here. But what he would love, *love,* is a peanut-butter banana sandwich. He hasn't had one in a million years and it would taste as good as Christmas.

   "You know what? I would *kill* for a peanut-butter and, ah—" It's pretty funny, saying you'd kill for a sandwich in a Buddhist shrine hall. She's walking off, pushing a dolly of food, not laughing at this one.

She says out the side of her face, "We have tuna, we have ham. And you already take a bite."

"*Excuse me* but this soup is too hot to eat." The angry one has erupted and the Tibetan turns back. Hal thought his soup—it's red, it's *tomato*, but it's too white—tasted like dust.

"Vera," says Sally, "if you leave a little bit. To cool down. Eat the sandwich first."

"I'll burn myself. It's too hot to eat."

"Here, I put over here. Let cool." She is infinitely patient, marvellous.

"Take it back. It's too hot to eat."

The server puts Vera's soup on the lower shelf of the dolly and departs. You can see how tired she is. She'll tip the soup bowl outside as an offering to the hungry ghosts. Her English is good, maybe she was born here. But she has the weary look about her of having come over the mountains.

"Would you like my sandwich? I'm not *touching* it."

He tells her, "We should do some prostrations together. Slap our anger right out there onto the ground." He's serious. This woman should do her entire *ngöndro* again, get all that crude stuff out. It's amazing she's stuck it out here this long with that amount of baggage.

"Finish yours and eat mine. I'm not going to touch it."

He wants to practise but he's left his mala somewhere. Go find it.

PEOPLE ARE INNATELY KIND. Everyone, it seems, went looking for his mala beads. Everyone but him! Apparently it broke. They're sandalwood beads, not expensive, but he thinks they were a gift. In any case, he knows them like his own little bones.

He is sitting on his bed and a Tibetan and the little one, Bea, present him with his mala, all put back together.

"It take two days, we still finding these little beads *everywhere*." The one with "Sally" on her thing hands him his mala.

"Thank you so much."

Hal wishes he could remember the neat saying, it went something like, When a Buddha dies it's like a mala breaking, his spirit scattering in one hundred and eight directions to benefit all beings.

"We find four more, so we tie up again. No way we find other one. Is disappeared!" She laughs, like this is a trivial thing. "Just one, though."

He starts counting on it, gets the thumb going, *tries* to get the thumb going, but it sticks. It's broken. The string is sticky.

"My thing, it, it doesn't—"

"We have to use dental floss," she tells him. "Is fine."

No it isn't.

"There's one missing?"

HAL SITS DOWN for lunch with some people he knows. Like him, they've been here a long time, maybe even living here like him, going for it. A Western novice, shaved head, sits beside him, eager, it appears, to make his acquaintance. Maybe last Saturday went well. But watch the pride. This fellow looks immensely sad. Usually these Western monks are too serious, no humour seeps in the cracks because there are no cracks, they're tight from wanting it so much. They think they started too late and now they're blind with hurry. This monk is older than him, he looks fifty. And he needs a haircut. Hal reaches up and fuzzes him anyway. The monk likes it. It does keep everybody humble. But he still looks burdened.

"Hal?"

"That's right." The monk has heard of him. Actually, they've probably met. "But you can call me … Hal." Laugh, please. Lighten up.

"Okay, Hal, I will. I'm Stuart."

"Haven't we met?"

"We have." He adds, "Sorry no one's been to see you in a few days."

"That's perfectly fine."

The monk points to a stack of three shoeboxes. *Cake* boxes. There's also a ghetto blaster on the table. "I brought some special things, for our lunch. Some special treats." He starts opening the boxes and lifting things out.

"I'm not sure we can eat in here."

"No, we can. Look." He points around at the other meditators, who are, indeed, eating at the tables. It's lunchtime. How did he miss lunchtime? He's very hungry. A tray wheels by, and there go some good-looking sandwiches. He calls to her.

"No, Hal?" The monk touches his elbow. "I brought something special, just for you. From your, your daughter. She wanted you to have some."

"Nice!" Look at those fancy hors d'oeuvres. "Will she be joining us?"

"No. She's travelling. She's going to visit as soon as she gets back."

This monk is just not himself. A hidden knot of sorrow.

"Will there be presents?"

The monk feigns levity. "There will be presents."

"She better!"

The monk mumbles something about her also wanting them to hear music while they eat and he punches some wrong buttons on the ghetto blaster, then finds the right one and something jazzy comes on, lots of bass. Something comical about it. The monk turns it up.

"Hal? This," the monk reads from a little instruction manual, "is called 'Forest Floor.' It's mostly cream cheese. In a mushroom cap. It's pretty good. I had one. Yesterday. There. Right. Yes, with your hands." The monk panics. "No, you don't eat the plate, that's just a— Right. Ha ha. Good one." The monk relaxes, he's far too serious. "Actually, Hal, those little plates are made of bamboo."

"Forest *floor*?"

"That's right."

Good name. There's bits of dirt, or twigs. Rosemary? And that was, wow, a whole crunchy thing of pepper. It's good. It's really weird.

There's more in the box. What else. Well—*here's* something you don't often see up in the mountains.

"This one has a funny name too." The monk consults the text. "But Hal? You should probably leave it for last, it's *really* spicy. Burns your mouth up, actually. It's, um, 'Prawns Afterlife.'"

"I'll have one of these, then."

"These are like devilled eggs. They're good. She called them 'Duck Satan.' No, you can eat that. It's a caper."

"I know what it is." It just resembles something disgusting. And tastes like dirty pickle. Rug pickle. Now the monk looks like he's going to cry. Hopefully it's nothing he's said. The new monks can be so homesick. They've left their whole world behind. "Are you all right, sir?" Hal asks.

He has trouble speaking. "She just— She really wanted you to like all this."

"I do." Let's show him how much. How about one of these. A jumbo shrimp, way up here? Can't be fresh. "I really do. And this one's—wow." He has to stand up. "Wow."

The monk is trotting over to the drinks cart.

Hal manages, through white-hot prawn meat, "I'll have th' tomato." He blows in and out like a weightlifter. Wow. But it's good. There's this stuff that grows around here, ghost pepper, which he's never had but would like to try. Out there in the town you do get some good spice, but they don't usually let it in here. One lama called spice "entertainment." Fair enough. But everything coming in the eyes, nose, and mouth is entertainment. The *Vajrayana* is not for prudes. His mouth is *burning*. Poison for the peacock.

"Wow. Okay." He sucks and blows. "Have we done the meal chants yet?"

"Yes. Yes we did. Here." The monk has brought him some cold tomato juice, wonderful, just what he wants.

"Should we do the closing chants?"

"Do you want some more, first?"

"Yes! I'm hungry. What is this stuff?"

"It's from your daughter."

"*Is* it." There's something going on here, something he knows nothing about. He recognizes the music coming out of the little stereo here on the table. It's—

He's had some kind of brain thing.

The fear can go out with the breath.

"So, this one's called—" The monk consults a menu, and smiles for once. "'Mouth Balloon.' It's a partly hollowed-out fig, filled with warm gorgonzola cheese, it's probably not warm anymore, and hidden in the cheese is a— There, taste it? It's a cherry, and inside of that there's a blueberry. It's weird, eh?"

"It is." This is extremely good. He doesn't remember the food here being this good. He should visit the kitchen and thank them. The monk opens another box.

"I know what those are." He takes one up. Celery with the stuff in it, and the raisins. "Ants."

The monk reads the note. "'Ants on a Log,' it says."

"That's right. They're good." Crunch-crunch. He doesn't like them much, never has. "She makes them for her a lot."

The monk nods at him, watching him like he's never seen anyone eat before. So he eats some more. It's very rich. He eats a tiny lobster, they used to call them scampi, maybe, and—*holy cow* it's hot.

The monk has stacked a bunch of little plates, which look to be made of wood.

"Would you like me to read to you?" He punches a button on the little stereo, cutting off a classical piece, slow horns of some kind.

"We'd be grateful." Good thing *he's* not reading. His mouth is burning.

Some others gather and settle. The monk, whom Hal is certain he knows, takes out a worn white book and turns to today's teaching.

"Have we done the closing chants?" It's good to maintain the boundaries. Chaos in a container.

"Yes," the monk tells him.

"Is it storytime?" asks the snarky one.

The monk indulges her. "It sure is!"

Hal wonders what's in those shoeboxes.

Raymond's boat was frighteningly fast as it slapped through the small waves. He shouted over the engine roar, "She actually moves better in chop like this." Raymond, the friend of a friend, was charging fifteen dollars each way to and from D'Arcy Island. He would be picking them up the following noon.

Her hip and shoulder pressed to his, Naomi gazed about her, alert as a seabird. She had twice pointed out the glossy black bowling-ball head of a seal. Reminding Michael of a housewife on an outing, she wore a yellow chiffon scarf on her head, tied under her chin, so cute. Though she had kept to her odd and gloomy path of late, she couldn't hide her excitement at seeing the island. At one point, when she closed her eyes as if to the sheer pleasure of the breeze on her face, Michael could not help but marvel that, if they spent the rest of their lives together, he would know her deeply, better than he knew himself, and yet he wouldn't know her at all. In a way that had not happened before, she made him aware of his utter difference from another human. At first he thought it was racial, and he was ashamed. Then he saw it wasn't that, not at all. It was that he was a man, and she was a woman. They could be no more different. And yet, at the same time, because they were equally obsessed with spanning the gap, the *same* gap—this was called love—they could be no more alike.

Looking at her beside him—his lover, so sweet, so beautiful, so able and aware—Michael reaffirmed his decision. It was a surprise for her. When the book came out, it would have her name on the cover, in the

same font as his. And when she saw the cover, he would
ask her to marry him.

From the beginning, Michael had wanted to go
to the actual site of his research. It could only help
his writing if he knew first-hand the two-hundred-acre
island they referred to as "the World." The slope of the
beach on which they had stood waiting for the supply boat; how the daily low tide smelled; what the
mainland looked like from their own dismal shore;
the stars at night, the wind in trees, the birdsong, everything! And how could all of this not inform Naomi's
work, too? Her poetry of the heart, as she put it.

Michael thrilled as the island grew close and he
could see the tan strip of beach where they would
land. Li, Sang Seen, Quince, Chin, all of them—this
is where they had lived and walked and breathed and
died! He inhaled deeply the scent coming off the
island. It was vital and fresh, salt and pine. Its cleanli-
ness was proof to Michael that even death was mortal,
and left no trace. And in this way, perhaps, all was
forgiven.

Raymond pointed up

"What is there," Hal asks, "to forgive?" He keeps his mala
going, watches the labour of his thumb. Whenever he talks,
it's two things happening at once, a thumb and a tongue. It's
not easy.

"I'm— I'm not sure," says the monk, apparently not in the
mode to field questions.

"Sounds a little Christian, doesn't it?"

"I guess it does. Well, these people who put them there,

they were probably Christian. But the Chinese would have been, um, I don't know."

What is this fellow talking about? He'd only been joking. He should tell the monk the one about sin, that to a Buddhist the only sin is—but how does that one go? Something about guilt. He knew a joke about that.

"The Chinese are *everywhere* now," says the little one. Bea. Bea! What a name!

Through a window, wind blows an orange drape wildly up, so you can see that the other side has lining, white lining sewn to it, probably to keep out the sunlight. On a table someone's paper napkin goes flying. You don't often see a wind in here.

"Should I keep reading?"

"Just read," says an angry one.

"We would be grateful," says Hal. He hefts his mala, bounces it so the beads rattle. Something's wrong with it. It sticks, the string's sticky. Too white. This isn't the one she gave him. It barely works.

The sad fellow starts reading.

Off in the distance, in some room, someone yells, a pure plea to it, rough and from the guts and then garbled, as if muffled. It would have been comic, overacted agony, had it not sounded serious. What's there around here to yell about?

Raymond wouldn't let his boat touch bottom, not even sand, and Michael and Naomi had to get wet to the knees. Naomi pulled up her stretch pants, but Michael couldn't get his jeans over his calves and they were soaked, his only pants. He should have just taken them off, shoes too, but for some reason things became hectic at the shore, as if things had to happen quickly. Raymond handed down their tent, sleeping bags, food bin, a one-burner stove. When Naomi whispered, "We should throw a pebble in and make him scream," Michael didn't know quite how to take it.

He knew it was natural to feel at least a little forlorn as they watched the boat depart, and shrink, and finally disappear. And now there was nothing but them, and the island.

Up in the trees they found the campsite, which was three small clearings for tents, and a single outhouse. No water, no picnic tables. The outhouse, despite the camping season being long over, smelled. Without speaking they walked to the clearing farthest away from the outhouse and dropped the gear. Michael eyed the bundled tent. He had planned, while erecting it, to make a joke, a romantic joke, about Sang Seen and Li's "mansion," but it didn't feel quite right. Everything felt very different, actually being here. He felt cautious, and compelled to move quickly and quietly, as though the trees were watching, absurd as that was. But Naomi looked tentative as well, even shy, as she cleared twigs from their sleeping site.

He went to an adjoining site to drag over a make-shift table, roped-together driftwood. He also wished he could have shared an odd thought with her: on smelling the outhouse he'd felt embarrassed, as if a smelly outhouse had something more to do with him than with her; that is, more to do with men than with women. He sensed it was something he could tell Naomi, and she would find it funny, or at least interesting. He had never known a woman he could have shared that with. It would also be something of an apology, though for what, he didn't know.

It was fun setting up a tent, as it always is. They chose to have the tent-mouth face the fire pit. It felt as if they were creating a soft and warm place not just to sleep but to make love. It was almost more than he could bear to watch: on her knees, wearing her little kerchief, with smooth expert flicks Naomi unfurled the mats and sleeping bags—there was something alluring in the efficient determination of a young woman building a nest. Had she done this before, with someone else? He didn't want to think so.

When the tent was up they walked the hundred yards down the beach to the lazaretto site, evident only for the several foundation stones and mound of stones from a hearth and chimney. The sizeable garden in behind had been reclaimed by alder trees, and black-berry wherever the sun penetrated. That seemed to be it. Which was a bit disappointing. Though what had he expected to find? Anything wood would have rotted back to earth, and anything usable or curious would have been looted. He turned to face the water. Across Haro Strait was the Saanich Peninsula, and over that hump of hills, Victoria. At least he could see what they saw, smell what they smelled. They must have stood and stared in the direction he was staring now. Planted on their numb feet. He tried to imagine having no feeling below the knees. How long before their hope numbed and died, too?

"Maybe if we dug around a bit," he said to Naomi,

who stood a little behind him, "we might find an opium pipe or a fork or something."

With an intensity that startled him, she whispered, "Don't." She had her eyes closed and head down. It looked like she might topple.

"Are you all right?"

She asked if they could please just go hiking through the woods.

"Let's." He took her hand. Maybe he would find where Li's tin was found.

They walked and walked. Two hundred acres could take a long time to circumambulate when paths were non-existent or wound mindlessly around trees. Sometimes the trail took them to rock outcrops near the water's edge, where they could enjoy a vista.

"It's beautiful," Michael repeated, at one point, unsure if Naomi heard, because she didn't answer. She still didn't. They were standing on a ledge of sandstone the size of a porch, backed by a lovely, contorted arbutus whose bark was dropping its orange layer and showing green. In front, a calm little bay. It was *beautiful.* Michael grew angry.

Then he remembered the thought he'd had last night, when they were making love. They were just used to it now and things were entering a phase where he could see a possible pattern. Things they liked, things they would do for each other. Last night, in the middle of it, Naomi revealed a disturbing side. Lying beneath him, her body enjoying their movement, her eyes were on his but appeared to be focused on something that had nothing to do with *him.* He wanted to ask, Who are you fantasizing about? But he didn't have to. What he saw, and understood as clearly as he understood a pie, was that Naomi was fantasizing about a Michael Bodleian that he *wasn't.*

"Naomi. I'm saying they had a beautiful place to live. I'm *not* saying they had an easy time of it."

"Most could not even walk here. Their world was that little grassy place."

"I'm not saying that wasn't the case. I'm saying that you and I can still appreciate things." He fought his anger. The entire walk he had been looking for a spot to stop her, and kiss her, leading to unquenchable passion up against a tree. While the wind

The little one has turned to him and says matter-of-factly, "They do that in Scotland. Up against a tree."

"*Do* they," he says.

"Or a wall," she says. "It all depends on where you live."

"In Scotland." Bea has interrupted something serious. A fight. Li.

"No. If you live in the city, or not in the city."

"Ah."

The monk has been waiting patiently. Hal smiles an all-clear to him.

While the wind, the drizzle, cools them. My God. But it didn't feel like this would happen now.

A thought came to him. "We can appreciate things even *more* because of them. The contrast. Our *luck.*" He didn't know if what he said next was true, but he said it anyway. "We *owe* it to them to see beauty." And the next, which felt lecherous even while saying it: "We owe it to them to have a good time."

Without a word, Naomi put a hand under her sweater and rustled with something. For a hopeful second Michael thought she might be wrestling the sweater off, unlikely as that would have been. Instead, she removed some folded paper, the same unlined paper she used for her translations.

"I want to read you what I didn't show you last time."

"Why didn't you show it to me?"

"I needed to work on it more. I was unhappy with it."

"You took it home with you?"

"And it bothered me. What it was saying." She wouldn't look at him. He saw that she had been crying.

"Part of our arrangement, a *big* part, was that everything remain at my … *None* of this can be seen until …"

Naomi simply began to read. Because of the breeze he had to strain to hear her. A keen interest took over and he leaned in.

A morning came that took me by surprise. When Sang Seen appeared at my door early, I was happy to see him, as always. His big quiet face, his face a map with almost no lines, a map I had to guess at, but could do it endlessly, because he had secret depths. I was grateful. This morning he took my arm and led me away from my mansion, my heart. He led me not to the common garden but to the area of private plots, and he told me I had to

work in Toy's garden today. His face showed nothing new
as he instructed me. I was to pick slugs, then thin seed-
lings, then hoe. And then my next job was in the garden
of Chin.

I did not know what to think. I was used to doing
certain chores in the common garden, finger work that
the others found difficult. And sometimes in the private
plots, too, if the owners asked me nicely, or offered trade.
But this was different. I did not know what to think. I
worked all day, and when Sang brought my food out to
the garden for me to eat it there, it meant I was to remain
there working.

A week passed this way. I did not know what to do.
In the middle of the week I tried refusing to work in the
garden anymore, and though Sang did not hit me, he
reminded me of all he had done for me, and I felt miser-
able, so I returned to work. I still did not know what to
think, but trusted that I would understand, or that it
would soon end.

At the end of that week, my new wooden door came
on the boat. Sang and another, Fon, whose lips have
thickened in a way that they are cruelly bent up into an
oversized and permanent smile, carried the door to my
house and, with my help, fastened it to the frame with
simple iron hinges, which also came. When the job was
done, I laughed, and told Sang Seen thank you, and
wanted him to lie with me in warm friendship, as we
had that day under the cedar boughs, but this time in an
actual house, of which we could both be proud. Sang told
me I was most welcome, in a formal way, speaking in a
voice so soft that I could hardly hear him. Nor could I

see his eyes. I had put the hammer and nails and metal square back in the tool bag so they could be carried, and I handed the bag to Fon, and I thanked him as well, hoping that just he would leave. But they both left. I missed Sang even as I watched him go out my door. So I called out.

"Sang!" I said. "The mansion is finished!"

Not turning to look at me, Sang Seen said, "Stay there." And he closed the door behind him.

I still did not know what to think. Nor do I know why I noticed it then, but as soon as Sang left, I saw that my new door did not have a lock.

I spent a quiet hour by myself, in my finished home. I tidied up what was already tidy. I swept what didn't need sweeping. I filled my lamp to the brim with oil. I opened my door, looked out and down the hill, closed it again, opened it and looked down the hill again. It was when I opened it maybe a fourth or a fifth time that I saw him, Lung Toy, coming up the hill. I still did not completely understand.

Though I closed the door to keep him out, he came in anyway, and then he closed the new door behind him. I called and called for Sang, and Lung Toy said, "Sang will not be coming."

Now I understood. And Lung Toy was not the only man to come up the hill that day.

To any who read this, a warning. Love must be dragon-eyed.

When Naomi finished reading she was no longer crying. Michael didn't know how to respond to what he had heard. He hugged her, and she let him.

"Well that," Michael said, "is a *sad* section. A bit of a shock." It was clear now, Naomi's mood. Li had become her friend. It was understandable. And it seemed as though Li's sometimes uplifting tale, as surprising as that was, had taken an awful turn. It would also mark a turn in his own work, because this new information would demand another angle in his writing, of gender and power politics, and it would ask a certain delicacy of him.

They made their way back to the campsite, taking the most direct route. It was time to eat in any case. Michael had made some chili to bring and heat up. They could talk when Naomi wanted to. As it stood, he would let her be in mourning for Li, as it were. There was no strategy for lightening the mood other than being there for her. He did want to remind her that their entering the life of a leper colony was never going to be a bowl of cherries, was never not going to be painful, would be by its very nature excruciating, but now of course was not the time.

"It certainly wasn't," says Bea.

He hadn't been paying attention and he wondered what the matter was now. He'd forgotten where he was. In fact, he— He has some sort of brain injury. And his hip hurts, so much. But he's ... just here. Fear is extra. Maybe it was a car accident. Did he crash Rose's car? No. Was Melody all right? *No.* There's something wrong with Mel.

The monk is eyeing him with patience. Not patience. He's considering something. He's staring at him pretty hard.

"Hal?" the monk asks.

"Here." He raises his mala.

"I'm actually reading this for you."

Singled out. Watch the ego. "Thank you."

The angry one stands up already walking. "I don't think so."

"Hal. Does 'Bengali tea boy' mean anything to you?"

Bengali tea boy. He makes you see yourself.

"Of course."

Bea asks, "May I stay?"

Hal rises to give her his chair. He doesn't know why—she has a chair of her own. So he says, "Let's trade chairs." And she does, pleased. His hip is hurting like hell.

At the campsite, Naomi gruffly insisted on doing the work of lighting the stove and reheating the chili. In a tinfoil bag was a small loaf of pre-made garlic bread to warm up.

Still feeling somehow blamed, Michael wandered to the gravel beach below. He kicked a rock over and watched tiny crabs scatter to find new holes in which to hide. Did the lepers eat these creatures? If it was protein, the Chinese ate it. But how would they catch them with their useless hands? And how would they prepare such a thing? A stew of crunchy spiders?

Naomi was cheerful enough when he came up for dinner. They laughed lightly at the picture they made, sitting far too low on their log for the table, which came up to Michael's neck and Naomi's nose. They ate the chili out of plastic bowls, in their laps.

"Wow, can you imagine, Naomi, boiling up some

crab here? How good that would taste? Do you like crab?"

"Yes."

"I had it once at a beach party where you just throw the shells back in the ocean and wash your hands."

"Mmm." And then she said, "Chili is Mexican food, but not Spanish?"

"I think that's right."

"Is there any Canadian food?"

"Um. That's funny. I'm not sure. It's probably all European, somehow."

"No, there is."

"Oh, so it was a test!" Michael reached over to squeeze her knee.

"There is a meat pie in Quebec. There is a maple sugar pie as well, and there are several dishes made with moose meat."

"I've never had moose. Have you?" At least she was talking again. Her odd grammar he usually found sweet, but it sometimes made him restless.

"Yes, I had moose sausage, in the North. The article I read, it also made an argument that apple pie was first made in Canada."

Michael pointed to the eagle sitting on the same snag where it had been for an hour at least, off on the farthest point. He told her that, speaking of apple pie, American tourists were often disbelieving and sometimes it seemed even a little angry at all the eagles up here, as if Canada had taken their national birds.

Naomi whispered, "Shan ying."

"Is that …?"

"Eagle, yes."

"In …?" He didn't have to say "old Cantonese."

Naomi nodded.

They finished eating and, without a word, Michael did the dishes. Few as they were, it took a while. He hunched at water's edge trying not to get his shoes wet again as he scooped gravel and scant sand onto them to scour. He had heard this worked, but even after a long time hard at it, everything came away greasy and disgusting. And he had fingers.

"I'm going to help," the little one says, and she gets up. Bea. You can hear plates and pots banging faintly up the hallway. Bea likes kitchen duty apparently.

"Bea," says the monk, flipping the page, "we're almost at the end of the chapter."

"Keep going," says Hal. He must have drifted off. But he remembers this part, he knows what's coming. He hates tents. Sleeping on a mat too thin to cushion your weight. And the smell of yourself in the morning.

And—he got caught. Rose said, *I know about your little camping trip.*

"I can skip ahead a bit." The monk scans, flips another few pages forward.

Hal says, "Please read it." He doesn't want to miss anything. Even though he hates this story.

They failed to make a fire, burning all the newspaper but nothing else. Handling the wood, he could feel how damp everything was, and soon it was hopeless. A fog had begun rolling in, and a breeze. It got cold even to sit on their log.

"The tent might be warmer," Michael said.

"Yes," Naomi agreed, and wasn't that a slight smile? And wouldn't you know but she rose and took his hand and let herself be led to the tent, at whose mouth she stepped in front and drew down the long zipper. He had been dreaming of this moment, had lived it again and again.

Inside, on her knees, she took off her coat. She made comically loud shivering noises—just like a Westerner, he thought—but then climbed into her sleeping bag fully clothed.

This was fine—it was only early evening. He climbed into his as well, leaving his arms out, as had she. He slid an arm over so their outer wrists touched, even though the mood in the tent was palpably one of talking rather than touching.

"What is 'dragon-eyed'? Li said love must be 'dragon-eyed.'"

"Li is poetic."

"Is 'dragon-eyed' a single character?"

"'*Love* must be dragon-eyed' is a single character."

"That's kind of amazing."

"Yes, and it means three things."

Michael waited.

"It means wise. It means to penetrate. And it means … lucky."

Michael told her that dragons sounded like formidable creatures.

"Dragons are best."

"Naomi," he told her, softly, not feeling overly ashamed, "I think that *we* are the best."

"Yes," she said, but she was passive to his moving closer, to his climbing onto an elbow so that he loomed above her. In the tent it was already hard to see.

He descended for a kiss. His lips an inch from hers, she averted her face and calmly stated that it would be a cruel insult if, while here, they enjoyed something that the lepers had been unable to enjoy themselves.

No, what was being cruelly insulted was his fantasy of Naomi and him in a tent. How was it possible that she would not make love, she who was always eager to make love, she who humbled Michael in her hunger.

Michael flopped onto his back, groaning, not caring that he sounded like a frustrated boy.

"Michael, I'm sorry. But … I have to ask you again, to promise me that you won't try to publish a book about this place."

Michael blinked on his pillow, which, like hers, was a folded towel.

"Okay, so what am I supposed to do with it?"

"Write your book, yes, but people must not read it!"

Michael told her that was absurd and impossible. He had hardly begun to list the reasons when he heard her crying. Her shoulders jerked and rustled the nylon.

He didn't know what to do. He knew the night he had dreamed about was almost certainly over before it began. So, he decided to tell her.

"It's too late."

She went rigid and fell silent for him to say more.

"I've already sent it out in its unfinished form to several publishers."

"No, Michael." And then, "You can ask for it back before—"

"This was some time ago. I've heard from two publishers, Naomi. They're both excited. Naomi—" He climbed back onto his elbow. "It's that good. I think there's going to be a small auction. For an academic book? Are you kidding? A bidding war? Naomi?"

He couldn't hear her breathing. The breeze had grown to wind, and its rush through D'Arcy Island's treetops was an oddly knowing music.

"I didn't want to say anything because I didn't want to jinx things."

"You can't."

"Naomi, I can."

Some hard silence, and then the awful "But, do you love me?"

"*Yes!*"

"And, Michael," she said, pronouncing it 'Myco,' sounding like a child from across an ocean, "wouldn't you do anything for me?"

"No. I wouldn't kill myself if you asked me to, and I wouldn't kill this book either, because both would be very bad for my life."

They fought, Naomi resisting any hint of good sense. She returned again to claims not just of ethics but of curses, a craziness Michael tried to approach gently, but which mostly angered him. It was impossible to abuse people one hundred years dead. And if no one else was going to tell their story, why shouldn't he?

Naomi shouted, whimpered, and begged. Craziest of all, she told him a joke, about lepers, which wasn't funny. She was trying as hard as he was to win, if not harder. At one point, not thinking too highly of himself, he considered giving in to her demands and then enjoying the grateful love that certainly would follow—then in the morning having a tragic change of mind. But he couldn't do that. Then, her smaller body resting beside him, for the briefest moment he even imagined forcing himself on her, wondering how she might respond if he were more insistent, not violent, just insistent, his hands strong and irresistible. This notion died quickly, withering in the harsh light of what Naomi had read to him today at the other end of the island. How absurd and ruinous it would be if his own actions were even to hint at Li's treatment in her new prison.

Exhaustion conquered Naomi first. He lay beside her, listening to her breathe, then went on an elbow again to watch her, to see her aching beauty, but it was too dark. He could no longer see her. For the first time, tears came. How was it possible, that the two best things to happen to him in life—Naomi, and this book—were now enemies, were somehow trying to cancel each other out?

In the morning, though she joked about their breakfast of cold garlic bread, Naomi remained weird. Even her posture leaned out of tune, though she pretended to enjoy herself. He could see that she was spooked, simple as that. Never once did she glance toward the lazaretto.

Michael felt no ghosts. He felt no censure coming from the land or the trees. Not that he particularly liked the place. It was no source of pleasure imagining anyone imprisoned and living out their life here, let alone dying a slow, horrible death. For some reason, he couldn't shake the image, the *feel*, of last night's greasy dishes. Their dead hands, slick with grease, and often blood. And the latrines, and no bathing—he couldn't think about this. At one point, while they waited for Raymond's boat, it started spitting rain and blowing, and it was chillier than any September should be. Michael commented that it was such a cold, grey place, and Naomi cried, "That's it! It's what I've been saying."

"What have you been saying."

"These rocks, they sucked hell up, like a sponge."

Michael thought, my goodness. "It's just weather, Naomi."

"It's no different. They were the weather too."

He would not let her delusions scare him. In any case, he had no answer for this. But as if she had just offered up enough evidence and proved her point, she took both his hands in hers, looked up at him with sweetness and what resembled long-suffering patience, and said, "So. Can you please stop this book? Can you do it for me?"

He held her gaze. Her face shifted and twitched, searching for another strategy. Tears welled, and from one eye fell. With her kerchief on, and her Chinese face, she looked unknowable. She looked possibly insane.

Unbelievably, she tried a smile next. She said, "We will have a long life together, and I will help you with lots of books."

"No."

"Michael. Please. You don't understand. I—"

He spun away from her. It was his turn to be the child. He wanted to wander off and sulk. But he stayed put and sulked on the spot. She stood behind him. Raymond's boat was buzzing in the distance.

What she said next froze him. It showed a direction in which she might be heading. Standing behind him, she said, "You can be a better man than this."

They waited as the boat grew louder. Their shoulders were a foot apart, but it could have been the entire island. The boat came in; Raymond cut his engine. Naomi said something else. Michael wasn't sure if he was meant to hear, but what he heard was, "I loved you too much and now we're in trouble." His stomach fell, even as he caught Raymond's tossed rope. His stomach fell further as he helped Naomi tread the slippery rocks. Because now he understood that what he had heard was, "And now *you're* in trouble."

The monk closes the book, finished for the day, and Hal says, "It's so sad we can't trust people."

"Why do you say that?"

"We're too complicated!"

The monk gives him a goofy, patronizing look and Hal realizes he isn't a monk at all. Now he doesn't know where he is, or anything else for that matter. Mel will tell him. *Mel should be here.* The hip, it hurts, but it doesn't feel that bad, he should be leaving this place. He's sitting here with— Who are—?

He's just here. Fear is extra.

He gets up to look for someone he knows.

HAL STANDS, PEERING AMAZED at this old man here in this, this big window, who might be his father, but then what wakes him up is a little monster in the corner.

It's like he was sleepwalking—it's a nice bathroom, warm and it doesn't smell, even though it lacks incense burners. But there behind the toilet, in the corner, a little … *thing*. What the hell is it? It's wedged headfirst into the corner, curled like a little tan turd, horrible. It looks like a leech gone pale. He can't see eyes. He needs to use the toilet, badly, needs to sit on it, but if he does he'll have his back to the thing, it'll be right behind his foot. It's probably not even alive. But if it is, he wants to be able to see its intention.

He sits, not pulling down his pants. His pyjamas. He can't sit here, it's right behind his bare ankle. He should just find another bathroom. But, so, where is this?

There's a hairbrush. He could mash the thing with it. He lobs it gently, misses. The thing doesn't even move. It's a demon catching its breath. It's escaped Diagonal Hell and is having a restorative nap. He *really* has to use the toilet. He's in his PJs, he can't just go out and find another bathroom dressed in this.

It's too hot in here, it needs a window on the mountains. No wonder there's a thing living in here, it's like the tropics. And it *stinks*.

Kathmandu was like this too at first, though you got used to it, up in the mountains, dry, but it smells too human. Corpse-of-food. Worst-of-human.

Walk. Can't even out-walk the smell! His bathrobe's open and he can't— He should go back to bed. Wherever that is.

In the hall, one of them, "Leah" says her thing, her banner, she has him by the arm soft but hard, turning him back into this doorway.

"You're Tibetan," he finds himself saying.

"Right you aren't." Leah's lips hard and showing teeth, mouth a smile in name only. "In here, Mr. Dobbs, you have a little accident, we get you cleaned up."

Leah whispering this so others won't hear, though some are looking at him, the hall is crawling with them, it's like rush hour out here, wheelchairs galore, striders in the passing lane. He must have missed the lunch gong.

A gal, not bad looking, in her nightgown carrying a purse. Is she in for a shock!

"In here, Mr. Dobbs."

"There it is! Look!" He points, won't take another step.

"Here!" The woman stoops beside the toilet, pinches up the monster. "Is just nut! Is peanut!" She thrusts it in his face, victorious and angry.

"It's a cashew."

"Is just nut!" The hard smile. Could be she's a nun who lived in the city and has come back, dragging insincerity with her.

"I'll flip you for it," he says, at which the hard woman tells him to stay put and then simply leaves. Whose fault is it when a Tibetan doesn't get your joke?

It smells. Everything smells like shit.

Good cashew, though. He taps his pockets for more—he's
in a bathrobe!

IT'S—

A roomful of steam. On a chair. Naked. Scrubbed, pulsing
with blood. Naked. No mala. Mantra falls away on the breath.

On a chair. See through floating steam.

Still.

Unchangeable, glory.

It's gone. When words come, it's gone.

A PLATE OF FISH STICKS. He's starving. He likes fish sticks,
always has. So does Melody, though she demands ketchup.

He didn't hear the gong but here they all are and thank
God. The secret to fish sticks isn't ketchup, it's—

"Excuse me? Do we have— Um, to, you know, for the fish?"
He mimes squeezing the yellow thing. Wedge. *Lemon.*

Fish, it's the best—if you're going to eat living beings, it's
the best. They have the nervous system of an insect, not much
pain felt. Or fear. Fear is pain. We forget this until we're afraid.

Hal asks a Tibetan if he can please have one of those, on
that table, right there, that red, that bottle—

"Ketchup, Mr. Dobbs? Certainly."

Best to eat these with the hands. Mmm. He went lake
fishing, as a boy. With his dad? *Sunfish.* Blue, orange, yellow.
And there was a black-grey fish, called a crappie. A black-
grey jewel. He was told to bonk it, so he did. A sawed-off oar
handle, painted sky blue but crusted with dark brown from
a summer's dried blood. That crappie's eye got smashed. So

he wouldn't bonk the sunfish, which choked to death on air instead, flapping tired around their feet. The beautiful colour fades when they die. A light goes off inside. The man called them panfish. That's how they were cooked, whole in a frying pan. Lots of little bones. *And these come with their own toothpicks,* his dad joked, something you know he'd heard, he never made up his own jokes. But good fish, when you're hungry. When you aren't hungry, ketchup helps. In Victoria he never took his daughter fishing, though he had the chance there and she was just old enough and it's what dads do. He should still take her! She loves to eat fish. She'll eat anything. They'll make a meal with spices, Moroccan, poblano, anything, watch to see if she'll eat it. Always does.

"Mr. Dobbs? Cake or jello."

"Both!"

"You know the rule."

He was joking, he was joking. "Snake." Oops. "Case."

She slides some cake under his face. It'll be dry probably.

"You eat Vera's lunch again! A miracle you not fat!"

"He *always* eats it," says the angry one.

"My brain's gotten fat."

"Ha ha!" She kindly slides him a cake spoon, too.

"He should *pay my rent.*"

"Or someone bonked me." He mimes getting clubbed with a sky-blue bonker.

"Ha ha!"

This is good cake. Chocolate, with cherries hiding in the middle line. Whipped cream. Sprinkles. It's black cake. Black floor.

"Hello, Hal, it's Stuart."

"Well of course it is! Sit down!"

"Thanks."

"No, here, I want to fuzz you!"

"I shaved it again. Just for you." The monk comes at him full bow and he fuzzes the spectacular head. All shaved heads are spectacular. Humiliated and bulbous, especially the women.

"I'm afraid of your shirt," he tells the monk. He meant to say "*brown* shirt," because it's the dark brown of blood that's dead and dry.

He misses someone. He missed that one who lived here all his life, but died. His name— The lanky clown, he'd fuzz every new shaved head, even a visiting lama, while everyone else stood stooped and worshipful. One of those crazy wisdom guys with no boundaries. He actually died, yes *he died*, he was way older than he looked. Chirden! Chirden, with his weird jazzy tunes of whistles, snapping fingers, and sometimes farts, but not to be funny. And the stagy smile after a tune. It reminded you of some old vaudeville thing, it really did, though vaudeville would be something Chirden had no clue about. The story was he became a monk as a young boy, no choice in the matter, and never took to discipline, or Buddhism at all if truth be told, but he had nowhere else to go. He wore robes the colour of liver, dead dried blood. Hal misses him. His name—Chirden!

OUTSIDE THE DOOR, it's crisp and cold, a lovely day. A monastery compound, with a manicured path weaving artfully through ornamental bushes. It looks more Japanese than anything else. He's pushing a wheelchair with an old lady in it. His hip hurts and he gets to lean down on the handles, though it's slow going this way. He tries to tell the old lady that he's also using her chair, but the words don't come out right.

"What?" It's the angry one he's pushing. What's she doing in a wheelchair.

"Nothing. Why are you in this?"

"It's *you*," she says. And then waves him away like he's an idiot.

"What?"

It's hard negotiating this tight curve while leaning so he eases off, and has to limp. His side hurts like hell. But pain—is extra.

He has a scarf around his neck, pulled up over his mouth. Here's that smell of wet wool and your breath coming back at you. It's the taste of walking to school. He's not heading to school now but he's been on this path before. He should watch where he's going, because now he's plowed the old lady's legs into some bushes and she isn't happy.

"It's fine," he tells her, but she's busy yelling. "I'll just go this way." He tries to back up, but it's difficult. A front wheel is jammed sideways.

"No, Mr. Dobbs, that's not for you to do." A woman, a teacher, has him by the arm, doesn't want him manning the chair apparently.

"Vera? Vera, calm down? I'll take her, now. Thank you." And off they roll.

He sits on a bench. They're here for people to sit and practise. But he's alone, it seems. It feels almost like winter. He sucks on his scarf. It's wet and the wool taste is scratchy and its smell is so familiar. He unwinds his mala from his wrist.

A teacher pushes up an empty wheelchair.

"Mr. Dobbs! This is supposed to be yours!"

"It is?"

A hand under his arm and he manoeuvres into the wheel-chair. Sometimes he likes these things. Takes the pain away. And wherever you go, here's a chair.

He's handed a steaming cup. It's perfect, how did they know? It's—brown, sweet. Hot. Burns the tongue a little, always does! Cold out, winter, a cup of— This.

THE MONK SHOWS UP just in time for lunch. He's staring at him like he's sprouted antlers or something. These sandwiches are good. Tuna or salmon. When it's canned you can't always tell which. Come to think of it. It's the mayo that makes it good, let's admit it. And the— The little crunchy green bits. The long, green stuff. You spread peanut butter in the hollow part. Plus raisins. His daughter calls it ants on a log.

A bug-eyed man approacheth.

"What happened to your hair?"

"Hmm. Well." He fuzzes himself up top. Nice fresh little crewcut. The guy is starting to scare him. "It's—"

"Hal. Who cut your hair?"

How should he know? Mr. Scissors.

"Did you *want* it cut, Hal?"

"Well of course I did." Why wouldn't he?

"Of course he did," says Bea, helping him out.

"Your hair was *beautiful.*"

"Well, thank you."

"Oh, it was," says Bea, all concerned, helping the other guy now.

The guy looked mad enough at *him* but he's more mad at someone else now because off he stomps, asking hair questions to any Tibetan name tag he sees. Hal hears a loud *How dare you* and *daughter not here to protect him* and *in homage to his teacher.* All rather dramatic. Must be some bad haircut! It's true he's had one, though. His, back here, his *neck* does feel awfully cold, come to think of it. He fuzzes himself again. Maybe next haircut he'll go the whole way, go the monk route, ask for the holy pig-shave. Except that it's cold in here.

The monk returns, hot under the collar. Hal will do some tonglen for him. He readies his mala. Which is sticky and fumbly these days. Awful. He can hardly count, and loses count. Maybe it's his thumb. Sticky thumbage.

The monk sits down hard. "Anyway. Phew. I'm pissed off. Sorry."

"Just let it go."

"Okay. Yes. I will." He takes a deep breath.

"Sit up straight and things clarify. It's automatic."

"Okay. Anyway. Hal?"

"No. Straight. It's a physical thing. It works."

But he sits up too straight now, and mindlessly.

"Would you like me to read to you?" Still angry, he pulls out his favourite scuffed old book.

He'd better say yes! "We'd be most grateful."

"And there's all four of us today." The angry one approacheth. There should be another body here.

"We're happy if you are."

His mala is already in his hand and he starts practice. It sticks, his thumb can hardly do it. *Om mani padme hum* for his dying thumb.

The monk settles in with the book. Finds his place. He reads

I have a plan.

The monk interrupts himself to tell them, "This is Li. She's a leper, trapped in a leper colony on an island. She's been betrayed by her, um, boyfriend. Sang. And she's being attacked. By the men there."

Hal knows this.

"That's horrible!" says the little one beside him. She's outraged. Bea. She's outraged but not really, she knows it's a story. Hal touches her arm. He doesn't much care for this story either. It sickens him, though it's a parable. But he hates what happens. He actually feels queasy.

"So," continues the monk, "Li has a plan."

> One of the more able men, Sulong, would often brag that he was a sailor and that he could build everyone a boat and sail them away from the World, and he would end his boasts by saying that the only thing preventing him from doing this was that there was no place for them to go. No city would have them, or farm, or job site, or army. Even if a compassionate family took pity and housed one of us we could never venture outdoors, for if we were spotted we would be returned here or more likely shot. So wasn't the World the only place for us? His listeners had already grunted and turned away.
>
> In any case, Sulong made halfway good on his bragging this week when he built a sailing trap for crabs. Up till last year, those few men who were able would tread underwater rocks to the depth they could manage, then toss the weighted cedar-strip cage a little farther, but it would usually not reach a depth that would produce

crabs of good size. Sulong's invention was a little raft
rigged with a sail. The crab trap sat balanced on the
edge of the raft. Both raft and trap had a length of twine
attached. When the breeze was blowing offshore, Sulong
launched his vessel and let it reach the end of its twine,
in deep water, perhaps fifty yards off, at which time he
would give the raft twine a mighty jerk, toppling the trap
over the edge, where it sank. He leaves the trap, baited
with dead rockfish, submerged for an hour, at which
time he drags it in. To do this he ties the twine around
his waist and limps into the trees, pulling like a mule.
The first day, checking four times, he produced fifteen
fat, meaty crabs, and numerous small ones which, after
making bets and setting up a racecourse for them, were
released on land. (Because of this festival of crabs no one
was much interested in me, and Sang Seen allowed me
to come down and see all of it. I had not seen an honest
human smile in weeks.) Sulong would have caught more
except that on the fifth check the trap snagged on the
bottom, and two more men joined his pulling, and the
twine broke. Still, tonight Sulong is a hero, and indeed a
sailor of great skill and renown. While the crab boiled, he
was already at work building a new trap.

　　The crab feast was wonderful. And so simple even
for the likes of us to prepare: boil sea water in a giant pot
then throw in creatures the size of a pie. No fear of being
pinched, though Lung Toy lost the tip of his smallest
finger, which did not hurt, but might mean future infection and rats in the night, so he smashed the scuttling
author with his boot and kicked the mess out the door
and off the porch. Several of us with good enough hands

struck the cooked legs and claws with pieces of firewood, cracking but not smashing them, and most everyone could use a twig to poke out the meat. As we bent to the task of eating, one could hear moans and little gasps of pleasure. I noticed that some of us soon turned from the meat and ate for a while the crabs' own dark green food in its guts—we have no more leafy greens but cabbage this late in fall and the body knows its needs. The guts tasted good, like cooked and mashed kale, already salted, not too fishy.

At one point we could hear the small young man, Chen, quietly weeping. He is the newest one besides me. I assumed he wept for joy, or perhaps remembering his mother's kitchen. But he pushed his crab away and shouted at it, and when asked what his damn problem was he said nothing at first, and then, when pressed, he said that his food had tricked him. When pressed further Chen told us all that the crab had bewitched his tongue and made him forget where he was and what the world had done to him.

But it was during this feast that I arose out of my own food dream and thought of Sulong's skills, and that he was the one to help me build a boat. Even a raft with a sail. If his question for me is, "Where are wooden planks?" my answer will be, "I sleep inside dozens of them." If his question is, "How would Sang let such a thing happen?" my answer would be, "I will feign illness for a week, and he won't bother to check." If his question for me is, "Where will you go?" my answer will be, "Anywhere." The only question I am unsure of is, "What will you pay me?" The only answer I have for that is, "Anything."

Blinking, Michael Bodleian looked up from the page, over—

"Bodleian's a library," Hal says.

"That's right!" says the monk. A bit arrogantly, like Hal was a little kid who knew something adult.

"It doesn't matter."

"Just read," says the angry one. She's had her hair dyed, a noble dark walnut. It doesn't reflect the red mind inside. And you can smell it, the chemical hair. What devils women put on themselves.

Hal rises to help the small one with her posture, which isn't bad, though her chin is too high in the air, an English thing. She likes the attention. The angry one he's afraid to help. She's too fierce and pissed off to slouch anyway, so thank God he doesn't need to touch her. A hawk with intentions.

Blinking, Michael Bodleian looked up from the page, overwhelmed with his own question, *Does Li get off the island?* He wanted so much to flip to the back of the book, so to speak, but the book was not written yet, at least not in English. And he couldn't ask Naomi. He could barely ask her anything lately. Ever since their camping trip, and their fight, if that is what it was. Even today, Naomi had delivered these new, terrible pages with a look that made Michael feel it was somehow his fault that things had taken a turn and the World had gone wrong.

Naomi sat pale and quiet on the couch

"Not *Naomi*," Hal hears himself say. He's irritated. This

monk has a strange copy. A different edition, maybe, than what he's used to. Because he knows this stuff.

"No?" The monk waits.

He can picture her clear as can be, though it's probably been years. She has a big nose for Cantonese. But beautiful. Her *skin*. Her eyes make you believe anything.

"Li."

"Ah!" The monk dips his head into the book, not believing him for a second. "Hal, actually, 'Li' is the name of the leper Naomi's writing about. Translating her, you know, pages."

"Silly me." He mimes a pistol to his temple and pulls the trigger. A scandalous no-no in a place like this. Burn the Buddha.

Naomi sat pale and quiet on the couch, across the room, head down, hands clasped, listening to him read. He couldn't bear it, another of these weekends. It was like she'd descended into … It was like Naomi had gone insane.

He had never been happier in his life. Doubly blessed, by a book that was building his career, heaping gold upon him, and by Naomi, the love of his life. How was it possible that one blessing could wither, and by its withering threaten all happiness? He could feel his future without her: bitter loneliness, empty pride. He could feel it even now.

From the couch, Naomi said quietly but forcefully, "Read."

"It's good, Naomi. But, 'author'? For the pinching crab?"

"'Author of another's misfortune.'"

"Are you sure?"

"Use 'thief.' It doesn't matter. Use 'criminal.'"

"But what was the character?"

Naomi paused over-long, and he didn't trust her answer even before she spoke. "Author."

"It's beautiful, Naomi. Your work is so—"

"Please read it, Michael." She paused again. "You might have other questions."

Myco.

Chin died last night!

It feels like augury of the grandest kind. Like one of his sticks cast with finality into the tide of life, Chin, who was weaker than he was young, expired in the night! He has finally suffocated in his own saliva, he could no longer swallow it away, and thankfully I was not sleeping close enough to hear how it ended. In the morning the others were mournful but severely tired. Their faces and their movements showed a judgmental mood they were not aware of but which comes from one person's noise never letting them rest all through the night. They were probably glad when he finally stopped drowning and fell quiet. Maybe one of them helped hasten poor Chin on his journey. It has happened here before, so they say. I won't judge. I judge only Sang Seen.

I came down the hill and emerged through the trees and into the main clearing to see four of them moving slowly and ineptly, dragging the body wrapped in a blanket, thinner than a spruce log. Chin's head bounced rudely on the uneven ground. Not feeling their own feet,

the men grumbled and stumbled, and argued over who
was not pulling his share. Surely, I thought, our time
here is doomed, the moon and the sun are broken, when
we cannot properly respect our dead. Surely, in bumping
Chin's head over the ground, these men were bumping
their own heads too, were grumbling and arguing over
their own foul and imminent death.

I wondered if poor Chin, with his pathetic flour sack
of sticks and shells, had augured any of this. Though
why "poor"? He has escaped.

Michael can't help but ask, though because Naomi
can't herself know yet, it's more an exclamation, "She
gets off, doesn't she? Li gets off!"

"I think she does. Yes."

"Where would she go?"

This Naomi didn't answer. In a kind of pantomime
she got up from the couch, and left the living room
for the kitchen. It was almost as if she had sniped, "She
would go to the kitchen."

Though there was another translated page to read,
Michael followed. Gentleness worked on her. She
loved him. He could almost always find her soft side.
He asked again, making as though she might not have
heard him, "I wonder where she could go? Her face. It
would be hard."

She was at the sink and he stood behind her as she
rinsed their tea things. It seemed that she might leave,
her quick movements had that feeling, and Michael's
stomach fell.

"There'd be Victoria," he offered, "but they'd just

send her back. There was Nanaimo, the coal mines, some Chinese women cooked up there, but one of those lepers on D'Arcy *came* from Nanaimo, so that would be a dangerous place, too. Maybe," he finished, aware he was babbling, "there was Vancouver. A place to hide there."

Naomi clinked dishes, putting them in the rack to air-dry, which she knew he didn't like, and which was why, he had explained to her, he always had two dish-towels hanging from the oven handle.

"Maybe," she said, "she'll dig a hole to China."

Michael had to tell her. Anything was better than this.

"They took it!" He grabbed her shoulders from behind. "They took the book! Danton, E.P. Danton, the best in North America. They want to go trade paper! They think it'll sell! They love Li! They love everything about her! We sold it, Naomi! We sold it!" He was surprised by the "we," but liked it. What's mine is yours. And it hinted at his big surprise. He would wait, he would wait. He loved her.

"Naomi?" He spun her around to face him. "We have a book coming out!" And I'm going to get tenure, I'm going to make full professor, and there will be no reason in this big blue world why you and I shouldn't get married.

"Except that he already is." He didn't know he'd spoken, except that now the monk is watching him and waiting for more.

"But your guess," Hal adds, "is good as mine." There's

nothing else to say about any of this. And after three or four breaths, the monk gives up.

To his huge relief, she stepped into him and hugged him, though weakly, as though she didn't know what else to do.

"Is everyone at work," she asked, softly, "very happy for you?"

"Of course they are!" He pictured, two days ago, ripped envelope in hand, marching to the Head's office, calling yippees and yelps, and shouting *Yes*. Telling anyone who'd listen. "Or they're jealous!" He'd also sat in his dark office, hyperventilating. There he'd enjoyed a memory, so clear it was almost a vision, of Kingston, of his old professor, Professor Wellborne, climbing out of his Jaguar, going into his lovely, fire-lit home, his lovely wife, his perfect life. He thought of his father, that awful pathetic smile as potential customers streamed past. At this point, Michael almost forgot how to breathe.

Now, in his kitchen, Naomi clung to him, and Michael realized she had begun squeezing him ever harder, until it felt like she was using every bit of her strength.

When she released her squeeze, and let out a huge rush of breath, he waited with her, still hugging, not knowing what to do. He brought a hand up to cup the back of her neck, under her hair. He loved holding her here, the feel of her creamy-soft skin, under which the two strong sinews ran the length of her neck, all sitting beneath her brain, her intelligence, which never stopped surprising.

"What do you think?" he dared ask.

Her answer wasn't immediate. Eventually she turned and began to lead him to the bedroom. He didn't know what to think. There wasn't the slightest hint of the joy, mixed with mischief, when she had led him there before. In the hall mirror he caught brief sight of her cheeks glossy with tears. In the bedroom she guided him onto the bed and began to make what he didn't know at the time was an already cursed and final bout of love. But he did know it, *he did*. She did not cry, and barely moved. Her stillness unnerved him. He thought of a stone that is hysterical inside.

HE KNOWS THIS GUY, who's shown up just in time for lunch. Could be he's a bit of a mooch because the, the janitor lady joshes with him about how he should start paying rent here.

"Hi Hal." Here comes a hand to be shook. "It's Stuart."

"Well of course it is!" Bowing's good, but you can stay inside yourself in a bow. Something about a good hand. Meeting halfway out there, eye to eye.

"Sorry I haven't been around for a few days."

"We all need a break." What practice might he be doing?

"I was up in Montreal, visiting my daughter."

"Mel!"

The guy's face flips and struggles like an upside-down beetle. He tries to chuckle, and says, "Mel's *your* daughter."

"Just testing."

"I went to see Jennifer, *my* daughter. Haven't seen her in three years."

"Well that's great."

"It was."

Though it looks like it wasn't. He searches for words. He looks sheepish. "I thought maybe we were fighting but maybe we weren't."

"That's great." The man is almost happy. He looks proud. He looks like a parent about to brag.

"She showed me around—I love Montreal! We ate poutine, we climbed the little mountain—"

"Really!"

"She has a boyfriend, nice enough guy, but he has this homemade wine that was actually really good. Made from this organic grape juice, just pure juice, not even yeast. It just— turns into decent wine."

"Sounds great." He hooks a thumb over at the angry one bossing the little one at cards, rolls his eyes. "We could use some here."

"Anyway, yesterday I embarrassed the hell out of her by sitting in on a class she teaches. It was a big one, but I couldn't hide."

"She's a teacher!"

"She's a TA. A grad student in English. She's into all the Jane Austen stuff, Victorian lit, but they make her teach one of those first-year-from-hell classes. Comp for engineers."

"I feel for her." They made him teach those big classes too.

"No she's doing okay. She loves it there." He pauses and darkens. "She has a busy life."

"They always do."

The monk nods. "I suppose that's a good thing."

A daughter. Beauty in human form.

"Hal?"

"Yes."

"Can I ask you something? I like talking to you, because you're open."

"I'm glad you think so." He should be open by now. It's his job.

"And because you had a daughter."

"Okay."

"I know it's hard for you to remember."

"Okay."

"Anyway, seeing my daughter, seeing Jen. It mostly just felt stilted. I don't really know how I fit in."

"Unconditional. Unconditional love. You spread it out. No fitting in required." What else to say? "It really is that big."

"All right. I suppose so."

"It's true. You just love. No thought of yourself."

The monk considers this. Though he's not made happy by it, the unhappiness seems to lift.

Both of them turn to contemplate a tray of cookies and juice being wheeled past by a smiling lady whose age is impossible to tell.

"But anyway, do you know what the title of her M.A. thesis is?"

"I do." Stops him for a sec.

"Get this. It's 'Female Agency and Domestic Economy in Austen's Later Novels.'" He's rolling his eyes but loves it. "Actually there's another big word in there."

"That's horrible!"

"I know!" Big smile, a dad proud as punch. "I told her about you, Hal. She wants to meet you."

"Does she."

SHE'S A DOCTOR, extremely young, and Western. Probably here doing some sort of service. Which he is doing too, though it's mostly in service to himself. Bodhisattva vow notwithstanding. You do your best.

First she's shown him how to work a wheelchair, which he already knew. Now she's jabbed him with a big one, and is drawing blood. The smell of the alcohol swab brings the word "hospital," though that's not where this is. She waits for the thing to fill with his wild red-black life. Black cherry—he has a car with a colour called that.

The young doctor hums in a way you can tell is habitual, and which maybe is supposed to make you feel at ease.

"Marcus Welby, MD," he sings softly, snugging his voice in with hers.

"I'm sorry?"

"You have a bedside manner," he says. "Even though it's a chair. Here." He taps the armrests with his palms.

"I try," she says. He sees that she isn't as young as he thought. She's tired.

"No, you're a natural," he says, overdoing it now. Sometimes he just wants to hear himself talk.

She's asked him to take down his PJ bottoms so she can see "the incision."

He keeps the waistband decently up over the dondalinger. Though in her line of work it would be no biggie. Ha ha. On his hip there's a humongous scar he'd forgotten about, it's an angry colour with no name.

His— Someone he knows has scars like this, exactly this colour. Her neck. She wears scarves, nicely folded and puffed. He called them ascots, teased her about being a snob.

"Has that bruising been there long?"

"Um. Yes." Couldn't really say.

"Do you remember how well it felt after the operation, Mr. Dobbs?"

I don't even remember if I've had breakfast. "It felt wonderful."

"I think we might be looking at a new issue. Not likely a fracture, of course. You're still walking."

"I am?" He grabs the wheels, moves himself an inch forward, then back.

THIS HAS HAPPENED BEFORE. It's this bathroom. Toilet rilling behind him, he's looking in the mirror. He sees himself *suddenly* an old man. Now he's himself again. Now into the future, *old*. But here he is. Is time what he's seeing? Is this *time*?

With any luck, we rot into wisdom. Words fall away, it's just here.

THIS MAN STUART, who he's very fond of, and who might in fact be an old friend, looks smug as a kitten.

"Hal? Can I tell you a true story? It's a funny one."

"It's true? That's unbelievable!"

"Good one."

He wants to tell him that all stories are true, but that will put the kibosh on this before it even gets going.

Stuart asks if Hal wants to be "pushed around the block" and Hal wonders if he's in trouble for his quip, but then Stuart's behind him and he's cruising in his chair. He'd forgotten he's in a wheelchair.

"Maybe even go for a beer," Stuart says. "There's a new

pub a few blocks down." They're zooming down the hall. Hal reaches to gather up his hair but there's nothing up there!

"You don't need a hat. It's beautiful out. Warm for November."

"I can walk," he says. There's something wrong about talking to people who stay behind you.

"Not till after your operation."

The guy steps in front and he's punching numbers on a wall thing. Something beeps, the door unlocks. What the hell kind of pub is this?

"An operation, you say."

"Your hip needs to be redone. Friday, a few days from now."

"Can they do my head while they're at it?"

"I'll put in a request."

"Who's— Who's there?" He meant to ask something else, *Will she be here?* It came out wrong and he's not sure who he meant. The guy behind him, Stuart, leaves it be. He's a tactful man.

Stuart has to punch buttons again at some glass doors and he can see trees and cars out there. Now he's tobogganing a slight ramp and they're outside. It's a beautiful day, a soft blue that feels kind more than anything else. He's not where he thought. He's not in the mountains at all.

"Okay, Hal?"

"Yes."

"I have a funny story. You ready?"

"Sure. But I can walk." He doesn't like a guy behind his head. In some practices, as an exercise in fearlessness it's where you hold a visualization of your worst enemy. But the guy won't stop. And he begins telling him a weird story about cat mummies, cat mummies as fertilizer, and buying a house, it all happened in Victoria—

"*We* lived in Victoria," Hal announces, though there's something about this notion he doesn't like.

The guy has gone on to say he started a house fire by burning his mortgage in a planter on his deck the same day he paid it off, and he asks how stupid is that—

"Stuart? I wouldn't go bragging about it, no."

Stuart stops talking in a way that says something has just happened.

"Hal. You've never said my name before. I wasn't sure you knew it."

"Of course I do. Jimmy."

"Anyway, so the house fire should mean I just renovate myself a *nicer* house, except, *boom*, I missed my payments and they cancel my insurance."

"Boom!"

"Exactly."

Hal isn't used to a voice behind his head, let alone the bumps of curbs and even the ruts in the sidewalk, which burn his hip like crazy. Turn each bump into mantra. Behind his head, he's being told about someone getting "unlucky in a tent," because someone broke some glasses—

"Wow!"

There's lice, an antique car, and he ends up in jail. Jail just a few hours, but it felt symbolic.

"It would!"

And then "your daughter" got him out and he stayed with her, and he talked to the insurance people downtown.

"Good for you," he offers. They're at some traffic lights and lots of cars. He doesn't like being in a wheelchair at an intersection. Shiny new North American cars. He wonders where they're going.

"But Mel did the nicest thing for me," the voice behind him says. Apparently, he can stay in her beautiful house for as long as he wants, and even start a little woodwork shop. It's a great gift because he likes it here, being closer to his own daughter, who is in Montreal. And, "I like visiting you every day."

"Well, I like that too."

"I'm glad, Hal." The chair slows up, a hand from back there squeezes his shoulder. "So, anyway, do you know what I found out this morning?"

"I do!"

"This morning, a phone call. The insurance company is honouring my claim."

"Well that's wonderful." Though the guy sounds mostly puzzled.

"But do you know what this means?"

Hal wants to say yes but he's wincing from a sidewalk bounce and, no, he doesn't know what it means.

"Two weeks ago I'm homeless. Suddenly, I have two houses," he says, almost as though he was happier with none.

"That's how it works," Hal says.

"Really."

"That's exactly how it works," he says again because it's something he knows about.

He's being pushed up to a door. Two young women, leaving, hold it open and he's pushed in from behind.

"Now you have three," says Hal, because look at this one. Leather couches and thick medieval tables you could dance on. A fireplace burns blue flames and big bright sports are up there on the thing and a beautiful woman carries frosty mugs and a tray of the best looking sandwiches he's ever seen. Burgers big as soccer balls. He calls to her, "Yes, please!" and, from behind, his shoulder gets squeezed.

He grabs the hand and says "Four," because your body is also your house, and your mind even more, so, five, though now his has jumped off an endless cliff, and why is he playing this game?

He didn't know he said it aloud, "I want to *go* home," but apparently he did and he says it again, to hear it, and it feels right, so, again, and now he's being pushed out of this place. He moans a little song, *namo amitabaya hree*, it's Sanskrit, Jesus. He doesn't know where home is but he hopes it's where he's being pushed.

Fear is this awful colour, surging like a wave.

Abide in *shamatha*. Breathe simply.

Fear is exactly the colour of a nightmare.

Breathe.

IT'S—

Mala, falls away. Mantra, falls away. Sitting up in bed, wedged in the corner. Breath. Body.

All—stillness. It's—perfect. It's—

HE'S PLAYING CLOWN-MOUTH. He knows he's played it before. Why not? It's good and silly. You imagine a calliope in the background, you try and get the beanbag perfect centre, right down the clown-throat, hear the clown-choke. Of course there's no throat, it's just a bagga beans hitting some wood.

The clown's an antique, old circus paint. Red, yellow, blue, white. It smells like dust.

"That's *absolutely* cheating."

The angry one doesn't like that old lady's partner, probably her daughter, helping out by lifting Mom's arm up and, well, actually sort of throwing it for her. But here's Bea nodding along and trying to look just as angry as her. As Vera. Jesus. Enjoy the clown. If you throw it hard enough it thunks at the back where you can't see and it sounds almost like the clown choking. *Gak.* You have to get it dead centre. But things are winding down, it looks like he won't get a turn. Though he thinks he's already played.

THE MONK HAS COME to the dining hall with all the rest of them, for lunch. The sandwiches are those strategic ones: white bread on one side, brown on the other, satisfy the fence-sitters. Of which he is one. Cannot abide whole-wheat pizza crust, for instance, it's sacrilege, it's the sixties gone too far. The sandwiches are a white spready cheese with, what's that, cucumber, and the other kind looks to be ham and lettuce. Could get nasty: some of the meditators here who were raised Jewish still have a weird argument with ham.

Instead of tucking into a sandwich, the monk hands Hal a mala, says it's his to keep! Wooden beads, pale yellow, colour of, damn ... It's on the sandwiches, the first thing you spread on sandwiches.

"They're yellow cedar," says the monk, nudging the mala with a finger as if prodding a snake to life, proud as can be. It was like he made it himself.

Turns out he did! Hal asks him how he carved each one

of these beads the same size. The monk, Stuart, explains at length how he did it on his "brand new used lathe," shows him with his hands how you clamp in a long, thin piece of wood, in this case yellow cedar, and it spins like crazy—Hal thinks he's seen a lathe go—and you sit there and you press your chisel in, along a guide, and make all these indentations, you hourglass it, he says, then one by one you cut the beads apart with a little saw. You sand them "to cream" and drill the little hole and—

They're the colour of butter.

"There's one hundred and eight?"

"Yes. And I have extras in case any break." He waggles a little plastic bag. "Smell it. It's yellow cedar. It's unbelievable. Wakes you right up."

Hal puts his nose to it and inhales like the monk did but, nothing much. "Smells wonderful!" Sometimes you lie.

The mala works, though. A pebbled stream, which is how he thinks of it, pebbles rattling, bip bip bip, in water. Works perfectly. *Om mani—* He isn't sure what he's supposed to say.

"Works great." He hands it back.

"No, Hal, I made it just for you."

"Thank you."

"I went to that shrine you took me to, checked with a guy about the string, which it turns out is special cotton they use." The monk eyes the sticky white string on Hal's old one, his mala, abandoned on the table beside that sandwich. Ham today, and another one, cream cheese and crunchy stuff, two kinds of bread. Black and tan.

"Works great." Bip bip bip bip bip, flowing pebbles, bip bip bip. He wraps his new one around his wrist. The words just aren't the same with it. The things, the little round things click and clack and don't sound like the old ones, there on the table. The one Rose— The one Rose *forgave* to him. *That* was the joke. After he asked her "Are you *forgiving* this to me?" Sometimes they could joke about the hard stuff.

"Hal, would you mind if I read to you?"

"I'd be grateful if you did." Hoping he's not being rude he takes up a sandwich, starving. There's too much cucumber to cream cheese. And the cuke is cold, so it dominates the whole thing.

"We're almost at the end." Stuart waves his scuffed white book. "I kind of want to find out what happens."

"Well so do I!"

Michael laid Naomi's fresh translation back on his coffee table, breathing shallowly, eyes unable to focus. *You can be a better man than this.*

Today, he'd felt the paper-thin elation of the condemned man who had been promised his perfect last meal and had finished it. Dinner was a phone call from his publisher, with their reiteration of excitement over the book and a ballpark negotiation of terms. The publisher ("Call me Morgan!") joked about an "advance" though the book was already written—it *is* mostly written, isn't it? "Mostly, yes," Michael told him, truthfully enough. Then, for dessert, his meeting with his department head, Dr. Philip Eaves, a man who had barely heeded Michael's existence but now clapped him on the back and said that an application for tenure and promotion was timely, best strike while the iron's hot and all that, and—joking but not—let's hope you're not suffering delusions about looking elsewhere, meaning UBC, whose History Department had both money and reputation.

The feeling of doom had been rising all week. It spiked today when he got home and took off his coat and there on the hall table lay her house key, with its forlorn key ring she had made from a broken shell from D'Arcy Island. She had let herself in. He knew he would find the manuscript on the coffee table, and there it was. He knew she would do it this way. He knew a lot of things. Part of him felt that he knew everything, and always had, but was too happily absorbed watching shadows on the wall of his cave.

He knew for certain when he picked up her translation, skimmed it, and spotted:

From behind his back, Li whispered, "You can be a better man than this."

How likely was it? *How likely was it?* All too clearly he could hear her saying that to him, word for word, on D'Arcy Island. *From behind his back.*

What about the other coincidences that were just too close, that at first caused him to smile, and then roused only the tiniest suspicions, little seeds that had gone unwatered till now. Such as when he mused to Naomi about the lepers' likely tooth problems, and the next batch of translation referred to Lon, who happened to be a lay dentist, and still good with pliers. Then, that reference to them eating crab and him wondering aloud how they caught them and, lo and behold, in the next batch of translation there was a

description of an ingenious trap. How *probable* was it
that he should ask Naomi if any of the lepers ever got
mail from relatives, and then the very next week there
was a letter from Li's father?

Michael turned, on the spot, and gaped out the
picture window, mouth-breathing heavily.

And Quince? Why had he not questioned what was
not even remotely a Chinese name?

Also on the coffee table lay the several pages of old
Chinese writing. He grabbed the top page and glared
at it. He held it up to the light, as if that might help.
He rattled it, as if to shake the secrets from its ridiculous characters. Bringing it to his face, he could smell it
more than understand it! He balled it up against his leg
and hissed "*fuck fuck fuck.*" He could feel it crack and
split and now it smelled even stronger, of greasy dirt.

What did it really say?

Did Li even exist? Of course not. His stomach
found a new, colder vacuum, as he recalled the time,
maybe it was the day they had met, when he had so
wistfully mentioned the lone female rumoured to have
been banished to D'Arcy Island, and wouldn't it be
spectacular to find some proof of her? Yes, Michael,
silly Michael, really, now what were the chances that
the following week he would get that very woman's
personal goddamned diary?

Michael grabbed up the sheets of fresh paper,
began again to read this next batch of "Li's" writing.

*Li found Sang Seen sitting on a bleached log at the
eastern beach. She knew he could hear her approach on*

*the gravel; she knew that he knew it was her. The frozen
set of his shoulders was that of a man too weak ever
to apologize. He was a man afraid of and blind to the
grand kindness that was all around them and as real as
earth, air, or water, and larger than them all.*

*From behind his back, Li whispered, "You can be a
better man than this."*

Michael whispered to himself, "Jesus. Naomi."

*She pointed a finger and touched his neck, which
she soon realized he could not feel. She closed her eyes.
She pressed harder, and harder, almost stabbing,
until he made a noise not unlike the plea of a goat.
After a last thrust, she turned away from him and
walked, leaving him alone on his private beach, to sit
with the piles of seaweed that storms had shoved up
upon the shore. The seaweed was beginning to stink,
and Sang Seen remained where he was, sitting and
rotting with it.*

Michael had sent photocopies of the Chinese
originals to not just his publisher, but to colleagues in
History departments in Toronto and San Francisco,
where both due diligence and curiosity would lead
to their own translations. Could be they had already
discovered the hoax. Tomorrow morning he would
pick up the phone and call the publisher. The book
was no more. The death of his career would not be
quite as fast, but it would be much more painful.

He lifted the rest of Naomi's offering and thumbed

through. He saw that most of it was a letter, from her
to him.

Dear Michael,

"She didn't write a letter."

"What?" asks the monk. He keeps reading the book quickly
to himself, unwilling to leave its world. Then the monk does
look up and meet his eye.

"It was just crazy" is all he can say. Because the whole thing
was crazy. *She* was crazy. Crazy sex, crazy eyes. Taking the ferry to
see her that time in Vancouver, surprising her, crazy Eastside,
other guys living there, and Quince. That guy Quince scared
the hell out of him. Left Rose and the baby for lust and chaos.
She was a witch. Jesus, there was no one like her. You could
feel her if you were within a city block. Li.

"A witch?" says the monk. And then, "Do you want to say
anything more, Hal?" Looking at him like he was looking over
his glasses. You got the impression he used to wear glasses.

"Sorry!"

There's an old woman beside him, he doesn't have a clue
who she is, but she's just come up, she makes her wheelchair
go by baby-stepping her feet and pulling herself along, little
breathy grunts, the most hideous thing you've ever seen. She
parks her chair in right beside his like this is where the wheelchairs go. Like this is a drive-in movie. He's seen her here.
She's never been able to catch up to him before.

The monk says hello and asks her name but she plays
it coy.

Treat everyone as the Buddha.

Dear Michael,

I don't know how to start so I will just
start. This letter feels like a dream. This world
feels like a dream. So dream-like, I can't even
feel it as bad, as the nightmare it is.

If you have bothered to read the new
translation, and you probably have, so hungry
are you for them, then I need to apologize
for it, because of course it is a picture of you,
and me, as it has been all along. But please
forgive me for this one most of all. I was
angry, I wrote it when I was hating you. To my
dismay I did learn to hate you as well as love
you, though the first one, love, happened
instantly and easily. Uncontrollably. But
they are that close, love and hate; they are
the real beast with two backs, apologies to
your Shakespeare. (I know I didn't tell you
this, but the week before I saw your ad was
the first time I was aware that I had begun
thinking in English. And then, when I met
you, I somehow put those two things together:
thinking in English, and falling in love with
Professor Michael Bodleian. It was just one
more lovely ornament I was able to wear, I
think.)

He pulled away from her letter, not breathing. He
looked again with a kind of fear at the dirty pile of
pages of Chinese writing, which Naomi had pretended
to translate, keeping up her ruse to the end. What kind

of gibberish, or poetry, was in those pages? What howls to the moon, or to God? Did the writer even have a God to howl at? The pages still looked like treasure to him. But he no longer wanted to touch them.

He was not so surprised by Naomi's words. He still felt he knew everything and always had. What struck Michael most was how much this letter, Naomi's own voice, sounded like Li's. It was as if Li did exist.

If you have read about Sang Seen rotting in the seaweed, and you know that he is you, again I am sorry. This harsh treatment of Michael-as-Sang is not fair, but that is how angry I have been. I did not enjoy writing it—though it did relieve some anguish and some frustration. Also, and you might think I am crazy (as I sometimes do, I confess), but I wrote it and left it that way because it felt to me like Li's true story and I did not want to edit it. So in that way it is nothing but honest. Mostly I want to apologize for comparing you to a monster. I could not love a monster. I do not love a monster. You are not a monster.

But Sang Seen was you, was always you. He helped Li, he rescued her and took her under his wing. He built her a place to live, she loved him, she tried to help him in return. But he thought only of himself and he betrayed her. When I wrote these portraits I wanted you to see yourself in him, and maybe change. That's how foolish I was. How arrogant.

I know I have ruined you. I have also ruined myself, because I have ruined us. How did this happen? How did I ruin my life? (I am drinking scotch. You know how little I drink, but it seems to calm me, the more I drink. Less wild and despairing. When you read this I am in a city you have never been, and that's all I will say about that.)

At first. At first I only wanted the job and the money you offered. I needed the money desperately, but I will not tell you why. I was no longer a student, even then. I did not know why you needed the translations, some research project I figured, despite the secrecy. (You told me nothing, and you can feel blame for this if you choose.) When I gave you the first one, the lists of foodstuffs, and lumber of different sizes, and nails, and bandages, your profound disappointment affected me. I was afraid you were going to terminate the job I so much needed. But now, also—this is where things changed, because now I had begun to love the man, to love Michael Bodleian. I can't say how it happened. You know how it happens. And then, wanting so much to please you, I invented. You were like a broken boy, a boy whose world had shattered. So I invented Li. You can't know how happy it made me, to see you so happy. How could that be wrong? I was unable to stop, anyway. It was an instinct, to make you happy. I was a wolf following the scent of food. My other favourite pastime was to imagine the size of our children's noses, and how sweet and smart they would be. Michael, we would have had four. Two boys and two girls. I see them clearly still, because I am not over the habit.

I was able to give you gifts! You wanted the writer to be a girl, and I gave her to you. I gave you the lepers' pain, but in ways you could understand. (It was also my instinct not to hurt you with the truth—not that I know the lepers' truth, either. No one can.) I gave you the glow of Victoria on fire, I gave you kites, and most of all I gave you Li and Sang Seen. It was our story, it was you giving me employment, and a shelter, and your quiet, steady love.

I knew my lie would lead to trouble, but I couldn't help myself, and therefore I didn't care, because each weekend was its own world, each weekend was worth everything, a lifetime of recklessness, good and bad. I did not know what you planned to do with my work but I knew it was only a matter of time before you discovered my deceit. You would discover me and hate me. I began to panic. How could I get you to stop your project so I could keep my dream alive? I had to try. Love kept me stupid and made me try. One way was to argue that our work was morally wrong. That the dead should be allowed their peace. That we had no right to pretend to know the life of the lepers. That we had no right to profit from pain. That we could be in some way cursed by it. The more I thought these thoughts, the more I actually began to feel their truth, and also, yes, a curse. It is a simple equation, to profit from another's pain. It is as simple and clear as the sun and moon. Greed is a blade that draws its own blood. You and I are both the proof of this.

It did not matter that the lepers were my creation, and that I gave birth to Li. The intent was the same, and so was the sin. And, Michael, I confess to you now that I began to think that you were more the sinner than I, because for you it wasn't a fiction at all. You were trying to profit from the life of these lepers, whose life you did not know. Whose world you didn't care about except for what might prove interesting to your readers. Who were Chinese, about which you know nothing, yet asked very few questions. Whose main voice was a woman's, another world you are not so clear on. Could you not smell the rot in this? Can you smell it now? Are you sitting in the seaweed? The scotch keeps me calm, but is its own welling hill, and possible volcano—you never asked many questions of me, either. I am an English major who studied your language enough to study your authors. You never asked me my favourites. They are

D.H. Lawrence, Sylvia Plath and Ralph Waldo
Emerson, and if you ever care to know more
about me, perhaps knowing this will help. But
you never asked, and this means that you are
as easy not to like as you are to love.

And then. Michael, it would be a lie
to say that things did not get worse, for
us, when I discovered you planned a book
centred on this work of mine. I would be
lying to say I did not feel bitterness when
I understood what prestige, what kind of
livelihood, you stood to gain from it. From
the painful lives of others. And from the
work of someone to whom you were paying
a trifling wage, while sleeping with. Michael,
yes, this is only the outer world I describe.
The inner world, that we loved each other,
excused all of this. Excuses it still. And I
swear I would have told you the truth had I
known how far it had gone. I did not know
you were showing my work to your superiors,
and to publishers. I thought it was still just
between us. I didn't know what to do. I
need you to believe me when I say that my
only mistake was confusion. Unless it was
also a mistake to love you, then that would
be two.

I swear I would have told you had I known.
My anger at you using me, and using my work,
was already being vented in the story of Sang
Seen, when he shows that all along he'd been

setting Li up, that by building her safe house
he was building his house of prostitution.
That story and that alone was sufficient
revenge for me. I swear yet again that I did
not want this end, which looks like revenge on
the grandest scale. I can only tell you that it is
not my revenge. It is Li's.

I am drunk on scotch now and calm as the
dead. My life is over, because our love is not
possible now, and also because there are other
things you don't know about me and never
will. You won't be able to find me.

Because I love you I will not mail you
the real translations, which I also dutifully
produced, and which might make a good
study for someone someday, though I hope
not. They are more of the same lists of dry
goods that I showed you at the start. Many
daily weather reports, and some concern
about undersized beets and dying cabbage.
On one whole page some ranting because
someone has a better fireplace. It is boring,
and crazy, but mostly boring. The man (he
never reveals his name; no woman is ever
mentioned) was near illiterate, and often
wrote the same thing twice and three times,
practising his characters like any child writing
down his alphabet, again and again. For years,
I think. I came to see that his lists were of
things that he wanted, not what he, or anyone
else, actually had. (Li, she could love what

she had.) But I think he wrote things down because, to do so, in the World (yes, it is true he called it that), to write things on paper, made them more real. Writing gave shapes to his hope. It was hard for me to read, harder than what I gave to you. But Michael, his insanity and pain must be left in peace. Plant his hope back in the ground, Michael. If you loved me even a little, that is what you'll do.

Michael. (Michael Bodleian. I still love your name. Maybe I loved it first of all. Learning to say it. Then saying it. Michael Bodleian.) Michael, if you do read the last part of Li's story, I am sorry if it was writ too poetic. It was in Li's nature.

Naomi

Michael sobbed a first and last time, caught it in a ragged inbreath, and held it.

He picked up Naomi's last pages of translation. He walked with them to the window, barely breathing, and stood leaning in what he realized was his posture of waiting for her, spying on her arrival past the hedge. He raced to the kitchen, where above the fridge he kept his modest liquor supply, usually a bottle of wine or two, but where he also knew was stored a bottle of scotch, saved for a special occasion. He could be with her this little bit. Maybe he could find the same dead calm. As he swung open the cupboard, it was as if he knew this, too: there was no scotch. Her letter had been composed while drinking it.

Michael returned to the window, to the natural light of day. He angled the pages at it so the paper was lit up white, the ink going blacker, clearer, as if also gaining both in volume and portent. He began to read the last of the story of Michael and Naomi. Which was *writ too poetic.* Naomi!

The night Sang Seen and Li disappeared into their separate fates, a windstorm rose to whip the trees of the World and toss the waters that encircled it. Waves rose and moved onshore to become giants' shoving hands. The earth around the encampment and up Li's hill shuddered from these torrents of rain and sea, that all night raced through, taking with them all traces of campfires and gardens and footprints and pathways, and anything Sang Seen may have taken part in. All night long the men huddled in their fetid shacks, all their blankets gone, praying for an end to the night, praying even harder that they were not cursed for their actions in life. On her hill, surrounded by her toppled cedar mansion, Li sat up hugging her knees, staring into the night, forgetting even to blink as the water struck and pounded and tore her weak clothing away.

In the morning, as the sun's kind rays entered their cleansed shacks, the men rose as a group, stretching, and smiling at what they saw through the open windows and doors. None believed they had slept, but all felt refreshed. Reaching for the ceiling in a stretch, swinging his head this way and that, it was Saysay who noticed it first. His missing finger had grown back, pink and wrinkled and puffy as a baby's. As he shouted, already weeping in delight, showing his quick-wiggling finger to any who would look, such was his amazement and joy that he could not hear or see the other men leaping and shouting for their own delightful reasons. One man hopped up and down, cradling a foot, shouting ouch through his laughter, because he felt the joyous hurt of a peppercorn in his boot.

They could not only walk quickly, they could run, and they could feel with the soles of their feet the smallest pebbles and twigs, which felt like nothing but endless jewels to them. They ran and leaped like children, and three of them built quick and excellent kites out of their own shirts. As several skipped along the beach, feeling the glory of clams squirting water up their bare calves, they could smell wonderful spicy food wafting on the wind, and each realized at the same instant that they were smelling a favourite that their own mothers used to make, on their birthday; and when they followed their nose in the direction of the smell, which they couldn't help but do, they could see that the source of the smell was the several boats landing on their beach. Lining the boats' walls, crying, waving, or beaming magnificently with pride, were all of their families.

In their excitement, no one saw, far in the distance, the other boat, its sail large enough to take it anywhere on the oceans that connected all the lazarettos of the larger world. The sail was the dark grey colour of their own blankets, all of them stolen and crudely stitched together, of course, by Sang Seen.

But the men saw that someone was missing, and they ran up the path to find Li and tell her that it was her birthday too and that the boats with their families were here for them. Those whose dead feet had come to know the path too well followed with some difficulty and with no small guilt, for the storm had made it rough and new. They pushed into her clearing in the trees and gathered there. There was no sign of the shelter Sang Seen had built. In the centre of where it had stood, planted in the ground and gleaming so white in the sun that it was hard to look at, rested a single, perfectly round bone the size of a small human being. It was carved by wind and water to the smoothness and translucence of pearl. As the men peered in closely, under its surface and in its depths swirled light in faint colours never before seen, colours more haunting than held in the eye. If a man eased his breath and watched with a settled heart, he saw the lights endlessly taking shape to never quite become his own original face.

ACKNOWLEDGMENTS

For their support, I want to thank the BC Arts Council, the Canada Council, and the University of Victoria.

I am indebted to the wealth of research provided by Chris Yorath's *A Measure of Value*, a painful but excellent book on the lazaretto of D'Arcy Island.

Thanks as well to my agent, Carolyn Forde, and to Nicole Winstanley and especially Nick Garrison at Hamish Hamilton, for taking a chance on this kind of story.

I also want to thank those who read early chunks and drafts of this in progress: Amelia Humphries, John Gould, Joan MacLeod, Eve Joseph, Sri Ter Yong, and Dede Crane.

And finally, unconditional love to Dede, for whom, due to my flounderings in the World, I might have been sometimes unavailable.

A Penguin Readers Guide

ABOUT THE BOOK

Consider the world around you. What would you do if one day, you lost everything? If you lost your house, your car, your security? If you lost your health and your hopes for a long life? If you lost the memories of your past and of your loved ones?

Stuart is in the mood to celebrate after retiring and paying off his mortgage. His celebration is cut dramatically short, however, when his house burns down and he learns that his home insurance has been mistakenly, cruelly, cancelled. With little more than an aging car and the smoke-infused clothes on his back, Stuart sets off on a wild cross-country drive to Toronto, with the hopes of talking some sense into the faceless insurance agent in charge of his case, and of meeting up with Melody, a vibrant woman from his past who he hasn't seen in decades.

But Mel has problems of her own. Suffering from terminal cancer, Mel spends her days reflecting on the scents, sounds, and tastes that she soon will never know again. She has come to peace with the fact that her days are numbered and, choosing to take that decision away from her cancer, has set a date to take her own life. This decision gives her a much needed sense of stability—a stability that needs some adjustment when Stuart finally gets in touch with her.

Stuart and Mel rekindle their friendship, helping each other with the details of their disrupted lives. Mel gives Stu a place to stay and much needed support while he fights for his insurance claim, and Stu accompanies her on visits to her father, Hal, a Buddhist monk and former writer who has lost his past to Alzheimer's.

On these visits, Stu takes up the regular task of reading aloud from Hal's novel *The World*, a multi-layered story about a professor and the young woman he hires to translate a sheaf of papers discovered on the site of a Chinese leper colony on D'Arcy Island, British Columbia. And as *The World* unfolds, both the novel and the novel-within-the-novel, the reader recognizes that for all of the characters there is no escaping the chaos of life or the chaos within ourselves—for that is what makes us human.

The World is a powerful novel about mortality, loss, acceptance, and the possibilities for joy that life holds for the living, from Bill Gaston, the award-winning author of *The Good Body*, *Gargoyles*, *Mount Appetite*, and *Sointula*. ■

Q: How did *The World* come about?

I'll take the question literally, and admit a salmon started it. I caught a salmon; I smoked it well into the evening in my dad's old smoker, on the sundeck, dispensing the charred, spent woodchips into a plastic planter of dirt that sat against the side of the house. With no lit embers in the planter, I went to bed—and in the morning woke up to the smell of smoke and my deck and one wall of my house on fire. The paperboy woke me up by pounding on the door. I tried to put it out with my garden hose. Vicky, from across the street, tied her pink bathrobe around my waist because I was wearing nothing but wet underwear and dress shoes. And so on. Fiction takes over right around here, though not completely. Most of the book's research was done for me by life. I won't go into details, but I know something about throat cancer and feeding tubes, and I've spent too much time in dementia wards. I can see the real D'Arcy Island from a beach near my house (which was beautifully restored; and the salmon was delicious). But the house fire was the spark, so to speak. ■

Q: The point of view progressively switches from Stuart to Mel and then to Hal. Why did you choose this structure over a more traditional one?

One reason short stories aren't as popular as novels might be because readers don't get to have as deep a relationship with the main character. It sounds corny, but reading a novel with a strong main character can be like making a friend. In *The World*, I wanted to allow that possibility of friendship by hanging out with a character long enough for it to happen, or not—and let me say that it's the same for the writer as it is for the reader, this making-a-friend, or not—but I also needed multiple main characters in order to tell the stories I wanted to tell. I also wanted a book that would hang together only as much as real people meeting in the real world would hang together—so, sort of a random feel. What I also wanted to do, because I hadn't done it before, was to spend time in one mind, for instance Stuart's, while he remembers and fantasizes about another person, Mel. And then, pop, we're in Mel, seeing through her eyes, and Stuart is on the sidelines, and we get her version of things now. And then Mel is thinking about Hal, who we see only from outside, and then, pop, now we're in Hal's head. We don't get to see Hal all that well, because he's almost gone, but when we read his book we get more sense of him, or at least of who he once was. Another reason I needed an intimate portrait of three people was because I had three distinct stories to explore, involving the loss of three kinds of "world": one, the loss of your home and family; two, the loss of your body; and three, the loss of your mind. ■

Q: Hal's novel *The World* is an interesting thread that runs throughout each section of the book. What challenges did you face in crafting this book within a book within a book?

One of the challenges was to give each "book" its own style, or voice, in order for it to appear written not by Bill Gaston but by Hal Dobbs, and of course Hal had to write Naomi's leper journal as if it were written not by him but by Naomi, and of course Naomi had to write it as if it were written by Li. (I was tempted to add another "book," and have Li's father send her a series of letters, but I figured enough was enough.) But since I'm a short-story writer, and enjoy writing in different voices, this novel's various voices were my idea of fun. I had to make decisions, though; for instance, I didn't think that Hal Dobbs should be that good a writer, so I made his writing rather flat, wooden, and old-fashioned. But then his style is contradicted by the rather poetic flourishes from Li, so it seems he was a good writer after all, and playing his own games. (Maybe on me.) ■

Q: You've enjoyed a very successful career writing novels, short stories, poetry, and drama. Which form do you find most challenging or rewarding? Do you ever find that an idea intended for one medium, like a play, demands that it become a prose story or a novel?

Typically a new idea will rattle around in my head for a while before I start committing anything to paper, so I usually have a good sense of what something's size and shape is going to be. I've been asked on occasion to take a stab at adapting my fiction into screenplay, and a couple of stories into dramatic pieces, and it's proved torturous, like wrestling someone way stronger and slipperier than me. The feeling I get is, If this idea was supposed to be a movie, I would have written it as a movie. And I stopped being a poet long ago, if I ever was one. Now, whenever a spasm of poetry ripples through my body, I try to insert it into a story when it isn't looking. But to answer this question properly, I'd have to add that *The World* contains something of a surprise to me. For several years I was sitting on an idea for a tragic love story. It involved a young historian and a Chinese translator and a box of papers found on D'Arcy Island—I think I never got around to writing it simply because I don't write those sorts of stories. I didn't know what to do with it, and then I realized that it could be Hal's book. ∎

Q: What authors or books have been influential to your writing?

It's hard to know how you've been influenced, or when. I suspect the deepest influences might also be the most invisible. I'll discover an author and read everything—I've had intense affairs with Ian McEwan and Alice Munro and Jim Harrison and David Mitchell and Marilynne Robinson and Roberto Bolaño, and the list goes on and on, back through decades. Early on, my first "serious" authors were Tolkien and John Steinbeck, individual books like *The Yearling* and *To Kill a Mockingbird*. I loved anything at all Robinson Crusoe-ish, where you have nothing and you start from scratch. And I know I have a tendency in my own writing to take my characters to that place, almost as if I want to see what they can endure, and what they can find to help them survive, and how they begin to rebuild. In all my reading life I have most been drawn to books that combine humour with heart—but maybe the same thing might be said for most readers. ∎

Q: Why do you end the book on a passage from Hal's novel, on a highly whimsical scene ostensibly written by the female leper, Li?

All along, I felt the urge not to end this book in a conventional way, which would have been to have some kind of positive epiphany with Hal, then have Stuart reunite with his daughter in some way, and tie up all his loose ends in life. Though much of that is touched on, I resisted it as the ending. Instead, I felt it more fitting to end on an image—all these lepers trying to see "their original face," which is a concept central to the Zen tradition—that also very much reflects what all these characters did in the book, which was to discover their essential self. It also reflects the act of fiction, and lots in this book—obviously—is about writing fiction, and what's true and what's not true about fiction, how our memory is a fiction writer, and all the rest of it. Ending the book like this was sort of brave on my part (am I allowed to say that?) because I suspected that some readers wouldn't be satisfied with this ending. ∎

Q: The meta-story of Michael and Naomi's research into the D'Arcy Island leper colony provides an interesting counter-melody to the rest of the book. What sort of research did you do on conditions in the real-life leper colony?

When I first heard about the Chinese leper colony I was fascinated because I see D'Arcy Island whenever I drive a half-mile north from where I live. It's such a legendary, in some ways archetypal disease, perhaps because it's so horrible to be disfigured, dying, and shunned all at once. My research involved going to the island on a kind of lily-livered mission, much like Michael Bodleian's own; then some fact-finding at the B.C. Archives. But most helpful of all was Chris Yorath's book, *A Measure of Value*, which gathers pretty much all that is known about the place. The facts surrounding D'Arcy are appropriately excruciating: no one got off (except a few who in the colony's last years were transferred to another island colony, near Sooke); some had gone into debt to buy passage from China and never set foot on the mainland but were taken directly to D'Arcy; one man from Victoria was apparently tricked there and contracted

the disease after he arrived; and, finally, they weren't very contagious and there was no good reason for the leper colony to exist at all, and
the government authorities knew it. But almost nothing is known
about the individuals there—so I was free to, or maybe forced to,
invent my own lepers, and to a certain extent inhabit their minds,
though they suffered in ways I could never begin to fathom. I tried
my best. It helped that they were rendered somewhat poetically,
sometimes even whimsically, by Naomi imagining herself to be Li.
So can I blame any shortcomings on her? ▪

Q: Each of the main characters faces a profound life crisis and
it would be easy to tell their stories in a melodramatic or
melancholic tone, yet *The World* resists that impulse with a
certain amount of humour and lighter touches. How did you
maintain a positive approach to such dire circumstances?

When I describe this book in a nutshell—uninsured house burns
down, cancer, suicide, Alzheimer's disease, life on a leper colony—it
sounds ridiculously depressing. So if I'm proud of one thing, it's
that most people—reviewers as well as readers I've heard from—
don't find it depressing at all. Some actually find it uplifting. I don't
think the book achieves this by being Pollyanna or rose-coloured
or naïve. I think it tackles these "dire circumstances" head on. The
humour, or light touch, comes from the kind of characters I've
chosen to explore. As I mentioned earlier, I like to put my characters through the mill and see what happens to them. So it is here.
And what happens to them is they find a kind of strength beyond
the dire. I've come to understand that in my life I've admired most
of all those men and women who face extreme hardship, especially
death, not with a macho bravery but a certain kind of humour.
I've come to see that when all is scraped away—when it gets to the
point that even pain is scraped away—people can express dignity
and humour. Maybe I admire these people because I fear I'm not
up to it, myself. In any case, Stuart, Mel, and Hal are perfect in that
regard—though Stuart I think ends up more addled than wise, and
Mel isn't at all beyond fear, and Hal is operating on less than half a
brain. But they all keep their dignity. There's an odd but interesting
concept in Tibetan Buddhism called "the lion's roar" that refers to

363

a humour that happens when we see life's pain as a kind of cosmic joke. It's not frivolous, and it's not gallows humour, not quite; it's the outrageousness of seeing through the horror and smiling at it—something in this resembles a lion's roar. I suppose I've tried to surround Stuart and Mel and Hal with echoes of that sound, trying to have it come in through the windows, a little. ■

Q: After such a long and distinguished career, what still drives you to write? What can we expect from you next?

I've long given up wanting to be world famous, and I no longer write because, as Gabriel García Márquez once said, "I want everyone to love me." I do it because I enjoy getting up in the morning and writing sentences. It just feels good, so it's selfish. Occasionally a character will emerge and hang out for a while, and sometimes we'll actually make friends, so much so that it's sad to leave each other. (Sometimes it's fine that they leave, and if you've read some of my books, you'll know why.) So I enjoy it, simple as that, and when I no longer enjoy it so much I hope I have the imagination to stop. At the moment, I'm looking for ways to retire, or at least go half time, from this teaching job I've found satisfying but used as a means to support my family situation for the last thirty years. What's funny is that my attitude is that now I can finally get down to my real work, which is writing. So I have yet to begin! What's next is a collection of stories, *House Clowns*, all done except for a final story, with the silliest title: "Thumpadabump." What's after that, and half-written, is a memoir about my father, whose own father, Ozro, had a restraining order from entering the state of Washington. There's some lion's roar in that story too. After that, if the muse is kind, another novel. I hope it'll be unlike anything I've done before. ■

1. What are your first impressions of *The World*?

2. Which character's story did you find most personally resonant, and why?

3. Each of the main characters reflects on their past in the process of dealing with their present. Explore the different ways in which memory is used throughout the novel.

4. The narrative structure of *The World* is not only divided into three character-specific sections, but also features extended passages from a book-within-a-book, also called *The World*. Discuss the different tones and narrative voices of each section and how they thread together to tell a greater story.

5. The section of the novel told from Hal's viewpoint is a deeply touching look at a man struggling with the loss of his memory and his place in the world. How does the author use language and imagery to evoke what it could be like to live with Alzheimer's as well as to craft a satisfying ending to the novel?

6. In what ways does the meta-novel *The World* and its story of life and loss in a leper colony reflect or reinforce the themes found in the rest of the novel? How does it become an important part of the lives of Hal, Mel, and Stuart?

7. The novel explores some pretty tragic circumstances, but its tone never turns maudlin and is rife with humourous touches. How does the author maintain such a balance of light and dark? Do you feel the book is ultimately optimistic about life?

8. Stuart is a talented woodworker as well as a teacher, Mel is a musician with a passion for the culinary arts, and Hal was a novelist before becoming a monk. How do these forms of creativity marry practicality with personal expression? How is this important to the themes of the novel?

9. How does Hal's mala (set of beads) play an important symbolic role in the last section of the book?

10. Stuart gamely sets out to confront a faceless, monolithic insurance company, Mel has come to terms with terminal cancer, and Hal is living literally moment to moment. How

do these characters summon the courage to challenge the inevitable? What is the author saying about the spirit of perseverance?

11. A very simple understanding of Buddhism involves becoming aware of one's place in the world and then exploring desire and suffering to attain a more fearless and wakeful state. Discuss the ways in which *The World* explores these Buddhist values, not only in regards to Hal's beliefs, but to the journeys that Stuart and Mel undertake as well.